DELPHI'S CHOSEN

To Nick,

Great to be back
with you.

Enjoy the
adventure!

Best wishes

A K Patch

AN APOLLO SERIES NOVEL

DELPHI'S CHOSEN

BY

A. K. PATCH

PEDACEUM
PRESS

Copyright © 2016 A. K. Patch

ISBN-13: 978-0-9908724-3-6

Visit the author at: www.akpatchauthor.com.

Cover Design: GKS Creative

First Printing

Printed in the United States of America. Worldwide Electronic and Digital Rights. 1ˢᵗ North America, Australian and UK Print Rights.

Photos:
Map of Ancient Greece, *Preface*
Map of Persian Empire, *Preface*
Trireme, page 319
Apollo Belvedere, Vatican Museum, Rome, page 320
Trireme Olympias, Palaio Faliro, Greece, page 321
Greek Gods and Goddesses, page 322

To our parents
Rosella and Milton Maly
Edith and Philip Patch

All the great things are simple, and may be expressed in a single word: freedom, justice, honor, duty, mercy, hope.

— Winston Churchill

Acknowledgements

I have a wonderful group of readers and advisors who guided me in the creation of this second novel: Micheal and Enriqueta Sullivan, Dr. Anthony and Bobbi Marciante, David and Betty Feldman, Jeanette Rigopoulous, Wendy Philips, Larry and Jean Patch, Leslie O'Brien, Marianne Stamos, and Lisa Tabor Fleischer. Special thanks to publishing professionals Antoinette, Richard, and Jared Kuritz, Laura Taylor, Shelley Chung, and Gwyn Snider.

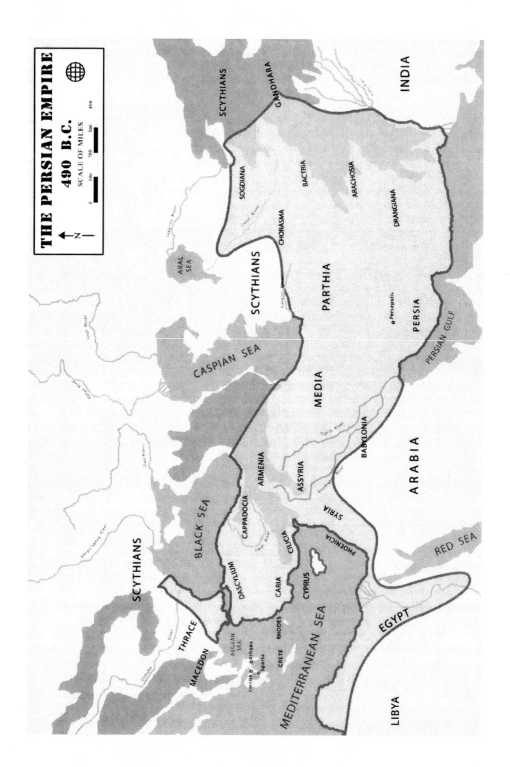

THE PERSIAN EMPIRE
490 B.C.

SCALE OF MILES

0   100   200   300   400

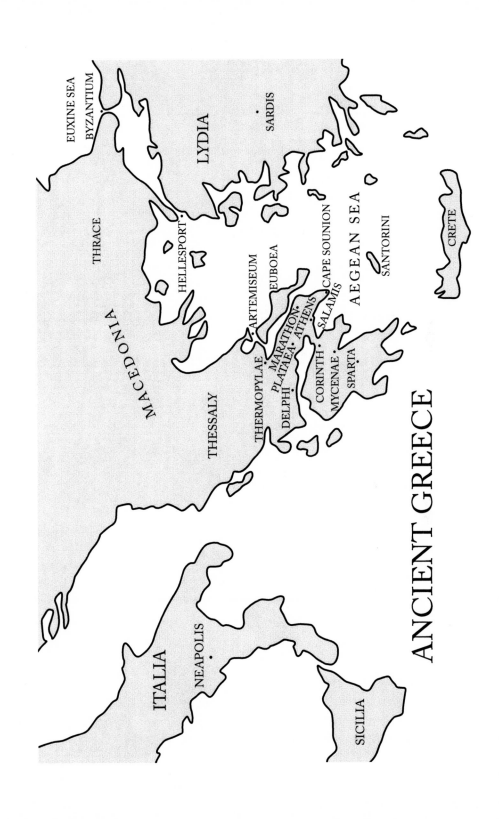

ANCIENT GREECE

Chronology

BC

1650	Approximate date of volcanic destruction of Santorini (Thera)—Minoan Civilization on Crete weakened.
1450	Mycenaeans from mainland Greece dominate Crete.
1200	Dorian invasion from north of Greece. Mycenaean cities destroyed.
1100-800	Greek Dark Age
776	First Olympic Games
590	Solon establishes foundations of Athenian democracy.
550	Foundation of the Persian Empire by King Cyrus.
490	Persian King Darius sends invasion force to Greece and his army is defeated at Marathon.
480	Persian King Xerxes invades Greece. Battles of Thermopylae Pass and Salamis.
479	Battle of Plataea. Persians defeated.
448	Construction of Parthenon begins.
431-404	Peloponnesian War. Athens is defeated by Sparta.
334	Alexander the Great attacks and conquers the Persian Empire.
323	Alexander the Great dies in Babylon.
264	Punic Wars between Rome and Carthage begin. Carthage defeated in 146. Rome becomes the dominant power in the Mediterranean Sea.

Delphi, Greece

There were many oracles in ancient Greece, but none more famous and trusted than Delphi, Apollo's sanctuary in the mountains west of Athens. For almost two thousand years, pilgrims traveled from near and far to reach Delphi, at the time believed by the Greeks to be a site of divine inspiration.

The trance-induced ranting of Pythia, a chaste holy woman, converted into versed prophecies by temple priests, was considered to be the will of the god Apollo. This foretelling of the future influenced not only decisions of everyday life, but also the prospects of colonies and the fate of kingdoms.

Unforgettable are the simple virtues carved into the forecourt of Apollo's temple: "Know Thyself" and "Nothing in Excess." These proverbs demonstrate how the triumphs and tragedies of ancient peoples could serve to guide our lives in the modern day.

A.K. PATCH

Prologue

Married professors Zack and Lauren Fletcher live the good life. Teaching at San Diego State University means living in one of America's finest cities. And their respective fields of history and ancient languages means summers abroad, immersing themselves in their fields. If they can agree on when and if to start a family—if Lauren can get Zack to commit past the next dig – life will be perfect.

The breaching of the academic cocoon in which Zack and Lauren exist is both unexpected and violent when an enraged warrior from the past appears in their lives as a present-day, albeit eccentric, thug. Yet, while frightened, their focus returns to their work and the ongoing discussion of having a child.

Embarking on what Lauren believes to be a second honeymoon and what Zack knows is yet another dig, their ensuing quarrels continue in Athens, until they are threatened by the same thug. Now alarmed and feeling hunted, they escape to Delphi. But their escape is, in truth, a manipulation, and they are hurled into the fifth century BC.

The histories they had studied and immersed themselves in pale in comparison to what they are experiencing first-hand. With no idea of who is pulling the strings or why, Zack and Lauren are embroiled in events that test their grip on reality. Beginning with the attack in San Diego and continuing in Greece, they find themselves fighting for their survival both in this century and one long past. But it is their eventual separation that hits them both hardest.

Zack misses Lauren. Despite the danger he faces, his wife is at the forefront of his thoughts. Did she make it back to twenty-first century San Diego? Was the killer who had stalked them across time and continents still pursuing her and the girl in her care? Their past disagreements became trivial in light of what they had faced together and apart. Commanded to focus on his mission, Zack finds that he cannot totally comply; not knowing Lauren's fate consumes him.

Many centuries removed from her husband, Lauren is no longer angry with Zack. The man she had come to resent had changed, tempered by their struggle to survive. Lauren wants Zack back, wants their life back, even wants their quarrels back. But inexplicably separated from him, and now protecting an orphaned Greek girl transported with her from ancient times, Lauren discovers she has more fortitude than she realized. If she can escape the wrath of Bessus, an enraged warrior of the fifth-century BC who has vowed to slay her, whether in her century or his, then she will focus on finding Zack. Whatever it will take.

Desperate to change a future unacceptable to him, Apollo has enacted his plan, one in which Lauren and Zack are unwitting, but important pawns. Having selected and drafted them, he still wonders if they are brave enough, wise enough, strong enough to be the leaders who will counter the threats he knows that gather from without... and from within.

Experiencing history's brutal lessons in real-time, Lauren and Zack begin to understand what has been sacrificed by so many over the centuries for a way of life now in jeopardy. And in recognizing this, they come to realize what is really at stake.

The trail of this odyssey will be marked by peril—for Zack, for Lauren, and for the world into which they were born. Selfless devotion to this cause will be necessary for them to become the heroes needed to forge a promising future. But as history teaches us, heroes don't always return home...

PART I

Delphi, Greece

PRESENT DAY

Apollo, the god of prophecy, dug at the sacred soil of Mount Parnassus with his heel. After creating a hole, he selected a triangular rock and set it into place.

I need a home. I will have a home.

With a cornerstone laid, he picked less-perfect rocks and arranged a square.

He had come to know strength at Delphi, seat of the oracle and a site of ageless wisdom.

Apollo gazed out over the sloping terrain that ended on the Corinthian Gulf. He would build a stout hut with a porch to watch the turning of the day.

"I vow that I will share this land with all who love peace," he said. This alcove would be his sanctuary, a place where he would finally know eternal comfort.

However, an arduous road must be navigated before he could rest.

History had recorded how the West had fallen.

And it was not far off.

Heroes fight and die, but peace between men and nations can be made with goodwill. He shouted, "Goodwill is stronger than the sword," and heard his words ricochet off the mountainside.

Apollo reset a curly forelock behind his right ear. The last echoes of his declaration faded.

But even gods can lie to themselves.

Peace is not what happened. The western world collapsed and all the gods agreed it must be restored or there would be no future. When the other gods had perished, he knew it was his duty to make their decision to act…a reality.

If, despite the training, his heroes—Zack, the "Traveler," and Lauren, "Golden Hair"—did not survive the fight, Apollo would have to find others to serve or alter history himself, something he did not want to do. Even Bessus, the Bactrian warrior from 480 BC, misaligned in time also, must unknowingly play a role in the sacred mission's success.

Apollo kicked at the new cornerstone for his home and dislodged it.

He would have to be honest with himself.

No more lies could be told. Victory would be hard bought or there would be no peaceful home for him, or anyone else.

Delphi, Greece

SEPTEMBER 480 BC

The serpent's head on the stone wall brandished a forked tongue, but it tasted no air, nor did it pose any threat. For having been carved in bas-relief, the snake guided the lost, or the knowing, and served as a reminder of a powerful civilization long departed.

Undulating along the wall of an underground passageway, the body of this colossal python, a remnant of archaic times, guided the way to the surface temples at Delphi. Professor Zackary Fletcher, long-haired and bearded, separated from everyone he loved, trudged downhill in the dark. He ran his hand over the artistry for a hundred yards or more, across a seismically shifted trail and a forest of roots. After negotiating these subterranean obstacles for nearly an hour, he reached the tail of the snake, knowing the ladder to the upper levels would be just beyond.

Zack halted and caught his breath. What he really needed was time to rest and heal.

But physical wounds were just the beginning of his torment.

The first time Zack had been on this path, he had no idea of the disasters that awaited him and Lauren. At least then he had his butane lighter to help illuminate the way. The memory of Lauren, all she had endured, and the young girl from ancient Greece, Cassandra, and their desperate escape, felt like a burning, guilt-tipped knife in his guts.

How had everything gone to hell?

Actually, he knew the answer to the question, and there was still no consolation.

Apollo was responsible, to some degree.

The rest was on him.

He had made decisions, disastrous ones, out of arrogance, jealousy of Lauren's success, and his own selfishness. He needed that one project to gain tenure at the San Diego State. And he was obsessed about the past. Manipulating Lauren to go to Greece had been a bad idea, with dire consequences for everyone.

Somehow, he would have to make it right.

But now, he didn't know what to do, having been sent back through the tunnel by Apollo. What awaited him wouldn't be clear until he could get topside.

The odors of dank air and rotting earth permeated the route. Relieved to have escaped an injury in this trek along the blackened maze, he ascended the stone-cut ladder, Nestor's Marathon sword in a scabbard, and his long-traveled leather satchel over a shoulder. Finding the hatch door still open, he lifted himself into the room above. He crawled toward the doorway and felt strands of hair on the floorboards. Zack jerked his hand back, suspecting something spidery, until he recalled what the hairs might be attached to. Flashbacks of violence commanded his thoughts. He followed a clump of severed scalp to the double-bladed axe, the one owned by the man he hated most on earth.

But this monster wasn't even of his world.

Bessus, a Bactrian warlord of the Persian Wars period of ancient Greece, born twenty-five hundred years before him, could not have brought more ruin upon his life and those he cared about most. It took only a moment for a cauldron of anger to build up inside him. Zack, Lauren, and Cassandra had barely escaped the fight at the farmhouse and in the tunnel room. He lifted the heavy axe and it struck something. Searching with his hand in the dark, Zack felt pointed horns fastened to a bronze helmet.

"Someday, I will make you pay for what you've done," Zack said, heaving the dreaded axe and helmet down through the hole. He slammed the hatch door shut.

It was as much revenge upon Bessus as he could manage right now.

Zack wondered if he had returned to approximately the same time period. He could assume he was back in 480 BC. If it was still summer, and shortly after the Battle of Thermopylae, then he could make it back to the farm.

He had always dreamed of living in ancient times.

Only, he never could have imagined all this.

Zack kicked aside the fractured pieces of the wooden door that Bessus had smashed earlier during the chase to the tunnel room. He negotiated more underground passageways until he passed the *antron* of the Pythia, the sunken chamber where legend says that the mysterious priestess breathed in the fumes of the python's decaying carcass and went into a trance to receive Apollo's prophecies. The three-legged stool was empty and no priests were in attendance. Zack knew from geological studies in modern times that the invisible gas, ethylene, leaked from a fissure in the bedrock. Now it occurred to him that if they accepted males, he'd be a hell of a Pythia.

He alone knew the future.

Well, that was partly true. Someone else did, too. Apollo knew.

Zack had studied this period of ancient Greece for so long that he took risks. And now Lauren had paid the price, and so had the generous family they'd met.

Not interested in a serious drag of whatever noxious fumes leaked from the earth, Zack took the stone stairs two steps at a time and arrived at the top. He avoided the egg-shaped omphalos stone he'd whacked his knee on last visit. He dashed past surprised priestesses in white gowns guarding the sacred flame in Apollo's temple. Ignoring their protests and pushing bronze doors open, he ran between pillars and exited down a stone ramp with dawn creeping over the horizon. More flashbacks attacked: Cassandra screaming for Athena to save them, Bessus straining to open the chamber door and Lauren's quick kiss on his cheek as she said good-bye. He had some fleeting memory of seeing her some-where else, talking to her—recent conversation, too—but it wouldn't hold in his mind.

Zack just couldn't remember, and he was sure doing so was really important.

He staggered down the Sacred Way, caught a poorly set stone, and fell at the foot of a statue. Grasping the pedestal, he hoisted himself up. Statues of the gods lined both sides of the switchback trail. They appeared almost alive in the moonlight, sculpted motion in stone. Getting to his feet, he found himself holding on to of the statue of Apollo.

"It's you," Zack said, stunned by how the likeness of the statue matched the farmer he had met on the road north of Athens, and the god who had surprised him in the tunnel room.

Here was more proof that he had, in fact, met a god.

Zack scratched his temple. Scenes of violence raced through his head, but he couldn't slow them down enough to concentrate on when they happened or what they meant, almost like trying to catch a silvery trout in a fast-flowing river. His chest ached. Zack dug his fingers into his chest muscles and felt soreness. Something had happened to him. He'd been wounded several times, and not from a Persian sword like before or the stones of the slingers. He drew a blank and petitioned the statue instead.

"If you're in there, I'm begging you to help. What's happened to me? I need another medallion to get home. I've got to know what's become of Lauren and Cassandra." The painted marble face of Apollo looked off to where his arrow had landed.

"Now I'm talking to rocks." He stormed down the Sacred Way, past treasuries and temples, statues of military heroes and mythological creatures.

Nearing the gate entrance, he saw two hoplites standing over the guard that Bessus had beheaded the evening before. That meant he'd only been unconscious for a few hours. Zack stayed out of sight of the guards. He climbed onto a crate, hoisted himself over the top of a wall, and landed hard on gravel. After waiting a minute for aching in his knees to stop, he headed for the trees at the side of the road. Trumpets blared behind him, signaling dawn. It would only be a matter of time before foot and cart traffic clogged the roads.

He ran past the sacred Castalian Spring and around a curve in the road, toward the square temple of Athena Pronaia. Just beyond, the front door to Nestor's farmhouse was open. Zack saw no Persians and wondered if they were still down the road awaiting Bessus's return.

They might have to wait a hell of a long time for that. As far as he knew, Bessus had followed Lauren into the time tunnel, and to wherever she ended up with Cassandra. Bessus could already have killed both of them. He felt a grinding in his stomach. He'd have to block it out of his mind if he was going to function.

Cautiously entering the farmhouse, he and made his way to the back door. Chickens and goats called from the pens. Birds chirped, oblivious to the devastation he knew awaited him. Entering the courtyard, the hard reality of slaughter caused him to slump against the door frame.

Zack went to Persephone first, finding her on her stomach, head turned toward the courtyard, with eyes open and fixed, in a vain search for her daughter. He gently closed her lids and brushed the bloody tangles of hair back from her forehead.

"Cassandra is in good hands. Lauren will love and fight for her as you did."

From her wrist, Zack carefully slid off the snake bracelet, something Lauren had admired upon their first meeting. He placed it in his satchel. As Zack lay her arm down reverently, he saw the massive cleaving that had severed her spine.

He averted his eyes from the wound. "I promise I'll avenge you."

Zack then turned to the task he dreaded most. Nestor had been a welcome friend in this twilight zone of existence. Nestor lay on his side with his eyes closed, his fingers gripping loose stones. Zack pulled the shredded cloth away from the blackened mess that was Nestor's shoulder. He muttered apologies, wiping the gray hair from his friend's face.

But Nestor felt different than Persephone. Not as cold. Zack quickly checked Nestor's wrist and then placed his fingertips over the notch of his neck. It was faint but unmistakable. There was, miraculously, a pulse.

"You're alive, you beautiful son of a bitch. I can't believe it."

Nestor's condition was grave and he'd have to act fast. He bolted to the barn and hitched the horse to the wagon as Nestor had taught him earlier. Lifting Nestor's weight was a job for two men, let alone one weakened by wounds. But Nestor's only chance to survive was for Zack to get him up to the temples. He hoisted him up and onto the open bed of the wagon.

Zack guided the horse through the side gate, much to the displeasure of the goats and sheep waiting for their morning feed. The wagon wheels creaked as the makeshift ambulance rambled up the roadway to the temples.

"Please, Nestor, hang on," Zack begged. He reached the guard post as the morning became fully lit. A squad of hoplites hovered over their murdered comrade. Zack shouted, "Help me."

The guards raised their shields and spears.

"Raise the alarm," Zack said.

"Declare yourself," the captain of the guard said. "Are we to be attacked?"

"The barbarians are camped down the road," Zack answered. "One of them killed a woman in a farmhouse nearby and wounded this man. Do you have a physician here?"

One of the soldiers leaned over Nestor. "This man is the architect. I've spoken to him many times."

"Sound the alarm. The barbarians are here!" the captain said.

Horns blasted out a series of long notes. Priests and officials ran out from doorways. Guards helped Zack drive the cart to the physician's house. They gently laid Nestor on a cot inside the small clinic and called for the doctor.

A slim, bearded man emerged from an adjoining room. He fastened a gold-colored headband over tousled white hair. "Why do you rouse me?" Minander, the temple physician, asked. Before the guards could answer, he slapped his cheeks hard.

"Nestor? This is a disaster." He felt for a pulse in the crook of Nestor's neck, shaking his head while murmuring the name of the son of Apollo, Asclepius, the god of healers. He dipped a linen cloth in a shallow bowl that held leftover wine and squeezed it, drenching the deep axe cut in Nestor's shoulder. After cleaning away the twigs, stones, and dirt, he dug yellowish-brown paste out from an earthen jar with a bronze spatula, and spread it on the wound.

"What medicine is that?" Zack asked, moving closer.

"A poultice made of honey, lentils, and mustard," the doctor replied, sounding irritated. "Afterward, I'll bleed the evil vapors from him before they foul his insides."

"Over my dead body you will," Zack said in ancient Greek. "I'll be damned if I'll allow you . . ." Zack felt suddenly faint. He reached for a table corner.

The physician ignored Zack. He handed a metal cup to one of the guards, instructing him to heat it in a fire. He turned to Zack. "Tie your tongue, stranger. I'm the physician here. Disturb my work and I will have you thrown out by the guards. I must make haste or Nestor's eyes will set forever."

Zack watched the doctor poise the heated cup on Nestor's wound, holding it with a hot pad. He couldn't believe what he was seeing.

"What the hell are you doing?" Zack said.

"Drawing out the harmful fluids," the physician said. "Get out of my way."

The wound sizzled. Nestor groaned, stretching his fingers, but weakly.

"This is a good sign. He stirs."

Nestor rolled his head.

"There, my friend. I will do what I can for you." The physician placed a dampened cloth on Nestor's forehead.

"Can we get him something to drink?" Zack said.

"Are you a physician?" Minander asked, flinging his hand at Zack.

"In my land, we have a different method to treat so much blood loss."

"But you are in Hellas and this is my patient. Stand back and see to yourself instead. You look dazed," the physician said flatly.

"He's my friend, too," Zack countered. "I'm an envoy and Nestor is my host. Persians did this to him and killed his sister-in-law." Zack saw Persephone's blackened blood on his fingers.

"Not Persephone? She lies there now?"

"She was slain by the same barbarian."

Nestor groaned. Minander turned back to him. Zack pointed at the half-filled krater cup on the table.

"If that is wine, physician, get him to sip it. In my land, this is how we treat a man who's lost a lot of blood. We keep him warm, make him drink, and raise his feet. We would never draw more blood from him."

"Your land must be full of the dead. Only the gods know if he will recover," Minander said, walking to a cabinet where he searched through a tangle of metal instruments. "We'll have him drink his own blood when I've eliminated the evil vapors."

"What? You can't have him do that! I—" Zack raised his hand to his forehead. "I need to sit." The physician picked up a ceramic bowl. He held Nestor's forearm and dragged a small iron blade across a faint blue vein.

"No!" Zack shouted, leaping to stop him. The physician raised an arm to protect Nestor. A guard cracked Zack on the jaw with his fist. He crashed to the floor in a heap and passed out.

"Set him on the other cot," the physician said. "This barbarian has lost his mind."

Later, Zack awoke to the tickle of a fly perching on the tip of his nose. He jerked his head to send it away only to see an attendant adjusting the bandage on Nestor's shoulder. He watched his friend's chest rising and falling rapidly. Nestor licked his lips and strained to breathe.

Nestor blinked and said something unintelligible. Zack rolled off his cot and crawled to Nestor's cot while the attendant ran to get the physician.

"Wine," Nestor managed to whisper. Zack dipped a cloth in the wine bowl, parted Nestor's lips with his fingers and dribbled the diluted wine into his mouth. The physician rushed through the doorway.

"Move," he said, pushing Zack aside. "Nestor, how do you fare?"

Grimacing, Nestor said, "Minander, my friend."

Zack managed to stand up. He smiled at Nestor. His grin turned when he saw the urn next to Nestor's cot.

"No. You idiots," Zack yelled.

Nestor's blue eyes brightened when he recognized Zack. He murmured weakly, "Praise the gods." He raised his hand but it fell back. Zack hugged him gently.

Nestor said, "I revel . . . in your embrace." He smacked his lips and asked, "Cassandra?"

"Lauren and Cassandra escaped from the barbarian. We defied him."

At least I think they escaped.

Nestor cringed. "His axe . . . left a scratch."

"Oh, Nestor, you are a tough bastard."

Nestor raised an eyebrow. "Zack, you look poorly."

"I also had a dance with the barbarian."

Nestor seized Zack's robe, gripping it tight. "The boatman calls me, but I will head to Eleusis, instead."

"You must drink all the watered wine you can to live. Do that for me, will you, Nestor? Stay with me."

The physician directed his attendant to fetch more wine and then left for his quarters. While he was gone, Zack's mind raced with the idea of devising some kind of intravenous drip for Nestor. Rubber tubing and hollow needles hadn't been invented yet, and forget about blood-matching tests. He stood over his friend. Nestor's breathing quickened and he looked shriveled and gray.

Nestor eyed him sadly, "Persephone?"

Zack shook his head. "I will see to her funeral."

"That monster . . . destroyed my family. Somehow . . . you must make him pay. Where did Cassandra . . . go?" he asked, grimacing.

"To the Western lands. She and Lauren are safe." Zack blinked, guilt swelling within him. How could he tell Nestor that he had no idea where they were?

"Praise the gods."

Nestor gripped Zack's robe again and his eyelids fluttered. "Go to the cave." His voice weakened.

"Bring three torches. Go through the hole in back of the cave." Nestor cringed. "Crawl straight...then left at the fork, down...the right fork and into a chamber...look for a rock in shape of an owl." His voice cracked. "Dig below it...find my wealth. Take it...to my niece. There's enough gold for all. Take care of my Cassandra. She is my...light."

"You need to get well and we'll all be together. Hold on. Stay with me," Zack said with an urgency that soon he might be alone again, in a time not his own.

"Nestor, I sent Lauren and Cassandra to safety. They'll travel west until they reach my land. I told you it was Atlantea, but it is better known as America. You may not believe what I will tell you next." Zack took a stabilizing breath.

"If you make the journey to Eleusis, I want you to revel in the knowledge that the future is bright. Lauren and I are not of your land . . . or of your time. The gods have allowed us to travel through the course of the ages . . . in a flash."

Nestor blinked and muttered, "Faster than the flash from your fire stick?"

Zack grinned. "Yes, my friend. I know that what I'm saying is confusing, but it is your god Apollo who allows this. Lauren and Cassandra are back in my land, in my own time...over two thousand years into your future."

Nestor sucked in his breath and let it out forcefully. "Then...you are...a god, too?"

"No. I am flesh and bone and mind, as you."

"Truly, you must be a mortal." Nestor coughed. His throat rattled. "A god could never look as bad as...you do."

Zack turned his face, hiding his smile. When he turned back to

Nestor, he said, "I know what's going to happen. The Greeks will win this struggle. Greek ways will spread to the limits of the earth, for all time."

"I believe you," Nestor said, but then struggled with his next words. "Use my wealth wisely...protect my Cassandra."

"Revel in what is yours, Nestor. Peace is in your mind, just like they told you at Delphi. We will love Cassandra as our own daughter."

Nestor strained and tried to sit up, gripping Zack's injured shoulder. Zack barely winced as he tried to comfort him, "There is so much to tell you, Nestor. Greek culture will be the basis for the future of the Western nations that love freedom. Our lives will see its influence at every turn. King Alexander, a Macedonian, will conquer the Persians many years from now and spread Greek ideas to the Far East . . ."

"Macedonians, they're nearly . . . savages."

Zack laughed. He held Nestor's head up and lifted the cup of wine to his lips. Nestor took a small drink but coughed out the rest.

When his throat cleared, Nestor said, "Protect...those who love freedom."

"Even in our time, Greek ideals are the basis for our government, our art, philosophy, and culture."

"Hold onto the best . . . of what . . . we are. Discard the bad."

"You must drink more, Nestor."

Nestor gripped Zack's forearm. "Live for me." His breathing hastened. "Save Athens." He licked his lips. Zack dribbled more wine in to his mouth.

After he swallowed, Nestor continued, his voice raspy, "I agree with you...about fate. A man decides what path...to take in life."

Nestor's words jolted some kind of memory in Zack. Visions of screaming people in the streets of modern-day Athens permeated his thoughts, but it flashed by and he couldn't retrieve it.

Nestor's eyes blinked twice and he tried to swallow unsuccessfully. "Eleusis awaits me." Red spittle sprayed out of his mouth. Nestor gurgled out, "Live boldly." He took a deep breath and struggled to speak. "My eyes, they cloud. Save Cassandra . . . my Honeybee."

His head rolled to the side. A long release of breath signaled the end of Nestor's life. Like his grandfather before him, his blue eyes held a steady gaze.

Minander walked into the room to find Zack openly sobbing. Minander closed Nestor's eyes and said, "Rest well. You will share a funeral pyre with Persephone. Your shades shall travel together."

The physician told his assistant, "Send a wagon down to the farm. Fetch the body of the lady and prepare a pyre. Take guards with you in case you find Persians."

Zack draped himself over the lifeless form of his friend.

The physician held up a papyrus scroll. "He signed this before you awoke. He bequeaths the farm and all he has to you. My attendant bore witness to this."

Zack clutched Nestor's body. He was alone.

It was several minutes before he would let Nestor go. When he did, he asked for cutting shears.

The faces of the dead had been propped up to greet visitors in the courtyard behind the physician's residence. The bodies of Nestor and Persephone, cleaned and prepared the day before, lay prone in white gowns on a crisscross of timbers with crowns of vine leaves around their heads. Coins placed on their eyes would pay the boatman's toll to row their shades across the river Styx and into the underworld. Both bodies held honey cakes in their hands as offerings to the gods, and vials of anointed oils lay beside them. Visitors wept openly for hours, ceremoniously sprinkling water over themselves before they left, for their protection following a visitation with the dead.

It was barely dawn when Zack and Minander stepped outside the temple of Apollo, accompanied by a group of temple priests, guards, and locals. Zack and Minander helped carry the litters of Nestor and Persephone to the funeral pyre. Zack had shorn his own hair nearly to his scalp, in the manner of the bereaved. It was an uneven cut, and with his beard whiskers longer now, he fit in easily with those attending. Two young men with wooden flutes played lyrical tunes softly in unison, slowly up and down the musical scale. Zack gazed upon the bodies.

They send you to Hades, Nestor. But I know, having vowed yourself to the Elysium Mysteries, you dwell now in the fields of Eleusis instead. Peace is there and a happier eternity for you and Persephone. Now I wonder if Eleusis could have been an earlier version of the Christian heaven.

The pile of logs and sticks of the pyre were interspersed with chips of aromatic cedar. The morning breeze brushed across Zack's face and sent the flames of his torch leaping. Minander stepped forward and read Nestor's will.

"My friend, Nestor, was well-known in these mountains and a legend in Athens. His brother died long ago at Marathon, his sister-in-law lies on the bier with him now, and his niece is lost." Minander gestured toward Zack with his hand.

"I testify that Nestor has bequeathed his farm and all his holdings to this man, Zack, the Atlantean. I bear this as the truth, and it is further witnessed by my assistant, Meanna. Nestor cannot be replaced. He worshipped the gods. He fought for freedom at Marathon, too. He answered to no man. What higher praise could a man receive?"

Zack withdrew a dagger from a scabbard at his side, cut a strand of hair from each of the bodies, and wrapped them in a leather folder. The muscles of his face twitched. He clamped down his emotions. If he let it, grief would break him down. He bit the insides of his cheeks. Both of his friends looked so small, caricatures of who they'd been in life.

Zack clasped Nestor's crossed hands, those that had slapped him on the back after long practice sessions with spear and shield. This man had fought at Marathon. Years from now no one would know he did. Neither of them would be remembered, lost to history. He stared at the shrunken corpses and wondered where the spirits of his dear friends had gone. Nestor's eyebrows would no longer lurch when Zack asked a question. Penelope's lips would never separate again to smile in a motherly pride for her daughter.

Zack stared into the cloud-filled sky and silently asked Apollo why it had to work out this way.

Holding the firebrand, he looked to Minander for the signal to begin. He touched the flame to the prepared wood of the funeral pyre. Tongues of yellow fire rose quickly, along with thick white smoke. The pungent odor of cedar pervaded at first until the smoke turned black. The fire sizzled and crackled. In a few minutes, the two forms of his friends disappeared in a yellow and red blaze.

Zack swallowed repeatedly in a losing attempt to hold back a bestial cry of agony. Something, some memory nagged at the periphery of his thoughts, distracting his torment. The mourners wailed, turning away from the overwhelming heat and odor of the pyre. Finally, Zack stood by himself. He held his breath and let himself be immersed in the rising, smoky remains of Nestor and Persephone. When he could take no more, he walked away, soot-faced and solemn. He had not wrought all this disaster by himself. Bessus was responsible, and so was Apollo.

I know there is something I'm supposed to remember.

The next afternoon, Zack sat on a stool in the courtyard of the farmhouse, a few feet from where his friends had been killed. He had combed stones to hide the bloodstains. He stared at the two barns, one containing food and supplies along with the bedroom that he and Lauren had shared. The other barn, about twenty yards to the left of the first, housed the horse and some oxen. Toward the southwest and the Corinth Canal, a narrow path shrouded by trees and brush led toward the creek emanating from the Castalian Spring. A hundred yards farther along the hillside was the hidden cave.

Like a magician practicing a trick, he twirled a gold coin in his fingers, examining the uneven contours. This was a single coin taken from one of five large jars of gold, silver, and precious stones that represented the life work of his friend. Nestor's directions had been exact: the treasure was easily located, buried under the owl-shaped stone. Zack had left the jars in place, hoping that Cassandra and Lauren would somehow get his correspondence in the future and find them. He had packed other items and buried them with the jars, withdrawing coins to pay for his upcoming expenses.

Zack had decided not to live at the house, the memories too vivid and painful. He couldn't care for the livestock, so he considered selling them. He couldn't stay because the Persians were still close by and could stage another raid at any time. History taught that there had been no successful assault into Delphi, yet historical accounts of the war could not account for every occurrence.

He had learned that the hard way.

Herodotus, the famed historian, had written that the Persians had attacked Delphi, but the gods and supernatural heroes had supposedly blunted the attack by rolling giant rocks down upon the Persians, sending them reeling back down the mountain.

Zack tapped his feet on the pebbles, pondering his next move.

Within the week, the Battle of Salamis would take place in the Saronic Gulf, near Athens. He couldn't trek the same mountain road to Delphi, since it would be guarded by Persians. His choice was to cross the Gulf of Corinth to the south at the port of Itea, go over to the Peloponnese, then head east toward Corinth, and join the allied forces at the island of Salamis. With only himself to worry about, there was no reason not to witness the next climactic battle in the Persian Wars, another that would decide the future of Western civilization.

He extracted a notebook from his leather satchel and began a letter to Lauren.

Dear Lauren,

If you have found this package then I am overjoyed.

Zack returned to the cave and deposited the letter into a pot hidden within a wall alcove. He reconstructed the stone obstacles that protected the entrance and hid it with branches.

Zack gathered his belongings, made final arrangements for the animals, and left the farm that afternoon.

He realized he had gotten what he asked for. He lived among the ancients, but now he'd also have to accept that he might not survive the experience, or ever return to his own time. Apollo had told him there were greater struggles ahead.

Talk about a vacation gone bad.

3

Salamis

SEPTEMBER 480 BC

The fifty-oared penteconter under Zack's feet glided toward the island of Salamis. It scraped the sandy shore at the lead of ten other transports. The crewmen hoisted their oars vertically to make room for the other ships to unload their cargo of supplies and warriors.

A long gangplank hit shallow water and a twenty-five-man squad of archers disembarked from the ship. With bows slung across their backs, they shared in the hauling of large leather sacks of iron-tipped arrows, stacking them in rows onshore. Hoplites cheered and made a path. The archers wasted no time hitting a trailhead that led to the other end of the island.

Other ships dispersed similar cargo.

These famed archers from the island of Crete had been pulled from duty at the wall at Corinth, and transferred quickly to Salamis in an effort to thwart the plans of the Persian king to build an earth-and-rock mole across the bay. Upon completion of the mole, his navy would surround the island, and his enormous army would march across toward Salamis, easily trapping the Athenian forces, their allies, the displaced population of Athens, and the trireme dry docks. With the

Greek navy defeated, and the hoplites aboard captured, Sparta would be isolated and overwhelmed by a land and seaborne assault.

Zack slung on his satchel, relieved that the movement no longer hurt. The archery unit marched along a dirt trail that followed the shoreline. The path headed uphill and, at the top of a rise, revealed the narrow bay just outside the town of Salamis.

Across that bay, clouds of dust and smoke obscured the shore. Up above the dust, a bluff jutted upwards to the top of a mountain. There, Zack knew, Xerxes had set his throne to watch his naval victory unfold.

From Zack's perch, he could see the battle-ready triremes of the Greek allies lying in rows along the shore with their masts set down to hide their location. The Greeks knew that Xerxes's view from across the bay to Salamis would be hindered by inlets, hills, and a small island in the middle of the narrows.

Nearing the triremes docking stations, Zack sprinted to the head of the line, anxious to find the Athenian admiral, Themistocles. He recalled staying at Themistocles's residence in Athens. He had argued with Lauren, vehemently, over his desperate need to go to Thermopylae. Both Nestor and Themistocles agreed with Lauren. The look of terror and anger on Lauren's face should have convinced him of their wisdom. But, he wouldn't listen.

He found an Athenian hoplite speaking with the captain of the archers. The captain wore the innovative composite armor that he had seen some hoplites wear at Thermopylae. Layers of linen glued together, creating a kind of ancient Kevlar.

"Your archers are most welcome," the hoplite said. "Those ships you see in the distance are waiting to carry you out near the mole where you can fire on the barbarians and disrupt their work."

The captain of the archers pulled off his leather cap and wiped his brow with his forearm. "Keep us supplied and our arrows will surely find their marks for you. I'll take the archers aboard the ships now. They're itchy as a pack of hounds dancing around a rat hole."

Two hundred archers moved out to the docks, leaving Zack standing with the hoplite.

"Where can I find Themistocles?"

"Who wants to know?" the Athenian said. He scanned the short-haired, bearded giant before him from foot to head. "You are no Hellene from what I can see."

"I have been to his home in Athens," Zack replied, fully aware the allies would be suspicious of any foreigners that might be Persian agents disguised as locals.

The Athenian captain placed his hand around the handle of his sword. "Then you would know the name of his most trusted slave."

"Sicinnus," Zack answered.

"A home that is surely in flames now," the hoplite said, relaxing his grip. "Look for him in Paloukia or at the docks. He's not a hard man to find, but his guards will gut you if they think you are a spy." The man pointed toward the ships, abruptly turned, and jogged off to catch up with the archers.

The crackling of campfires commenced with the coming of dusk. Zack approached the fleet of triremes lined up on the shore, their hulls painted with pitch. He ran his hand over one of the battering rams protruding from the hull. These three-pronged, solid bronze protrusions were hammered and bolted onto the nose of the ship just below the waterline. Zack felt the serrated edges of the ram with his fingers, aware that no triremes from Greek or Roman times had survived to the modern day. It was not until the 1980s that an effort was made to reproduce one and test it on the water.

Soon, you'll be stuck in the guts of a Persian ship.

A knot of hoplites and men in civilian dress surrounded a bonfire. Outside this circle of men stood Themistocles, dressed in dark leather armor with white borders, holding an eight-foot spear. He halted before entering this meeting of the naval squadron captains and the hoplite commanders. The warriors stood with their feet set apart and their arms folded.

Themistocles entered the circle with his chin set high. He was middle-aged and thickset, with a broad forehead and short hair. A long mustache fell into a clipped beard. For all his groomed appearance, he looked more like a boxer or a wrestler. He peered into each man's face while standing in front of a fire that shot hot embers into darkening skies.

Zack found a spot outside of the ring, towering over the warriors in front of him, with a good view of the man Nestor had introduced him to in Athens just over a month earlier. Northern Greece had fallen. The Spartan king, Leonidas, had been slain with his elite warriors. Now, Athens lay in cinders. The allied navy of three hundred triremes had been cornered here, near Salamis, holding onto this small island. It was a daunting task for Themistocles to keep the allies together. The Greeks fought for their lives and homes but Zack knew more was at stake. The birth of Western civilization hinged on this naval battle.

Themistocles hoisted the spear high over his head. He closed his eyes as if gathering his will. He transferred the spear to his right hand and drove it into the sand beside his sandaled feet.

"These are our lands. Our ancestors lived and fought here. The temples and sanctuaries to our gods have been built of stone cut in our mountain quarries. Would the all-knowing gods have set their thrones upon the snowy peaks of Olympus if they had any intention of being dislodged by the god of upstart barbarians?"

Themistocles walked around the fire, halting his speech to allow the impact of his question to take hold.

"I tell you the answer is nay. Our gods expect us to fight; they expect us to be victorious and in doing so, earn their devotion and trust. Yet we fight not only for our gods, who might easily vanquish the foe if they chose to, but also to continue our ways."

He stared into the eyes of each official and warrior while he spoke.

"A free man wakes and decides how he might best spend his time. Will he till and harvest the barley, or pick succulent grapes heavy with juice drawn from our fine earth, or smooth the splinters from his fishing boat and cast off early to ensure his catch? A free man can do all this and more."

Now he stood in the center and folded his arms. The crowd remained silent.

"His sons may improve themselves; go to academy, argue to the best of their intellect, prove to friends that they are noble men and seek justice in all matters. Might they change their mind and decide to take on a new vocation, they may do so. We have seen this life take seed and begin to blossom in our land."

Themistocles raised his voice and pointed at the Persian camp on the hills across the strait.

"Yet I ask you to examine the day-to-day life of those who foul our land and shores, over there, just across this tight but gentle strait. May he pick up his sword and return to his land? May he tell the barbarian king he does not wish to fight the brave warriors who oppose him? Must he approach the stacked shields and the bristling points of our spears with a whip licking his shoulders? I ask you fair and brave men of Hellas, which of these lives will you choose?"

Themistocles now quickened his pace, walking the circle of men. "Will you fight and expire, if need be, to pass freedom to our children? Will you strike out at the enemy, until your limbs have no more strength, as did the Spartan king at the Hot Gates? Did he not perish to buy you this time to gather your strength and put iron into your will?"

He thrust his hands at the sky, bent his elbows, and threw them skyward again.

"I ask you to choose the finer manner for a man to live. I ask you to test your character and come away with victory. Choose now, warriors of Hellas. There is no more time to bicker. There is no more time to consider new lands to move our populations. The barbarian king will follow us until we will have no place to bring our ships ashore. The enemy is here for us to slay. They have been drawn into our pit. We will now coil and strike out at them. Make them regret they ever set their eyes upon our rocky shores, our mountain meadows blanketed with wildflowers, our teeming peaks tipped with snow, and the scratchy soil from which only we can bring life?"

Zack watched Themistocles, the craftiest of politicians, moving fast now within the circle of men, searching the faces to see if he had won them over.

"Tell me that you will all stand together and share the danger. Unending glory will be ours; even on Olympus they might say that we are worthy of them. Will you fight when the signal is given? By Zeus and Athena and all we hold dear, tell me your reply."

Some screamed their resolve and others argued to retreat. The surging voices, amid hurled firebrands and kicked sand, hit a crescendo. Fists were thrown and others wrestled their opinions out on the sand. Above the swirl of opinion, someone demanded silence. It was the voice of the Spartan admiral, Eurybiades, given command of the entire allied fleet by Themistocles and the Athenians, a brilliant political tactic even though the Spartans brought fewer ships to the battle.

"Curb your tongues. Save your arguments and anger for the barbarians," he bellowed, joining Themistocles in the middle of the circle. The arguments continued in whispers until finally the voices were raised again in disagreement.

Zack slid through the throng of warriors to position himself close to Themistocles. Eurybiades pulled Themistocles closer to him. From a distance, Eurybiades would be seen as jabbing his finger in Themistocles's chest, giving the impression that they were arguing. "It would be well that we speak alone, noble Themistocles. Let us set ourselves near that rowboat and debate each other there."

"I see the sense of it," Themistocles replied, pushing his hand away. The two separated themselves from the surge of leaders still casting their opinions and stratagems at their backs. Zack hovered near the rings of bodyguards and heard Eurybiades speak first.

"What a fine speech from a fishmonger. Do you think any of the king's agents swallowed it whole?"

"I hope so," Themistocles said. "They must believe that no two voices in this fish soup of allies will agree. As long as you and I see eye to eye in secret, the plan will carry forth in the dark hours. My trusted pedagogue, Sicinnus, will deliver a message to Xerxes, declaring to him that we cannot agree and that we will attempt to escape by both sides of the island channels. Xerxes will hear that I secretly covet his alliance so that Athens will survive. He will be forewarned that during the night, or possibly at first light, the Greek navy will attempt escape. If there are agents nearby with eager ears, they will corroborate what Sicinnus will tell them."

Themistocles knew that the eyes of all the allied captains were upon them from afar. Eurybiades pounded his fist in his palm, continuing the theater of discord.

"I will inform my Peloponnesians to be prepared at first light to let the Persians pass, if they swallow the bait."

"Let us pray to the gods we are better actors than leaders," Themistocles said, his eyes reflecting a popping bonfire. "We part ways now, but when dawn lifts the veil of night, we will be as one."

"It is the only way to victory," Eurybiades replied before leaving to rejoin his captains. Themistocles walked to the edge of the bay and soaked his sand-crusted feet in the channel. Zack saw his chance and hurried in his direction, hoping for a short audience. Two sets of strong arms latched themselves onto him and a dagger was pressed to his throat.

"In haste, are we?" one of his captors whispered in his ear. Zack, his neck stretched and his arm twisted to the brink of agony by guards far shorter than he, gagged out a plea.

"Themistocles will know me. Tell him I am the friend of Nestor." Zack didn't see that Themistocles had come up behind them.

"Let me see this man," he said. "I am confounded by the darkness. What companion of Nestor's are you?"

Zack realized that he no longer resembled the man that had met Themistocles earlier. Now he was grateful for his increasing command of the language of the ancient Greeks. He spit out through gritted teeth, "I am the envoy from Atlantea, noble Themistocles. I came to your home, with my wife, Lauren, accompanied by Nestor."

Themistocles, straining his eyes in the darkness, stared in Zack's face.

"Your hair is shorn on top, and you have a face full of fur. Was not your name Zack? Why the disguise? Have you any more of your medicine? My temples pound harder than the beat-master's hammer on a trireme."

"I bear sad tidings. There is no other way to say it. Nestor is dead."

Themistocles took a step back. "How can this be?" he said, putting his hand out as if to stop the news from reaching him.

Zack said, "A detachment of barbarians, sent up to Delphi, came upon his farm. Persephone is slain also. His niece and my wife escaped."

"Ye gods, the world is crumbling around us. I lose his counsel at such a time?"

"These are the times that try men's souls," Zack said, stealing the phrase from the desperation of the American Revolutionary War for his response, but it fit.

"Truer words were never said, Zack. Yet alas, I have no time for mourning, there is much to do. Seek me out after the battle. You will find me, or my head."

Zack breathed in deeply. "Themistocles, I want—"

"Can I assist you somehow? Or should I? You make a nasty habit of tempting the gods." A guard tugged on Themistocles's forearm, pulling him and pointing to the rowboat, barely lit in the distance. A figure lurked near the rowboat. When the man turned, Zack could see it was Themistocles's slave, Sicinnus, the one he and Lauren had met at the house.

"I must take leave. Seek Poylas. His trireme lies yonder." He pointed to a ship pulled up onto a *neosoikoi*—a stone boat ramp, its hull being painted with another coat of pitch.

"Keep heart, victory will be yours," Zack said.

Themistocles stopped suddenly. He raised his thumb and forefinger to his chin. "And Zack, will it be our will or the will of the gods that will decide the victor tomorrow?"

Assured by his experiences with Apollo, Zack replied, "It will be both. You are the strong arm of the gods. You do their bidding."

"You are a changed man, Zack. Tell that message to all our Hellenes, and speak more loudly, so the gods will hear you as well." Themistocles left with his guards.

Zack's sandals kicked up sand running to the ship. He saw a shadowy figure up on the deck.

"On board there, I seek Poylas," Zack said, panting.

"Come out of the darkness. Who seeks him?"

"A friend, my name is Zack. Will you tell him?"

"There will be no need. It is I, and as soon as I can believe my eyes, you may come aboard."

Zack ascended a rickety gangplank and met the curly-haired sea captain at the top where they clasped forearms.

Poylas said, "You didn't wait for us at the Gates. Where is your wife?"

"It's a long tale," Zack said. "She has gone west to safety. Walking south from the Hot Gates was not a good choice, but I am here and offer my assistance to you."

Poylas narrowed his eyes. "You want to fight. Do you know which end of a sword is the sharp one?"

Zack laughed but was aware that most knew that he had no experience in battle.

"I am not even sure that I could row for you." Zack grinned. "I've been in some fighting and my shoulder was cut." Zack turned and showed him the raised scar that crossed from the front of his left shoulder, over his deltoid, and ended just before his shoulder blade.

Poylas said, "You won't be much good to anyone with that, but I couldn't put you on a bench either way. Rowers train for months to pull their oars in unison. One bad oar and the ship could go dead in the water or fail to catch enough speed when we're ready to ram." He pointed at a hill about a hundred yards from shore. "Go to the camp of the Mycenaeans, where you see three fires up on that rise. Seek out Prince Diomedes. He'll put you to work somewhere."

Not exactly what I had in mind.

"I'll see you off in the morning, Poylas. May the gods be with you tomorrow if the battle commences."

"It will have to be soon. We cannot hold these rascals together much longer." He sniffed at the air and rubbed his arms. "It's a bit colder tonight. That means there might be some fog in the morning. Take off now, I must attend to my ship."

"Sink one for me, Poylas."

"You are not greedy enough, my friend. I will wreck five, just for you."

Zack began to hike to the Mycenaean camp, but turned to view the beached flotilla. There was no chatter and few campfires. The sailors worked quietly, aware the noise would carry over the water to alert the enemy of their activities.

Reaching the top of the rise at the edge of the camp, Zack met a team of hoplites, fully armored. After he explained why he was there and who sent him, they escorted Zack to a blazing campfire. A haunch of steer smoked over the flames, making Zack realize he had not eaten since he started his day at the wall in Corinth. It had taken many hours to hitch a ferry ride over to Salamis. The aroma of roasting meat assaulted his stomach, distracting him from the warrior who now stood before him.

"You are the envoy from Atlantea, the husband of Lady Lauren?"

Zack studied the warrior before him; taller than most, oddly clean-shaven, lean but muscular, dark hair tied in braids that fell across his back.

"I am, but how do you know this?"

"I am Diomedes. I fought at the pass. I am among the men grateful for the attention both of you gave to our wounds. I didn't recognize you at first with the whiskers and chopped hair." Then he froze. "But wait, where is Lauren? She left for Sparta and then to search for you. Only the gods knew if you were a corpse."

"She awaits me in the west."

Diomedes exhaled heavily. "It is well that is so. She was a welcome guest in our palace." He looked away momentarily, concern on his brow.

"There is much I don't know about her travels without me," Zack said. An unexplained shiver ran through him.

"A man should guard his woman," Diomedes replied, staring into Zack's eyes.

"How may I assist you tomorrow?" Zack asked, not wanting to dig deeper in what the hoplite might have meant.

"You didn't fight in the north, if I remember well. Ever stick a man with one of these?" Diomedes held out his eight-foot spear.

"No, but maybe someone could teach me."

Chuckles erupted around them as other hoplites sidled up to listen.

"A warrior is not made overnight and a shield grows heavy quickly. Tomorrow, if the barbarians reach this island, you will surely need it. If they unload their Immortals, you will have to stand with us. When their sailors wash up on the shore, we will spear them like carp in a barrel."

"Teach me what you can tonight."

"Then come over by the fire, but don't think my men will treat you like a child. You will rest this night, but not too comfortably."

While a near-full moon rose overhead, Zack alternated between being slammed to the ground as his feet were knocked from underneath him, to rising to take on a spearman or a hoplite darting in, slashing him with a wooden practice sword. He had learned to parry a sword cut with his shield and drive a man back with a series of swipes and stabs. He remembered his lessons with Nestor and attacked his instructors with a spear, bending his knees and coming in low.

After an hour, Zack held his hand up. "That's enough for tonight," he said. "I must reserve some strength for tomorrow." Zack peeled the bandage from his shoulder. Diomedes raised his eyebrows, as did others who had done the sparring.

"You didn't say you were cut."

"Did you not continue to fight when wounded at Thermopylae? I must also."

"You may yet be a warrior and a worthy opponent. Come and eat with us," Diomedes said, walking away.

Zack nodded, confused by being called an opponent.

What the hell did he mean by that?

Zack awoke with a start when someone tripped over his leg. The man swore in hushed tones and then continued on in the dark. Quickly, many others rose and quietly donned their linen armor. Zack rubbed his shoulder, finding that he had overdone it the evening before.

It was a hard lesson and Zack realized more than ever that he had a long way to go before he could survive hand-to-hand hoplite warfare.

Now I could use some pain pills.

No fires were allowed. He went to where Diomedes and his guards were strapping on their leather sandals and fixing the clasps of the greaves covering their shins.

"This is a day that will be remembered," Zack said.

"For those of us that still stand after the barbarians are beaten," Diomedes answered. "If you have no armor, I have a leather jacket you could wear."

"That would be appreciated. I go to see Poylas off. I will return to stand by you."

"You have no stake in this war. Why do you fight for us?" Diomedes asked.

"But I do, Prince Diomedes. I do."

Zack approached the line of triremes, all with their masts and sails down, stripped for battle. The crews crept up and down the gangplanks in the dark, loading the last of the battle ware. He heard a loud splash and a series of groans. Zack stepped aside as a line of twenty Athenian marines—carrying two spears apiece, their helmets and shields slung over their backs—boarded Poylas's trireme. They took their stations at the bow, behind a raised superstructure, much like a castle wall. The last of the hoplites carried grappling hooks to cast aboard the enemy ships when the signal was given to board and attack. The rowers already sat in their tiered rows. Oars were pulled up and in, creating a crisscross pattern under the two long walking planks that stretched the length of the ship. Zack ascended the gangplank and saw Poylas standing at the stern, where the captain's chair, called the trierarch, was bolted to the deck. He heard muted cursing coming from him.

"Greetings, Poylas."

"The day is not starting out well. My shield bearer fell off the gangplank just now and broke his arm. By the gods, what a foul fortune blows my way."

"What's his task?"

"To shield me from the missiles that will pelt our decks when we close in. I can't watch them fly at me and direct the helmsman at the same time." He looked out at the glimmers of dawn. "We must embark while it's dark."

Zack waded through a jumble of thoughts in his mind. Was it sheer foolishness to offer what he knew might cause his death? Abandoning all temperance, Zack blurted out before he could stop himself, "I will take his place."

"Are you mad?" Shortly thereafter, Poylas said, grinning and scratching his chin whiskers, "Can you swim?"

Zack nodded.

"We may not come back. Do you venture to tempt fate once more?"

"I will accept the fate the three sisters have set for me."

"Then take my shield and stand with us. I cannot spare marines." Poylas pointed his index finger toward a bronze shield lying on the deck. On the face of it was a blue dolphin leaping from the sea.

"A dolphin," Zack said. "A good omen and a symbol of Apollo?"

"It is so. He came to the oracle long ago from Crete disguised as a dolphin. We will require all his grace this day. Now eat some bread and ready yourself."

Zack picked up the shield and felt its weight, almost twenty pounds of oak and beaten bronze. He stared at the dolphin. Delphi was the Greek word for dolphin and thus was named the temple site dedicated to Apollo.

Apollo must be watching me now. Am I choosing to do this, or is this my fate?

"What am I getting myself into?" Zack whispered in English. There was no one to answer him, just the resigned efforts of men facing their fate. He wanted to live real-time history, but not as an observer, like at Thermopylae.

The order went out to sleeve the oars through the hooks and lower them into the bay. Dockworkers pushed the trireme down the oiled ramp into the still waters, as did many other crews among the other inlets and coves. Darkness still blanketed the sky. The allied fleet could only be so quiet. A fleet preparing for battle is noisy. The Greek oarsmen and marines only heard the thump of pulse in their chests and in their ears.

Zack felt a muscle twitch on his right cheek. He rubbed it, but it came on stronger. And it wouldn't stop.

King Xerxes wore purple-beaded slippers. He strode upon a white drape, laid over a dirt path leading to a bluff overlooking the narrow waterway. Courtiers accompanied the royal person, ready to catch the king if he tripped. He arrived at his white throne chair, positioned to allow him to direct the entrapment of the Greek rebel navy lying out in the darkness.

Xerxes, lord and king of much of the known world, ruled from where the eastern sun rose in Bactria near India, westwards to Anatolia, Ionia, and Thrace, now studded with the colonies and cities of these same Greeks. He commanded the riches of Egypt and Ethiopia in the south with its wildcats and population with skin the color of coal; over Medes, Iranians, Assyrians, and Babylonians in the middle lands; Scythians, Armenians, and Thracians who dwelled in the north; the prosperous port cities of Sidon, Tyre, Halicarnassus, Tarsus, and Ashkelon along the shores of the inland sea. King of a brave and devoted aristocracy, Xerxes dedicated himself to expanding the empire his forebears had created. The invasion so far had not been without its difficulties. An oversized black eunuch spread a tasseled shawl over Xerxes's shoulders, shielding him against a morning breeze.

"Mardonius, did word reach us of the Greek navy making their attempt to escape through the west channel of the island before us?"

Mardonius, marshal of the army, answered, "No, my lord, the Egyptian squadrons report no movement, so far."

Xerxes scratched his ear. "And the Phoenician admiral below signals no attempt by the main Greek navy to escape either?"

"Nay, sire. They are trapped like sows in a pen, ready for slaughter.

Perhaps they wait for light. The messenger who came to us last night revealed their discord. It may be they chatter and scramble and cannot yet decide a course of action. Soon all will be revealed. The signal flags are ready. They will move on your command, my lord."

Xerxes's fleet of four hundred triremes waited in the bay, down to his left. A screening detachment beat a slow path back and forth across the channel opening, waiting to catch any Greeks hoping to make it to safety in the open sea.

"My crews," Xerxes asked. "Have they been awake all night?"

"That is so, my lord," Mardonius answered. "Yet, they know you watch them from this point. They will not tire."

"They must not fail me. Are the admirals and captains aware what their fate will be if the Greeks escape?"

"I am sure they enjoy the manner in which their heads are fitted now, my lord."

"When Ahura Mazda sends forth his first burst of light from the east, I shall pour the sacrifice and the sacred fire shall be lit. Victory requires only one climatic sea battle to destroy the Greek navy. Then I will march upon the meager wall the Greeks built on the isthmus to the south. My army, without end, will then smite the southern Greeks, including the hated Spartans, and the war to conquer Greek lands will be over."

"I welcome it," Mardonius answered, sensing a stiffening breeze. He sniffed the air. The high ground of the island lay silhouetted in the first glow of light coming up on their left, from the east. Xerxes stood, holding a golden chalice, and dribbled wine on the ground beside his throne. Next he waved his hand and a firebrand holder lit the stone hearth. Ahura Mazda was properly sacrificed.

"When the Greek fleet is crushed, I want only the women and children spared. The fire of rebellion in the men must be stamped out. The slave markets will prosper."

Mardonius did not seem to hear the words of his monarch. His eyes strained to pick out the ghostly shapes revealing themselves with the coming of dawn.

Xerxes prattled on. "Without the Greek navy to stop us, and as you have planned, we will land troops on the southern island and corner the Spartans in their homeland. The Spartan troops will withdraw from the wall, and with no navy to make their escape, we will surround the remaining Greek warriors. They will all be on their knees begging for mercy before the moon makes another cycle."

Mardonius walked to the cliff edge for a better look.

"Mardonius," Xerxes said, irritated at being ignored.

"My lord," Mardonius shouted back. "There to the right, up in the channel. I see sails, many of them. The Greek ships are turning to flee. A trireme does fight under sail. The Egyptians will catch the Greeks as they round the island on the other side. Victory will be ours."

Xerxes stood on the pedestals before his throne, craning his neck in the gathering morning to witness this news for himself. He nodded his head and said, "Then the message the Athenian leader sent to us was truthful. Signal the Phoenicians and Cypriots to enter the narrows at full speed. Close the trap and chase them down."

Signal flags unfurled as a rose-colored hue cast itself upon the sky, mountains, and peninsulas in the distance. The bay began to lighten below as the first squadrons beat their oars and triremes surged forward. Xerxes saw that many of the Greek ships still sat at their docks.

Xerxes said, "We have caught them sleeping." He clasped his hands together in front of his lips. "We will smash them before they can run."

Off to the right, the Greek ships under sail still ran north. The leading triremes of the Phoenicians and the massive numbers of ships behind them were now all moving into the channel in pursuit. The royal party slapped each other on their backs. Xerxes's eyes remained locked on the chase.

Then they heard voices coming from the narrows of the straits.

"Do you hear that, Mardonius?" Xerxes said with a puzzled look. "What is that commotion bouncing off the rocks? I hear singing. Is it our oarsmen singing so mightily? How proud I am of them."

Mardonius leaned his ear toward the narrows below, attempting to filter the voices from the slap of oars.

"It is as if one voice can be heard," Mardonius murmured. "Could all of our ships sing the same song? Do they not speak different tongues?"

Mardonius sensed spidery fingers of fear lancing through him. To their right, the Greek triremes in flight stopped. Sails fell, then their masts.

Mardonius stepped back and braced his stomach with both hands.

Xerxes leaped to his feet, thrusting his finger toward the Greeks. His lips moved but no words came from his mouth. Down to his left, just when his squadrons cleared a tiny island in the middle of the narrows, lines of Greek ships came out of the morning fog.

And the voices, louder with each stroke of the oars, came from the Greek decks.

Xerxes bellowed, "What treachery is before me? The Greeks are to flee, the messenger told us so. Yet their oars beat a path to strike my ships. This cannot be."

Mardonius mouthed a response but instead it became lost in the tactical dilemma developing before his eyes. A chill ran the length of his back, something he had not felt since his precious Immortals lay slain before the Spartans in the north.

"Call our ships to return, Mardonius. Make haste," Xerxes spit out.

A blast of trumpets echoed across the straits. The Greek ships came on in even lines, like arrows to a target.

"Signal them now, I demand it. Summon them back." Xerxes covered his cheeks with his palms.

Over the voices of the Greeks and the beating of oars, the strain of ropes, the wind whistling, and trumpets echoing off the mountainside came a sickening crunch from out in the bay.

Xerxes groaned hideously and leaped from his throne, shaking his fist at the scene unfolding before him.

"I will not allow this. This cannot be." With lips curled, Xerxes croaked out, "No, no, call back my ships. Call back my ships."

A new breeze blew in from the north. Zack heard shrill flutes and the voices of oarsmen and marines on his ship. He tried to sing but no words came out. All he could do was continue staring at the lines of Greek triremes, leaping forward with each sweep of their oars. Ahead, the Persian fleet packed themselves into the strait, all eager to join the fight.

His arms lost their strength. Spreading his legs for balance, he held on to the rim of his shield with one hand and a railing with the other. The timbers creaked and groaned at the simultaneous dig of three banks of oars into the still waters of the Saronic Gulf. One hundred and seventy men labored, singing at the top of their lungs. Zack's heart beat faster. The drum master pounded out an increasing cadence. Zack concentrated on the singing, trying to understand the words. It was a paean, a prayer to Apollo.

He heard the Greeks sing, "Onward, sons of Hellas. Free your country, set free your children."

With the Persian ships getting closer, he latched onto the back of the trierarch chair. It was time to thread his arm through the sleeve on the inside of his shield and grip the hold cord. Zack didn't know the words of the song. He hummed it, faint at first, as a distraction from what he knew was about to happen. Then louder, he belted it out, when the words were repeated over and over again, till his voice matched the others. He made up words at times. He didn't care. He sang. His heart beat faster. The song took him over.

Zack wanted to fight. He could do it. He could be one of them.

Poylas shouted, "On ye hounds, wade into them, harder now. Pull, you freemen, pull!"

Poylas's commands jogged Zack back from his song-trance. Before him, the Persian fleet surged into the bay like a jam of logs coming down a river.

Zack could see the archers running to the rails on the Persian ships. His trireme surged toward them.

"Marines, hold on to your rails," Poylas instructed. "We'll ram them."

To their left, an Athenian trireme outraced them and crashed into the side of a Persian ship with a resounding smash that echoed off the mountain heights. Screams followed from the struck ship. Men ran from the impact area. Some leaped overboard. Cheers erupted from the other Athenian ships closing on their targets.

"Helmsman," Poylas barked, pointing. "Turn and spear that one amidships. Steady, steady now. Dig your oars faster, men. Now hold on."

Zack saw the terrified eyes of the Persian oarsmen. They scrambled to escape the imminent collision. Many were chained down and could only throw up their arms in defense.

"Faster." Poylas said, holding on to the forearms of his chair and planting his feet on the deck. Zack saw fire arrows pelt the other Athenian triremes until the Persian archers turned their attention toward his. He raised the shield to protect both Poylas and himself.

The collision hurled Zack into the trierarch's chair. He heard wooden beams cracking. Both ships shifted violently in the water. He regained his footing and lifted his shield again. The impact knocked the enemy archers from their feet, giving Zack enough time to recover his position.

"Backwater, you dogs of war. Backwater." Poylas boomed over the cries of wounded enemy oarsman tossed into the bay. Marines with long poles pushed against the side of the Persian trireme, separating their ship from the damaged enemy ship's hull. Zack raised his shield higher and covered Poylas.

"Don't block my view, off to the side with that shield." Poylas seized Zack's leather vest, shouting, "Watch the missiles. Here they come again."

A volley of arrows flew at them, hissing as they passed. Some struck timbers. Others overshot their targets and sliced into the bay. Two of the oarsmen on the top outrigger row caught arrows, twirled, and fell onto the long deck planks. Zack's shield rang out as a few shots found his target. He breathed a sigh of relief.

"They'll roll over and have no time to shoot at us again." Poylas said, pulling on his rudder.

The trireme detached itself from the enemy hull. All along the line now, the splintering of oars and timbers was heard. At a right angle to them, the Persian fleet came on. The Athenian navy, smashing into the left side of their fleet, set a chain reaction of floundering Persian triremes that tried to turn, but could not. Each succeeding row of Persian ships collided into the row in front of them. Except for the leading squadrons, the Persian fleet was dead in the water. The Greek Peloponnesian and Aeginian ships, seeing their opportunity, attacked from the southern inlets, deep into the flanks of the enemy.

"That one there, helmsman, turn us," Poylas yelled above the din.

A new target presented itself for broadside. The oarsmen strained and grunted. The beat of drums announced the pace.

"Can we gain enough speed to ram?" Zack said.

"Maybe," Poylas said. "Marines, ready your fishhooks."

The Persian ship ahead saw them coming and attempted to turn.

The new angle gave Zack a view of the hundreds of faces manning the oars. They were all slaves, from mostly interior kingdoms of the Persian Empire, pressed into service for the navy. Most could probably not swim, with barely a chance of survival if their ship was struck or boarded. The Phoenician ship locked oars with another ship and neither enemy vessel could move.

Poylas saw the opportunity and shouted with his hands cupped, "Row and we'll skewer another."

The three banks of Athenian oarsmen couldn't see where they were headed. Facing the stern of the trireme from where they sat on their benches, the oarsmen slid on the greased lambskins under their flanks, enabling them to draw a longer pull. They sent their trireme forward, building speed.

Zack held the chair tighter this time. When the impact came, he was thrown, but still able to keep his feet. The ram smashed into the enemy hull, piercing it, but not too deeply. Railings splintered along the right side of Zack's ship. Crewmembers were thrown from the outrigger and oarsman sent sprawling from their long benches.

The marines regained their footing and formed rows at the forecastle.

"Throw your hooks," their captain said. Grappling hooks latched onto the enemy vessel. The Athenian crewmen tied ropes to ship rails, holding the ships together. The first marines climbed over the rail, deflecting darts and sword thrusts from the enemy marines protecting their decks. More Athenian marines followed, spearing their counterparts and working their way down the planks, dispatching crewmembers and oarsmen as they went.

Zack held his shield high, catching more arrows from the Persian archers aiming at Poylas. The Persian commander knew from where the Greek ship was commanded. Enemy oarsmen leaped into the sea, grasping for anything afloat. The sea was clogged with debris and thrashing men, crying to their gods for deliverance. Zack and Poylas viewed the progress of their marines who were now amidships, moving fast, fighting in two rows down both lanes of the enemy vessel's deck. Enemy rowers, having been passed by, escaped behind the Athenian marines, effectively cutting off the marines from their boarding point.

Zack's concentration on the progress of their marines evaporated when he saw an enemy trireme turning toward them. They were hopelessly locked in with the Persian ship and only four of their marines remained on board. Zack recognized the peril immediately.

"We are going to be rammed." Zack said.

"By the gods, we're trapped," Poylas screamed over the pandemonium. "We'll be struck, watch out." Some heard the order and took hold.

The impact sent them sprawling. Speared below their waterline, their trireme had suffered a deathblow.

"Dammit." Zack said, regaining his feet. Within minutes, dozens of enemy marines lined up and hopped over the rails, holding small shields and swinging axes, maces, and swords. The unarmed oarsmen fought them with bare hands, but many leaped into the frothing bay, knowing well their ship was doomed. The four marines left on board defended the two center long planks that served as a deck. They parried axe blows, killing some with their long spears, but they were steadily driven back.

Poylas shouted, "We must help them, Zack. Keep the shield and follow me."

Zack picked up a broken piece of the outrigger and ran with Poylas to join the Greek defenders, who were losing control of the decks. Fire arrows lodged in their hull. With Poylas at his side, they reached the two hoplites on the left side of the ship. They put their weight behind the hoplites, pushing into their backs to shore up their balance. The weight of the enemy attack was too much, and there was little traction on the slippery deck. Run through by a spear, one of the hoplites fell and his body was kicked aside by the Persian marines.

Zack took his place in the line. His mouth went dry. A sword came in a downward arc toward Zack's head. He blocked it with his club and then backhanded his adversary across the face, sending him to the deck. Poylas came in low with his sword and gutted another Persian swinging a single-bladed axe. Zack alternated forehand and backhand, knocking weapons from hands and smashing arms and heads, anything he could hit.

With their backs to the stern hull, the remaining two marines from the right side joined them and locked shields.

The enemy stopped momentarily, gathering their courage to continue the attack. Their advance along the desk had cost them. Half of the enemy marines lay wounded or dead on the decks.

Zack caught his breath in great heaves. They were trapped. Blood pounded in his ears. Black smoke enveloped his ship.

We're on fire.

He bent his legs to receive the charge that he knew would come.

Flames and smoke billowed behind the enemy. Shouts and screams filled the air. Zack heard unceasing crunches as more Persian ships were struck by the Greek triremes. To his right, the Athenian marines who had bordered the enemy vessel now saw the peril on their own ship. They doubled their efforts to cut a path back to their decks.

With a battle cry, the enemy marines rushed at them. Zack and the two Athenians with shields ran forward to block their advance. Poylas swung his sword over the top, gashing an extended neck and severing an upraised hand.

Axes crashed onto his shield. The faces were close now. Wild-eyed and filled with bloodlust, Persian marines drove onward, knowing victory was near. Another Athenian took an axe cut and dropped to his knees. Zack, gasping for air, felt his back foot against the hull.

I've run out of ship.

There was little in the back of the ship to brace against. He wedged his back foot along the floorboard rim and prepared himself for the end.

Lauren, why didn't I listen to you and stay away from the fighting?

Javelins were thrown at them but they were easily blocked by the shields. Arrows flew by. Zack swallowed and licked his lips. He had no saliva. His heart pounded in his chest. Smoke obscured the sky, at least partly. He glanced skyward and wondered if you can always see so clearly just before one dies.

The rush came again. He bent to receive the jarring impact. Metal rang. He swung his club and connected. The last Athenian marine fell. A blur of motion came from the right.

Poylas blared, "Watch out."

A sledgehammer smacked Zack's jaw. He lost his eyesight. Stars burst in his head. Hot blood sprayed across his face. He spun, lost his footing, hit the rail, and toppled over the side.

He fell like an iron anvil, unable to flail his arms for balance. He hit debris before the sea, smacking on top of mangled bodies and desperate men, fractured rails, floating hulls, and rigging.

The saltwater revived him. Zack choked and gurgled. Hands grasped for him or anything else to halt their owners from descending to the bottom of the strait. A trireme raced by, unknowingly whacking the sea-tossed survivors on their heads. The swimmers screamed cries of terror in languages he'd never heard before.

Two hands grasped his shoulders from behind and pulled him under. Zack thrashed and thrust an elbow into his assailant's soft underbelly. Rising to the surface, he connected with his right fist, and gained his release.

He kicked with his legs and found himself in a scene of complete chaos.

Zack grasped a shattered plank, held onto it like a paddleboard, and willed his legs to move. He heard a deep groan, not from a man, but of a ship, capsizing to his right. He spit the briny sea from his mouth. On the surface, the blue sea was mixed with the blood of countless men. Barely holding on to consciousness, saltwater filled his mouth, making him gag and cough.

Zack closed his eyes while catching his breath and summoned his remaining will to live. Oddly, Lauren, in her wedding gown, flashed into his fading consciousness. She had asked her father to give her away dressed in his Marine Corps dress blues. They all stood together. Who would know that he died here?

An oar missed his head. He put one arm over his head to keep from being clobbered. He kicked away from the sinking trireme. Men cried their last cry and sank below the sea chop.

To both sides of him, Athenian triremes sped by, hulls above the bronze ram painted with blue eyes. Drums beat from their decks and fifes played. The men still sang the paean to Apollo. Zack saw the shore of Salamis, a hundred yards ahead. He pushed aside floating bodies and wreckage. He found a plank that would support his weight. He pulled himself halfway onto it.

I can make it.

He kicked with slow, even strokes.

Nearing shore, still hugging the plank, he heard screams. All along the beach, hoplites skewered the washed-up sailors from the enemy fleet with their lances.

No mercy today. Help me, Lauren. Help me . . . Apollo.

A wave caught him. Exhausted, he fell off the plank. He floated on his back. Seawater flowed into his mouth. The wave left him rolling in the low surf on the shoreline. He dug his fingers into the sand for traction. He crawled onto the shore, gagging.

He heard in Greek, "Another, over there, to add to our collection." He heard splashing feet and clanking armor.

Zack looked up, but couldn't see too well with the sting of salt in his eyes. Coughing out seawater, he saw a spear raise and the sun glinting off its shiny blade.

He cried out weakly, "Diomedes." Zack twisted enough so the point missed his leather-covered chest and plunged into his shoulder, the same one injured before.

"Diomedes," Zack gurgled out, absorbing the bite of the spearhead. The hoplite twisted the lance and then pulled it out to strike again. Zack arched his back and raised his right hand to halt the finishing strike.

I'm sorry, Lauren. I did all I could. It's over.

"Go to your death, Persian," the hoplite shouted.

Zack mouthed the words but nothing came out. Why couldn't he speak? Then a third time, he screamed through clenched teeth in Greek, with all the strength he could muster.

"Prince . . . Diomedeeeeees!"

"Choice words then," the hoplite said, holding back the butt spike of his spear just above Zack's breastbone. "Drag him to the physician. He might be one of ours."

Later, Zack awakened on the sand. He heard voices drawn out, like bad videotape, and the aroma of newly cut burnt wood. He attempted to rise but his left side refused. The muted voices coalesced into cheering men, waving spears and tossing their helmets high.

Jubilation erupted all along the shore.

His tongue stuck to his palate. Zack coughed and waved his right hand, hoping to catch the attention of anyone nearby. He saw a man spin, fall to his knees, and throw his arms in a reverent act of supplication. The look on his face bespoke pure joy. Others joined him. They threw their arms over each other, fell, and rolled in the sand. The words rang clear now: "The barbarian navy has sailed away."

Zack raised himself on his right elbow and tried to get up. Forget it. His left shoulder was wrapped in tight bandages. His left jaw was tied tight also. He ran his tongue around the inside of his mouth and felt hamburger. The Persian navy had sailed away and the Persian king would now be racing to the pontoon bridges at the Hellespont to make his escape. The history books had said so.

"Lay back, sailor. There's no need to rise. The battle is over, at least for now," said a man with dark locks held back by a golden forehead band.

Zack said in scrambled English, "We won?"

"You're difficult to understand with your jaw wrapped up," the man said, squinting and trying to block the sun with his hand. "You have been dreaming a full day. I put the iron in your shoulder while you slept. Lucky man you are, not to feel the bite of the hot iron."

"I've been out a whole day?"

"Do not deny the gods what they require of you."

Zack raised his chin and felt a circular burn mark on his chest.

Oh shit, I hope they didn't bleed me.

"You'll have more time to rest. Prince Diomedes will be back soon. You should have heard him laugh when he saw you. He guessed for sure that you would have been slain. He asks that you accompany him to Mycenae. The gods favor you, sailor. They truly do."

Zack turned his head to the gentle lapping of waves on the shore. Then he heard the smack and piling of wooden beams.

"What?" Zack asked through clenched teeth, understanding now how hard it must be to make a living as a ventriloquist.

"They will be making piles all day and then maybe for the next seven thereafter. Except they gather not wood or ships; what you hear is the stacking of corpses."

"Pull me up?" Zack asked, levitating his right hand to signal his desire to be hoisted to a sitting position.

Damn, he thought, I'm the Mumbler again. He remembered his time in the makeshift aid-station outside Athens. After he was struck unconscious by the slingers, he mumbled for days in and out of sleep and was given the name Mumbler by the Persian surgeon.

Cheering hoplites packed the shoreline, running amongst the trireme crews, screaming thanks to the gods. Fractured and half-submerged ships lay beached all along the shore, and across below the heights where Xerxes sat the morning before. As far as Zack's eyes could see, an unending string of beached corpses lay on the edge of the water.

Just like the shoreline at Thermopylae. The midday heat potentiated the aroma of death.

"We haven't enough wood in all of Hellas to feed the funeral pyres that will be needed," the physician said. "They will be tossed in holes before they corrupt. Until I pass to the land of Hades, I will never forget the unceasing crunch of bronze rams upon wooden hulls out in that bay. The Peloponnesians hit them on their left flank, trapping them in a rabbit's snare. They fouled each other and strove to retreat backwater, but to no avail." The physician sifted sand through his fingers as he spoke. "The sea echoed with the dirge of desperate men, knowing well they would die. The paean our sailors and marines sang, methinks, was the last sound they ever heard, 'cepting the gurgle in their throats." The physician broke only the faintest of grins.

Zack ran his fingers along the bandage that secured his jaw. He winced and rolled his eyes. The physician stuck three long sticks in the sand and placed a cloth over them to make him a shade.

The physician prattled on. "Worked all night to repair our ships, we did. This morning, we sailed out to meet them again, but their triremes had gone. Not to be seen at Pireaus, nor past the bend of Cynosure, or even docked at islands just beyond our shores. They tore down their king's throne in the time it takes to drain a krater of wine. With so few ships and no food, Xerxes had to flee, too. They say he bypassed the smoking ruins of Athens and made haste up the inland road to the north. I declare before the gods, this is a day I will never let loose from my memories."

Zack's teeth were bound so tightly he could barely speak. He pumped his fist instead.

The physician said solemnly, "The cost of failure for them has only begun. They were so sure of victory. Last night, when the light left the skies and the only sound to be heard was the screams of men filling their lungs with water or the others that were slain by our hoplites, it ran certain in my thoughts that our gods would not allow their temples to be sacked by an inferior race of men. Our gods are far stronger than theirs. The barbarians must know that by now."

The physician gathered wood and made his own pile of smaller pieces.

"These men are all dead because of the arrogance of their king and the brilliance of Themistocles. The dead lose everything. Who knows what gods they travel with now?"

The physician handed him a cup of wine with a sandy bottom. "There now, partake of this before there is none left. It will deaden your pain. If your cuts fester, have someone bleed you and drain the evil vapors."

Not a goddamned chance, Zack said to himself. I almost got my head handed to me again and I wonder if Poylas made it off the ship.

"Leave that bandage on and don't try to spit out that resin holding your jaws together. It'll have to stay that way for almost two moons for the bones to mend. You'll be drinking your meals for a spell. I must leave you now to bind the broken limbs of our wounded."

The scene on the trireme replayed itself in his mind. He was alert now, and the throbbing that was faint earlier had now increased and spread throughout his left shoulder where he'd been stabbed. *Where the hell is my satchel? Maybe Diomedes has it back at camp. That's where I left it. There's still penicillin and pain pills left in it. I hope it's enough.*

The physician turned to walk away. "They'll come by later with a wagon and load you on with the shields and breastplates. Two days of bumpy road and you'll be under the Lion Gate of Mycenae."

Zack tried to grunt a thank-you, but the physician had left.

The whirlwind of events, from when Lauren and he were captured by the Persian cavalry to his encounter with Apollo, coursed through his imagination like film clips. He closed his eyes, willing the pain to cease its domination over him. The drink in the cup had to have some kind of opium in it. The tension began to leave him. He unclenched his fist.

He remained lost in recollection.

Lauren, you would have been proud of me. But I almost bought the farm. Would Apollo let me die? He said he had some kind of plan in store for me; a mission to save lives. Does that give me some special protection?

Zack tried to take a deeper breath and winced. He couldn't rise.

If Apollo's got my back somehow, he isn't doing a very good job.

The wind picked up and a corner of the sheet protecting him from the sun blew loose. The sun warmed his face. It felt good on the raised black-and-blue bruises on his cheek and chin. He must look hideous.

I have another reason to live. I'm going to Mycenae and nothing is going to stop me from seeing that citadel. Maybe it won't have the grandeur of earlier Mycenaean times, but . . .

He heard a creaking wagon approach.

Zack surrendered to the shadows that crept from the periphery of his thoughts. He turned his head to the side, with his cheek burrowed into the white sand comfortably. Drool from his gummed-together mouth leaked out and soaked the sand under his chin. He saw the blurred image of a tall man pulling the wagon and an amused grin on his face. When he bent to load Zack onto the cart, a long curl, tucked behind his ear, loosened and fell across his face. The man lifted him up effortlessly. The stab wound in Zack's shoulder caused him to cry out loud.

"There, there, Traveler," Apollo said. "I will tend to you soon enough and see you safely to your next stop in Mycenae. I fear you will choke if I let you drink. I will bathe you in the healing potions instead."

Zack saw blue light, and an instantaneous electrical charge that encompassed his body. *How many more times can I escape alive? I have to get back to you, Lauren. Can you hear me?*

Then he sensed soothing warmth, and let it encompass him.

Delphi, Greece

PRESENT DAY

Lauren cracked her head on the cave ceiling. Rubbing her scalp, she felt sticky blood under her nails. Stalactites hung from the top of the cave passageway, like chopped-off dragon's teeth, making it no place for a tall woman.

"Darn it all," she moaned. "Wait up, sweetheart, you're going too fast and I can't see."

She followed Cassandra, her thirteen-year-old orphaned friend from ancient Greece, deep into the mountain from the main chamber of the cave. After everything that had happened to them, crawling ahead into a blackened abyss seemed a trivial risk to take. Still, there was something terrifying about descending into the depths of the earth, a place that could swallow you whole and never give up your body.

"Please, Cassandra, slow down," she yelled, rubbing the new gash that she knew would made a perfect triangle with the others on the top of her head.

"I beseech you to hurry, Lady Lauren, and keep your head down."

"Too late—for my knees, too," Lauren said, running her hands over an uneven stone floor. "Stay where you are till I catch up."

Ten yards ahead, Cassandra halted along a curve in the pathway. "I cannot believe Nestor survived, if only for a while," Lauren said.

They navigated a long, grueling obstacle course, one that required them to clear debris, climb ledges, and descend blind drops where earth movement had altered the pathway over the past twenty-five centuries.

At least Lauren had the flashlight.

"The gods kept my uncle alive. How else could Zack have left us his words?"

"Somebody made it happen, and I think I know who." Lauren crawled slowly to spare her kneecaps. This time, she kept a hand over the top of her head. In the light that the flashlight offered, Lauren could see crude scrapings that had widened the cave tunnel.

She wanted to smash that flashlight against the wall when she found it, knowing Bessus had held it in his hand earlier. They only had a pack of matches lifted from the police station's duty room to illuminate their way through the tunnel entrance, and she had the singed fingers to prove it. Then she found the flashlight on the cave floor. It would have to do for now. Still, holding it, she felt a waves of revulsion. Where could Bessus have gone? The terra-cotta pithoi still lay broken. She could see blood in a puddle where he had collapsed. Could he be alive in the cave right now? But that didn't make sense. The entrance to the cave had been covered again, hidden actually. The rocks set in place carefully. Bessus wouldn't do that.

She hoped.

"Your ancestors left their marks on the walls," Lauren said, wondering how long it would have taken to hack enough space for an adult to pass through. "I just wish they had smoothed the floor, too."

"My uncle wrapped pads over his knees and wore a bronze cap he made just for this passage."

"Not the best time to tell me that," Lauren said, knowing her honey-colored hair was now a collage of blood and cave soot.

Cassandra continued on relentlessly. "Follow me to the left and at the crossroads, left again. Then it curls to the right; farther beyond is the stream."

"Will it make us sick if we drink from it?" Lauren asked. She licked her lips. Only Cassandra knew the way to the secret chamber.

"It will, and so will the vapors if we stay too long."

"It figures; there's water, water everywhere, and not a drop to drink."

Just don't leave me alone here.

They crawled another half hour.

"Come, it's a short distance now."

"Check the chamber first to make sure that Bessus isn't in there."

"Would he sit in the dark by himself, lady?"

"I'm just saying."

"Fear not, I've arrived and I'm alone, except for the snake."

"What?" Lauren screamed.

When Lauren entered, she saw Cassandra on her knees, praying to an owl carved from stone and painted in blue, perched on a rocky pedestal. At the owl's feet, the tip of a stone serpent's tail began to twist around the pedestal, then down concentrically around the perimeter of the walls until it reached the ceiling at the opposite end of the chamber. At the end of the smooth scales that ran the length of its body, the snake's head had fangs and a forked tongue.

Cassandra finished her prayer with the words, "Bless and protect us, Athena."

"Holy snakes, Batman," Lauren said, scanning the room. The chamber rose almost thirty feet, appearing to have been extended vertically and engineered wide enough to fit twenty people or more. Snakes and Athena; Lauren recognized the dual power symbols of the goddess religions.

"Are you speaking the words of your land?" Cassandra asked. "Can you teach me?"

"I will in time," Lauren assured her, speaking ancient Ionian with an easy fluency gained by the months she spent in the Greek world of 480 BC. *A long time ago*, she thought, and a time that still held her husband captive. Too much competed for her concentration. She had told lies to the police, big fat ones about what had happened to all of them. That next morning, being that they weren't prisoners, Lauren told the police she had to get breakfast and do some shopping. And when she and Cassandra were able to break back into the cave, they discovered Bessus was gone. She remembered the unbelievably vivid dream Apollo had sent her. She knew Zack had been sent back to 480 BC and had no idea when he would return. At least she got to say good-bye, sort of.

When will this nightmare end?

"This is my uncle's room," Cassandra said. "My mother told me that long ago, ceremonies were held here to worship the serpent. His name was Python, the son of the great earth goddess, Gaia. My mother belonged to their order. She said the priestesses held much power then. She said the old ways should not be let go and that I must pass them on to my daughter."

In the torchlight, Lauren could see the stream of tears on the young girl's cheeks. Cassandra sniffed, pushing tangled hair away from her dark eyes and faced Python again. "I vow to you, Mother, I will carry out your wishes."

"The owl is beautiful," Lauren said. "It represents Athena, I think."

"Yes, it is the lady. My great grandfather carved it. The serpent and the lady are allies. They will protect us. I feel safe here." Cassandra dropped to her knees beneath the carving and dug at the dirt with her fingernails. She turned to see Lauren laughing at her efforts.

"When I was little, we had a black dog with pointed ears named Castor. This is how he would dig," Cassandra said. She spread her legs, bent forward and scooped the dirt back between her legs.

Lauren's mind remained tortured with the revelations of the last couple of days. Zack had said in his letter that the god Apollo existed and had a hand in what had happened to them. Then she met Apollo in the dream. She shuddered, a cold chill, made more penetrating since the temperature had dropped as they descended into the mountain. Lauren wondered when the world would start making sense again.

Cassandra's efforts finally uncovered five pithos ceramic pots, each with a leather cap sewn tightly over the opening. Inspired, they both joined in the digging, finally uncovering one to its base. Lauren stopped, holding her dirty fingers and nails before her.

My husband held this dirt in his hands. He was here.

The wide-mouthed pot would be too heavy to lift out of the hole. She worked on the caps instead, cutting through the thread with a jagged stone and peeling the leather off. Underneath the rim of each jar was a thick layer of hardened wax. Cassandra ripped at it with her nails.

She uncovered a cache of silver coins and gold ingots.

"Athena, it's a treasure." Cassandra said, grasping handfuls of irregularly shaped coins and gold sticks. She let them fall through her fingers, like a one-armed bandit voiding its mother lode.

"My God," Lauren said slowly, unable to break her gaze from the horde of ancient coinage. "Did you know your uncle held such wealth?"

"I am told he was a famous builder."

Lauren dug out the wax covering of each of the remaining pots revealing similar stores of wealth. Some of the pots held more unexpected treasure: shiny stones, rubies, sapphires, beautifully cut and polished, others roughly shaped and dull. One pot held a thinner layer of coins and was sectioned from what was below by a thick slab of bronze.

"This may be the one, Cassandra."

One of the plastic freezer bags Zack and she had brought to protect archaeological findings lay underneath the bronze cap. Cassandra held the bag closer to the torchlight.

"I can see through this. It slips from my fingers. What manner of cloth is this?"

The Ziploc resisted the young girl's efforts until Lauren broke the seal at one end. She handed it back so Cassandra would have the pleasure of uncovering the gifts Zack had left for her.

"There's something heavy inside," Cassandra remarked while unwrapping a lambskin that bore Zack's writing. Lauren held it under the torchlight. Tremors returned to her hands. Lauren read

Cassandra and Lauren,
I'm overjoyed you've found my surprise. It means you're both safe.
Nestor did well for himself.
Cassandra, you must be careful with the knowledge of this treasure. Do not
tell anyone else it exists. It is your birthright, left to you by your uncle, and it

will allow you to prosper if it is protected and used wisely. I wish I could be here to see your face when you open these gifts. Nevertheless, I'm with you and I smile at you from across the ages. I hope someday to be your father, if you will have me. I yearn to be with both of you.

Please do not forget me.

I love you,

Zack

Lauren wiped her eyes with her sleeve. "Go ahead, sweetheart, open it."

Cassandra held a package of tightly wrapped linen, feeling the bumpy outlines of what lay inside.

She unraveled the covering, revealing the snake bracelet her mother had worn, along with a small box made of bronze. Cassandra screamed, falling to her knees. She slipped the bronze coils over her wrist it and held it to her heart.

"My mother, my mother, my mother," she cried out.

Lauren reached for her, fighting despair herself from the realization of their simultaneous loss of the people they loved the most. The barbarian, Bessus, had made a train wreck of their lives, and so had Apollo.

And there was no going back.

"Sweetheart, let's see what's inside the box."

Despite the meager lighting, Lauren could see that on the cover was the figure of a woman holding long stalks of grain: the goddess Persephone. It was a poignant moment, being that the goddess was responsible in Greek mythology for the seasons and the rebirth of life from the earth after the cold winter months.

Like us. We're also reborn.

"It is my mother's box. She held her jewelry inside." Cassandra opened the tiny clasp to find another note from Zack.

Cassandra, I thought you would like to have some additional remembrances of your family. Of course, the white hairs are your uncles and the dark

*hairs, your mother's. The earrings are so beautiful. I hope to see you wear them
when we are reunited.*

Love,
Zack

Cassandra ran her fingertips gingerly over the hairs. A gentle smile
of gratification replaced her tears. "May the gods praise you, Master
Zack," she said, lifting the golden loops Persephone had worn when
Zack and Lauren had first met her at Nestor's farmhouse.

"Sweetheart, it may be best to put them back in the box, so nothing
is lost. We should rebury everything for safekeeping, even the bracelet,
until we know where we stand."

Cassandra looked up at her and smiled. "May I hold them a
little longer?"

"Certainly, but the flashlight might run out soon."

Thank you, Zack. We won't forget you.

After savoring a few more minutes, they reburied their possessions,
including Zack's letters, and crawled back to the main cave. Lauren had
told the duty office at the police station they would be back to answer
questions. The thought of meeting the barbarian again set within her a
dread she couldn't shake. She just couldn't figure out what could have
happened to his body in a matter of a day. She thought about the old
legal line about a body being proof of death.

That meant he could still be alive, and by some miracle, waiting for
them somewhere outside the cave. Where the hell could he be?

Delphi, Greece

SEPTEMBER, PRESENT DAY

Lauren hid behind brush that obscured the front of the cave. She crawled forward on sore hands and knees. In the light of mid-morning, she scanned the vicinity one last time for the sight of Bessus the barbarian. She dashed for a clump of bushes to the left of the cave mouth, and listened. Not hearing or seeing him, Lauren scampered back inside their cave sanctuary. She was met by an armed Cassandra, grasping a bronze pot by the handle.

"We're gonna need better weapons than that," Lauren said. "We have to get back to the police station. I didn't see the monster."

"What about the screaming birds? Will they descend upon us?" Cassandra looked at her grimly.

Lauren had to imagine that the ambulance they heard early in the morning would sound like screaming birds to someone from the ancient world. "Don't be afraid of that noise. It is the wail of a chariot and the people within are sworn to protect the wounded or innocent. The chariots are large and shiny and they need no horses or oxen to propel them. The loud wail announces for all to get out of the way. Remember, I told you there are wonderful inventions here."

Cassandra made a face like she wasn't sure.

"I have such a chariot myself," Lauren said.

Cassandra shot back fast, "Do you cover your ears when you ride?"

"It doesn't make the same sound."

"A woman can have such a possession?"

"You will see that women in my time have many freedoms that were not allowed in yours. You will attend an academy when you are older and decide whom you shall marry."

"My mother would have enjoyed living in your land. She complained to me that she was capable of much more but was restricted by custom. She said that is why my uncle moved us to Delphi. He did not wish us to live in the city and draw the anger of the officials."

"An intelligent man, your uncle. I shall miss him greatly. Now, we must prepare to leave. After we reset the stones in front, when I give you the signal, we'll run for the cover of the trees." Lauren massaged her kneecaps. "When we know we're safe, we'll dash for the orphanage. It's the closest building in town and the museum isn't open yet."

"Toward the home you showed me for children that have no parents?"

"Yes."

"I want to go back to the pot that sucks down the pee in a swirl of water."

Lauren grinned and took her in a tight embrace. "The barbarian might be somewhere nearby. You saw that his corpse was gone when we entered the cave."

Cassandra gulped.

"Someone covered up the entrance with those rocks, too."

"How could he have survived? I stabbed him three times and twisted the blade. The pithoi were on fire. They cracked and fell on him."

"I don't know, but I'll care for you and protect you, just like a cave bear," Lauren said.

The moment was broken by loud gurgles of hunger from Lauren's belly. The two broke into peals of laughter.

"You can't argue with your stomach for very long. Stay close to me and do not speak or cry out. If we see the barbarian, you must dash to safety. Don't go back to the cave. Flee to the house with the men dressed in blue. Are you ready?"

"I am."

Lauren bent down and kissed Cassandra on the cheek. "Remember this, if we meet other people, do not speak. They won't understand our plight and may seek to separate us."

They bolted from tree to tree, making their way across the hill toward the remains of the temple of Athena Pronaia. The risks weighed upon her as Cassandra ran beside her. They made it to the road and scampered to a cover of trees. A car drove past them spewing gas fumes from a broken tailpipe.

Cassandra covered her nose and pointed. She whispered, "If your chariot stinks like a sick bull too, then I don't want to ride in it."

Lauren put a finger to her lips to signal Cassandra's silence. She whispered to the young girl, "We'll make a fast run for the doorway of the orphanage."

I know Bessus is out here, waiting. He survived, somehow.

Cassandra looked up. Her eyes spoke of fear. Lauren held out her fist.

"When I raise the third finger, we go."

Like hunted gazelles, they burst out of the trees, streaked past the parking lot and headed to the orphanage. At the top of the short stairway, Lauren tried to open the door but found it locked. She pounded the doorbell with her palm. She turned and prayed she wouldn't see Bessus lumbering up to them. She saw the dark figure of a large man in the distance. Could it be him?

His body wasn't in the cave. I can remember his horrid breath and when he ...

Lauren pounded on the door. Through the glass window of the door, Lauren saw a middle-aged man rushing down the hallway toward her. She was never more frightened than now, at the moment of their deliverance. She looked back one more time to see if Bessus had found them. Not seeing him, she turned and saw combed-over dark hair through the window as the man bent over to release the lock on the door. When it swung open, Lauren and Cassandra ran for a room to hide in.

"What, what is this? Who are you?" the man demanded.

Lauren hid Cassandra under a desk. Lauren seized a letter opener and held it up, ready to stab.

"See here, what's wrong?" the older man said, wide-eyed.

Lauren blurted in Greek. "There's a kidnapper out there. Lock the door, he's chasing us."

He quickly secured the door. Motioning for them to come with him, he led them to an office across from a small cafeteria. Lauren held Cassandra's hand. Minutes passed. They caught their breath.

Now she was seized by another terror: Was the story she devised believable?

The man looked into her eyes. "Now, what did you say about a kidnapper? What did he look like?"

Lauren took a deep breath and let it out. *Here goes*, she thought.

"We were kidnapped by a man, a huge, filthy madman. He blindfolded us, held us for weeks. We escaped when my husband fought with him. I don't know where my husband is. He hasn't returned."

The man stood up quickly. "Can you describe the kidnapper?"

"Huge, bushy black hair, scars on his face, he's horrible." Lauren listened for the smashing of the door, certain that the barbarian must have seen them and would stop at nothing to get her.

"Are either of you hurt?"

"No, just frightened."

"I'll be right back. I need to call the police."

Lauren gripped the letter opener.

The man walked across the hallway and made a phone call while watching them through the open door.

"Remember, Cassandra, don't talk," Lauren whispered in the girl's ear. "Just do what I do and if for any reason they try to separate us, fight like a hoplite. Do you understand?" Cassandra affirmed the instructions. The man returned a minute later.

"I'm Mr. Avtges, the director of this orphanage. Could you please identify yourselves?"

Lauren coughed, weighing her words. "I am Professor Lauren Fletcher. I'm an American." She hesitated. "My husband's name is

Zackary Fletcher. We're from San Diego, California. I don't know this girl's name, but we escaped together. She either doesn't speak or won't. The girl was already there when we were kidnapped. She doesn't seem injured but I doubt she will leave my side. Can we contact the American Embassy?"

"Of course, but the authorities will be here shortly. They said you stayed at the police station last night."

"We did, but we went for a walk and I thought I saw him again. Can you get police here fast? The guy might be outside and unless you have a gun?"

"They'll arrive in a moment. We've had a murder recently and there was an intruder reported within the orphanage just this morning. One of our children encountered a man like you described and is now so terrified he won't leave his bed. A police inspector will arrive to speak with you."

Lauren's insides quaked.

"While we're waiting, could we get you something to eat and drink?"

"Oh, thank you. We are hungry, but please check and see if he's outside."

A boy with dark, curly hair walked past the doorway.

Mr. Avtges called to him. "Demo, please help these ladies. Set out for them whatever is left over from the midday meal."

"Yes, sir," the boy said unenthusiastically, not bothering to look at the women.

"His name is Demetrious, but we call him Demo. Poor lad, he lost a good friend recently. Terrible murder at the museum," Avtges reported.

"Are you sure all the doors are locked?" Lauren asked, sitting upright and keeping her eye on the letter opener she had laid down. She calculated that the murder had occurred on the same morning of their arrival, and close to when Bessus entered the modern world.

"They're locked and all the children are inside."

"Please Mr. Avtges, Do you have a gun or a baseball bat? Oh dang it, this is Greece. How about a shovel or ..."

He put his hand on her shoulder. Cassandra buried her head in Lauren's lap.

"They'll be here in a moment," he said.

Lauren wondered if she should act more frightened than she already was.

Avtges asked, "Will you feel better if I watch the grounds from the window? I'll be able to see anyone around the building."

"Yes, please," Lauren said frantically. She picked up the letter opener again and pushed Cassandra down under the desk.

The boy, Demo, returned, announcing the meal was ready, but did a double take when he looked at Lauren holding the letter opener like a weapon.

"You won't need that. We have forks and spoons," the boy said. "Is the girl going to eat under the desk?"

"Please, Demo, escort them into the cafeteria," Mr. Avtges said. "There is no sign of the man you speak of, Mrs. Fletcher."

Two full plates of chicken legs, rice, and green beans had been laid out on a long white table in the cafeteria. Cassandra swallowed. Lauren took a paper carton of milk and opened it at the side. Cassandra, watching her, reached out for one and attempted to squeeze the ends in the same manner. Before Lauren could utter a warning, the carton burst and soaked Cassandra's shirt. She put her hand to her mouth, but didn't say anything. The boy laughed out loud.

"I should have helped her," Lauren said, shaking her head. Mr. Avtges grinned, but then excused himself to keep a watch on the perimeter of the grounds.

"I can get another," the boy announced, removing his unyielding gaze from Lauren. When he returned, Lauren placed a straw inside the carton, put her lips around it and sucked, demonstrating the technique to the girl.

Cassandra, more careful now, did the same. She drew in too much, however, coughed, choked, and spit it out of her mouth and nose. She covered her face with two hands.

Demo clutched his sides, cackling hysterically. "She's funny, is she from Pluto? Hasn't she ever used a straw?"

"Apparently not," Lauren said.

Lauren looked past the boy's curly hair to the doorway, expecting any moment to see the barbarian barge in.

She used a plastic fork to spear green beans. Cassandra, being extra careful, copied Lauren's technique. She held the fork in front of her eyes, inspecting the design. Having eaten with her hands or spoons made of wood or metal in her previous life, she delicately speared a fork full of beans. She chewed furiously and smiled.

Finally noticing the boy's measured stare, Lauren dabbed her face with a napkin, signaling Cassandra to remove the pieces of rice stuck to her chin. Demo returned with more milk and a plate of white-powdered cookies.

Lauren felt oddly vulnerable. She wondered why a teenage boy could make her so nervous.

Cassandra took a bite of the small round cookie. Her throat filled with powdered sugar. Unable to maintain her airway, she coughed it out, all over Lauren.

Demetrious doubled over again.

"She's too much. Are you actresses at the museum?"

"We're visitors," Lauren said.

Cassandra went for another cookie, this time taking a measured bite. She closed her eyes, smiled, seemingly savoring the crunchy sweetness, but careful not to make a sound. Her face gave the appearance of having been through a blizzard.

"Have you been to our orphanage before?" Demo asked.

"No," Lauren said.

Demo sat in front of them. "It's mostly boring here, except lately. I've been here since I was five. My parents were killed in a car accident."

"I'm sorry to hear that."

"Is she your daughter?"

"No, but . . ."

"She just ate the whole plate of cookies."

"We're really hungry."

"Why doesn't she talk? Is there something wrong with her?"

"I don't know. She hasn't said a word to me, either."

"I work up at the museum sometimes, have you been there?" The boy waited for Lauren's answer.

"Just a quick visit," Lauren said, continuing her clipped answers. She needed practice for the police inquisitors.

I've got to get my story straight.

"I work at the museum afternoons and weekends. That is, when I don't have a soccer game. I work the refreshment stand or help my friend Maria in the kitchen. Sometimes, I empty the trash cans and help take care of the grounds. Tourists leave jackets and garbage out on the mountainside...and other things." Demos stopped talking and looked at Lauren as if expecting her to say something.

"You are a very industrious young man," Lauren replied.

Cassandra watched the conversation, turning her eyes to mwhoever spoke. She scooped the rest of her rice into her mouth with her fingers. She smiled at Demo with her lips closed.

"She seems nice enough."

"She is, but she's been through a lot," Lauren said.

"We all have, since this morning." Demo turned his head. "Mr. Avtges keeps locking the doors. It's going to get really boring if we can't go outside. You know, you look familiar to me."

Lauren raised an eyebrow. "How so?"

They were interrupted by the swift entry of Mr. Avtges.

"Mrs. Fletcher, the police will be here in twenty minutes. Would you care to bathe? I have some spare T-shirts and shorts you could wear."

"That would be wonderful." Lauren hadn't noticed how filthy they were from the cave expedition.

"Then I will show you to our guest room upstairs. Please come with me."

Demo stayed behind. Lauren felt his eyes on her as they followed Mr. Avtges out of the cafeteria.

Upstairs they stopped at a closed door. Beyond that, the whole second floor was filled with evenly-spaced beds. "I will send Demo to tell you when the police arrive." He opened the door to a small room painted in light gray with two white-sheeted single beds, a dresser, and a desk. Lauren was pleased to see it had its own bathroom, and a cross decorated the wall between the two beds.

"We occasionally have officials that stay with us. I hope you find it comfortable."

"Mr. Avtges, you're a lifesaver."

"It is my pleasure. I will see you in a few minutes."

Lauren shut the door. Cassandra went over to the bed and ran her fingers over the sheets. She hesitated before she hopped onto the bed and bounced.

"Sweetheart," she whispered in Ionian, lowering herself directly in front of Cassandra's face, "very important officials are coming here to see us. You must not speak, just keep hugging my knees and don't look at them. You must act frightened. Even if someone pinches you, don't cry out, do you understand? Only speak to me in that little room with the door closed."

Cassandra stopped jumping. She locked her knees together and rocked.

"Do you have to relieve yourself?" Lauren asked.

Cassandra nodded her head.

"I know. You want to use the water pot again."

Cassandra sat on the commode, smiling and tapping her fingers on her cheeks. Then she jumped up abruptly and flushed the toilet. She clapped and jumped up and down.

"I want to make it work again." Cassandra stared at the swirling water as it disappeared down the toilet bowl.

"I'll shut the door. There is tissue here instead of sponges or moss." Having endured three months of ancient times lacking modern bathroom luxuries, Lauren couldn't have been happier to be back in modern times herself.

Shampoo, lotions, razors, and toothpaste!

Lauren lay on the bed and closed her eyes. So far so good, she thought to herself. After Lauren had listened to the toilet flush for the tenth time, she went to the door and knocked.

"Come out now, Cassandra," Lauren whispered to her in ancient Greek. Cassandra opened the door and then returned to the mirror, a sheepish grin on her face as she studied her image in the glass.

"I have never seen myself in this way."

"You are as beautiful as Aphrodite. Now come, I will teach you to wash your hands." Lauren turned on the faucets to the further amazement of her young protégé.

"My uncle and my mother should be here to see this."

"I wish it could be so, sweetheart."

"What is the marble enclosure? Is it for bathing?"

"Yes, and we must hurry to prepare ourselves for the authorities. Remember, do not speak and do not let anyone take you away from me, understand?"

"I will obey you, lady."

Lauren clasped Cassandra's head to her shoulder.

Maybe in time you will call me . . . Mother.

Demo knocked at the door, calling to them to come downstairs.

"We are on the way," Lauren replied nervously. She drew in a deep breath and let it out between closed teeth.

A man wearing a dark brown suit stood next to Mr. Avtges. He was not quite as tall as Lauren and the graying hair at his temples signaled a level of experience in police matters that set her heart pounding. His dark brown eyes searched Lauren's face as if sizing her up. The eyes revealed neither threat nor friendliness.

There's danger here. Lauren knew it. On top of that, he seemed vaguely familiar.

"Am I to understand you are Mrs. Lauren Fletcher, an American?" the policeman asked with a neutral tone and with passable English.

"I am."

"I am Inspector Peter Trokalitis, homicide division, as you would say in your country." He pulled out his wallet, revealing his badge and ID. "I hear you have been through quite an ordeal."

Lauren nodded her head, hesitant to speak, wondering if this man would be able to see through the story she had reported. His full head of graying hair was slicked back and he wore a neatly groomed salt-and-pepper moustache that reached the corners of his lips. The police always saw through stories. She was doomed.

"It has been very difficult," Lauren answered.

"And who is the young girl here?"

"I'm not sure. She hasn't spoken and she has no ID."

Inspector Trokalitis raised a thinly manicured eyebrow. He strolled around the office and hung his suit jacket on a hook.

Oh no, here it comes. I'm gonna fry.

"And your husband, Mrs. Fletcher, you have both been listed as missing for some time. Where is he?"

"I don't know. He helped us escape and we ran. We hid in the rocks and worked our way through the mountains in the dark. He hasn't shown up."

Inspector Trokalitis had a sudden coughing fit.

Lauren thought she'd heard that cough before.

"Tell me about the man that held you captive and perhaps for the director's benefit too, we should continue in Greek. I understand you are quite proficient in our language."

Lauren took a deep breath before beginning her fabricated tale of captivity, horribly insecure fearing that a veteran detective would see through her story. "He's enormous, foul-looking; has bushy black hair and beard, is missing a lot of teeth, smells like a sewer. He wears leather over his chest, black leather like they did in the army centuries ago. His eyes scare the hell out of you; they're deep set and dark, and the bone is pronounced over them, like a gorilla's. He wears bronze bands over his biceps and scars crisscross his face. He's terrifying."

Trokalitis pulled out the drawing made by the young boy, who was still too terrified to leave his room after his run-in with the intruder. He studied it, pursing his lips, breathing out through his nose. "Your description resembles what the child has drawn. Is this him?"

He handed the drawing to Lauren.

Lauren gasped, "It's him."

It was an accurate drawing, in a young child's hand. The basics were there: a big, black stick figure, wild hair, crisscrosses on the face, and something curious—the child had drawn a shiny armband in yellow crayon over only one of the monster's biceps. "He was in this orphanage?"

"Just this morning," Mr. Avtges said.

"I can't believe any of you are alive," Lauren said. "He's searching for us . . . for me."

Trokalitis stopped his pacing momentarily. "Fingerprints all over the kitchen may give us a lead. Is there anything else that would help us to identify him, or anything to assist us in locating your husband? Zackary is his name, am I correct?"

Lauren put her face in her hands. The mention of Zack's name had chipped away at her control. What had occurred, their travel in time, the ordeals they had survived, and her return without him had truly shaken her. Finding his letters in the cave made it official. She was in front of the police, in her own time, and he was gone. Lauren wondered if faking a melodramatic reaction to Trokalitis's questions would help.

"I apologize for bringing up your husband at this time, Mrs. Fletcher. Perhaps we can come back to him later. Can you tell me more about the young lady who is with you?"

She wiped her eyes with a sleeve. It was as much play-acting as she could muster.

"May I offer you a tissue, Mrs. Fletcher?" Mr. Avtges asked her in Greek.

"Thank you." Lauren swathed her eyes. "She was already there when we were kidnapped by this guy. We were hiking in the mountains, north of here. He came out of nowhere, with a large knife and a club. He hit my husband with the club, then blindfolded and handcuffed us. He didn't remove them till he brought us to his 'lair.' The girl was already there, tied to a stump."

"She has never spoken to you, not even then?"

"No. All I know is she would wrap herself around me and wouldn't leave my side. Maybe she's traumatized . . . I know I am."

Trokalitis kneeled down in front of Cassandra. He spoke to her in modern Greek. Unable to obtain a verbal response or catch her gaze, he continued his questioning of Lauren.

"Does she understand Greek? She appears to have Mediterranean features."

"I don't know. I take her with me and show her what to do. I imagine she trusts me. She won't leave my side and I won't leave hers."

"We'll take her picture and see if she matches the description of any missing children in this and neighboring countries. With the upheaval in the economy, perhaps she's a refugee?" Trokalitis smoothed Cassandra's hair with his hand. She cringed.

"Nice girl," Trokalitis said and walked away to the window.

Mr. Avtges interjected. "Living by herself, all the way down here, inspector? Wouldn't it be more likely she is Greek? I would be happy to house her here until Social Services can determine who she is."

"That would be agreeable, Mr. Avtges. I will send a medical examiner here, if I can find one. Everyone is on strike these days. Do you know if she was assaulted?"

"I'm not sure, not while I was there. Actually, neither of us was," Lauren answered. "I'm not sure why he kidnapped us. He wouldn't know who we were. Just brought us food and kept us tied up. Spoke a language we didn't understand."

"Very strange," Trokalitis said, rubbing his chin. "If he is a murderer, I'm not sure why you survived at all."

"I can't figure it out, either. He moved us about every week at night. We stumbled along blindfolded; a hand on each other's shoulder, like the mustard-gas victims in World War I. Zack told me to get ready. He had gnawed through the rope that had us tied together. Then he threw himself at the guy. I removed my blindfold and hers, and we ran. I heard them fighting. Zack told me earlier to keep going and not to stop. Later, we heard the man coming after us. Zack never showed up. We hid in the woods for a few days, waiting for him." Lauren hung her head.

"Very gallant, your husband is." Trokalitis coughed again and it dawned on Lauren that she had met him at the museum fundraiser.

"You are both professors," he stated.

"Yes, of ancient history; we studied in Greece for a couple of years."

"I saw the poster the late professor had put up all over Greece looking for you."

"What?" Lauren said, trying to look stupefied. "What did you say about the professor? Do you mean Professor Papandreou?"

"I'm sorry. Of course, you wouldn't know."

Lauren face turned pale. She was quite sure she was a horrible actress, but she now knew for sure that the dream Apollo had brought to her, with Zack, was real. Papandreou had been killed by Bessus. This stark reality wasn't helping her control, either.

"Are you . . . telling me . . . the professor is dead?"

Trokalitis's stark look only reinforced that devastating truth.

Lauren jumped up from her chair. Cassandra held onto her leg.

"There, Mrs. Fletcher." Mr. Avtges leaped up to comfort her, holding on to her arms.

Lauren blurted out, "This is too much. What happened to him?"

"We found him murdered, beyond the temple grounds, up the mountain near a hollow."

"This is horrible, horrible," Lauren lamented. Mr. Avtges guided her back to a chair.

Inspector Trokalitis said, "We don't know if the man you describe is the same man who murdered the professor. We've interviewed the museum staff. No one saw anything. We still aren't sure why the professor was roaming around up there in the early morning."

Trokalitis kept his hand within his coat pocket, rummaging underneath as if searching for something. "Few people in this area seem to have known the late professor: only just the director of the museum, Mr. Avtges here, and the young boy who lives here."

Cassandra peered into Lauren's face momentarily, and reassured, she nestled her head back onto Lauren's knee.

"We're so tired, so much has happened. I don't know what to do next. I need to notify my family and the US embassy."

"You may stay here temporarily if you wish, Professor Fletcher,"

Mr. Avtges said, his face one of compassion for the loss evident on Lauren's face.

"And the girl, can she stay? I don't want to leave her."

Mr. Avtges checked for confirmation from Trokalitis. Receiving it, he affirmed that they could move in immediately.

"Of course, Mrs. Fletcher, or should I say, Professor Fletcher, there is an ongoing investigation and you may not leave this area until I say so. Is that understood?" He extracted a golden case from his pocket, opened it, and withdrew a cigarette. "There are many very odd happenings here lately. I will need to bring in Social Services for the young girl. Do you need medical attention?"

Lauren stared at the black-and-white alternating linoleum pattern on the floor.

"I don't need a doctor. Maybe a bartender would help. I won't leave the area and I will help in any way I can. My husband might still show up and I want the girl to stay with me. Can you work with me on this?"

"For the time being," Trokalitis said, searching for his lighter in his pants pocket. "We'll send a search party out for your husband and a bulletin on the suspect. Stay inside in case he lurks nearby."

Lauren shot a look at the window. "This man is horribly cruel. You have a gun. Please don't leave, Inspector."

"I'm shorthanded right now. We'll come up the mountain frequently to check on you. We're sending the fingerprints from the murder scene to the lab to see if they match prints on the door and other areas of this facility. There are local police who can assist you."

"This guy can break two ordinary men in half at once if he wants to."

He grinned gratuitously. "I will warn them. Now I must attend to other business. Here is my card if you have any information that might be of value to us. A police artist will arrive tomorrow."

He took a first drag from his cigarette and filled the room with hazy smoke. Cassandra sniffed, glanced at him, then at Lauren for a moment. She reburied her head in Lauren's lap.

"Remember, Professor Fletcher, do not leave this area without my permission. I am not yet satisfied with what has been reported here."

Lauren paled. "I will contact the embassy. Perhaps I can find assistance there."

"Do what you feel you must, but if you leave, the consequences will be severe. I bid you good-bye." Inspector Trokalitis left the building quickly and headed in the direction of the parking lot.

Lauren turned to Mr. Avtges. "May I use your phone? I want to call the US embassy, and I think I need a lawyer.

PART II

6

Mycenae, Greece

OCTOBER 480 BC

Mold coated the stone under Zack's toes, like a thick layer of butter on bread. He took another step near the top of a winding stone staircase, but slipped, reached for wooden railing, and halted a disastrous tumble. More carefully now, he held his torch at foot level, as did his two burly palace guards descending before him, each step bringing them further into the bowels of the Mycenaean citadel. The stairs glistened with water that percolated from buildings and the ground above. He smelled dank air, but not so cold. More scorching was evident on the walls, just like in the foundations of the royal buildings above, evidence of a calamitous fire, maybe the one that ended Mycenaean rule in 1100 BC, after Troy herself had been razed.

This was Zack's kind of place.

His hand ran over yet another bas-relief of a serpent, a sentinel from the early Bronze Age, he estimated, just like in the tunnel hallway underneath Delphi. The serpent coursed, helix-fashion, along the wall, leading them deeper into the blackness. Zack knew this had to be a far more ancient place than the palaces and temples up on the citadel. He gripped the railing. It was a long way down those stairs.

The stairway ended on a rough-cut landing with stones rounded by the footsteps of those long departed. A guard reached for a bronze ring on a door and rapped it. They stood aside, leaving Zack standing before this studded bronze door, easily ten feet or more in height. Holding his torch, he could see the raised figure of a goddess in the center of the door, dressed in a pale blue gown with long sleeves edged with vibrant red piping. The goddess's prominent breasts were bared in the style of Minoan Crete. The figure was split down the middle by a barely recognizable seam, delineating the two sides of the door. The goddess held in each hand a curled snake, painted black with yellow eyes. Zack ran his fingers over the embossed bronze, and then up and over the goddess's breasts.

He wondered if the fondling was the curiosity of an archeologist, or something else.

Zack heard the pop of a vacuum and felt a rush of air. The breasts separated. He stepped back.

The two sides of the massive doors creaked as they were pulled inward. A bluish haze and the aroma of flowered incense sifted out from the chamber, escaping up the stairwell.

Inside, Zack saw a larger, painted terra-cotta statue of the female figure he had seen on the doors. Two tall, dark pillars flanked the seated statue that was illuminated by a dozen torches on each side. The goddess statue sat on a throne, her legs and feet together in an archaic style that could only be Egyptian-influenced. Several highly polished bronze cauldrons were set beneath the spaced torches, throwing off dazzling reflections.

Zack's attention was diverted to a large fresco painting of leaping bulls, its vibrancy dimmed by centuries of smoke from oil lamps and torches. Then he heard a rhythm of metal, like a Slinky descending a stairway. A priestess entered his view from the right, emerging from clouds of incense billowing from metallic tripods.

She wore an orange gown that rippled when she moved, jingling from rows of tiny bronze balls sewed onto the hem. The gown was trimmed in blue with a pink apron, back and front, which tied at the waist and further accentuated the voluptuous figure that moved beneath it. She halted before the massive statue on the altar.

Diomedes, clean-shaven, dressed in a white chiton, and seemingly unwounded in the battle at Salamis, followed the priestess, his neatly combed hair tied in the back.

"Enter, honored envoy," the priestess said with a bold voice that echoed inside the chamber and gained his attention. "I am Io, queen of the Mycenaeans."

Light blue accented her eyelids. Her thick eyebrows were painted dark with lines that extended almost to her ears. She wore her dark hair swept up, displaying large gold earrings.

Zack stepped through an arched entryway. Two young female attendants, one of whom had met his glance beforehand, diverted their eyes. They pushed the doors closed behind him, and then walked together out of sight through a stone corridor.

Zack bowed, not sure what else he should do. He recognized Diomedes with a nod and squared his shoulders.

Why did they bring me here?

"Twenty nights of rest have brought you back to your feet," Prince Diomedes said, sitting upon one of two white throne chairs draped with purple and gold sashes.

"You may recline if you wish," the queen said to Zack, pointing to a brown couch with round pillows on one side, and positioned before the altar. She collected the back of her gown so as to not crumple it and sat down on her throne chair. "You are welcome among the Myceneans."

"I am honored, Queen Io," Zack replied. He had not met her when he arrived, drugged and bound with bandages on a wagon with the other wounded. Zack could only guess that she was just slightly older than his thirty-two years, having probably given birth to Diomedes as a teenager. She was more bronze-skinned than her son and her face was barely lined. Her nose was just a shade long, but balanced by red fleshy lips and a square chin that had a very subtle cleft.

Zack sat in the center of the couch, wondering if he should recline on it, as was the custom in ancient times. Leaning on his side might cause him to wince, and he didn't want to show pain.

"You have a warrior's build," Io said, scanning Zack slowly from head to toe. "How do your wounds fare?"

"They heal. I am happy to have the bandage over my jaw removed," Zack answered, relieved that he didn't suffer a fractured jaw. A few weeks of gruel and mashed fruit sloshed into his resin-bound jaw had been bad enough.

"Did our celebration please you?" Io asked. "Your wife saw one much the same when she visited our citadel not long ago. Diomedes revealed to me that you have sent her to safety in the west. Is this so?"

Zack shifted in his seat. He adjusted the sling that held up his left arm, lessening the strain on a shoulder twice sliced open in the span of a month.

"He speaks the truth," Zack said. "She protects an orphan girl and journeys back to our homeland."

Diomedes nestled his chin into his palm. He emitted a brief but recognizable sigh. Zack heard him and wondered why Diomedes would emit such an emotion.

"Did you send her away with trusted guards?" Io inquired.

"She journeys alone with the girl," Zack said. He didn't know himself if they were safe. The side of his face that didn't suffer the hammer blow twitched.

"Your wife is truly a woman of fortitude, yet I am confused that she would be sent on such a journey unprotected." Io stared him down.

Zack sucked in air through his teeth.

"You are a difficult man to fathom, Atlantean," Io said. "You fight in a war not your own and cast away your wife to the west, without a champion to protect her. You should know that she was well thought of here by all of us." Io folded her arms. "Explain this to me, if you can."

Zack searched for words. He ran his tongue around the inside of his right cheek. The wound felt better, though the tissue still felt serrated and hard, like the rubber on the bottom of a boot.

"Queen Io, brave Diomedes; every morning that Helios lights the skies, I ache to return to Lauren. The more I think of her, the more it hurts, far worse than wounds . . ."

Io interrupted him. "Lauren has demonstrated her courage, yet danger abounds on the seas and in the settlements. You risk her safety for that of the Hellenes? You have seen fighting at the Hot Gates and fought bravely at Salamis, though my son says you are not a warrior. I say again, your deeds confound us."

Both she and her son leaned forward to him for the answer.

Zack had the advantage of history on his side. Yet he could not appear to be so reckless with his wife's safety that his hosts would think that he didn't care about her. He worked his jaw around, stretching it before he spoke.

"In Atlantea, we live much as you do. Our forebears earned our freedoms, and we do not take them lightly. The enemy you face is massive and would take every nation into slavery. If the barbarian is not stopped here, then there will be no one else who could halt his march to the western seas."

Zack stopped for a moment. He'd barely spoken in weeks and his jaw muscles were already tired. He seemed to have little difficulty speaking the Ionian dialect and wondered about it for a moment. He had practiced it with Lauren, but had not conversed at this level.

Did Apollo implant some special knowledge of languages in me?

He refocused on the conversation at hand. "In time, they will learn of my land and mount an invasion to our shores. Our land is strong and prosperous, and we would prevail, but there will be much suffering among our people in such a war."

Io and Diomedes listened intently, absorbing Zack's statement. They turned, conveying reaction to each other with their eyes.

Zack continued, "I must know the true nature of this threat so I can warn my countrymen. Lauren knew well the challenge of seeking safety in the west. She concerns herself more for the child than her own well-being."

Diomedes sighed yet again.

"I ask you now to assist me," Zack said, standing up. "I want to hold the shield and master the spear and sword, so to stand with you in battle. I will pay for my keep with silver. I beg you to grant these wishes."

Zack bowed and awaited their answer.

"You will make a formidable warrior, when you heal and if your heart is in it," Diomedes said. "If our lands are similar as you suggest, then in time, our peoples could share the danger together and combine our might."

Zack nodded. At this point, he thought, there was no reason not to agree with the idea of an alliance between the ancient city of Mycenae and the United States. Since Lauren's and his arrival in ancient times, they had told everyone they were from Atlantea. Maybe they didn't have to disguise the fact of the later existence of the United States. But hell, there was history to consider.

"And I know now the fortitude of the man that Lauren has wed," Io continued. "My son will be pleased to teach you the arts of war and he yearns for a male companion. A prince can only befriend his men on the surface. He must keep a certain distance from them, for the day will come when he will be their king."

Io turned her gaze away from Zack for a moment. "The gods did not allow us another child after my husband was injured in battle many years ago. Do you have heirs, the fruit of union between you and Lauren?"

"We do not."

The queen recoiled. "You both are well into childbearing age. How is it that so well made a couple does not bear children together?" Io asked.

"My wife . . . has had difficulties bearing a child. We have not been blessed."

Diomedes leaped from his seat.

"Do you bespeak that she is barren?" Io asked.

"It may be so," Zack answered, uncomfortable now, wondering if he should have volunteered that information.

Diomedes and his mother locked eyes.

"Lauren and I had little time together and we did not speak of children," Queen Io said, glancing at her son. "She was eager to deliver the ring of Leonidas to Queen Gorgo. There was a mystery about your wife, but I could not calculate what it was." Io hesitated. "I felt she was the favored of the gods, now I wonder . . ."

"We may yet have a child. We are young and there's still time. I am curious, however, about this chamber. It is an ancient place," Zack said, hoping to change the subject.

Io stood, stepped onto a footstool decorated with ivory shells and then onto the marble flooring. She strolled slowly to the twenty-foot statue. Her gown swayed and the tiny bells tinkled in unison. She was a living representation of the bronze goddess on the entry door.

"Your fate and that of your wife is in the hands of the gods, Atlantean. If they choose for you to return to each other, or to bear children, it will only be if they desire it to be so. Accept their decisions and your fate, whatever it will be. You ask me to tell you of this temple." Reaching the massive statue, she ran her hand reverently over the bronze folds of the goddess's gown. "This ground has been sacred from the beginning. I am the chief priestess of she who made the heavens and the earth. I hold the goddess most dear as do the women of this citadel."

She moved again, the sound of the tiny balls jingling accompanying her. Movement on her periphery caught Zack's attention. Amid the swirling smoke from incense and within the dimly lit enclosure, black serpents peeked out over the rims of the bronze cauldrons and slithered down the sides of the pole-stands.

Zack froze.

"The serpents bring fertility to our womenfolk," Io declared. She saluted the statue by placing her right hand across her forehead, palm out.

Zack noticed the golden snake bands Io had on both arms.

"In times long past, the goddess ruled over all. She protects the serpents that enrich our wombs. But now, the serpents must dwell here, driven underground by the gods who rule above. Here is the serpents' domain. Here they thrive."

"Could I attend your ceremonies?" Zack asked.

Io halted her prayer and turned slowly. "You do not know what you ask."

"In my land, I am a teacher at an academy. I study the lives of people who lived long ago," Zack said, hoping an academic angle would gain permission from her.

"It is well to learn the ways of others," she agreed. "The ceremonies I guard are the memories of mother to daughter, surviving conquest and countless generations. The mother goddess protects us all and she will be given her due. Few men have seen this worship. What you wish to witness . . . may not be what you expect."

The snakes curled around the cauldrons, flicking their tongues, made far more terrifying with the torchlight illuminating their eyes.

"Then I shall concentrate my energies on the spear and sword, for now," Zack said, a hint of disappointment in his tone.

Diomedes interjected. "Why had you not learned these skills in your own land? Do not all your men, as ours do, take up these practices as boys? Your land must be a soft place, since all do not learn to fight."

"Our armies are massive. All are not required to fight." Zack didn't like the direction of the conversation. The same uncomfortable feeling he had discussing this issue with King Leonidas arose within him.

Diomedes countered his statement. "The fortunes of war cannot be foreseen except by the gods. To fight is to survive in these lands. I say the time will come when all your men must learn the art of war, as we do."

Diomedes left his throne chair and stretched. "Remain with us. Take up our war if you wish. The gods have a plan for you. You will know what it is soon enough."

He pointed at the two girls who reappeared from a side corridor. "You will be escorted back to the citadel to continue your mending. When you are well, we will begin your training. For now, the crops are ready to harvest. Work in the orchards will bring strength back to you."

"Become one of us. Join in our labors and you will be accepted by the people," Io declared, her chin raised. She clapped and the female attendants escorted Zack back through the doors and up the long staircase.

When the Atlantean envoy had departed, mother and son dismissed the attendants and remained by themselves. Diomedes reached into a bowl of honeyed figs harvested from citadel orchards and snatched a sticky handful. He bit the end off of one and licked the sweetness from his fingertips.

"A worthy man, but his wife still haunts my dreams, Mother. I cannot forget her actions at the Hot Gates. When blood covered the ground, when our limbs were weary and sweat blinded our eyes, she was there to heal us."

Diomedes closed his eyes, "I can see her covered in the gore of friend and foe, hair clumped and hanging over her face as she gave heart to those who had none left. She could not have been more desirable or respected to an army of men who had given themselves to death and the dealing of it. Am I foolish to yearn for this woman?"

Diomedes finished off the fig he had grabbed but stopped and stared with vacant eyes at a clump of them stuck to his palm.

"I can see in your face that you hold her dear," Io said. "Don't dwell so long on her, though. A woman that cannot give you a son is of no use to you."

She draped a comforting arm over her son's shoulder.

"You know your father is not well. A sickness lurks within him and his physicians bring no cure. We do not have enough warriors to ward off invasion from the barbarians, no less our neighbors who covet our orchards and vineyards." She ran her hand affectionately over his hair.

"Zack is a sturdy, comely man with the height of Ajax. You can build his muscles and teach him the resolve of a warrior. You must erase Lauren from your thoughts. She will likely never return here." Io stared into her son's eyes.

"Instead, look to the survival of our people and our city. I will consult the goddess and ask her how best to forge an alliance between the Atlanteans and the Myceneans. He must have the ear of his king to be their envoy. An alliance might save us from conquest in the days ahead."

"We also don't know for certain that she cannot bear a child. "Diomedes countered. "We must survive the barbarian invasion first. No alliance can move fast enough to save us from Xerxes."

"That is so. I cannot bear the thought of our citadel razed, our men slain . . . our women and children sold into slavery abroad. I refuse to provide bedroom favors for some savage from barbarian lands." Io walked toward the statue again, the hem balls tinkling.

"I fear your father will not last to the next harvest. We will know by then if Hellas can turn Xerxes back. We must bond you to a powerful neighbor by marriage soon or I will have to take the survival of our people into my own hands."

Diomedes chewed on his cheek, deep in thought.

"Do not think me cruel, Diomedes. We must survive so you can be king. I can still bear a child. If I must join myself to a royal family in another city, I will do it."

Diomedes shucked off the handful of sticky figs back into the bowl. "I have lost my appetite, Mother, but I see the sense of it."

"Train our men well, dear son. We do what must be done ... to survive."

"He could have easily perished in the sea battle. My men stuck him on the beach. It would be well for me if he died, so I could find Lauren and make her mine."

"You must remove her from your thoughts, Diomedes. The truth is she belongs to him and you are the prince of a city in deep peril. Forget her and train him. We need warriors."

Mycenae, Greece

OCTOBER 480 BC

There, Stranger, hold the ends of the net for me," Zack's over-seer said. "No, no, fumble fingers. Don't drop the olives. Hoist it higher."

Zack held the ends tight, pulling the net over the ground to the oxcarts. Up and down the orchards, all the teams gathering the crop did the same. Zack grunted, lifting the tightly woven nets tied with twine at the top, and set them with others on the cart placed there earlier.

"Quickly, back to the trees and put your stick to work. There's a long day ahead, Cyclops. If I had ten of you, I could clear the tops of the trees before the others wet the bushes on their first break."

"Do we stop when darkness falls?" Zack asked Attalus, who responded with a look of disgust. The farmer was a short, thin man with unkempt hair and a dark and leather-worn face. His brown tunic was torn and looked unwashed for some time.

"You cannot be a Hellene or even from the colonies," Attalus said. "What land is it that knows not the toil of bringing in the fruit of the olive orchards? Come now, is this truly your first picking?"

"It is, I am sorry to say."

"Curse of the centaurs, how did I draw such a beginner? We will fall behind the others and lose our chance to win the olive bough from the queen herself. Oh, why me! Hasten your work. Now quickly, cover your head with a hat, wave that stick and get on to the next tree. You'll stop when I tell you."

Zack did not relish being branded a barbarian, no less an incompetent embarrassment to his overseer. The morning came in crisp, but now the sun had brought its warmth to the October air. Men were dropping their tunics, working in their loincloths. Zack did the same, doubling his efforts.

"If this is your first picking, then from what barbarian land do you hail?" The man did not stop to look at Zack and neither did he give him a chance to answer. "Don't tell me. If olives and wine don't grace your table then you must feast on cattle and drink their milk; truly not the food of a civilized land."

"I am from a land far to the west. We do know the grape and the olive there, but I never joined in their harvesting."

"Here now, carry this last load with me. We'll lead the oxen to the presses."

Zack led the team with his companion to the side of the orchard where several circular stone presses awaited. Men and women scurried to unload their cargo and then return for more.

"And what is the taste of the oil in your land?" Attalus asked, slapping the oxen. "Does it draw the flowers or fruit from the soil and air as ours does? I cannot wait to dip my finger into the first press."

Zack frowned. "I fear I'll disappoint you with my knowledge of oil, or wine for that matter." The line of carts was dwindling ahead and they were next. The nets were taken from the cart in front of them and the olives dumped into the stone basin. A round stone, connected to a harnessed ox by a wooden beam, was rolled over the clumps of tiny black fruit. The oil was crushed out, draining through a stone portal into ceramic pots. The pots were lined up off to the side with their sides glistening with sunstruck liquid gold.

"Why is there such a hurry to capture the olives?" Zack inquired. "If they don't fall from the trees, they must not be ripe."

"What god torments me with your presence? Surely, I have lost their favor. It's the fruit, Cyclops. The fruit must be pressed in one day, or it will spoil."

"Do you mean we must clear this entire orchard?" Zack cast his eyes at a beehive of activity among the hundreds of trees extending as far as he could see into the plains beyond the citadel.

"This one and many thereafter; we shall toil well into the night. Torches will be lighted and you will fall to the earth exhausted with the rest of us. Afterward, we'll praise Athena for delivering to us a hearty crop." Attalus jumped to beat tree branches with his long stick. More breathlessly he said, "We can't live without our oil." After another leap, he said, "Light our lamps…cook our food." He took a quick break and wiped his forehead. "Fill our ships with it to trade for goods abroad. For these reasons, if anyone is caught harming a tree, they'll be put to death. Remember this well. Now hoist the nets."

Zack and his companion lifted the nets and dumped the olives into the stone vat. In the vat, a black mash, the residue of the olive skins, crept up the sides and was scooped away by women with long wooden spoons and further saved in clay pots.

"There, your efforts are pleasing me, Stranger. Now take these leather stockings and tie them over your shins. The next orchard is not groomed and the sticks and briars will cut your legs. Take a switch to the oxen and find a new tree."

Zack rubbed his shoulder, stretched, and shook it loose.

"I know, I know," Attalus said. "I can see you have wounds. Many do. You'll not hear them whimper."

Horns blared and hoplites bearing lances formed lines leading to the presses. The queen approached under a fringed gold canopy held by her attendants.

"How goes the harvest, manager?" she asked Attalus.

"Your people tend to their labor, so even the largest pithoi jars will be filled to the brim." He held his chin high.

"I am pleased." Io set her eyes upon Zack, chest bare and his loincloth wrapped above tanned thighs. The queen's face twitched just a moment. Her eyes lingered.

"Honored envoy," she said. "The people of Mycenae appreciate your efforts."

Zack bowed. "The work builds my strength. I am pleased to assist."

"I see that the colors have left your wounds. Soon the prince will be able to fill your grip with an eight-footer. I will not delay your efforts here any longer. Attend to your oxen, guest of our citadel."

Zack smiled. He didn't know for sure, but he thought he felt the queen's eyes on his back.

When they were again among the trees, Attalus pulled on his arm.

"You are a favored guest of the queen? Why did you keep such a secret hidden from me? What a fool I am. My tongue has wagged too sharply."

"Be not concerned. Let's return to our sticks and see if we can win the contest. You can call me Cyclops if you wish, but I prefer Zack."

Dawn rose and still the trees held olives. Zack shivered. The day before, he'd sweated with others, and then with them all night while they worked, stopping only to chew on chunks of bread thrown to them by children. The morning air blew in colder now than the day before. He pulled a makeshift bandana from around his forehead and wiped the grime from his face. He was worn out but wasn't going to complain. Too many women, children, citizens, and slaves continued working beside him.

By midmorning, the brassy blare of horns announced the imminent end of the harvest. Exuberant cheering followed. When all the nets were in, the workers collapsed near the presses. Hundreds lifted clay pots and drank their fill of wine to the sounds of the slowly churning stone wheels, whose work was not finished until every olive had been drained of its oil. Five-foot-high pithoi jars, four to a wagon, were filled with oil from smaller barrels and taken by teams of workers up the long ramp to the citadel. There, the oil was once again transferred into pots and deposited into even larger pithoi within a stone building, which served not only as a storage facility but also as a bank. In those massive jars rested the wealth of the city.

"You toiled hard for me, Cyclops," Attalus said, resting on an elbow. "But, we didn't win. How I would love to have the queen place the bough on my forehead; to breathe in her perfumed hair and get lost in the dark sea of her eyes."

Attalus laid back and rested his hands under his head. "I have watched her since she was a young lady of the court, I being of the same years. Since I first saw her stroll with her companions to draw water and myrtles from the streams in the valley, I have dreamed she would be mine. But I am a farmer and she is a queen; how cruel are the gods?"

Zack gulped down the rest of his wine. "She is a fair woman, Attalus. And there is no law against dreams."

"We haven't much time for dreaming anyway, Cyclops. When Helios rises tomorrow, we must begin the reaping of the barley and the wheat crops."

"Don't make jests with me," Zack said, searching the man's eyes for the hint of a joke.

"I make none. In the few days hence, you will only dream of sleep."

"Training for war might be preferable to pulling in the crops," Zack countered. In the distance he saw rain clouds streaming down from the north.

"If you cannot stomach the harvest, then neither can you endure the clash of arms."

"It was a stupid thing to say," Zack uttered, a little embarrassed. "I've seen what it takes."

"Don't tell me tall tales, Cyclops. Your eyes give you away. If there's a warrior in there, then I am a prince."

8

Delphi, Greece

PRESENT DAY

Demo darted away from his perch outside the doorway where he had been eavesdropping on the conversation between the policeman and the woman. He peeked around the corner and watched the policeman strut down the hallway and out the door.

The woman was lying, but why? Demo was sure she was the one on the video he had found, showing her and her husband being swallowed into a spooky hole up on the mountain. His friend, Professor Papandreou, before he had been killed, had told him that there was a great secret up there and to keep it quiet. She must have a reason to lie. Would she be angry with him if he asked her about it? Since the professor's death, he'd felt too scared to talk to anyone about the hole or the video.

He had spent the last day with Stephan, curled up beside him in his bed, calming his fears about the big man in the kitchen. Demo wondered if that man was the one who'd killed Professor Papandreou. So much didn't make sense.

Lauren closed the door and collapsed on the bed. Cassandra rolled in beside her.

Lauren said in a soft voice, "I've never had to lie like that before."

Cassandra tilted her face upwards. "Were all of you speaking Atlantean?"

"No, sweetheart, but you must realize these are your people, just many years after you were born. I'm sorry this is so difficult to explain, but if we are good actresses, like in the plays your family took you to in the theater in Delphi, then we may be able to stay together."

"Only men are allowed to act in the theater."

"You will have to learn fast."

Cassandra said, "I will pray to Athena and I will put on an act that would be victorious at the Pythian Games, lady. You will be witness to this."

Lauren ran her fingers through Cassandra's hair until she fell asleep. Lauren couldn't rest, not yet. The revelation that the professor's death had taken place near the tunnel entrance jolted her. She wondered why he would have gone there in the middle of the night. *Something isn't adding up. Probably just what that inspector is thinking about my story. My performance was decent, but if he keeps asking questions, he'll catch me somehow.*

At eight a.m., Lauren sat in Mr. Avtges's office, rubbing her temples while she spoke on his private phone.

"Yes, Mom, I miss you, too . . . they're searching for Zack now . . . Was Dad's bypass extensive? Three coronary arteries . . . please call me after you get back from the hospital and tell him I love him. Mom, there could be a lot of trouble here—I know you'll come when Dad is better—I don't know how long I'll be here. I won't leave this girl. We have been through so much together. I'm going to need access to our bank accounts . . . That's wonderful of you, Mom. I'll have to set up an account after I talk with the embassy people. Mom, I miss Zack—there's a lot to tell you. I'm so worried about him. I need to call his family, too . . . Yes, you're right; they deserve to hear it from me. I know I'm my father's girl. I'll make him proud. Ok, I love you, too. Bye."

Cassandra sat next to Lauren, waiting for the translation of Lauren's conversation. "My mother says she cannot wait to meet you."

The young lady smiled broadly.

"She is even more surprised that you have the same name as her mother does."

"Will I meet her also?"

"I will make sure of it. Come here. I need a hug, a good strong one."

Oh, Zack. What is Apollo doing to you now? I miss you. I need you.

After a long embrace, Lauren suggested they go get breakfast before she had to get back on the phone to call the embassy.

Most of the children were crunching on cereal, but they stopped eating and stared at Cassandra as she and Lauren entered the dining room. Shy, Cassandra scampered behind Lauren.

"Ah, our guests," Avtges said. "Children, these are our new friends. They may be staying here awhile. I would like to introduce Professor Lauren Fletcher and . . . oh my . . . I do not know the girl's name."

"I call her Cassandra," Lauren answered in Greek, pulling the girl forward. "We are very happy to be here. But children, I'm asking for your help in making Cassandra welcome. She does not speak and also does not understand your language. She is scared and we have had a difficult time. Perhaps, there are some games we could teach her later. Thank you for your help."

The bright faces looked up, most of them smiling at Cassandra. Lauren didn't see the boy who had served them lunch the day before. She learned that he worked at the museum on Saturdays. Cassandra settled herself behind Lauren until she was directed to sit at one of the long tables strewn with the remains of breakfast. She looked over the breakfast items: small single-serving boxes of cereal, one with three boys on the cover. She tugged on Lauren's sleeve and pointed at it.

Lauren said, "What, the Rice Krispies? Oh right, you've never eaten cereal, at least not this way. Oh, shoot, you can't understand a word I'm saying anyway."

All eyes watched them until Lauren made a bowl of cereal by opening one of the miniature boxes and pouring milk inside. The bowl emitted snaps and crackles. Cassandra smiled, leaning her ear into it.

"Do not be concerned, Professor Fletcher. The children will enjoy the company. A distraction is what we need anyway, with all the tension."

"I'd be happy to pull my weight in any way I can. I need a little time to make more calls. Could I use your phone again after breakfast?"

"Inspector Trokalitis is not an easy man to deal with. Then again, he has a difficult job to do."

"Yes, he's a real sweetheart. Would it be all right if we helped out in the kitchen?"

"Grand idea," Avtges said, slapping his thighs. "It would also be a good way to get to know everyone, for the girl also."

"Things are looking up, Mr. Avtges. I've already landed a job."

"You may start this afternoon."

"Will do, and I am more than happy to reimburse you for the calls." Lauren saluted him. The children laughed.

At a minimum, she'd bought time and a place to stay.

Lauren put the leftovers from lunch into the freezer. When she returned to the kitchen, Cassandra had her hand on the controls to the gas stove top. She would turn on the burner, leap back, and clap her hands. Then she turned it off, staring at the burner mechanism, and then ever so slowly, turned the dial until the flame appeared once more. She heard Lauren's laughter and turned nervously, as if caught in the act.

"Sweetheart, every day you are going to be more amazed with our inventions. But, do not touch the fire maker unless I am here with you. Understand?"

Cassandra bowed. "I understand."

Lauren raised a forefinger to her lips. "Now do not speak."

The boy they had met earlier, the curly-haired one, entered the cafeteria and plunked himself down at the table. "Are you going to do the dishes, too? We won't have to help clean up? This is great."

Lauren smiled. "What was your name again? Was it Dem . . . ?"

"It's Demetrious."

The boy watched Lauren as she stacked pots onto shelves that lined the walls.

"I worked up at the museum today. You can call me Demo."

Lauren dodged the subject, but didn't quite know why. "These are beautiful mountains. I feel like I am a part of the past, like when the great heroes lived: Hercules, Achilles, and Leonidas. You must know of these men from the past?"

"Of course, I am Greek."

"It's good for a young man to understand his heritage. What's your favorite kind of Greek food?" she asked, changing the subject.

"Oh, I like gyros and moussaka the best." Demetrious licked his lips.

"We make them where I live, too."

"What is America like?"

"It is a wonderful place to live, for the most part."

"Have you been to Disneyland? I have heard that they have haunted houses and pirates."

Lauren grinned while closing the kitchen cabinets. "They do. America has many different kinds of places to live and play. There is snow and beaches, great forests and mountains, miles of grassland, bears and horses."

"I want to meet a real Indian. Do you have a headdress of feathers?"

Lauren laughed out loud. "Well no, but we could make them, have a campfire, and dance around it."

"Really, can we?"

"We'll make them out of paper, color them, and put them on our heads. It's easy."

Demo leaped up. "Yes, yes, when?"

"Maybe I could teach you to make one. Then, you could help the others decorate them with crayons."

"This is the best day of my life; I'm going to tell them all right now." He dashed out of the room.

Cassandra whispered, "Why is he so very pleased?"

"We are all going to play together."

"I do not think they like me. They point at me and whisper." Cassandra hung her head. "Do I still need to be silent?"

"Yes and now would be a good time to stop talking. We do not want anyone to catch us. Come, let's go for a walk. There is so much to teach you."

"Can I turn the fire on once more?"

"How about if you press your finger on that button and turn off the lights in this room instead?"

Cassandra galloped to the light switch and turned off the lights after flicking them on and off a few times.

They walked outside to enjoy the temperate afternoon sunshine. Fall had come to the mountains and the wind whipping through the pine trees added fragrance to the air.

"You are doing well, sweetheart. I know it must be so hard not to speak, but anything you say might be used to take you from me."

"It was not long ago that the barbarian chased us up that hill." Cassandra shuddered. Lauren felt it also.

"Maybe we shouldn't be outside. Let's go back in."

Delphi, Greece

PRESENT DAY

Not such a great time for the air conditioning to go down," Lauren said to Mr. Parsons, the US Embassy representative interviewing her. The orphanage was stuffy and hot. The windows had been ordered closed and locked on the ground floors. In a corner, a fan rotated on its base. Each time the breeze approached, Cassandra closed her eyes and let it wash over her face.

Mr. Parsons sat at Mr. Avtges's desk. He scratched at a yellow notepad with a pen. His fingers were long, like the rest of him, and he looked uncomfortable sitting in a chair too small for him. He stretched his lips minimally and managed a smile in response to Lauren's small talk, but it was a gratuitous attempt, like a limp handshake.

Lauren did'nt know what to expect from this man. He might help her or destroy her. He seemed a little distracted, as was she. Lauren had met him at Professor P's fundraiser also. She remembered he had been very pleasant and complimented her on the books she'd written about the Persian kings. She nibbled on a nail. Inspector Trokalitis had unnerved her and she could not stop dwelling on it.

She looked at Parsons pensively. His black hair was clipped short, neatly parted on the side, very businesslike. He looked back at her and then sniffed quickly through his thin nose. Mr. Avtges begged his leave after the introductions and closed the door behind him.

"Professor Fletcher, could you please tell me the whole story in detail? I understand you have been through a difficult experience." Parsons sat up straight, his pen poised.

Lauren told him the same story she'd told the police.

Mr. Parsons rubbed his chin after hearing her tale, as Trokalitis had done before him.

"Professor Fletcher, I want you to know we're on your side. We are used to managing many different problems presented to us by US citizens. We will do all we can to help you, but as I am sure you are aware, the laws of this country are different from yours."

He tapped the point of his pen on the desk. Lauren wondered how many times each week he had to utter the same soliloquy to tourists in trouble.

"Your husband has disappeared, as has the kidnapper. It seems probable that the kidnapper and the murderer may be the same man. I have spoken with Inspector Trokalitis and he's told me that the description of the intruder into this orphanage two mornings ago matched the description of your kidnapper. Nevertheless, these events, as you have revealed them to me, are quite remarkable. Imagine yourself in his position: two Americans have been reported missing for a couple of months. One finally shows up, accompanied by an unidentified, seemingly handicapped girl, and relays a story about kidnapping. This occurs while the Inspector is preoccupied investigating the stunning murder of a very important man. A murder, I might add, with no suspects."

Parsons stared at her. "He will take his time studying the evidence. You must be very careful, being a foreigner. Do exactly as he says and do tell him the truth, Professor Fletcher."

"That's exactly what I am doing," Lauren answered, not sure if she sounded more defensive than convincingly candid.

"I suggest nothing *but* the truth, Professor Fletcher."

Lauren shifted in her seat. "I have nothing to hide."

"I believe you will need legal counsel. I have a list of very proficient lawyers that I can recommend to you to assist you through this difficult time."

Lauren swallowed hard. "I will need your best recommendation, Mr. Parsons, and I will need your help in establishing an account over here so that I can transfer money for my expenses and legal bills. I am very worried for my husband. He is out there somewhere and I can't help him. The kidnapper is ruthless and will kill us on sight. He needs to be apprehended quickly."

"Perhaps he's gone from this area."

"I hope so," Lauren said, the strain clear on her face. "I'm going to stay with this girl, she's very important to me."

"Does she understand anything we're saying?" he asked.

"I don't know for sure but I doubt it."

"You must realize of course, Social Services will arrive to evaluate her. She may need medical attention."

"I understand that but I will not leave her side. We've been through too much together, and I need your assistance in preventing our separation."

"That is not a simple task, Professor. There is no guarantee that either of you can remain here."

"Mr. Avtges and Inspector Trokalitis have said that we can stay."

"Then let us hope that it remains that way. Have you notified your family that you are well?"

"I called this morning. My parents will not be able to come over to help me since my father is very sick. Other family members may arrive to assist me. How long have you been stationed here, Mr. Parsons?"

"Five years. It has always been my goal to work in Greece. I love it here."

"Do you have a family, Mr. Parsons?"

"No, I'm a bachelor."

"Can you understand me then when I tell you that I will not leave this girl until she is taken care of properly? If it turns out somehow she has no relatives or cannot be identified, then I want to become her legal guardian."

Mr. Parsons raised his eyebrows and blew out a deep breath. "Professor Fletcher, are you serious?"

"Very."

"Don't you think you have enough problems to deal with?"

"If my husband is alive, he will show up at some point." Lauren lowered her eyes. "If he isn't, then there is nothing that I can do about it and this girl will forever be an emotional connection to him. He risked his life to save ours."

Mr. Parsons did not avert his eyes, as if weighing her truthfulness.

"I know a legal firm that can handle this. Is there anything else you want to tell me?"

Lauren raised her chin. Parsons waited for her answer. She wondered if he believed her story. She was desperate to tell someone the truth, the whole truth, but he was not the right candidate. She might not be able to tell even her own family. "No, just please help me. You have no idea how comforting it is to have the United States to rely on when you're in a foreign country."

"Yet, we cannot work miracles, Professor Fletcher. But I promise you I will do my best."

"Maybe what I need is a miracle. Or divine intervention."

Mr. Parsons stood up, retrieved his briefcase, opened it, and withdrew a folder. He handed a list of legal firms to Lauren. "I suggest you call the firm at the top of the list. Give them my name. They will be happy to help you. I'll tell them of your predicament."

"Thank you for your assistance."

"It's my job. Here is my business card. Call me if you have any questions."

He stood, extended his hand, and shook her hand firmly this time. He patted Cassandra on the top of her head. She looked at him and smiled.

"I will call you if I have any information but do not expect fast results. In fact, you may be here a long time, a year or more. You must prepare for a very rocky road ahead."

"It has been a rocky road for some time, Mr. Parsons. I will survive it."

"Good-bye then." He opened the door and walked out.

Lauren stared at the open doorway.

Cassandra cupped Lauren's ear with her hand. "Will he help us?"

"I hope so, sweetheart. I really hope so."

"I shall pray to Athena. She will come to this man in a dream and convince him."

Lauren held the young girl closer. "We need all the help we can get. I told them I want you to stay with me always. He said the road to this would be long and hard." Lauren went to the door. She looked down both hallways and closed the door.

"I do not want to be a slave, I beseech you," Cassandra said, pleading. "Don't allow them to sell me in the markets. They strip the girls and poke them."

"Oh sweetheart, that will never happen. Slaves are not allowed in this time, at least not in this country. The officials will want to see and examine you for injuries, even your private parts. They may flash bright lights in your eyes, but do not be frightened. I will explain it all to you. Do not talk or cry out, even if they pinch you. We have to trick them. Do you understand?"

"I loved to play tricks with my mother."

Lauren put her fingers to her lips. "Be silent now, I hear footsteps."

The clicking of loafers on the tile announced the arrival of Mr. Avtges from the stairwell. He knocked on the door and entered.

"Ah, I see he is gone. Was the visit satisfactory?"

"Yes. I will need to hire a lawyer. May we stay here for a while? The process may be longer than I imagined."

"We shall see, Professor Fletcher. For now, this is fine, but we should take it day by day."

Lauren bit her nail. She had no idea what would occur now. It might have been better to remain in the cave. She could have scavenged for food and escaped somehow. She caressed Zack's folded lambskin letter in her pants pocket, a letter that never left her person.

Lauren said, "We're going to rest. I'm not feeling well."

"It is understandable. I will have you called when it's time to prepare the evening meal. The ladies that volunteer their time will be happy to have a break."

"Someday I'll pay you back, Mr. Avtges. I promise."

Late that afternoon, gentle tapping on the door awoke them.

"Ladies, ladies, it is time to wake up. May I speak with you?"

Lauren motioned with her finger to her lips for Cassandra to be quiet.

"Who is it?" Lauren asked, hearing a boy's voice.

"Demo. I have a question for you?"

Lauren ran her fingers quickly through her disheveled mane of hair. She needed a hairdresser, a manicure, a massage therapist, but most of all, a psychiatrist. She tucked the hem of a red blouse into her jeans.

"Just a moment," she said, pointing at the bathroom with her finger, directing Cassandra to move inside. She closed the bathroom door and opened the other to find Demo standing there in a worn blue jogging suit, his knee exposed through a hole in the pant leg.

"It is time to make dinner, are you coming down?"

"Yes, right away." Lauren yawned. She heard her jaw crack, up near her right ear. She put her fingers there, hoping to massage away a discomfort. "I must be grinding the heck out of my teeth," she complained aloud.

"Will you teach me English?" Demo asked, peering around the doorjamb, looking for Cassandra.

"If there is enough time, I certainly will."

"Are you leaving?"

"I hope not. I would like to stay here a long time."

"Could I help you in the kitchen?"

"Certainly, Cassandra will rest and I'll bring her down later. I'll meet you in the kitchen then."

Demo and Lauren snapped long strands of pasta in half and dropped them into a boiling pot. The boy didn't say anything for a time. Lauren hummed, happy for the distraction of cooking to keep her mind off the complicated scenarios she continued to ruminate over.

"I hope I can work at the museum when I get older or maybe become a policeman." Demo broke the conversational silence.

"I will catch all the bad guys."

"How is the boy who saw the big man in the kitchen?"

"He stays in bed. Mr. Avtges speaks with him. He's still very scared. I hear him crying in the night. I told him that I would protect him."

"That is very brave, Demo. Can you put all the plates on the table? We need about twenty plates, correct?"

"Yes. When I help my friend Maria in the museum kitchen, we make food for hundreds."

"You're experienced as well as brave. Will you protect us, too?"

"Of course I will. You know, one day something strange happened to me."

"Oh, really? Tell me."

"It was a rainy day, during the summer. I had finished picking up the soda cans and trash. Maria had given me a big plate of food to eat. Later, I wandered out past the temples. You can see a long way from this mountain."

"I love to look out at the mountains from the temples, also," Lauren answered.

Demo tossed the plates onto the table. The silverware clinked as he set it in place.

Lauren retrieved a bag of frozen peas from the freezer while the water simmered in the pots.

"I hiked up the mountainside."

"Could you get the milk containers when you're done with the forks?"

"Sure." Demo stopped and fixed his eyes on Lauren. "I saw a sinkhole."

The declaration caught Lauren in the middle of ripping open the bag of peas. They showered on the floor and flew out in all directions. "Oh, my," she said, kneeling to pick them up.

"I'll help you." Demo helped sweep the peas into a small pile with his hands.

Lauren said nothing. Her lip quivered. She put the recovered peas into a small bowl. Demo held a handful and let them fall from between his fingers filling the container. He looked into Lauren's eyes.

"And at the bottom was a stick and on the end of it . . . a camera, hanging from it, not a picture camera, a handheld movie one."

Lauren slumped to the floor and sat with her back against the counter. She closed her eyes and shook her head slowly.

Game over.

Lauren smiled at Demo nervously. He didn't wait for her to say anything in return. He continued on, like he was in a confessional and had a lot to unload.

"I was not sure at first if it was lost, but then I thought who would leave a camera like that? I hid the camera in my locker for a while. There was no place to play it because the battery was dead. If I brought it to any shop nearby they might think I stole it."

He looked into Lauren's eyes. "I took a long bus trip to Athens. No one would know me and I've seen camera stores where all the tourists go. I watched the video. I saw your face, talking and laughing, and the man, the one who is missing."

Lauren raised her head from her arms. Teardrops streaked her face.

"I saw him dig out the hole from the piece of rock, and then he fell in . . . and then you as well. Then I saw the cloud."

"Ok, Demo, now I know why you have been looking at me so strangely."

"That's not all." He paused. "I recognized you as the missing people. Flyers were posted at the museum. I knew a professor from the museum in Athens was looking for a missing American couple."

"Oh, my God," she said. Her face bore the realization of the implication of what he was saying.

"I went to visit him and he watched the movie. He was so pleased, brought me back to the orphanage, got me out of trouble, and then he arranged for me to study with him." Demo's face descended into a grimace. "He told me not to say anything," his voice broke. "I promised him, and now he's dead."

Lauren shuffled over to him and hugged him tight. "Professor

Papandreou was my friend, too. I knew him a long time."

"I thought so. You were upset when you heard that he was dead."

"But you were not in—"

"I was outside the door. I knew I had to talk to you."

"Well, the cat is out of the bag, as we say in America."

Demo dropped his head back onto Lauren's shoulder.

"Have you told anyone else?" she asked, expecting the worst.

He shook his head.

"Can you continue to keep our secret?"

"Will it help to catch the bad man?"

"I don't know, but it may help my husband. He's lost and if anyone knows about the hole, they might spoil it, dig it up, and ruin it forever."

"The professor said the same thing. I will keep my lips . . ." He made the motion of zipping them shut.

Now Lauren's mind raced with the implications of this new information. *The late professor had seen what had happened to them. Could he have deduced that what had actually occurred was a supernatural event? Maybe he thought we were swallowed by a mudslide. But that doesn't make sense. If so, he would have notified the police to dig there, hoping we could be rescued. I need the video, just to keep it out of others' hands, especially the police. Again, if the inspector had the camera as part of his evidence, wouldn't he have seen it and mentioned its contents? She would be clearly caught in a lie. She would likely be in jail already, having given a false statement.*

"He played the movie in his office, right?" Lauren inquired.

Demo nodded.

"Then it must still be there."

"After he played it, he put the camera in a video box on the second shelf from the top."

Lauren bit her fingernail. *The video camera could be anywhere now—at his home, or even in police possession.*

Mycenae, Greece

LATE WINTER 479 BC

Trumpets announced the arrival of a long train of guests from the neighboring city of Argos. Guards rushed to parapets to present an honor guard along the walls. The people crowded behind the guards to catch sight of the canopied wagon bearing the king of Argos, his wife, and their young princess. Hoplites on horseback rode beside the royal family, along with a string of officials and attendants. The travelers trudged toward the Lion Gate, the slow pace speaking of their fatigue.

Queen Io greeted the visitors with a bow, made apologies for her husband's absence, and introduced Prince Diomedes to the veiled princess holding on to her father's arm. Io locked eyes with the queen of Argos in a silent approval of their arranged visit. After all, she knew this was a time for alliances, by marriage or otherwise. Although, any act of state might be in vain with the Persian army winter-camped in northern Greece. Their fleet had left for Asia, but Xerxes had left a powerful army to continue on with the conquest of the city-states of Greece, and they would begin their campaign in the spring. She shook the trepidations from her thoughts and displayed a gratuitous smile.

Zack had heard about the coming visit and kept trying to remember some vague fact about the city-state of Argos from around this time period. Education can be a trial of facts and memorization. He felt like he just couldn't remember something of importance, like a cloud filled his head and he couldn't get rid of it.

It was going to bother him all day now.

Standing beside Diomedes, Zack saw him stiffen slightly when the princess was introduced. They had not spoken much in the last days before this meeting, with Diomedes consumed with the preparations for a state visit. The princess, elaborately clothed in a red and yellow gown, lifted her white veil.

Diomedes made no sound or movement. Queen Io complimented the princess on her beauty. The princess had dark hair and eyes. Her hair was pulled back from her face and tied with gold ribbon. Rouge colored her white cheeks. Zack estimated this girl could not have been more than fourteen or fifteen years old.

She should be in middle school.

Zack nudged Diomedes in the ribs with his elbow and whispered to him, "You better smile or say something. Everyone's looking at you."

Diomedes let out a short breath. "Welcome to Mycenae, King Pheidon, Queen Acantha. The goddesses themselves would be hard-pressed to win a beauty contest against your daughter."

The young girl smiled first. All present followed. Zack whispered again, "Lucky man."

Diomedes nudged him back with more vigor, signaling for Zack to shut up.

Queen Io said, "We shall accompany you to your quarters. There will be time to bathe and rest. King Pheidon, your presence is requested tonight for symposium."

"I am pleased," Pheidon said, extending his arms for his queen and daughter to join him in the walk to the upper city.

The party departed for the long walk uphill to the citadel. Zack stayed with Diomedes to dismiss the royal guards and see to the housing of the visiting hoplites.

"The women stir a heavy pot of tricks to marry me off," Diomedes said to him. "Is not my life my own?"

"Everyone is on edge," Zack pointed out. "All are concerned with survival."

"But I do not favor being a sacrificial bull."

"Have you thought about how the girl feels? She may be thinking the same as you. She has no choice but to be married off to a stinking ox like you."

Diomedes cracked a smile finally. "Atlanteans think oddly. A woman belongs to her family and then to her husband."

"I beg to differ with you, noble Diomedes, but maybe we can discuss this tonight at symposium."

"We'll serve our reserve wine from Chios and our finest oil for bread-dipping, but it is still not an evening I relish."

"You have to lighten up, Diomedes. Enjoy the party tonight. Talk to her tomorrow. You might like her."

Diomedes started to say something but stopped. He looked out towards the faraway mountains. "Let us go lift some bags of sand and then bathe for tonight."

"What tortures your thoughts?" Zack asked.

"Something only the gods can answer."

Zack folded the long end of a white himation over his right arm while following Diomedes through an off-center doorway into the *andron*, the men's drinking quarters. He handed his sandals to a male slave. Red-sheeted couches were arranged head to toe against the wall with small tables set in front to hold food and drink. Zack saw a striking mosaic of the god Dionysus that covered the entire floor. He stepped over the god's mouth, which was open to receive a bunch of grapes held aloft by a nymph. Diomedes directed Zack to recline on the couch next to him. On the wall behind his couch, a long tapestry hung from the ceiling, depicting a bevy of seminude women accosting a centaur.

"There isn't going to be any of that tonight, is there?" Zack asked smirking, pointing at the tapestry.

Pheidon and Andokides entered, nodding their heads at their drinking companions. They took their couches, leaving three others ready for occupancy.

Diomedes whispered to him, "The night can be anything you wish. Flute girls, as many as you want. Maybe one of the boy attendants might be to your liking?"

Zack rolled his eyes. "I think I'll stick to drinking and eating."

"Do not worry yourself. Empty your cups at will. I'm the symposiarch and will determine the mixture of wine and water to keep us all from fouling this fine room. Even so, this room has no memory. Do not fear that your actions will be held against you."

Pheidon pulled his feet up onto the couch and laid his back against a round pillow. Recognizing Zack from the reception, he said, "I see your giant friend is attending our party. I hope he will leave enough wine and food for the rest of us." He smiled at Zack, letting him know he spoke in jest. Then he sighed. "I'm happy to enjoy the evening after our trip today. It has been many years since you invited me here, King Andokides."

"It took that long to fill our caverns with enough wine after your last visit." The corners of Andokides's eyes crinkled.

Pheidon burst out laughing. "Well, let us see what cups we will be using tonight." He held his shallow drinking cup aloft and inspected the painting of an older man with a hand resting on a young man's shoulder. "You remember my tastes. This will be a fine night indeed."

Zack turned to Diomedes. "What is he talking about?"

"Look at your cup, Zack."

Turning it in the candlelight, Zack saw a picture of a man with a figure of a woman bent over a table. It was obvious what the characters were doing.

Diomedes cackled, watching for Zack's reaction. "Oh, don't be such a prude. In a moment you'll see what your choices are."

Zack stirred uncomfortably. Moments later, two boys walked in, one muscled, the other slender, holding a round table that they set in the middle of the room. Pheidon sat up on his couch. Directly behind them, four of the young female attendants Zack had seen periodically around the citadel followed the men. Garlands of red and white flowers complemented their dark hair and they wore short-cut yellow chitons that showed off their legs. One carried a krater, a decorated mixing bowl for the wine, and set it on the table. Another held a jug for mixing the water in the wine, and the third handled a more elegant jug for pouring the diluted wine into the cups. The last carried an armful of lei-like garlands that filled the room with a rosy fragrance. She handed one to each of the men with a smile.

Pheidon licked his lips. "Bring on the food, me boys. I'm famished. And do not stay away too long. I have other appetites." The stone-faced boys left for the kitchen. The young women awaited the order from Diomedes to mix the wine.

Diomedes scratched his chin. "Let us begin with a four-to-one dilution. I don't want my friend's eyes to become so wanton this early in the evening."

One of the girls looked at Zack briefly, giggled, and turned her eyes away.

The girl with the water jug poured a long draft into the krater. The second dribbled in purple wine to the proper calculation. With Diomedes's approval, the girl dunked a pitcher into the krater and filled it. Each of the men held out his kylix and thanked the woman with his eyes for this first serving.

"A toast then," Andokides declared, "to the gods for their blessings. They give us wine to lessen the burdens of men and bring back our thoughts to the joyous side of life." Andokides stopped speaking, almost out of breath. He took a sip from his cup and motioned for Diomedes to take over the toasting duties.

Diomedes lent a furtive glance at the king of Argos. After a moment he said, "I agree the gods bless us one moment and the next they torture us." He looked at Zack. "Tonight, I think there will be a very pleasant torture."

Everyone laughed but Zack.

"Here now, good man," Pheidon said with the four girls standing in front of him. "I'll not be greedy, pick one now to sit on the couch with you. Let her sing in your ear of her charms. The scowl on your face would offend the gods, Atlantean."

Zack lifted his cup and took a long drink. The wine was diluted, almost grape juice. "I see your wisdom, King of Argos, but I prefer to await the meal, and then maybe music before our ladies here must attend to other duties."

Maybe, if I can get them all drunk, they'll leave me alone.

"All finish the first cup," Diomedes said. "We must stay in unison. The gods favor the moderate."

With the aroma of baked bread and fish cooked in olive oil, the boys returned with platters, setting them down on the round table next to the krater. The girls made four plates of grapes, apples, bread, eggs, and cheese and placed them on the individual tables in front of the diners.

Zack ripped off a chunk of bread and dipped it in the oil, wondering if he had handpicked the olives from which the oil was made. The flavor tasted of herbs, but he couldn't place which fragrance or taste it was. He'd never been able to decipher wines either. He just knew when they were good.

Pheidon raised his kylix and said, "And to our great cities, may the gods keep us safe." A slender boy-servant had to move aside for one of the girls to slide by him with a plate. Pheidon pulled him over and kissed him on the cheek. Not knowing what to do, the boy froze. Pheidon chuckled, "Ahh, a beginner! Come sit by me."

Andokides interrupted, "Let the boy alone for the time be, the lad has duties to perform here first. Have one of the maidens entertain you until he has set the table."

Pheidon stammered, "Oh, if he must. Come to me girl, and bring your flutes. I want to sing while you play."

He hauled one of the four girls onto his couch and twirled a finger in her hair. Another of the female attendants brought the twin flutes. Pheidon wrapped his arms around her and buried his face in her dark curls. Zack laughed nervously.

Diomedes said, "Go on, Zack, you can have two if you like. Mine is yours."

"I appreciate your generosity, truly I do. But for now . . ."

"Do you think of your wife often?" Diomedes asked with a grave look. "I can see you are troubled. Here now, have another cup." He pointed at the tallest of the girls and told her, "Two-to-one dilution, I command you. Maybe we *will* drink like barbarians tonight."

Pheidon came up for air and flashed his eyes at Zack. "You are an Atlantean, I hear, whatever that is." He bellowed laughter and squeezed the young girl tighter. "If you refuse the girls, are you going to fight me for the boys?"

"Fill my kylix with haste, I beg you," Zack said. "Are there not any songs we could sing, a game perhaps?"

Andokides said through a spattering of wheezes, "Oh there will be games. Drink up first. We must all finish the second toast soon."

Pheidon lifted his head again from the neck of the squealing maiden and sang out in a booming voice, "Come to me little nymph, bring me your precious flower . . ."

"Now we must toast to love," Diomedes interrupted. Rising off the couch, he raised his kylix and said, "To the women who hold our thoughts by day and haunt our dreams by night." He looked at Zack. "Whether they be flute girls, concubines . . ."

"Or wives," Zack added.

"This man pines away for his wife," Andokides said, wrapping a blanket over his shoulders. Two of the maidens ran to his side and tucked it in. "The winter winds chill me."

"Is there a chance Lauren might return to us?" Diomedes asked.

"Only the gods know," Zack said glumly. "It is doubtful."

Diomedes's grin fell away and furrows appeared on his brow. "Drink up, gentlemen," he said in a depressed tone.

"Have you ever loved another woman but Lauren?" Diomedes asked.

"Well, yes," Zack said uncomfortably. "I've had women."

"But you married Lauren. Why?"

Zack sipped from his kylix. "We have so much in common. We both are teachers of the past, pedagogues in our country."

"A woman can be a pedagogue in your land?" Diomedes asked louder, rousing Pheidon from caressing a serving boy's cheek.

"Sounds like a land of weaklings," Pheidon said sneering. "What men can you be if you cannot control your women?" The servant tried to get up but Pheidon forcefully seated him down.

Zack countered, "King of Argos, in our land we recognize that women are just as capable as men."

"You must be a nation of fools," Pheidon said, flinging his hand at Zack as he returned his attention to the boy, nibbling on his ear.

"We should raise a toast to mothers also," Andokides returned, grinning at Diomedes. "We should not forget their love above all."

Pheidon groaned. "So many beautiful sentiments; must we be distracted with all this dripping honey?"

Another of the girls sidled up to Diomedes, draped herself over him, and pulled down her top. Diomedes shunned her, saying, "Pay attention to my friend here, instead."

He pushed her towards Zack. The girl smiled, but didn't go to him. Instead, she walked back to the krater while resetting the top of her yellow chiton.

"Never mind then, drain your cups, but leave a little wine and sediment at the bottom. It's time for *kottabos*," Diomedes said.

The boys hauled in a bronze stand supporting a two-foot-high statue of a goddess with her arms raised and outstretched. The slender boy slipped from Pheidon's arm and pulled a metal disk from a pocket in his chiton, and placed it between the statue's hands. Below the statue, a bronze cup was positioned to catch the disc as it fell, giving off a bell-like ring.

Diomedes said, "Take your kylix, Zack, hold it by one handle, measure your throw, arch it backward, and fling the sediment at the disc. If you hit it and sound the bell, even the gods will cheer. I shall throw first, watch me."

Once again, Pheidon yanked on the arm of the slender boy, pulled him onto his couch, and stroked his thigh. "Go ahead, Prince Diomedes. Let me know when it is my turn."

"The prize for winning is a wreath of olive branches and your choice of the attendants, more than one if you like." He looked directly at Zack.

Good thing I don't have a clue how to play this game.

From his reclined position and without practice, Diomedes slung the residue at the disc. The mixture of wine and sediment flashed toward the target. The sludge hit just to the right of the disc and splattered against the wall. Diomedes cursed. Andokides laughed hard until he coughed. Zack wondered if he would get a throw past his own lap.

"You don't appear to be too interested in our game, Zack," Diomedes said.

"If your thoughts turn back to your wife, tell me true, was your marriage arranged by your father and what was her dowry?"

"Come now, Pheidon," Andokides said. "Show me if you still hold the skill of your youth."

Pheidon let the boy go free. "You will see not only my throw, good Andokides, but I will prove my youth later with the boy." Pheidon slipped his finger through the ring handle of the cup. From his sitting position, he bit his lower lip while taking a few half motions to measure the weight of his cup and the length of the throw. "When I win, I will claim the attention of this fine young man and that girl you just turned away."

"We do not arrange marriages and there are no dowries in our land. You don't seem to have your heart in this party either, Diomedes," Zack answered.

Pheidon hurled his mass and splattered the bronze stand, well short of the mark. "I'd better make a fast sacrifice or I will lose my company for the night. Fill my bowl, girl. I'll have another try."

Andokides grinned. "Perhaps a gust of wind disturbed your throw."

"Wind you say? I felt only the winds of your Atlantean, running on with talk while I'm trying to concentrate."

Diomedes interrupted him. "Give our guest some leave. You have a try at it, Zack. Drink your kylix almost empty and leave the sludge."

After downing the red wine, Zack held the shallow cup in both hands while setting his finger in the hole of one of the arching circular handles. With the kylix hanging from his finger over his shoulder, he whipped it forward. The kylix fell from his hold. The sludge splattered Pheidon and wet his couch.

"I'm so sorry," Zack said, horrified, leaping from his reclined position to help clean up the mess.

"Have you no brains?" Pheidon erupted.

"Lay back down," Diomedes ordered. He told the attendants to fill the cups again and others to dab the stains on the couch and Pheidon's robes.

"I will show you again, Zack. It does take some practice."

"Must I compete against this . . . this barbarian?" Pheidon complained.

I'll bet none of you could hit a baseball the first time, either.

Diomedes drained his cup in one gulp, wiped his mouth, and hurled the dregs at the disc. He hit the disk with a portion, but it didn't fall from the goddess's hands. He let out a hoot.

"There, I am close and will try yet a third time. Fill my cup, girl. Keep the dilution at two-to-one. We must all drink the same number of cups. Father, it is your turn."

"I will pass tonight on the heavy drinking and hurling. It is entertainment enough to watch all of you soil each other."

"There, Zack, raise your cup. Did I fill your eyes with dew mentioning Lauren?"

Zack obeyed and spit a small stick out of his mouth.

"No," Diomedes shouted. "That will thicken your sauce. You need the refuse to hold the throw. Otherwise, it is just a hurl of red piss."

"Forget the barbarian. I'm ready," Pheidon declared. He reached back and emptied his cup at the target. He splattered the wall just to the left. "Too far away," he complained. "Move it closer while I fill my cup."

"I am symposiarch and it stays where it is," Diomedes said forcefully.

"A firm man; you will make a good husband for my daughter," Pheidon said, tipping his kylix in salute. "Her dowry will be talked about around hearths for some time."

There was no joy on Diomedes's face.

Pheidon rattled on, "Chests of embroidered robes and polished furniture made of strong oak will be yours. Ten of our finest mares and teams of oxen will pull carts with pithoi brimming with our oil. She will bring twenty breastplates made of bronze, a brace of lances, and long iron swords so sharp that enemies will run upon seeing their sheen."

Andokides face brightened. "And she is a beauty, that one. Your girl is a living goddess. My son will be proud to have her as his queen."

Diomedes buried his face in his kylix.

"Silver cups, golden ones too, adorned with scenes of hoplites for your feasts in the megaron," Pheidon continued.

Zack slung his cup and hit the disc. It fell from the goddess's hands, turned end over end, but didn't land on the bronze bowl. The disc clattered when it bounced on the stone flooring.

Diomedes erupted, "What a throw. You are favored of the gods. Who hits the target on the second try?"

I did pitch baseball in high school.

"But it's not a winner," Pheidon pointed out quickly. "We must load up our saucers and try again."

Zack reached for a bowl of black olives, bread, and fried fish fillets.

Pheidon chastised him. "No time for feasting. I will not be bested by a foreigner. Drink up and prepare to lose."

"Do not cut the wine this time, young girl," Diomedes called. "We will see who shall be the victor."

"Moderation, young man," Andokides warned with a hint of anger. "The gods do not favor arrogance. Do not offend them."

"I will tease them, Father. No more."

"Tease, that's all your servants do," Pheidon complained. "Send them all in here at once for me to make my pick."

"You order people around, like Xerxes," Diomedes said. "Must we all do your bidding?"

"What kind of host are you?" Pheidon complained.

Diomedes snickered, "One who will fill your cup for the next round." He motioned for the cups to be poured.

"Where is your reverence for your elders? Do not disrespect me, young man," Pheidon said with narrowed eyes.

Diomedes looked at Zack and saw him gazing at the wall.

"I lost my reverence, my respect for blind obedience at Thermopylae. The Persians drove their warriors into our spears with whips. Those men did not have a choice. Here, a man fights because he wants to."

Andokides laid his head back and began to snore.

"And he came at you with an endless number of those warriors, didn't he?" Pheidon asked. "In the end, he took the field of battle. He won."

Zack sipped from his cup. He stayed out of the conversation purposely. He wasn't sure if it was the wine, but he struggled to hold on to a vision that seeped into his head but flew away each time he tried to concentrate on it. He walked in the streets of modern Athens alone. It didn't make sense. He had only ever been in Athens with Lauren. The image of a handgun tried hard to capture his attention. He heard distant echoes of shots and explosions.

Diomedes roused him. "The gods play with your thoughts, Zack. Tell them to leave you alone, and join us. Come now, we must all down the next cup. Ready?"

Zack obeyed. One of the girls reset the disc into position.

Pheidon did not let the subject go. "Xerxes can build more ships. He will never give up."

Zack threw off his garland of red blossoms. His face felt hot. He knew he had sucked down too much wine.

"Xerxes's army will descend upon southern Greece and he will bring northern hoplites with him, and cavalry that will hit the flanks of your phalanx and break it apart. There will be no narrow pass to constrict his warriors." The king of Argos wiped his mouth with his sleeve.

Andokides roused suddenly and threw Diomedes a worried glance.

Pheidon continued, "I do not want to see my city burned, my wife and daughter raped and sent away to slavery; my fields burned. You cannot tell me that I am a fool."

Suddenly, Zack drew back his kylix and made his toss. Almost in slow motion from his haze of wine, he saw the dregs fly true and strike the disc. It dropped and hit the bronze cup with a metallic ring, stopping all conversation. Pheidon watched with slack-jawed awe as the flute girl leaped up and ran to hold the disc up, declaring Zack the winner. Diomedes attempted to get up for a speech, but fell backward.

"He did it," Diomedes declared on his rump. "Gods on Olympus, he bested all of us. You must drink two cups in a row, victor."

Pheidon scowled. Andokides clapped his hands. Diomedes ensured that Zack drank the contents of his cup and poured him another.

Zack lifted the kylix yet again to celebrate, but not so cleanly. Red splashed on the already stained folds of his white himation. The room wobbled and started to spin. He caught himself falling backward.

Diomedes watched him with a mischievous grin. "That's what you get for winning. It is time to pick your prize."

Zack stabilized the seemingly bottomless cup of wine. Red wine, uncut now for the last kylix, or two even, slid down his throat and he dreamed of Napa Valley. He had a fleeting vision of a gondola ride to the top of Sterling Vineyards winery and a long afternoon in the tasting cellars of V. Sattui Vineyards in St. Helena. Lauren was with him. He envisioned her smile. There was something he needed to remember about her, something that had happened. His head ached. Was she safe? Where was Apollo?

But he was alone and that wasn't going to change anytime soon.

Zack replied, slurring, "Oh, I don't know which girl to pick. Can I have another cup of wine instead?"

Zack took another gulp. "Oh maybe I'll choose after this last cup." The kylix fell from his hands. The last of the wine spilled on his lap and made a stain in a strategic spot like he'd urinated on himself. The kylix clanked on the mosaic flooring, one handle snapping as it struck the likeness of Dionysus. Zack collapsed backward and passed out with his mouth open.

Watching the fall of the mighty, Andokides remarked, "It appears that neither of the Atlanteans can hold their wine. His wife collapsed at a banquet we held for her."

Diomedes stared a hole in his kylix. "They have other qualities, dear Father. How do you feel?"

"Never better, my boy. Soon enough, Morpheus will claim me to a pleasant rest this night. I will surely converse with our good friend

Zack upon arriving in the god's realm after him."

The king of Argos guffawed. "Now who was it that asked for the wine to go uncut?" Pheidon asked.

"You did," Diomedes answered in garbled speech, "and I approved it. We have never gone to five cups." He tried to stand but thought better of it. He reached for a plate of dates, lay down, and looked up at the whitewashed ceiling of the *andron*. "The gods cannot be explained. What fate do they have in store for me, for all of us here?"

Pheidon pointed a finger at Diomedes. "I can reveal your fate to you, young man. I'll tell it to you just like Apollo himself would. But only if you listen to me."

Andokides snored again, but woke up when Pheidon began to shout.

"Marry my daughter while you can, young prince. But I will not allow it if you join these stupid bands of rebels who defy the Great King of Persia. Do you think a few small battles will keep him from conquering this tiny patch of rock?"

Diomedes's face reddened. He squeezed a date in his hand, and the sticky pulp burst through his fingers.

Pheidon rose to his feet, holding his empty kylix by the handle. "He will be back with warriors that cannot be counted. So you defeated them at Salamis. What about next year, and the year after that?"

Andokides blinked his eyes and said to Pheidon, "You cannot believe what you speak of." The wreath of laurel on his head tilted to the side, blocking his vision. He fought to straighten it out, but finally ripped it from his head.

"Join our cities together and quit this foolish display of hubris that will only bring ruin upon your household and city," Pheidon, king of Argos, declared, falling back on his couch. "Separate yourselves from the Spartans and Athenians and I guarantee you Xerxes will give us power over the whole of the Peloponnese."

Diomedes lurched upward.

Andokides cried out, "Be calm, Diomedes. Do not let the Furies take you over."

"My daughter is fair. Her dowry is generous." Pheidon failed to halt a loud yawn before continuing. "But only if you see reason. What say you?"

Diomedes sneered. "I will not marry your daughter." He stood up, but teetered and had to hold on to the couch rail. Andokides started to breathe harder. Pheidon's eyes widened.

"No matter what you try to arrange, I love another. I will always love her."

Andokides blurted out, "What are you saying, boy?"

Zack unconsciously gurgled with his face half-buried in the couch.

He pointed his finger at Zack. "It is his woman that I love. There, the gods already know what I declare willingly. I love Lauren."

Pheidon balled a fist. "Stupid boy," he shouted. "You offend my house!"

Gesturing with a nod of his head at a prone Zack, Andokides said, "Lauren is fair to be sure, but she is far away and she is this man's wife."

Pheidon, despite his age, swung at Diomedes, missed him, and fell on the floor. Enraged, he grabbed a small table and threw it at Diomedes. Ceramic dishes fell and cracked on the stone floor. Diomedes blocked the thrown table with his arm. A slave, arriving with a new amphora of wine, turned and ran from the room.

"Even if I found the marriage acceptable, I would never join your house." Spit flew from Diomedes's lips. "You are a traitor to the Greeks, Pheidon. If my father will not tell you, I will. I've heard enough of your betrayal. I will not marry your daughter. Leave this city in the morning."

Pheidon drew a tiny dagger hidden beneath his himation. "Half-wit, you chase a woman who belongs to your friend? Better you die now." He lurched at Diomedes.

Diomedes caught his arm and wrenched the blade from his grasp.

Andokides gasped out, "You are right, my son. Tell my staff to gather the king's advisors and send them all home." Andokides held his forehead. "And get me to bed."

Pheidon shouted on his hands and knees, "I will not forget this insult. Your city will be razed. By the gods, I will tell Xerxes and he will smite your city. He will give me this palace as a reward."

Diomedes stood over him. "I will tell Xerxes myself, just as we did at the Hot Gates."

Zack awoke with a start, his face red and eyes misty. He smacked his lips, reached for his stomach, and hurled a volume of red vomit that covered Pheidon from head to toe.

Mycenae, Greece

WINTER 479 BC

Zack waited, holding a shield tight, his wrist through the leather sleeve and hand gripping the cord on the inside edge. He stood in a line of hoplites, fifty men long and four deep. He set his right foot back and sought purchase in the scrub grass, watching a dense pack of warriors approach him, equal in number, all pounding their shields with their lances. They halted not twenty yards away from each other, with dust swirling, spears leveled, and battle cries shouted. Then the two formations moved as a solid wall toward one another.

A thunderous crash of bronze upon bronze followed.

Diomedes had given him instructions before the contest.

You must experience the crush on the face of your shield while standing in the front line of the formation. There is little to compare the sensation to. You will feel it in your legs and in your chest when your heart threatens to burst. Stand fast when your balance is tested, when you are bowled over and spears search for a weakness in your armor. Then you must attack when you hear the horns and flutes. Even if there is no strength in your limbs, or you're out of breath. You don't allow the line to be broken. Never.

Zack's team heaved back, but his line wavered, and then recovered, in a great tug-of-war. He gritted his teeth. He heard the grunts of those beside and behind him.

Don't let them collapse the left of your line, Zack. You are the largest and strongest man in the seam. Stand your ground or they will split us. Step back slightly and do not allow them to surge around to the left.

This was different than what he had seen at the pass when an unorganized mass of Persians encountered the dense shield wall of the Spartans and their allies. Here, the two sides were evenly matched in skill and weight. Zack felt the weight of the shields behind him, pressing into his back and giving him support.

"Advance," Zack shouted in Greek. The four lines condensed further. As a solid mass, they pushed like linemen on a football sled. "Harder, harder," Zack shouted. A half hour later, breathless and spent, they forced the "enemy" back until they had crossed the line of crushed lime, signaling victory for their side. Shields were raised and helmets hoisted from sweaty brows in the ranks.

Diomedes smashed his fist on the face of each shield that formed the front line as a reward for their efforts. When he reached Zack on the far left, he emitted a war cry that all could hear.

"This man will hold the left." A roar of approval erupted down the line.

"These many months of drill have made you a warrior, Zack. You have earned their respect."

Zack nodded his head just slightly, accepting the accolades with humility. This was his sixth month of drill. The first month had hardened the muscles of his shoulders, legs, and back with the lifting of sacks of sand and boulders. He made long marches in armor and hours of slow movements with heavy weapons. The second month, nearing winter, he endured cold, made swordplay with experienced warriors, and ran races in full battle dress. Then, thrown daily into a circle of trainers, all thrusting at him with sword and spear, he mastered the "pit," as it was called.

He was taller than all the men beside him and almost in as good condition now. When the winners of the mock battle were paraded before the faltering king of Mycenae, who sat on his throne and could only raise his hand in recognition of their efforts, Zack held the banner as recipient of most honored warrior.

Not bad for a university professor. San Diego State would be proud.

The queen stood behind the king at the pedestal. Flags swirled and ripped in the strong wind.

"Husband, the chill runs through you. Come inside, I beg you," Io said. She wrapped a woolen blanket more tightly around him.

"In a moment; I want to see my son at the head of his troops and the envoy he calls his companion."

"The Atlantean is a worthy man."

"He did show fortitude in the sea battle, I am told. A man's worth can only be measured when the trumpets call him to the shield line."

"You are such a man, dear husband. You were triumphant on so many fields of battle."

"You are kind to speak of me thusly. A sick man must rest on his laurels. I fear there will be no more wreaths planted on my brow."

The queen sat in her chair beside him. Andokides smiled.

"A courier delivered the news today that the barbarians are moving in the north," Io reported. "They will descend into our midst by summer. The Athenian admiral, Themistocles, has been cast from power in favor of the men who field the hoplite armies. They send away a hero who knows how to win battles."

Io shut her eyes for a moment. "Trouble brews and we are vulnerable. Mycenae needs your steady hand, my love."

"Then the bickering will begin, Io. It cannot be long before the Athenians and Spartans posture for the site of battle. The Athenians will not wish their city sacked again since the rebuilding has already begun. The Spartans will be reluctant to send their entire army beyond the wall at Corinth. The heralds bearing offers and threats will wear out their sandals running between the cities. You are correct my love; it is a most dangerous time."

Andokides tried to stand but failed. He collapsed on his throne, his face a mask of agony. Gripping his side, the air suddenly smelled foul with lost bowels. Io signaled attendants to aid the king. They carried him to a pallet. Io cradled his cheeks with her hands until attendants whisked him away to his physicians.

Each episode of his uncontrolled sickness frightened her more. Her son was not yet twenty years of age. He needed more time for the seasoning necessary to run a kingdom. Two other children she had borne died in infancy. One expired in his crib, a younger brother to Diomedes, found lifeless in the morning by his nurse. Io put her hand over her heart. The other infant, a beautiful girl with shining hair and bright eyes, succumbed to a sickness that no physician could cure. Then her husband had been wounded in battle and no longer could he deliver. Io had thought she was over the grieving and realized quite suddenly that she really was not.

Io peered out over the massed rows of Mycenaean infantry. The Atlantean envoy could not be missed. He cut a fine, towering figure with a crested helmet, shield, and spear. She had watched him train and blossom these many months, sometimes from a distance, other times at the banquets and with Diomedes. Each meeting twisted her heart and fed the fire of her desire for him. She secretly told her staff of female attendants that no one was allowed to seduce him or accept his attentions.

He could be seen above all the other hoplites, even above Diomedes by a head, at least. A son from the Atlantean's loins would be tall, muscled, and respected in all of Hellas. Her husband might not see many more moons and her hand would be forced. With invasion imminent, panic would prevail. Populations might have to evacuate. Who would accept her people? There wouldn't be enough food for the city-states to feed their own. The alliance she tried to arrange with Argos ended in disaster. No princess from any other powerful city-state had been offered to Diomedes. Had Mycenaean prowess sunk so low? Tears pooled in the corners of her eyes.

"The storm clouds gather," she said soberly to no one in particular. Her lip quivered. She massaged it with her hand. She must decide what to do. She raced to catch up to the litter bearing her husband.

12

Delphi, Greece

PRESENT DAY

Inspector Trokalitis's morning cigarette burned slowly in the ashtray, a habit his ex-wife had despised. She would harp on him to take his morning smoke outside, complaining that she and the children had to put up with the fumes.

It was just one of the issues that had caused their divorce.

Alimony payments left him with only enough money each month to afford a studio apartment, up in the hills, away from everyone. By the end of his workday, he didn't much feel like being around others anyway. He tapped out the burning ember of his cigarette. After tightening his necktie, he threw a navy blazer over his arm, locked the door to his apartment, descended two floors, and walked to his company car, an aging four-door Citroen. He slammed the door twice, cursing the station mechanic who told him that it had been repaired. He hung his sports coat meticulously over the passenger's side headrest, careful to prevent any wrinkles.

The air had turned crisp. He switched on the heat in the vehicle for the first time. He stepped on the gas and sent stones flying from tires that were nearly bald. The traffic had yet to obstruct the roads this morning and it gave him time to think. The upraised hairs of his moustache tickled his nose and he sneezed. His vehicle swerved momentarily until he straightened out his wheels and coursed down a long thoroughfare to his precinct.

Each morning as a routine, he shut off the radio and contemplated the facts of his cases while he drove the three kilometers to his office.

There was no suspect for the Papandreou murder. The man had probably gone into hiding. Could he be the same man responsible for the unsolved murders a year earlier, marked by pins on his office map of Greece, all leading north to the border with Turkey? The new evidence taken at the death scene and in the orphanage would reveal if it were the same perpetrator as the year before.

Now, what about the American professor? She has a solid description of the kidnapper, all corroborated by the drawing from the boy. The kidnapping confused him though: She was almost two months in captivity with no report of sexual violation. The young girl, mute and kidnapped previously, added another odd aspect to this case. Pressure from the attorney general to find the professor's killer continued to mount.

Papandreou was well-known, internationally too, as evidenced by the stories on American news stations. His murder caused an uproar in the papers. The only person he could connect to all of these events was the American.

This woman knew the truth. He was sure. He wondered if he should have pursued his dream and continued on in the classical studies. But for now, he would shake the bushes and see what dove flew from within. Pressure her until she reveals the truth. He had a sneaking suspicion she harbored more than a bountiful chest.

Trokalitis arrived at the police station, an aging stucco building with two wings. Cars entered through an arch into a central courtyard. He pulled up into his reserved spot, a perk he had earned when he was promoted to regional inspector five years earlier. He held an important post locally, but he knew that if he did not produce results soon, the investigation would be taken from him and given to his superiors in Athens. Dishonor would come upon him and there would be no further advance in grade or raises.

He entered the main office, waved his hand to greet staff, and closed the solid wooden door to his office. He lit a cigarette, sat back in his chair, and removed the bronze armband from his pocket. He held it up to the light and imagined the sizable bicep this would be clasped around.

Trokalitis would need to submit it soon for evaluation by police forensics, yet he remained curious as to why he had "neglected" to turn over this piece, as he was legally obliged to do. Something about it held his attention. His guts told him to hang on to it. Can it be so old, and yet be so shiny and undamaged? He imagined it must be bronze, yet it had a sheen that was uncommon to even the most polished of artifacts. He wondered if he wasted his time; it could be nothing more than shop-keeper's tourist trash. But he knew better. The boy in the orphanage had drawn a picture of a wild-haired giant with one similar armband . . . and one missing.

The door reverberated with solid knocks.

"Inspector, I have the estimates from headquarters."

Trokalitis stuffed the armband into his desk drawer. "Let's have it."

His young and ambitious lieutenant walked in. Trokalitis knew his understudy coveted his position, wearing a tie and pressed clothing every day to work.

He handed a folder to Trokalitis while holding back a yellow envelope. "Contains the new budget and you're not going to like it."

Trokalitis withdrew a stack of neatly typed pages filled with headings and numbers. He flipped to the last page where he coursed through the lines to the last entry.

"Damn. How can I run the department with this pittance?" he yelled so his voice carried beyond the shut door. The implications were drastic for all of their salaries. Not only would there be no raises, they must all do more with less. Trokalitis slammed the folder onto the desk, scattering the pages.

"This could set off more strikes: airlines, banks, teachers, and public services staff are part-time already."

"All we can do is hope the bankers keep handing us euros, inspector. Austerity was a hard bitch. We'll see if this new government can save us."

Trokalitis tempered his anger and gathered the papers. "Well, we still have a job to do. A police strike is unimaginable. The country would spiral into chaos. What if we have more fires? What about the terrorist strikes? At least the elections are over."

A strike by law enforcement would not be condoned, but inwardly, that is just what Trokalitis thought they should do. He could not reveal this to his staff or even speak of it. He was still in charge and he needed all of his staff to attend to their duties. He reached for his Lucky Strikes.

"We will need to schedule a meeting with all the staff. There are going to be questions."

"Yes, inspector, I'll put the time on tomorrow's schedule. This also came in by courier from the museum at Delphi." His understudy handed him a bubble-wrapped yellow envelope and left the room.

Inspector Trokalitis clutched at his lower back where the stress of recent events accumulated to torture him.

He said quietly, "I tire of all this." His hands left his back and went to his temples. He could barely pay the alimony and child support. A ten percent or more pay cut might send him out of his apartment and to sleeping in his car. No inspector of the police department should suffer such embarrassment. He opened the envelope with a knife. Inside was a note from the museum staff explaining that contained within were the security videos on memory sticks from the night when the professor was murdered; one of multiple views of the museum entrances, and another with a single view of the gated entrance to the grounds. He stuck the memory stick of the security gate to the grounds into his computer.

Trokalitis fast-forwarded until he saw two figures moving on the screen. He backed up the recording and played it at normal speed. Very clearly, he saw the American professor and young girl, both looking filthy, climbing over the entrance barrier. They kept looking behind them and up toward the museum, as if searching for someone. Quickly, they moved away from the wide-angle camera lens viewer in the direction of the remains of the Temple of Athena Pronaia. Shortly afterward, a car parked in the street lot. To his amazement, Professor Papandreou went to his trunk and pulled out digging equipment and a handheld movie camera. He climbed over the fence and disappeared uphill.

Twenty minutes later, an enormous bushy-haired man covered in filth, but wearing two smudged bicep bands, casting his glance left and right, climbed over the same gate entrance, also heading for the street, but in the opposite direction toward the town.

Trokalitis lit a cigarette. He now had a suspect and a decent picture of him. Already imagining the notoriety gained by solving the murder, he watched the recording again, noting however, several flashes of light that couldn't be defined even when he slowed the motion to frame by frame. Finally, he watched the museum door recording. The enormous bushy-haired suspect walked up to the lens, maybe not even aware it was there. Trokalitis could see dark eyes and swaths of mud on the man's face, maybe even the hint of scars across his nose. The suspect held a flashlight and tapped it on an outdoor lightbulb, breaking it. The suspect threw his arms up and appeared to shout something, finally running away downhill, where he was further seen on the gate recording.

Trokalitis rubbed his chin. *Good evidence, at least a start.* A few facts could now be discerned— the burly suspect, the woman professor, and the girl, were all in the same vicinity the night of the murder. Trokalitis hoped to see the woman's husband on the recording, too, but was disappointed. He had a reasonable facial shot of the suspect, and now he knew that the woman was telling him the truth, at least partially. Yet the events still gave him concern, and he wasn't going to reveal this evidence yet, not to his staff, not to his overseers, not even to the American professor, whom he knew he had over a barrel.

He thought back to the murder scene. The evidence from the suspect made sense now, but something was missing. Finally it came to him. There was no handheld movie camera at the murder scene and no camera in any of the others' hands when they exited the gate.

What happened to that camera and where was the husband? Additionally, when the murder suspect stood at the museum door, and upon leaving the museum gate, he had two armbands on. But in the orphanage and by the woman professor's testimony, he had only one. There were a lot more questions and he would have to answer them or be out of a job.

A.K. PATCH

Delphi, Greece

DECEMBER, PRESENT DAY

Lauren hated being a liar.

More than a month passed with no progress on any front. No murderer had been arrested, nor any kidnapper. The photographs Social Services had taken of Cassandra predictably yielded no result, either. No child fitting her description was listed as missing, or as a runaway in Greece or in neighboring countries.

Lauren worried about her father, who'd experienced a setback and required a second operation, delaying her mother's arrival. Zack's brother arrived, soundly irritated with the difficulties associated with flights into Greece during a strike. He searched the mountain areas and left dejected; maybe suspicious even. Lauren didn't know. He never accused her of anything.

She never felt more guilty and disgusted with her secret.

It was all going according to plan, or at least while the frail strings of her story still held. Lauren had sensed irritation in Trokalitis's voice recently when she had called him to check on progress. She wondered when the whole house of cards would topple around her.

"Professor Fletcher, it's time for the cookout. Can we go outside?" called a young voice, shaking her from an intense death stare into the wall.

"Ah, certainly Irena, I'll be there in a moment." She wondered what the children thought when she went around the orphanage with glazed eyes.

Lauren walked to the cafeteria and entered to find a circle of children sitting cross-legged. They had all made Native American headdresses out of paper, each one with colored feathers sticking out from the back of their heads. They had been painted with moons and arrows in red and yellow. One of the children came to her. Lauren grinned at the blue lightning streaks on the little girl's face.

"Do I look like a real Indian?"

"Why yes, you do, except we respectfully call then Native Americans." Lauren cupped her silky cheeks in her palms. "Is everyone hungry?"

"Are we going to hunt those big cows?"

"You mean buffalos? Well, maybe not today, but I am going to make you a special meal." Lauren dropped to one knee. "And we all have a lot to be thankful for."

What does this child have to be thankful for? And here I am wallowing in self-pity.

An eager face ran up to her. "When can we do the rain dance you promised us?"

"We can as soon as we all eat. Come now, back with the rest of the tribe."

Lauren put on the headdress Cassandra had prepared for her and stepped into the middle of the circle. Searching for the correct words in Greek, she raised her hands and said, "Great Spirit, grant us our wish, bring back the buffalo to the plains."

Demo crawled in from the doorway with a brown rug covering his frame.

"Behold the great buffalo," Lauren said, lighting candles to create an atmosphere of mystery among the long tables.

Demo mooed and growled. The children huddled closer. Cassandra held her hand over her mouth, only her eyes revealing her astonishment.

"Now," Lauren declared, "all warriors should rise and dance. Show respect to the great beast that rules the plains. Come, I will show you how."

Lauren entered the circle of tribe members, raised her hand to her mouth, and war-whooped like Sioux doing a ghost dance. The children all joined in line, mimicking her antics, bobbing their heads forward and back while hopping on one leg, then the other.

Mr. Avtges rushed over from where he had prepared a small campfire in a circle of stones. He emerged upon the scene, reared his head back, and burst out laughing. The dancing continued until Lauren announced it was time to follow her outside and then for all to gather at the fire for more dancing.

"Lauren, I have never seen the children so joyful. The costumes are wonderful," Avtges said.

"Well, it's not exactly how we celebrate Thanksgiving, but they had a good time."

I can at least give them my best while I'm here.

The next day, rain pelted the stucco exterior of the orphanage. The water ran in streams down the glass, obscuring their view of the roadway. Parsons arrived an hour late. Lauren wondered if he had been regretting meeting her with the driving conditions being so treacherous coming up the mountain roads. It had been difficult to contact him, his schedule taking him on different duties outside the office. Lauren decided it was time for a face-to-face again.

She looked at the calendar: December 1.

How long can this charade last?

Parsons entered the orphanage shaking the rain from his umbrella.

"Can I get you a hot cup of coffee?" Lauren asked, humbled that he would go to this length of effort on her behalf.

"That would be a welcome treat," he replied. "It was only misting when I left, then the heavens broke loose. At least the roads were not too busy for a Tuesday."

Lauren handed him a steaming mug. He cupped it in his fingers, blowing the steam off.

"Here, let me take your coat. We have the office to ourselves."

Lauren sat in the chair across from the desk as Mr. Parsons walked past her. His nostrils flared and he raised his nose, weighing scent in the air.

"I'm perplexed by the scent you wear. What is it?"

"J'adore. I've been wearing it for ages." The paradox of her statement was lost on her guest.

"Well, it's very nice. Now let's get down to business. I can only stay a short while. There is more business to attend to back in Athens. As you know, the State Department has been alerted to your situation. They're standing by, but paperwork cannot be filled out and processed with so little information on the girl."

"So, is she a Greek citizen or not?" Lauren asked.

"Complicated would be a euphemism to describe this situation, Professor."

"Please call me Lauren."

"As you wish, but nevertheless, you are not released from the investigation. Trokalitis has no suspects except you. It's been a few months and the pressure on him is steadily increasing. There is no rush to declare this girl as anything other than an undocumented alien or a ward of the state. She will stay at the orphanage only as long as they decide to allow it."

"I'm in really bad shape, aren't I?"

"I wouldn't wish to be in your shoes, but that is also why I would like to help you. Let's call this a challenge for me."

"How many nationals are adopted by foreigners each year?"

"Not many. But there are exceptions for the physically disabled."

"Wouldn't Cassandra qualify? She's essentially mute."

"The doctors have found nothing wrong with her, physically. Her mental state probably qualifies her, but then again she is not Greece's to give up. All this may be a moot point unless you can convince Inspector Trokalitis of your innocence, and that will not be likely, for political reasons. They may hold you as a suspect to buy time, with no options available. The US embassy has petitioned the Greek government officially on your behalf, in an effort to keep this issue under the radar, so to speak."

"Then you're saying we play ball and wait out their decisions?"

"It's the safe route."

Lauren walked to the window and noticed that the rain had subsided. Pools of water sat in holes in the road, creating a tiny archipelago. A car raced up the hill and dispersed the water, ruining half of them.

Someone always has to come and spoil perfection.

"I can't wait that long," Lauren declared, turning abruptly. "If I let them dictate the schedule, I'll be here forever. There has to be another way." She slammed rolled fists on the desk in front of him.

Parsons raised his hands defensively. "Do I have to remind you again that this is not the US?"

"You know, Mr. Parsons, I think like my father. He was a Marine Corps fighter pilot. Do you think he took no for an answer?"

"I imagine not."

"Then help me. What avenue will circumvent these obstacles?"

"If you take too many chances, you could get badly burned."

"But they might take Cassandra away. I couldn't stand that."

Mr. Parsons scratched the fine hairs on the back of his neck. "Well, if you're looking for an avenue around the bureaucracy, would you take a side alley instead?"

"How do you mean? Like cloak-and-dagger stuff?" Lauren sent one eyebrow skyward.

"I need to inquire. There may be a possibility. Someone I know."

"Seriously," Lauren replied with her eyes narrowed.

"I can only promise I will look into it. I will get back to you if an opportunity arises."

"My back is against the wall, Mr. Parsons. My claws are out."

"You have to decide how much risk you are willing to take and at what cost. Even so, Inspector Trokalitis holds your future in his hands; beating him with your fists will bring nothing positive."

Lauren nodded her head. "I'll entertain any proposal you bring to me. Please help me." She stared the man in the face and did not look away until he did so, something her dad had taught her.

"I'll get back to you, but first I need to feel out Trokalitis. I warn you, don't do anything stupid. He's waiting for you to slip up."

"Advice taken," Lauren answered, shaking the man's hand firmly. "I'll await your call."

Later, up in their room, Cassandra tried on a new sweatshirt Lauren had given her as a gift. On the front was the image of four men that Lauren had described to her as musicians.

"Pray, tell me again," she asked. "This one is called the Edge. Why should he name himself thusly?"

"He is the man who strums the lyre you saw on the box with moving pictures. He plays with other fellows in a band called U2. But let's talk later, now it's time for our first class with the children. I'm going to teach everyone to speak and write Atlantean, and if there's time, your Greek language from long ago."

Lauren took Cassandra's hand.

"You have been a perfect actress, sweetheart. Keep up the good work and I will buy you another garment with the image of the singing woman."

Cassandra clapped her hands. "You speak of the one that dances almost naked with wild costumes that would shock even Aphrodite?"

"She's called Lady Gaga and don't get any ideas. Come now. Let us go downstairs to class."

Lauren stood in front of the children, all sitting on the cafeteria benches. "Now children, we're going to start out with very easy words in all three languages. Does anyone here speak any words of English?"

Half of the children raised their hands.

"Very good, now when I point my finger at you, say a word of English, starting with Demo."

"Baseball," he said.

"Pepsi," shouted another.

A third shouted, "I'll kick your butt."

The class howled. It took a minute to calm them down.

"Now let's get down to business," Lauren said, but the children still fidgeted, their amusement dying hard.

"Please children, calm down. Now who can tell me why it is important to learn to speak the words of the ancient Greeks?"

Stephan raised his hand and grinned, something he had not done much since his traumatic experience with the scary intruder.

He said, "So we can order dessert." More howls.

"Very good answer," Lauren said, chuckling herself. "The real reason is that it is important to know about these people, how they lived and how they thought. The remains of their buildings are all around us and we learn from their discovery of the sciences, literature, playwriting, and philosophy. They can give us clues on how to best live our lives."

Mr. Avtges hid just outside the doorway to the cafeteria, listening to the lesson. His hands were clasped, prayer-like, and he shook them, thanking God for this wonderful new development. The American professor taught his orphans English and ancient Greek. It was a grand idea and the children sorely needed instruction, more than he could offer them. This woman, striking to set eyes upon, influenced his operation in a positive manner and in a way he never dreamed of. While the visits of the authorities disrupted his day and caused questions from the children, he had to admit all were pleased to have her companionship.

One person can make a difference, he thought. The children's lives would be enriched and their development advanced. How long this would last, he didn't know. The professor's predicament was complicated and worrisome. He sympathized with her. The loss of her husband must be devastating, but she seemed to refocus on the child. The girl seemed stable enough for the experience of kidnapping, but in a kind of walking trance most of the time. Her eyes revealed only fascination or ignorance, and he was not sure which one was more accurate. Everything she looked at caused her to stand and stare as if she had never seen a television or heard the ringing of a phone. She must have come from a very poor village in some remote area to the north. Was there truly any place now that did not have television? She could not have reached her early teens without a family or an overseer.

He listened to the repetition of English words, some simple ones he knew himself. Perhaps he would sit in on the course, too. After all, it had been many years since he had learned English and it had mostly faded from his memory. He walked back across the hallway to his office and resumed making phone calls to raise money for the orphanage. Donations were dropping off and a heating bill had gone unpaid.

Next year looked to be especially difficult.

Bang. Bang. Bang.

Lauren laid down the next day's lesson plan in her bedroom. "Geez, that door is going to get a hole in it." She answered more loudly, "Just a minute."

Lauren put her finger to her lips. Cassandra moved into the bathroom, well-versed in the drill. Lauren opened the door to find Demo standing in front of her, waving two sheets of paper in his hand. His dark curly shocks of hair were wet, fresh from a bath, and Lauren could not help grinning. She had never seen him with his hair combed away from his face and back over his head.

"Good evening, Demo." Lauren greeted him in slow, measured English, as they had practiced in the earlier lesson.

"Good evening, Professor. How are you?"

They proceeded through the standard elementary run of conversation until Demo ran out of phrases and returned to his own language.

"What brings you here, Demo?"

"I want to turn in my homework assignment now. I have a doctor's visit tomorrow and I will miss your class."

"That is very proactive of you. I will look these over later. If you don't mind me asking, why are you going to the doctor?"

Demo peered into the room, obviously hoping to spot Cassandra. Disappointed, he shyly tapped his toes on the doorframe and looked up at Lauren.

"I'm not sick exactly, but for a long time I've had a virus in my body. I don't feel bad really, but I have to go for treatments every once in a while. I feel sick after them, though."

"A virus," Lauren responded, quickly searching her memory for possible viruses that a boy might have: chickenpox, measles?

"It is called hepatitis, hepatitis C."

"How did you get that, Demo? I'm so sorry."

She ran her fingers against his cheek.

"I got it when I was a baby, from my mother. The doctors told me it affects my liver although I never feel it or anything. My mother was an abuser of drugs, bad ones. She gave it to me at birth. She died in a car accident." He looked away and scratched the doorframe with his fingernail. "I never knew who my father was."

Lauren reached out and hugged him, smelling the shampoo scent in his hair. "A young man shouldn't have to go through such tragedy."

"It's kind of fun being the oldest orphan. I get to tell everyone what to do."

"I've never seen you do that. You're always helping the other children."

Demo grinned but shuffled his feet nervously. "Where do you think your husband is?"

"I don't know. He's out there somewhere. I'm very frightened for him."

"A lady shouldn't have to go through such bad times."

Lauren hugged him. "You're a bright one."

"Where is the girl, Cassandra?"

"She's in the bathroom."

"Girls are always in the bathroom."

"So we can be pretty for boys like you. Now, I'll look over your homework and we'll see you tomorrow."

"Your secret is safe with me, just like I promised the professor."

"It's nice to know I can depend on you."

Demo stretched his neck, watching the bathroom door. "I wish she could talk. The kids are saying that she's dumb."

"You know better."

"She's nice, even though she doesn't say anything. It seems like she wants to."

"We may never know what happened to her."

"I tell the other kids not to say those bad things."

"You're truly a fine young man."

"When I was younger, the older ones made fun of me. They

told me I was infected with tiny bugs. They would touch me with their fingers and run away screaming."

"That's terrible, but then you know how it feels to be a little different."

Demo nodded his head. "Well, see you tomorrow."

He walked away from the door and down the hallway, but paused and looked up as if a grand thought came to him. He turned on his heel, tiptoed back to the closed door and put his ear to it. Inside, he heard voices in hushed tones and more than one voice. His mouth flew open. He covered it quickly and scooted back to the sleeping hall.

Once again, the morning came too fast for Lauren. The knocking was gentle but incessant on their bedroom door. Lauren leaped from her bed and quickly wrapped a bathrobe over her shoulders. The floor felt icy underneath her bare feet.

"Who is it?"

"Mr. Avtges. Sorry to wake you but Inspector Trokalitis is here to see you."

"You've got to be kidding. He's here unannounced, at seven a.m.?" Lauren complained. "What does he want?"

"He didn't say why, professor, but he's waiting in my office."

"I'll be there in a few minutes," Lauren said in a gentle tone, not wishing to scold the messenger. She bolted for the bathroom and started the water running, beginning the few minutes of countdown before any warm water would arise to the second floor. She peered into bloodshot eyes and cursed, "You're a real beauty." She rubbed her eyes with her fingers. "It's getting to you, isn't it?" she asked herself. The lips in the mirror answered back, "It is."

Lauren brushed her teeth quickly with cold water, eliciting a zing from a sensitive root. She warmed it with her tongue while letting the water run, testing the stream with her fingers and waiting for a more tolerable temperature. She brushed her hair back and fastened it in the back with a brown clip. A pair of thick woolen socks bought at a shop in the tiny town beyond the museum made her feet warm. She had purchased a functional wardrobe for them both there: jeans, blouses, sweatshirts. Anything warm with the temperatures dropping and rain falling more frequently. She tripped, struggling to get her long legs into the blue jeans, and fell on the bed. Cassandra turned over, the top of her head peeking out from under the blankets.

"I have to go downstairs. Please stay here. You know the rules."

Cassandra closed her eyes and sighed.

When Lauren entered Mr. Avtges's office, Trokalitis waited with his arms folded. His deadpan expression did nothing to improve Lauren's estimation of what the visit was all about.

"Inspector, this is a surprise," Lauren said, making a point of the inconvenience of his arrival. He returned to his seat and eased himself down, careful not to disturb the navy blazer carefully wrapped over the back of the chair.

"Getting along here well, I presume?" he said in English.

"As well as can be expected," she answered, waiting for the axe to fall.

"There's been no progress in the search for your husband or his remains." He searched Lauren's face for reaction.

She fought to keep her expression as unemotional as his was, but blinked several times.

"I am still not satisfied with your story, professor." He walked to the window and looked out over the main road, absorbing the early morning sun.

"No sign of the murderer, or a kidnapper." Just behind him, outside the window, a helicopter traced across the horizon. It looked like a police helicopter.

He continued, "My investigation is mired in complexities; disappearing husbands, kidnappers, murderers, tourists, a girl with no identity or even a voice for that matter. This is grand material for a novel, but not acceptable to a professional lawman." He waited for her response, sending a shiver through Lauren's plummeting confidence.

"I've told you the truth," she answered.

"Perhaps you have." His voice went down an octave and his tone became a bed of needles. "Perhaps not."

What does he know?

"I've refused your lawyer's request for release. Your embassy cannot sway me either. Something is rotten here and your story is . . . unconvincing."

"But I've told you everything—"

"Have you now?" he interrupted, peering over the rims of his glasses. Lauren's facial features registered surprise and fear simultaneously. She wondered if he was bluffing or searching.

"I've told you what I know, inspector. I've lost a husband whom I love dearly. What is it that you suspect I'm fabricating?"

Trokalitis clicked the top of the pen in his right hand and paced the room.

"You tell me why I should not consider you a suspect? Could it not be possible that an angry wife might perpetrate some hanky-panky on a husband that she wants to do away with?"

"That's uncalled for," she said in a calm and measured voice. "You can't be serious?"

"What else should I presume? You present a strange account, no suspects, no cave, no habeas corpus, no one to corroborate your story." He emphasized the word *story*, further piercing her delicate hold on her emotions.

"You must be aware of the difficulties I'm experiencing as a result of all this tragedy. I cannot leave and return to my own country. I do not have unlimited funds for an extended stay here, or an indefinite leave of absence from my university." Her tone remained steady. "My father is very ill after surgery and I desperately need to see him. I have a legal mess to unravel in my own country, and I have a scared young woman who depends on me for comfort. On top of that my husband is missing and may be dead."

"Interesting sentiments and I am truly moved, professor." He lifted his blazer off the chair and put it on, a tight fit across his shoulders. He placed one hand inside his coat pocket. "This is quite a dilemma. All of our time and effort spent to identify the girl has been unsuccessful.

Social Services has said that she is healthy, physically at least, but her loss of voice is perplexing. Further evaluation will be needed, but budget cuts in the public sector will slow down the process. This is all going to take a very long time."

Lauren dug her nails into the palms of her hand, willing herself to remain controlled.

"I'm sure you know that I'm willing to adopt this girl if no relations can be found. She is very important to me."

"Again, a lovely gesture, but until my investigation is finished, until I arrest the murderer and locate your "missing" husband, you are a suspect." He towered over her sitting at the side of the desk. "Let us speak plainly. I think you withhold the truth from me." He rummaged in his coat pocket as if searching for something. "Do not leave this vicinity. Any wrongdoing on your part will land you in jail. Not a cushy American jail either, serving tea and muffins, I might add. Then, I'll take the girl and place her in the custody of Child Services."

Lauren's hands trembled so she folded them together. She raised her chin. "I'm stunned, inspector. I've done nothing wrong." She forced herself to speak calmly. "Why don't you spend your resources chasing down that goddamned Frankenstein?"

Trokalitis stared blankly at her, but ran his eyes from her toes, along the length of her legs, across her chest, and into her eyes.

Lauren shivered inside.

"Professor, you have my card. Should you care to reveal the truth to me, do not delay. My patience is nearly exhausted." He headed down the hall to the door, leaving Lauren staring at his back and listening to the click of his shoes on the linoleum floor. He shouted without turning, "You have a week, no more."

14

Delphi, Greece

PRESENT DAY

Inspector Trokalitis strode to his car, quite pleased with himself. The beautiful American professor will break and submit to my will, he told himself. Pressure will be applied gently at first. After all, this is an American, and although a well-respected one, very likely soft from easy living. Then the hammer will be brought down. He had used this technique many times, soliciting panic in so many other suspects. Nevertheless, this woman will be easily manipulated, although she may require more prodding than most females. The heat will be turned on, and if she does not talk, it will be brought to a boil quickly.

He settled himself in the driver's seat. Withdrawing an envelope from his inside lapel pocket, he reopened the letter that reported a match between the fingerprints of the murderer of Professor Papandreou with fingerprints left in the cafeteria of the orphanage. Further than that, the fingerprints also matched those of an unknown murderer from a year earlier thought still at large. That case went unsolved, a string of homicides all leading to the Turkish border. It was all too clear; the murderer did enter the orphanage and may have kidnapped the Americans and the girl. The American *had* told the truth, at least in that respect.

But he wouldn't tell her that.

And it wouldn't get her off the hook, either, Trokalitis decided. The second sheet, from a trusted antiquities expert, announced that the bronze armband the police found by the stream coming downhill from the Castalian Spring in Delphi might be over two thousand years old. This did solve the mystery of the missing armband on the oversized suspect, reinforcing his instinct that the American, or a group of them, may have discovered artifacts. This information, as well, he would not reveal to her.

These were chess pieces he would hold to play later.

Quite possibly the murderer may have happened upon the woman professor and her husband while they were digging, took them hostage, figuring to keep the loot for himself. It reinforced his decision to hold onto the bronze armband in his coat pocket.

Trokalitis's gut told him that somehow the armband was part of a large cache of artifacts that would lead to the solution of his murder case. Now, he weighed his next action. It was clear to him that the murder suspect had probably returned to Greece after his string of murders a year earlier, and might escape from the country again. He might have to gamble that the lady professor had more information to offer. He would draw the truth out of her. Probe and pressure till a useful lead arose. Most criminals crumbled at the thought of being tossed in jail. He would have his confession, one way or another.

The car started without hesitation, the carburetor repaired properly for once. He drove fast down the mountain, obsessed with how the failure to find the killer would affect his career. He didn't have much time before he would stand in front of the chief of police in Athens and be castigated for incompetence. If he had the American arrested, he might placate his overseers for a few weeks, but she would be released for lack of evidence and for political reasons. He wondered if he would have days or weeks before he would be disgraced. Perhaps the tortoise-like speed of government would delay his summoning.

He stopped at a family-run store in the town of Plakeau and purchased a carton of Lucky Strikes. It had always been his brand, reminding him that at least the Americans were good for something. The owner knew him well but did not comment about the case. The newspaper headline offered him all the update he needed.

It was too cold to sit outside and enjoy a cup of tea. He decided to drive to the National Museum once again, speak to the new curator and sit inside the late professor's office. His stomach felt upset and the back of his throat burned. He reached for a plastic container of carbonated water.

This job is killing me. He had given his life to police work and what did he have to show for it: an auto any Balkan immigrant could afford, a trashy apartment, and a family who no longer loved him. The bubbles in the carbonated water brought him relief. He deserved more pay for all this aggravation. He pushed on to Athens, turning on the siren to clear traffic from the road. Everyone had better stay out of his way. The clock ticked, but not in his favor.

Delphi, Greece

PRESENT DAY

Lauren had to wait another week before she could arrange an appointment with Mr. Parsons. She knew she had no right to remove Cassandra from the orphanage and she was afraid to discuss developments over the phone with him. Most of all, there was no way she could leave her alone. She begged Mr. Parsons to drive up one more time, but his schedule conflicted. He promised that he would visit her as soon as possible.

A little diversion might help, she thought. Christmas shopping might be a good remedy for the desperation that had permanently fixed itself in her thoughts and feelings.

Lauren walked with Cassandra through the town beyond the temples. Shoppers left stores with plastic bags filled with gifts. This would be Lauren's first Christmas away from Zack and her family. Cassandra would catch on quickly to the celebration, especially if presents were involved. She stood still, marveling at the display of Christmas lights the town had put up.

"I see preparations to worship the gods. Is there to be a festival?" Cassandra pulled her aside to ask. She locked her eyes on the packages wrapped in multicolored paper, tied with bows. She stood transfixed when she saw a boy riding towards her on a bicycle. The boy thought she would move, but she didn't. He swerved at the last moment and ran into a light pole, propelling him in flight to where he landed on a trash can and sent debris flying. Cassandra gasped and ran to him with Lauren close behind.

"Cassandra," she cried out in ancient Greek. "Don't talk."

Cassandra helped the boy up and then got on her knees, bowed her head, and raised her hands prayer-like.

"She's very sorry. Please forgive us. Are you hurt?" Lauren asked.

The boy inspected the ripped vinyl of his parka.

"My mother is going kill me when she sees this." He righted his bicycle and rode away on a wobbly front wheel.

Lauren led Cassandra to a café restroom. "We can talk now but whisper quietly to me."

"He rides without a horse, on the wheels. He must be a great champion to have won such a prize. What race must I win to acquire one?"

Lauren giggled. "Our lives are so different. Every day you will discover a new invention. Which do you find the most interesting so far?"

"I wonder about the square box that shows plays, lady. I have seen others sit and peer at it with their eyes so they no longer know what occurs around them. I never thought there could be such a window into the lives of the gods, but I think the gods do not wish to be watched so closely. The other children are consumed by their desire for it. They forget the flight of birds or the settling of butterflies. I must think about it some more. I cannot decide if it is a trick played upon us by Pan or by some other god."

"You just dispatched two thousand odd years of human advancement." She smoothed Cassandra's hair and kissed her cheek. "Come now, I'll show you the face of the god who rules this festival. If you have good manners, this great, fat god will hear your wishes and then deliver the gifts of your dreams to your room."

"This cannot be true, lady. Do you mean gifts are lavished upon those for good temperament and *not* for giving the gods their due? My uncle would not understand such a festival."

"There is another god, Cassandra, and he is the real god to which the festival belongs."

"Who is this God?"

"He is a glorious God, full of forgiveness and hope; a God that became a man for a short time and lived among us. He taught us to love and to help one another."

"You speak of a god who was a man? Do you mean Dionysus? He is such a god. Twice-borne he was; of Zeus and a mortal woman."

"Not . . . exactly. Oh, this is getting complicated. Dionysus is no longer worshipped in this time."

Cassandra turned her face away, clearly disturbed.

"Why is this so?" the girl asked. "Gods do not die like men. They are immortal. My uncle told me so. Can this god you speak of make miracles? My uncle has attended the Dionysian rites. The priests would place three pots of water in an enclosed room. In three days, the water would turn to wine." Cassandra held up three fingers to emphasize her point.

"But Sweetheart." Lauren turned Cassandra's slender shoulders toward her. Cassandra pulled away.

"My uncle said that Dionysus is a god that you feel within you, that during his rites, the worshipers consume flesh of beasts and wine, to be closer to the gods. How is your god worshipped?"

"You won't believe it, Cassandra, but there's too much to explain to you."

"Have your people dispatched all of my ancestors' gods?"

Lauren had never before seen such a look of trepidation and betrayal on Cassandra's face.

"Cassandra, maybe your gods live on in our god."

I never thought of that before.

Cassandra took Lauren's hand. "I wish to return to our room. I must pray to Athena and ask for her guidance."

"We should go anyway, before someone needs this bathroom."

They walked outside into the cold air. A group of college students staggered away from a bar singing. One stopped suddenly and threw up on the sidewalk. Cassandra ran up to the museum grounds where there were no others around.

When Lauren caught up to her, Cassandra said, crinkling her eyes, sporting vindication on her face. "I am no longer concerned. Did you see that man void his belly? I can see that Dionysus is still worshipped here."

Mr. Parsons arrived promptly at noon the next day. He returned Lauren's smile, although his eyes lacked their usual sparkle and his cheeks looked hollow. He begged off a handshake.

"Please excuse me, professor. I have a cold that I don't wish to pass on."

"Well, that explains the black circles under your eyes."

"My sinuses are killing me. Every winter my head seems like it wants to explode. I hope I'm better in a few days. If not, I'm going to rent the first camel I see and ride to the desert."

"I can't thank you enough for rushing to get here." Lauren closed the door to Mr. Avtges's office.

"I'm pleased to see you, but I have nothing new on the progress of your case."

"Why am I not surprised?"

"How much will the lawyers charge for a possible adoption, if you don't mind my asking?" Parsons said. He snatched a handkerchief from his pants pocket and sneezed into it.

"They want ten thousand dollars more than the five thousand I already gave them as a retainer to help me with the police investigation. Of course, there are no guarantees, on either case."

"Not unexpected."

"Mr. Parsons, we both have been around the block, haven't we?"

"How do you mean, Lauren?"

"Could I get to the point? You mentioned there might be a way to get help for me. If I gave my lawyers the extra money, would that get me where I want to be?"

"Hard to predict, Lauren, for all the reasons I pointed out earlier. Inspector Trokalitis, for one, stands in your way before any other matter can be solved."

"Look, I'm willing to put all my resources into the bending of the rules. I know money talks."

"That is not necessarily true in this case. Honor holds far more weight here."

"Is it so different? I'm not sure I buy that."

"You don't have children. Is that correct, Professor?" Parsons flicked a pen through his fingers like a majorette whirling a baton.

"Not yet. We tried for some time, but . . ."

"Then could this be just a desperate stab at motherhood? Forgive me, but you should be concerned with your legal case and with the Greek police. It strikes me as unrealistic to carry on your desire for adoption when you're in danger of being jailed. Jail, professor, has it sunk in yet?"

"But I'm innocent and there's nothing that can stand in the way of that fact. So I'm confident I will be absolved of any blame. Is what I'm saying to you off the record?"

"This conversation is quite confidential." He shifted in his seat.

"Can we cut out the pleasantries?"

He narrowed his eyes.

"I need help. There must be someone who can expedite this process. The girl is my link to Zack, no matter what it appears on the surface to you or anyone else. I feel like her caretaker, her guardian . . . maybe at some point, her mother."

"I understand all this, but your wishes and desires will still not result in any faster or more positive actions on behalf of the Greek police or the legal system here. Are you aware that if a couple wants to adopt a child here, the women must dress like they're pregnant for months before the child is received? This is what you are up against. Furthermore, adoptions of Greek children by foreigners are very rare."

"Mr. Parsons, I need someone who can make things happen; someone like Radar on that old show *M*A*S*H*."

Parsons chuckled. "Yes, yes, by some miracle he got Colonel Blake what he needed."

"I'm willing to pay a lot of money."

Mr. Parsons walked to the window. A jet flew by, rattling the windows. His pant leg was hitched above his right shoe. He didn't notice it and Lauren bit her cheeks to keep from laughing. She was not sure how he would react to an embarrassment, and what they discussed was no laughing matter.

"How brave are you? Money may be a conduit, but how much risk are you willing to take?"

"I am going to take care of this girl," Lauren said. "I think the lawyers are going to rip me off and get nowhere."

"You may lose your teaching position and all your money in the process. They could put you in jail for a very long time."

"I'm digging in my heels. I cannot bear the thought of this girl languishing in some halfway house or deported to god knows where."

"I know someone. He is not without influence." Parsons turned toward her.

"Has he assisted you before?"

"On a few occasions, though I do not recommend that you take this course and I will deny it officially, do you understand?"

"How could I be in any worse position than I am now?"

"At this point, you still have your freedom."

"Just look me in the eyes and tell me that this guy can help me."

Parsons didn't blink. "I call him the Facilitator. You will never know his name. If I were to reveal to you who he is, I would not only lose his assistance, but it would be dangerous for me to stay in Greece, diplomatic corps or no."

The implication of what she heard startled her, but what country doesn't have influential individuals who can bypass the law for a price? Lauren wondered if he might be organized crime. She pictured Vito Corleone, the Godfather, except with one of those Greek fishing caps on.

Parsons sat down again. His pant leg fell back to its natural position. "You will only be able to contact him by phone. No personal meetings."

Lauren's stomach swirled.

"Great, this *is* real cloak-and-dagger stuff," Lauren said. She gulped. "Do you think you are bartering for a Tijuana blanket, professor?"

"So I give this guy the money and he will arrange things?"

"You'll have to trust him."

Lauren paced with her hands on her hips. From the corner of her eye, she could see that he was studying her, and not in an intellectual sense. *Perhaps there is leverage here,* she thought. She was desperate to think it, but she placed her hands flat on the desk in front of him. Her blouse hung a little lower.

Time to play tough; I wish I knew how to do this.

Lauren blinked. "I'll go for it. Please give me his number."

"Once you sign this release. I will help you, but I will not sacrifice my career for you." Parsons diverted his eyes.

I guess my bait isn't so great anymore.

Lauren signed the document that relieved Parsons of any liability in her case and handed it to him. She wasn't sure if it would hold up in any court, but time was of the essence now.

He withdrew a small square piece of white paper from his coat pocket. He slid it across the desk to her.

"The Rubicon is crossed, professor. I only hope that I have not given you false hope. A lot can go wrong. You must know that in some countries, it is still a man's world. You have two disadvantages: you are a foreigner and a woman."

"But I've got one thing going for me," Lauren said, keeping her eyes locked on his.

"I'm my father's girl."

16

Mycenae, Greece

JUNE 479 BC

The news of Xerxes's marshal, Mardonius, moving his army south from Thessaly into Boeotia sent ripples of panic through the palaces of the allied city-states. The morning practice session out in the training ground below the Mycenaean citadel took on a more authentic urgency. There was power behind the lance and sword thrusts now. Many went to the side for bandages, as did Zack with a spear cut in his thigh.

When the practice ended, Zack retired to his room, the same one Lauren had been in the year before. Following a good scrape with cudgel and oil, he lingered in hot water poured for him by his assistant. Finishing his bath, he sat on the stone floor, cleaning his thigh wound with wine and then dressing it. His mind wandered back to the days when he and Lauren were together.

He'd been told that Lauren had lain right there on the bed.

Gentle rapping on the door interrupted Zack's concentration. He jumped up.

"Master envoy," a female voice called out. "Your presence is requested by the queen."

Opening the door, he found three of the queen's attendants before him, hair loose, dressed in short yellow chitons.

"I, ah, will be ready in a moment," he said in Greek. He fetched a gray chiton. He heard whispering behind his back.

"Where am I to meet her?" Zack asked.

"In the goddess's temple," a short but shapely attendant answered, standing before him with her arms tight behind her back, pressing her unrestrained chest against the fabric.

"Why does she send for me?" Zack asked quickly, turning to buy time.

"We ask you to follow us," she answered. The three turned, the loose hems of their tunics dancing over their thighs.

"I don't know how much more of this I can handle," Zack muttered quietly.

"Did you speak, Master Zack?' the nearest to him said, taller and more lean than the others, flashing her white teeth at him.

"Lead on, ladies."

They walked through the covered colonnade decorated with hanging ivory and white blossoms. From there, down an oak staircase and across a courtyard where six gnarled olive trees were evenly spaced within a square. The wind swirled and the yellow chitons whipped up around the ladies waists. Zack took a deep breath and wondered why he was summoned.

The party entered a rough-cut stone structure through a doorway barred by a thick wooden door, guarded by Mycenaean hoplites wearing the ancient boar's tusk helmets, reminiscent of the bygone days even before the fabled King Agamemnon and the Trojan War. The white tusks were halved and encircled the helmet, tied to it by bronze wire. The guards drew back their lances and let them pass. At the end of the hall, two hoplites waited, each bearing a torch swabbed with pitch so that flames leapt from the ends.

They began the long descent down the circular stairway he had navigated on the last visit, the women planting their bare toes on the worn stone edges for traction. Zack followed behind, searching for an angle to keep the torch fumes from choking him.

The sumptuous breasts on the decorated door once again separated before him. The girls led him inside. The fragrance that wafted toward him was far more floral than on his first visit. The doors clanged shut behind him. He heard a bar placed on the other side of the door.

I can't leave. What the hell?

A blue haze swirled throughout the chamber, enfolding a double line of women, swaying in place, wearing green gowns held at the top by gold broaches and belted by thin golden cords. The statue of the goddess was barely visible behind them. When the haze cleared, Io stood atop the marble pedestal, a pale blue gown adorning her from neckline to feet. Zack's chaperones took positions behind Io. She clapped her hands. In one corner, the slow beating of a drum began followed by the gentle plucking of lyre strings.

"Step forward, Atlantean," Io said with a commanding voice.

Zack tentatively moved closer to the center of the room, just before the line of women. Their eyes were painted in the manner he'd first seen on Io many months before.

"You ask to witness the rites of the goddess?" Io asked.

"It is my wish."

"It may not be as you expect."

"I am here of my own free will."

"Then prepare yourself for that which no man's eyes have witnessed since the goddess ruled the land. These sacred ceremonies passed to us from the old times on Creta, the great island to the south."

A smiling priestess handed him a bronze mug, the surface of which bore the raised carving of a woman holding a dagger. She motioned for him to drink. Zack wondered what drink filled the cup. He took a small sip and waited. The drink was honeyed and he felt no ill effect, so he swallowed a deeper draught. The women moved into a circle around him. Even with their extreme makeup, Zack could recognize the bevy of attendants and priestesses who served Io. Flutes played low, haunting notes. The women began to chant. It quickly became evident to Zack, as the volume increased, that they were moaning, in unison.

He drank again and licked his lips. The women swayed, rolling their hips side to side in a long, luxurious grind, synchronous with the music. Zack could see Io on the throne pedestal. She raised her hands above her head.

"Great goddess, Gaia, you, who have enriched our wombs and blessed our fields with life, hear our prayers."

Io fell to her knees, her hands extended with her palms faced outwards. "Grant us strong seed that will bring forth grain to feed our people and stronger seed from our men to bear children."

The moaning of the women increased in volume.

"Keep our bodies fertile, our breasts full, and hold our men in the river of desire."

Zack's fingers tingled. His eyes surveyed the cadence of the slow rotation of hips beneath the tight gowns. He laughed and was met by the wanton glances of the dancers.

Io seemed to float over to a bronze cauldron. She dipped her hand in and withdrew a serpent that writhed and curled in her hands. She held it up. The snake flicked its forked tongue and slithered around her arms and over her hands.

"Behold the rites of fertility," she announced.

A priestess threw incense over coals and white clouds billowed upward. Zack finished a second cup, enjoying the drink too much. He staggered slightly but righted himself. He found a tripod set behind his legs. He lowered himself onto it, guided by gentle hands on his shoulders.

More of the cauldrons revealed their inhabitants, drawn by the music and herbed incense. The serpents cautiously made their way to the marble floor and stayed there, hesitant to go near the flaming tripods. The dancers increased the speed of their rotations, their arms curling and beckoning Zack. Io stood again with the serpent wrapped around her neck, tail in one hand and head in the other. She faced the tall statue of the goddess and declared, "You, who provide what we need, accept our sacrifice."

Her voice took a more urgent tone.

"Give rise to the stalk. Yield the seed. The seed must be young and strong. When winter recedes and planting is to be done, new seed must be found to yield unto the goddess. Give rise to the stalk."

In one motion, the ladies of the circle, all seemingly handpicked for their youth and beauty, wrapped their fingers over the gold broaches, unclasped them, and tossed them aside. The gowns fell, but were held from going past their waists by the thin leather ties. The women, each with a countenance of unsatisfied desire on her face, revealed their breasts as each passed in front of Zack. They ran hands from their hips, over waists, and across breasts of all sizes and shapes. They moaned, and as they passed him, each strived to outdo the one before in motions of erotica.

And they stared at his groin with looks of wanton expectation.

Zack recoiled. The women closed in on him.

"Sisters, how raises the stalk?" Io asked.

"He raises readily, priestess," they cooed in unison.

"Part the way," she said.

The dancers halted. More incense perfumed the room. Torches were extinguished. The room darkened.

Zack's nostrils flared. His breathing raced. He felt swimmy-headed. Through the haze, he saw Io step off the pedestal and walk away through a side portal. He could see the outlines of the women around him. Their hands moved in slow motion. His vision became doubled and Zack shook his head in an attempt to correct it. He nodded off for a moment. The women raised their voices in song and he opened his eyes, but in a dream state. Their motions became blurry. He tried to talk, but only babble came out. His hands were being gathered behind the chair and bound. Some of the dancers paired off. They melted onto the floor in front of Zack, one of each pair mounting the one beneath. Zack heard orgiastic moans. Blinking his eyes, he could barely see through the clouds of incense.

Then, through the red-tinged haze, Zack saw the outline of a female figure emerging from behind the statue. She had lighter hair falling over her shoulders, and moved toward him, one foot slowly placed in front of another.

She looked like Lauren.

The women on the floor all rose and stood in front of him. He felt hands, lots of hands, fondling him.

His last vestige of sense told him that he was being seduced in a way so powerful and so beyond his control. Desire commanded him, fired by the concoction in the mug, the dance of the women, and the hands beckoning him to their will.

Someone from behind held his shoulders down. Zack arched his hips and found he couldn't move his arm. They'd been tied behind him. Then, the faintest hint of a fragrance wafted past his nostrils. The scent he had known for so long: Lauren's scent, Lauren's perfume. Only she could have J'adore.

It had to be her.

"Lauren," he shouted, but the name stuck in his throat. Now the scent assaulted him, and the women grouped in front of him, partially blocking his view of Lauren's long honey-colored hair. He tried to shout her name again but no words would emerge.

Lauren, come to me. How I've missed you.

With eyes open just a crack and the haze of blue smoke obscuring his sight, the women parted and there stood his wife in a long white himation. She threw away her broach with one hand while grasping a motionless snake with the other. Her gown fell to her waist. She writhed just in front of Zack, threw her head back, raised her arms and bent down, then back up, luxuriously, slowly. She then pushed her gown over her hips and it dropped to the stone floor. Zack felt roaming hands over his chest. Hands covered his face and he couldn't see. Zack felt incapable of catching his breath and all he knew was that he could finally bask in the comfort of his wife.

Io stood before him, one leg slightly in front the other. With lips parted, she breathed faster. The loose clothing no longer offered Zack sanctuary.

"The stalk is ready, goddess," Io declared, her voice low and sultry.

"Ready it is," the women returned the chant.

She raised the ceremonial dagger, curved like a snake.

"The seed must be harvested," Io shouted.

"How we desire the seed," the women replied.

The Atlantean dropped his bronze cup, empty of his third round of drink. It rattled on the stone.

Io waved the dagger. She ran her finger over the curved edge. The tripods lost their flames and the chamber darkened. The Atlantean had sight of her for only a moment.

"When the seed is given," Io said.

"And our fruit is ripe," the women said together.

"The seed is gathered."

All together they cried out, "Then the stalk is . . ."

The Atlantean sat splayed on the tripod. More torches went out. From behind the statue, three long gongs sounded. The circle of women quickly gathered their gowns and scooted to the side alley. Almost in darkness now, Io leaned into Zack, placed her fingers on his shoulders, and then dragged the fingernails of one hand down his chest. She kissed his cheek delicately, and whispered in his ear.

"Zack, I have come back for you."

He rolled his head from side to side, "Oh, Lauren, oh honey."

Io straddled his thighs, positioning herself over him. She held the snake dagger behind his neck.

Barely above a whisper, she said, "Submit to the goddess; submit to desire." Io swallowed him inside her and stayed still for a moment. She shut her eyes and began to move slowly. Then, comfortably seated, she rocked a bit faster and harder. Abandoning all reserve, she arched her neck, pursuing him relentlessly, and greedily, like the priestesses before had taught her. She reveled in the long, delicious eternity of it, as if she were the goddess, herself.

She didn't want it to end.

But from deep inside her, the torrent rose. She couldn't deny the longing held down these last months. She rotated her hips faster still.

This man would be hers, no matter what it took.

She lost herself. She bucked and thrust.

Io's lips parted and she let go a shattering scream.

The snakes raised their heads.

Then she hoisted the dagger high over the Atlantean's neck. He groaned. Queen Io dragged the dagger over his neck and drew blood.

The Atlantean barely flinched. He rolled his head, lost in the potent poppy-laced drink. Io smiled.

The ceremony had been perfect. The priestesses had passed on, by word of mouth, that far in the past the male consort would be sacrificed. The dagger had been handed down, but now the cut was ceremonial.

The Atlantean had truly believed that Lauren was with him. The honey-colored wig worked. Queen Io would later thank Gaia that Lauren had given her the small bottle of flowered perfume when she had visited.

A brassy gong sounded behind the statue.

Io licked the tiny stream of blood from the back of the Atlantean's neck, emitting another luxurious moan and then lifted herself from him. She ignored her discarded gown and lay down on the floor on her back. Closing her legs tightly together, as if protecting the prize she'd earned, Io, rotating her shoulders and hips, slithered serpent-like back to the temple, holding the dagger in both hands.

"You are served, Mother Gaia," her voice echoed off the enclosed walls. "Strong seed is mine."

And she left by the same corridor as the others. The bronze doors reopened.

Cool air rushed inside and found Zack slumped in his chair. Two guards seized each arm and carried him up the long stairway.

Mycenae, Greece

JUNE 479 BC

Zack opened his eyes. Morning. He knew in an instant that he'd been drugged. His mouth was dry and, even lying down, his head ached. Rather than attempting to stand, he decided to roll out of his bed onto the floor.

A breeze filtered into the room from open shutters, bringing in the scent of wildflowers. He took a deep breath.

He conjured together visions of the day before. He had been in the earth goddess's temple and then all became a blur. Zack slapped his temple with his palm.

He had been with Lauren.

Zack circled the room. Could it really be that Lauren was here? He drank watered-down wine and his head cleared of the fog. It wasn't just last night that fought for attention in his memory.

Something else did, too.

If he could slap the memories from his head, he might get some real answers. He kept seeing Lauren's face. She was crying and saying good-bye, but it wasn't in the tunnel room with Bessus trying to force his way in, or in the goddess's temple the night before.

He saw tables, like in a restaurant, but only for a moment and the remembrance flew away, to be replaced by the memory of explosions.

This is what bothered him the most. He didn't have any wounds from the explosions, but his chest ached like he should have been injured by them. He sensed ghostly concussions under his feet, as if the memory of some detonation tried to surface in his consciousness.

Zack put on a gray chiton and slung his sword and scabbard over his shoulder. He fitted a belt around his waist and clasped it over his abdomen with a round silver buckle.

Grapes in a terra-cotta bowl sat on the table near his bed, and he ate a few quickly and washed them down with the diluted wine. At least his attendants brought his food and drink to his specifications. All his water was boiled in iron pots under coal fires. He showed them how to make the ash and olive oil soap to clean their hands before preparing his food. When sicknesses hit the city, Zack taught them to isolate the sick and to improve the disposal of human and animal waste to prevent typhoid and dysentery.

He had to know what the hell was going on. He had been with Lauren last night, but where was she?

Zack threw open the door to his quarters and strode along the palisade till he reached the back staircase that led to the megaron. Lauren had walked these same steps, he was told. Needles of guilt lanced through him. He clomped down the stone steps in his leather sandals, but his head swam again. A hand on the wall kept him from falling.

He wondered: since Lauren left with Cassandra through the portal, did she also use it to get back here, too?

Recovering, he walked through an open doorway heading into the central meeting hall, the megaron. Hoplites draped in purple cloaks stood in squads before the queen of Mycenae. Sunlight bursting in from opened shutters lit the room and seemed to focus a beam primarily on the queen.

No fire had been lit in the center pit. Zack heard the voice of Io echo inside the confines of the square-shaped room. Zack shuddered. Doubt consumed him. He saw her lips and the curve of her chin.

He didn't like what he was thinking.

Io said, "We have four hundred hoplites able to march for the Isthmus of Corinth. The royal guard must remain in the city to defend its walls. They number only two hundred. If we lose our hoplites in the battle to come, how will the city be defended?"

Diomedes walked briskly into the megaron from a door on the opposite side. "Forgive my delay, Mother. I have come from the posts on our borders. They have been reinforced, but are short of supplies and weapons."

Queen Io took a deep breath and let it out. She glanced briefly towards Zack and then back to Diomedes.

"We need more warriors," she said with certainty.

"The Spartans train their helots for battle. Could we at least train our common folk, even the field slaves, to fight?" Diomedes answered.

Io resettled herself on the marble throne chair. "After the fields are worked each day, take half the slaves and the poor to the training fields, Diomedes. Our crops may suffer, but will it matter if we are overrun?"

"Is there an alternative site we may escape to, like how the Athenians sent the people to Salamis before the sea fight?"

"That is a good question and one that must be answered by you, Diomedes. Go scout out a campsite in the mountains. Parlay with our neighbors if you must."

"I'm sorry, Mother, but there will be no time to bargain. I will find a site and send parties of workers to prepare our refuge in the mountains to the west. Let Xerxes come up the long road with his army. We'll roll rocks down and smite them.

"You will be a good king, my son."

Diomedes took the compliment with a smile. "I would like to take the Atlantean with me. We'll leave the horses behind. He could use a stretch of his long legs."

Io cast a fast glance Zack's way.

"Do so, Diomedes. Do not be away too long."

Diomedes slapped Zack on the back. "Your feet will cry out for mercy before we rest tonight."

Zack bowed and blurted out, smiling,

"Wait, where is Lauren? Where's my wife?"

All in attendance looked at each other.

"Have the gods possessed you, Zack?" Diomedes asked with his eyebrows creased. "Lauren is not here. You sent her west."

Zack pounded his forehead. "But, I saw her last night. I'm certain ..." His head began to swim again.

"You need to rest Atlantean," Io said, her voice echoing in the enclosed chamber.

"No, wait, I saw her last night in the . . ."

But he couldn't finish because his vision sparkled in from the sides and he collapsed. Diomedes rescued Zack from hitting his head on the stone floor.

Io ducked her chin. "Rest him for a couple of suns, Diomedes, and then take him on your journey. His head will be rid of fog after climbing the mountain, and he will be restored."

"Did he visit the goddess chamber and partake of the cups, Mother?"

"The Earth goddess does not reveal her secrets."

Diomedes lifted his chin. "Perhaps the Earth Mother will make him forget his wife."

Queen Io waved her hand and the hoplites filed out into the courtyard. When only she and Diomedes remained, she uttered, "Would it not be better for both of us?"

Two days later, the two reached the border fortifications near dusk, dust in their mouths and water bladders empty. Zack guessed they had hiked about twenty miles. With unfriendly Argos to their south, they headed west toward the border of the city-state of Tripoli.

The fort was square-shaped and made of stone blocks and timber planks, about thirty yards long on each side. Above the fort flew the double-headed axe flag, symbol of Mycenae. Diomedes hailed the guards on the ramparts and the wooden gate opened with a long grind. They followed two guards to a barracks. Other guards surrounded cooking fires, grilling butchered hares splayed on iron rods. Zack was hungry and the smell of grilled meat made his stomach gurgle.

The captain of the guard put his hands on his hips when Diomedes walked in.

"Greetings, Prince. Since you showed up with no wagons, I can only guess our supplies are not arriving."

Diomedes waved his hand. "Don't worry. They were loading wagons went we left. You'll have barley and olive oil by tomorrow night."

The captain blew out through his mouth and scratched his head. "That will be welcome. The rats in the compound have all run away. As you see, we've been setting traps in the woods for the hares."

"What about wine, anything to quench our thirst?"

"I have a nice bucket of piss for you, Diomedes, but you'll probably have to wrestle the tall one next to you for it."

Diomedes bellowed and smacked the captain on the shoulder.

"At least we still had wine to drink at the Hot Gates," Diomedes said with a quick nod of his head.

"Could have filled pails with Persian blood and drank that if we ran out." The three men looked at one another, with an understanding only those who had been at the pass could understand. "We lost many a good fighting man up there."

Silence ensued.

"Well, Atlantean," the captain said, "you are in training, I hear."

Zack nodded.

"Stay in the infantry. Border duty will shrink your balls."

Diomedes laughed aloud. "It's good to meet again, Perseus. I can't let a man who excelled in slaying barbarians starve, now can I?"

The captain smiled, showing a big space between his two front teeth. He was about ten years older than Diomedes. He had ragged scars on his arms and forearms. When he turned, Zack saw he had also lost an ear.

"We're going up into the hills tomorrow. We'll scout out a suitable camp for the city folk if we need to make our escape from Xerxes."

The captain coughed and spit onto the dirt floor.

"You need a campsite for almost five thousand people? What will they eat, pine needles?" the captain returned rather sharply.

"We're building stores of grain and dried figs right now."

"Even if you attain such a store of foodstuffs, you can't leave them up here. You'll need wagons and oxen to transport it while the people walk."

Diomedes looked out the window at the hoplite guards cutting meat from the rabbit carcasses.

The captain said, "And these hills aren't high enough to stop that army. We'd have to go west, across the Peloponnese, to the coast. You think our neighbors are going to allow us passage?"

"Maybe I should ask for a council with the king of Tripoli," Diomedes returned.

Zack spoke for the first time since they'd left Mycenae. He could not rid himself of his sullen mood. The realization that Lauren's visit had been a mirage angered him so completely he could barely think. He'd been drugged and used, raped actually.

Zack asked, "How long can you hide if Xerxes wins? You might be better off sending as many hoplites as you can to whatever battle will be fought. The citadel is not going to hold against any attack from the Persians. Any camp you build up here will only be a way station to the next hiding spot."

"We have thought of this already, Atlantean," the captain said an irritated tone. "Still, if escape is the only way our people will survive, then we must prepare a sanctuary."

"Are there any places you can hide in the Peloponnese where five thousand people cannot be found?" Zack asked, not liking the way the captain looked at him.

"The gods might know, but I don't," Diomedes replied with a defeated look on his face.

"Go up into the hills then, and see if such a hiding spot exists, maybe a cave big enough to hold a Cyclops," the captain said. "Just be on the watch for bandits from Argos. They're hunting deer and chopping down trees. By the time we follow the sound of their axes, they've gone."

"We will," Diomedes replied, "but now my hunger draws me to those hares. Come Zack, we can likely beg a mouthful or two before rest. Tomorrow we rise early."

Zack woke before dawn, roused by the clanking of spears and the banging of pots. A coal breakfast fire had been lit and blue smoke penetrated the bunkroom. He rose on one elbow. The thin rug he had slept on felt like a stack of bricks. He stood, rubbed his lower back, and headed out the door to the garrison grounds. Diomedes stood on the parapet talking with guards. He pointed to the high ground to the west. When he saw Zack, Diomedes waved and bounded down the timber steps. He stopped at a stack of weapons and grabbed two stout spears.

"Fill your stomach, Zack. We leave before Helios rises too high."

They hiked for a few hours through scrub brush and along rough-cut roads leading higher into the mountains. Then the road disappeared and became more of a track, closely bounded by trees and bushes.

"This path will have to be widened," Zack observed. "Even pack animals will have a hard time getting through this."

"We'll need crews to cut the trail."

"Are you expecting to find a cave up here?"

"I know there are caves up here. Dark, foreboding ones that even a Spartan would find uncomfortable. We'll store our grains there and guard it from robbers. Come now, we may have to crawl before we can go much further."

"Wait," Zack said. "I have to take a leak. Be just a moment."

"Water the brush if you have to. I'm going to see if there's a clearer path. I tire of these stickers punching holes in my hide."

Zack pushed aside brush and thorny branches. He put down his spears and lifted up his chiton to let loose his stream when he heard rustling in the brush ahead. He had seen Diomedes go in a different direction.

Did this mean bandits?

He held his pee back until he could retrieve his spears. He didn't want to call out for Diomedes until he knew who might be sneaking up on him. More rustling in the bushes commenced.

Then he heard a guttural snort.

Answered by another deeper and more threatening snort, followed by a high-pitched squeal. Zack saw smaller shapes on four legs dashing away through the underbrush.

Zack couldn't hold his bladder any longer, but the brush parted and an enormous hog with tusks shook his head and snorted. A second boar, bigger than the first, with a black swath along his back and eyes that looked tiny and sightless, squealed and kicked dust behind his hind legs. The beast apparently had not the slightest fear of the man before it.

Pee ran down Zack's leg.

The boar charged and was on him in a flash. Zack thrust the spear and caught the beast behind the shoulder. The boar screetched, turned, breathed hard, and wrenched itself free. A red flow stained his thick brown fur.

Zack heard Diomedes call out to him from a distance, "It'll be night before you leave your puddle, now let's go. I hear snorts, so watch out for boars."

The second boar came through a thicket and joined the first. Then together they charged. Zack held the spear out and braced the butt end in the ground. One boar, the smaller of the two, ran right onto the spearhead, squealing and twisting as the blade penetrated its belly. The second swung its head, ripping Zack's arm with its tusk.

Zack swore and grabbed his arm.

He heard Diomedes call again. The boar lowered its head and threatened to put its massive weight behind a thrust at Zack's stomach. He turned at the last second and the boar hit him in the back. Zack smelled the stink of the woods and the hot nasty breath of the beast in his face. It kept rolling him over, snorting and cornering him, looking for a better place to gore him. The first boar screamed murder and lay down, swatting at the wound in its stomach with its foot.

"Diomedes!" Zack roared. The boar reared back and stabbed Zack full on with its tusks, lifting him up and slamming him against boulders. Zack drew his Marathon sword. He stabbed at the boar but barely penetrated the thick hair. The boar growled and bucked its head, trying to smash Zack against the rocks again. Zack felt slick all over. He'd been pierced three times. The boar opened its mouth to bite him. Zack thrust the sword into the boar's mouth and twisted it. Hot blood spurted out. Just as the beast disengaged, Zack had a sudden flashback. The animal screeched and took off. A vision came to him of the Marathon sword in his hand, in another place, blood on the blade, and a man screaming, but in another language. He stared at the sword just as Diomedes pushed his way through the thicket.

Zack collapsed on the pine needles. Blood ran from a gash in his side, another on his back, and a third on his bicep.

"Atlantean, I told you to beware of hogs in these hills."

Zack couldn't answer. He wondered if being rammed against the rocks had broken bones, too. Diomedes held his spear defensively in case the boars came back.

"Oh Atlantean, you do have way of getting yourself cut up. Let me look at you."

Zack groaned when Diomedes turned him over and saw red blood coursing from a jagged rip in his back.

"We'll need to bind you up. Why didn't you call out to me?"

Through gritted teeth, Zack said, "Wasn't time. Stuck one, dropped my spear."

"We have to get you back to the guardhouse. Can you walk?"

Zack got to one knee, but fell over.

Diomedes took off his chiton. He doubled up the spears and tied crosspieces to each end, making an ancient version of a Native American travois. He stripped long pieces of thin bark and tied the ends together, creating a square. More pieces created strong crossbars for Zack to lie on. Diomedes helped him onto the travois.

He dragged him downhill over rocks and stumps, brush, and broken ground until the travois broke. Zack held back grunts and groans.

Tiring, Diomedes sat down, breathing hard.

"If you were a maiden, I could carry you with one arm. Instead I have to transport an ox." He grinned at Zack. "Are you still with us?"

Zack grimaced and said, "Screw you."

"Good, then you're still alive. I don't want to disappoint all the palace girls."

Diomedes stood up. "You'll have to walk. I can't drag you any longer." He pointed at the narrow path in front of them, bordered by rock and brush.

He pulled Zack up on his feet, and step after agonizing step, they made their way down the hillside until the parapet guards saw them approaching.

"Remind me not to bring you hunting again, unless you have a horn to let the beasts know you're coming their way. They probably had piglets to protect."

"You make a good mule," Zack said, managing a grin.

"They can wash the wounds with wine and bind you here."

"We must get back to the citadel. I have medicine there."

"Is that what you conceal in the leather sack you keep in your room?"

Zack nodded. He had some antibiotics left, but not many. The wounds could easily get infected, and he had to wonder about rabies.

"We won't linger here then. They must have a wagon and horses."

A day later, near evening, they reached Mycenae. Zack's wounds had already swelled and turned red. In the upper citadel they laid him on the cot in his room. Io and Diomedes rushed in along with the palace physician. The first thing Zack saw was a knife and a bleeding cup.

Zack blared, "No, not that. I won't allow it."

The physician said, "The cuts have festered. Let me help you."

"Clean the wound with fresh wine. I need my medicine and some follow-up stitches. That's all." Visions of Nestor lying in Delphi with his arm dripping blood into a vase terrorized him.

Io folded her arms. "I've seen many get the fever from wounds. The pus is already leaking from them. If you are hardheaded, Zack, you may go to Hades faster than you expect." Her lips were drawn tight, and she didn't appear to be in the mood to argue.

Zack winced when he turned in the bed to accommodate the swelling on his back. "Give me the sack. I'll take the round pills. You'll see in a few days, I will recover."

The physician looked at Io and shook his head. Io's face turned from intransigence to concern. She bent down next to Zack.

"We don't want you to make the journey to Hades. Listen to us."

"You don't understand," Zack said. "Give me the sack." Diomedes went to his locker, lifted the satchel, and handed it to Zack with a smug look. "I hope you have some miracle in there or all our training for war is for naught."

"The pus," Zack said, "it's like tiny bugs in the wound, from the boar's bite. They're called bacteria."

The physician snorted. "Tiny bugs you say, with six or eight legs?"

"You can't see them with your eye. They're too small."

The physician breathed in and out. "He's delirious. We'll pray for him." He tugged on Io's sleeve. "Speak with me." The physician nodded toward the hallway outside the door.

Diomedes stood with his hands on his hips. "Perhaps the boar left you with stars in your head, Atlantean."

In the hallway, the physician withdrew a small terra-cotta jar from beneath his white himation. "Put this in his wine. Once he is asleep, we can drain the evil humors. He doesn't have much time left."

Io's lip quivered. "He is adamant that he not be bled."

"These Atlanteans must be backward. He talks of bugs. If you want him to live, let me do my work. A good charm will cure him."

She closed her eyes for a moment. "I will attend to him myself. If your methods do not heal him, I have herbs that may help."

"We must act fast. His leg and arm are nearing twice the size and his back looks ugly. How many strong warriors have we seen go to their death with wounds like his? His fate is in the hands of the gods."

Io put a finger to her lip, thinking. "Have the sleep potion mixed into his wine. Come back later."

"As you say, Queen Io," the physician replied, waving his hand to attendants standing at the end of the hallway. "He will ask for wine. But he is the suspicious sort, so don't try to force this on him. Just put it on the table next to him. His thirst will mount. Once he is asleep, we will cut him." The physician walked away to the stairway, muttering, "Bugs, bugs he tells me."

With her brow furrowed, Io entered the room. She placed her palm across Zack's cheek. "You're a blazing fire." She dipped a clean cloth in a water pitcher and wiped Zack's forehead. Listen to us, Zack . . ."

"No," Zack interrupted. He tossed his head from side to side. His chiton was soaked. He saw concern on Diomedes's face.

"You don't bleed a sick man, or one that's lost a lot of blood," Zack said adamantly.

Diomedes and Queen Io stared at each other.

Zack clacked his tongue. "God, I'm thirsty."

Diomedes said, "I'll get you a drink, and me, too." He left the room.

Io sat on Zack's cot and said with a pained look, "In this short time, I've become fond of you. I will not lose you. Listen to us."

Zack shut his eyes. "Our medicine is advanced, beyond yours. Hand me my medicine. In two days, you will see me get better."

"Why are you healed in two days, Atlantean?"

"It takes two days for the bugs to die. If I keep taking the pills, I'll be healed in seven."

"Why have our physicians never heard of this . . . medicine?" She swept her hand over the satchel.

"People learn from each other."

Io wiped his face again with the wet cloth.

"Did you learn from the earth goddess?" Io asked with a gentle smile.

Zack coughed and made an unsuccessful attempt to reach the bandaged wound in his back. He was badly hurt. This was no time for talk, and not the right time to ask what happened to him in the chamber. It all might end badly for him.

Zack didn't know what to say—encourage her, scold her—he felt miserable.

"There will be . . ." he winced, "a time to talk about what happened in the goddess temple, but I need to take the medicine now. Give me three of the round tablets . . . please."

Io held the plastic bottle of penicillin in her hand. She peered at the writing on the side. "Are these Atlantean words?" she asked.

"Yes, and if you twist the top, it will open."

Io tried to open the childproof cap unsuccessfully. "What is . . . this?"

"Plastic. Let me do it." Zack squeezed the sides of the cap and twisted it off. There were only ten tablets left. He swallowed two of them. "I don't know if it's enough." He looked up at Io, into her dark eyes and a face of unusual beauty. "Clean my wounds with fresh wine and dress them with only boiled bandages. If I pass out, don't let them bleed me. I beg you. It will kill me."

"Atlantean, I have to care for my husband, too. I will be back, when I can."

"I thank you, Queen Io. But . . . there is more to talk about with you."

"There is much you cannot fathom, but I will beg your forgiveness."

Zack laid his head back on the sausage-shaped pillow. "You don't understand. I love Lauren, and it is my fault she struggles for safety in the west with the young girl. I brought her into all this trouble and I don't know if she has survived."

"The gods will decide. Perhaps both of us will have to endure the death of our spouse. Be on guard, fate may knock you down soon enough, Atlantean." She flipped her gown and left through the door.

A boy soon entered the room and set a large kylix holding wine on the table next to his bed. "Be well, master Zack," he said and left the room.

Zack struggled to get out of the bed. He staggered to the door, his breathing shallow and forced. He flipped the wooden lock on the door jamb. He put his weight behind the dresser and pushed it in front of the door. Grunting, and weakening, he lay back on the cot and accepted the onset of pain.

"You bastards aren't going to bleed me," he shouted. "It ain't going to happen." He took another drink of the wine. "I've got to rest." His mind raced with the implications of such tremendous blood loss. Nestor finally died from it. Even in 1799, physicians repeatedly bled the first American president, George Washington, when he contracted a fever while inspecting his property on horseback in cold weather. He died from being bled, too; so much for the advances of medicine from ancient times to the modern age.

Through the haze of his sleep, he heard rapping on the door and pleas for him to open up. Despite the incessant voices of Diomedes, Queen Io, and others, Zack couldn't wake. He fell back asleep until the hammering started again. Deliriously, he shouted out for them to leave him alone. He descended again into a deep slumber.

Finally, the door burst in. Men dropped a log on the floor. Io and Diomedes ran to Zack's side.

"Atlantean, how do you fare?" Io placed her hand on his forehead. "The fever remains."

"Drink, please," Zack rasped out, raising his hand. He grasped for the tablets and took another. "Have to take, three times . . . a day."

The queen unwound his bandages. Her lip trembled. "The pus still oozes, but it is a little less red."

Zack swallowed two more pills. He had no idea how long he had slept. Had he taken enough to kill the infection?

"How long . . . have I been sleeping?"

Diomedes said, smirking, "Most of a day, Atlantean. You are full of tricks, barring the door. We thought you had died."

"I think you spiked my wine."

"What?"

"You put medicine in my wine to make me sleep."

"You needed the rest," Io said affectionately.

The physician bolted into the chamber, out of breath. "Let me help him." He drew a slicing blade from his leather instrument wrap. "Hold him down," he ordered. His attendants rushed in past Io and Diomedes. They grabbed Zack by the arms and set their knees on his shoulders.

Zack yelled, "No, you can't. Don't let them bleed me . . . no . . . God, no."

The physician dragged the blade across Zack's wrist. He held the urn under the flow of blood. Zack only saw his life leaking out of him. Summoning the last of his strength, he hurled the attendants away from him. He seized a cloth and wrapped it tightly over the wound. Lips curled, he pointed at the physician while bellowing at Diomedes, "Get him out of here. If that asshole comes near me again, I'll kill him."

Io, unable to stand any more, shook her fist, "Begone, all of you. I will attend to this man."

"But Mother, if he . . ."

"As I said, all of you leave this instant." She pushed them out of the room.

The physician's shoulders drooped. He left with the blade hanging from his hand, the tip bathed in red. He whirled toward Io, declaring, "I am not responsible for this. I've done all I can."

Io said, "You are absolved. I will petition Gaia for his recovery."

Zack looked at the blood-soaked bandage on his arm. Diomedes left the room. Io slammed the door shut.

"Atlantean, I will guard you myself. No one will ever bleed you again."

Delphi, Greece

PRESENT DAY

In her bedroom, Lauren twirled the paper with the phone number in her hand. The typed phone number held either promise or danger and she couldn't decide which was more likely. She could only determine on some base level that this man must be somewhat reliable, since he was a contact of Mr. Parsons. She noticed the bitten ends of her fingernails.

"What troubles you?" Cassandra asked.

"Adult matters. Take a bath, sweetheart. I'm going downstairs. What if we go for a walk later?"

"That would please me," Cassandra said quietly and then sheepishly returned to the secrecy of the bathroom to continue her lessons. "Hello, good-bye, and thank you," she whispered in English, followed by the same words in modern and ancient Greek.

"Good. Keep practicing until I return." Lauren marveled at the changes that had come over Cassandra. This girl would have had minimal instruction in reading and writing in ancient times. If not for her mother, she'd be like most women of that time: efficient in weaving and the arts of cooking and keeping house, but kept out of public sight, and maybe not even fed as much as a boy. In the farmhouse outside of city, Nestor had allowed his women more freedoms so he wouldn't suffer the severe criticisms of his peers, had they stayed in Athens. He had said to Lauren once, in that time long ago, that his women were not to be kept as pets or prisoners in his house. They were his joy.

Mr. Avtges said that he had errands to run, leaving Lauren in charge of the orphanage. She sat at his desk picking up and then resetting the telephone receiver for the third time.

She was on her own.

Lauren seized the phone. Like a leap into freezing water, she punched in the numbers.

It's time to step across the Rubicon. Where the hell is that river in Italy, anyway?

"Kalimera, good morning," the male voice said in Greek.

"This is Professor Lauren Fletcher." She heard a mature but raspy voice, like one a heavy smoker would have.

"Professor, I've been informed that you might call me. Would you prefer to continue in English?"

"That works for me." Lauren's heart ran at a stallion's pace.

"I've been briefed by an associate of yours. I must say you have an interesting predicament."

Lauren closed her eyes, imagining a face to go with the deep voice; someone with silver hair, like Aristotle Onassis, the late Greek shipping tycoon.

Great, I'm going to get eaten for lunch.

"I know that we cannot meet," Lauren said, testing the waters.

"I have my reasons, Professor Fletcher. Your situation presents a very difficult challenge, maybe one that is unattainable."

Lauren's stomach fluttered.

"I hear you have a lawyer already and there has been little progress?"

"That is correct."

"Are you prepared financially to tackle these problems? That is, seeking to circumvent our governmental policy on adoptions?"

"Tell me if I am wasting your time, sir, but do not be mistaken that I am not quite serious about what I propose."

"Of course, there is a police investigation to contend with as well. I am a polite man, especially with women. Yet business cannot dwell in niceties forever, my dear professor. This will cost twenty thousand US dollars to start."

Lauren dug her fingers into her temples. This was already out of control. She ran through their bank statements in her mind. She had already paid her Greek lawyers five grand. If she gave him what he wanted, she'd be nearly broke.

The agony of her separation from Zack hit home again.

"I see," Lauren said, trying not to sound desperate.

"Professor, there will be no guarantees. I can only promise you that I will do my best." In the background Lauren heard clinking glasses and noise from a restaurant.

"Sir, I am a woman and a foreigner. Furthermore, I cannot look in your eyes to get a feeling as to what I should do. This is a leap of faith that holds dramatic implications for my future."

I could tell if he were lying to me if I could meet with him.

"You will have to trust your instincts, professor. If you do not wish to proceed, there will be no feelings hurt. I have so many projects to occupy my time. My experience in police matters and what I know of your case tells me that the investigation may take many months." He took a breath. "There remains a great deal of public and official pressure to find the killer of Professor Papandreou. The death or disappearance of a foreigner is another complication. Adoption will take more than a year, if it is possible at all. You have a heady list of hurdles to leap."

Maybe this man is my only chance. Zack, I need your help. What the hell should I do?

Lauren held in a deep breath and then exhaled. She drummed her fingers on the desktop. "I'll have money wired from the US. Please help me."

"I will give you a numbered account to deposit the funds. When it arrives, I will begin."

Lauren scribbled down the bank information and verified it twice.

"Contact me if you have questions, professor, but not too often. Otherwise, wait for my call."

"Wait. What do I call you? I was told to call you the Facilitator."

"That's far too dramatic. Call me Samaras. It's not my real name, but it will do."

He ended the cell call.

Lauren wondered what she was getting herself into. She cradled the phone, slick with her perspiration. Heading to her room, she wiped her palms on her jeans.

Lauren closed the door to the bedroom. She shut her eyes.

Cassandra looked worried. "Why do you breathe so hard?"

"Come hug me. I need you." This time it was Lauren who dug her head into Cassandra's shoulder. Afterwards, Lauren laid a cold washcloth on her forehead, taking deep breaths, holding them and exhaling slowly.

She wondered if there would be any escape from trouble.

I need a plan, and fast.

Demo tossed in his bed for hours, thinking about the trick Cassandra was playing on all of them. He could not figure out why she would not speak to him, or to the other children. He was always nice to her. The professor lady had so many secrets. He wondered if all Americans held secrets and why anyone would hide such a thing as talking.

He woke up tired and stomach-sick from his medical treatment the day before. He struggled to hold his attention in class, preoccupied with the mute girl sitting at the table across from him. She glanced at him frequently with little smiles breaking across her face. What did she hide and why? He wanted to stand and announce to everyone that Cassandra could speak. They would stop calling her bad names and he wouldn't have to defend her anymore.

Demo slumped in his chair, rested his head in his palm, wondering when recess would be called. Finally outside, they started a soccer game. He picked Cassandra for his team. Cassandra raced down the left side of the field. Demo punched the ball toward her. She deftly handled the pass and kicked it past the goalie. Demo ran to give her a high five. She smacked his hand and broke a smile from ear to ear.

"You're really improving, nice shot!"

Cassandra nodded.

"I know. You don't have a clue what I just said."

Cassandra wiped the dark hair back from her face and ran back to the other children. Demo followed her, wondering how he could get her to talk. If she can trick me, he thought, I could do the same to her.

After dinner, Demo stayed to help with the cleanup. He sent the other children up to the television room, hoping to get a few minutes alone with the lady professor. She said little while they stacked dishes. Her face looked sad. She sat on a chair finally, resting her head on her arms. Cassandra nestled in beside her, as always. Demo seated himself across from them, wondering whether this was the time to talk to her. She seemed not as friendly as she usually was.

"Thank you for your help, Demo," Lauren said, beginning to comb the girl's hair.

"You're welcome," he answered in English. Cassandra lifted her head, like she understood what he had said. "Was she ever able to talk?"

"I don't know. It's very strange, isn't it?"

"What if she stubbed her toe on the bedpost? I did that yesterday. It hurt so much I said a bad word, really loud."

"I've never heard her say anything, even when we were kidnapped."

"Really, you swear, like we were in church?"

"Why do you ask?"

"It's hard to believe. I think . . ."

"A lot of very strange things have happened to us lately."

"What happened to you in that hole?"

"I was unconscious for some of it, kind of asleep. It is difficult to describe."

"But there was that cloud that sucked you in, like in the movies."

"It was some kind of smoke and then lots of mud."

"Then the earth closed over you, it was weird, on the film . . ."

"I wish we could get that film. If the police watch it, I could be in trouble."

"Your secret is safe with me, any of your secrets would be."

Lauren looked at him but didn't say anything.

"Are you lonely for your husband? You look really sad."

"I need him to help me. I have very serious problems and I'm scared."

Demetrious stood. "I will be your man. I will protect both of you."

"You are a man, Demo; maybe well before you should have to be. The only things that keep me going are this girl and friends like you. I love Cassandra and I have to protect her. Do you understand?"

"Why don't you just make her your daughter?"

"I'm trying, every day."

"Will you leave if that happens?"

"Probably, but it may take a long time."

"I will miss you both, if you go."

He said good night to them in English, and walked upstairs to the sleeping hall. He rubbed his eyes and he didn't feel so good. Tonight he would skip brushing his teeth and just get into bed.

Tuesday night arrived with high, billowing clouds and a brisk wind coursing through the pines behind the orphanage. Lauren zippered her blue parka, left by the rear door, and scooted across the parking lot, staying away from nightlights.

I wish I could run away.

Lauren halted when she reached the stream, dazed by the change in her fortunes since she had arrived in Greece almost five months earlier. She searched the perimeter for Bessus. "You're gone, you bastard. Forever . . . I hope."

She had a completely different set of problems now, and more enemies. What was Zack doing? Was he living in some parallel time? Lauren wished she had listened more in physics class. Even the most expansively minded scientists wouldn't believe this story.

Birds took off from a dense thicket of bushes, startling her. She headed along the mountain path, silver flashlight in her hand, with kneepads, and a thick wool hat with a cardboard lining she had cut for the underside. Jogging towards Nestor's cave made her feel like herself again. *Maybe this is what's been missing. I need exercise. I'm turning into a wimp. My parents wouldn't tolerate this behavior.*

Lauren parted the concealing branches, undid the barrier of rocks, took one last look behind her, and entered the cave.

She felt the infiniteness of peace inside. Here, she could confer with Zack. She knew his spirit existed within these walls, and thought back to his marriage proposal. He told her that he had sensed the souls of people who lived on Thera before the volcanic explosion ruined their world and weakened the Minoan civilization.

"I know you're here, Zack. Help me figure out what to do," she said aloud.

Her voice echoed within the cave. "What should I do, Zack?" She heard the same question, again and again.

It would be a matter of days till whatever new disaster Trokalitis would force on her. She sat on the rough stone floor, rereading Zack's letter written on lambskin. He wrote that he loved her and would never stop, no matter how long it took till he returned. How many disasters had he faced? She felt the blood pump in her neck. She thought about Apollo and came to the same frustrating questions without answers that she always did.

How can I tell you I love you, Zack?

She decided it's us against them.

These bastards have really pissed me off.

The cave returned her shrill call, "The hell with all of you."

If Zack could survive, so could she. She placed the lambskin letters back in the clay jars where she had found them.

Her flashlight was fortified with new batteries, and spares in her pocket. She had a lot of work to do.

Mycenae, Greece

JUNE 479 BC

Diomedes sat on a rock, chin resting on his palm, a pose perfect for a future French sculptor. He had been sullen and distant in the week since his father had died. He held his sword by the rounded pommel and drove the point repeatedly into the ground.

Zack sat in the same pose, his own problems detaching him. He had not seen Lauren in almost a year since they had arrived in ancient Greece in the summer of 480 BC. He had not felt so depressed since that time. His wounds had healed and he concentrated on rebuilding his strength. But the truth of it was that he couldn't shake the guilt that swamped him. His experience in the goddess's temple, even through the veil of his inebriation, shook him. He had been raped. Lately, he'd been unable to concentrate on his military training and separate himself from his nagging personal problems. Io had destroyed his discipline, his control.

Diomedes drove the sword deeper into the soil and twisted it. Zack did the same. Besides her nursing him, to his relief he had seen Io only three times since the ceremony in the temple. The first at a meeting of the hoplite captains as the city-state decided where to deploy the troops and discuss evacuation by land or sea. The second time she wore her ceremonial purple robes and golden diadem, marching in her husband's funeral procession with Diomedes by her side. The population filled the route to the majestic, round tholos tombs where the king's cremated remains were to be interred with those of his ancestors. Distraught by the loss of their beloved king and the gathering threat to their homes, the people wailed and prayed to the gods for deliverance. Diomedes and Queen Io marched stoically, presenting a face of strength in a time of uncertain future. Zack thought of Jackie Kennedy and wondered how these two women could be so composed in such times of tragedy, set apart by two millennia.

"Your father was a great king," Zack said. "I can speak of this because I saw how the people loved him. That, by itself, tells of their respect."

Diomedes had cut his hair short, as Zack had done for Nestor and Persephone's funeral. His clean-shaven jaw was replaced by dark whiskers.

"My mother and I knew well the day was coming when father would leave us for the realm of the dead. Yet, we both feel like a dagger has been stuck into our ribs. No amount of preparation can dull the agony." Diomedes turned away from him. "I cannot remove the sight of his face from my thoughts, the hands that clasped mine when I was a lad, his arm over my shoulder, and the wooden swords we played with. Then the pride I felt when he sent me off to the Hot Gates at the head of our hoplites."

Diomedes ceased the digging with his blade. He stood, looking out over a vineyard. "You will be king one day, my father said to me, and you must lead your warriors. Endure their hardships, take their risks, and they will follow you." When I saw him lying on the funeral pyre, and the flames consuming the shell of the man I loved so dearly, I felt the gods had abandoned us. I wanted to kick the fires away and hold him again, or be swallowed up by the fires myself and be done with this agony."

"Yet, you have the love of your people, Diomedes, as does your mother," Zack pointed out. "You both care more about them than you do yourselves. I believe they know that. Allow yourself to grieve. Your mind must be in the right place and soon, for a battle is coming, one for the ages. The Spartans will have to decide soon whether to join the allies beyond Corinth or fight the Persians alone when all the city-states fall because they waited too long. Your people will need you. Your mother can only endure so much."

"You are a good fellow and your counsel is wise." He looked at Zack. "What of you then? Do you favor our city and our people?"

"I do, Diomedes. Close friends were slain by a barbarian before I arrived in Salamis and I mourned, as you do now. At the same time, I sent Lauren to the west and loneliness plagues my soul. Your generosity has restored me."

"We are but mortals, molded by the gods for their aims. We know not when they will end our days. How do you know if you will ever cast your eyes upon her again?"

"Only the gods know, as you say."

"If your wife is gone and it is unlikely the Fates will bring you together again, why waste your youth in want? You have strange habits, Atlantean."

"Our ways may be difficult to fathom. Is there no woman that you love?"

Diomedes sighed and looked away. "I know how you feel. There is one that clouds my vision and holds my heart, too."

"Who is she?"

Diomedes snatched his sword and cut the branch off a tree in one stroke.

"She is the woman of my dreams, but living is not for dreams, Zack, especially the life of a warrior. Be content with that which is beyond your control. Trust that the gods have thought this through for you."

Now the events of that one night pulled Zack's attention away from Diomedes as he continued on about the hoplites that marched for the Hot Gates and perished in the bloody muck. They, he pointed out, died heroes, but would beg the gods on their knees if they could for more days to be back among their families and countrymen. They would deny themselves no pleasure that the gods would allow, for life was fleeting.

Zack nodded his head, stabbing at a gnarled root, but his mind wandered back to that same muggy night after the funeral when he had just begun to feel like himself. The rough stitches had been cut away, and the wounds in his side and back closed finally. Blue and red scar tissue made a latticework over his torso. After sleeping on his side for weeks uncomfortably, he fashioned a lounge chair from his pallet, lifting up the headboard with blocks of wood and covering it with soft ram's wool.

He had fallen asleep that night thinking about how an aqueduct could be built from the mountains and where to dig outhouses. He had finally convinced the population to dig outhouses away from food-preparing areas and wash their hands after going there. He could bring some simple modern innovations to this ancient culture, even though he was no engineer. Even little advances like a tiny screen for his window made of thin filaments of twine made life easier. These ancient people lived with such nuisances: flies and crawling insects everywhere, lack of bathing and basic hygiene, food and water contamination. He just wondered how people survived infections and sicknesses. A restful sleep finally came to him, and he dreamed of armies in battle until he heard his door creak open early in the morning. He had been sleeping turned away from the door, and couldn't see who had entered, but understood why Alexander the Great had always slept with a dagger under his pillow. He slid his hand underneath the feather-filled pillow and grasped the dagger handle.

Who would want to kill me in my bed? That meant he had enemies in the citadel and his mind raced quickly to discern whom he had offended.

Then he smelled lavender perfume, and breath laced with mint whispered in his ear, "Do not rise or move, Atlantean. I have come to you."

"Io?" Zack stammered. She covered his lips with her fingers. Then she dropped her nightgown and nestled into the linen beside him. Zack froze . . . and waited. She laid her arm over his shoulder and kissed his neck.

"Maybe I am Aphrodite, or a Bacchae come to ravage you. Either way, submit to me, Atlantean." She blew hot breath onto the nape of his neck and reached for him. Zack squirmed and protested before Io once again shushed him.

"Speak not, Atlantean," she whispered in husky tones. "You are alone, and so am I. All I want to hear from you are your cries of joy to the gods."

"You raped me in the temple. You gave me no choice."

"You asked to witness the ceremony. The goddess requires devotion to her ways."

"You drugged me and made yourself to look like Lauren. You even smelled like her."

Io spooned into his back. "Then I apologize, Atlantean, for all my tricks. But I ask you to think very clearly about the will of the gods. What if you were to find out later that Lauren has perished, and you wasted your days here, with us . . . with me?"

Zack didn't reply.

"I am here. I want you," Io said, squeezing him. "You must set your thoughts on what the days ahead hold for you. You must submit to the gods, and me, willingly."

Zack had heard that before, somewhere. Apollo's face commanded his thoughts. Lauren was somehow with Apollo, too. Had they a meeting together? He tried to concentrate, but once again, any attempt to hold the memory failed.

"You do not answer, Atlantean. What thoughts fill your head?"

"I'm sorry, Io. I . . . am remembering."

"Then remember for a time, but not for too long." She whispered in his ear, "Come to me, when you have settled in your head what you have lost and what awaits you here."

She donned her robes and slipped from the room.

Back to the present, Zack rested his chin on his palm. He had succumbed to the realization that maybe he would not return to his own time, to his family, and ultimately, to Lauren.

Then what would he do?

He was lost with no center, no sense of whom he was any longer. Worse still, he still could not gather his thoughts in certainty, in clarity.

Scatterbrained is how he could describe it. Memories fought to be recognized but always seemed beyond his grasp.

"You look like a centaur has shoved his stinky buttocks in your face," Diomedes said. "What is your worry?"

"You have a way with words, Diomedes. Maybe I will never return to my home."

Diomedes brightened and smacked him on the back, hard. "Enough. We need a distraction. Let us test your skills in boxing and wrestling. A spear and a sword are good to fight with if you have them, but many a hoplite has conquered an enemy with his hands."

Zack jumped to his feet and spread his legs for balance. Diomedes did the same, grinning and raising his fists, his left one forward, ready to jab.

"Dispense with fists, Zack. We need no bruises to contend with if the war begins anew. Just show me that you can take me down."

Diomedes lowered his head and attacked. Zack sidestepped him, but Diomedes knocked him off his balance with a foot sweep. With catlike quickness, Diomedes pounced on Zack, curling a steely bicep around his neck. Zack gasped for air but he would be damned if he would raise his finger in surrender so soon. Unable to break the grip, Zack rolled his head within the hold, giving him a slight reprieve. He slung his arm between Diomedes legs, hoisted him up and smacked him backward onto the ground, breaking the hold.

Diomedes leaped up, away from Zack, rubbing his back. "You are learning well, my friend. But behold the skill of a finalist in the Panathenaic Games!"

The Mycenaean prince jabbed with his fist, forcing Zack backward. Then he swung with his right to keep his opponent off balance. Zack recoiled, kicked straight out with his heel, catching Diomedes in the chest, halting his advance. Diomedes recovered and jabbed again, but Zack locked arms and threw him over his shoulder.

They fell together in a heap. Quickly, Diomedes wrenched Zack's arm backward. Zack grunted, threw an elbow, catching Diomedes in the forehead, causing his release. The two separated, snorting like bulls.

They both raised fists in anger. Winning took on a new urgency.

Diomedes's features had changed. He bared his teeth and his face contorted into a sneer. He picked up the sword at his feet. "I will beat you and Lauren will be—" but his words were cut short by a volley of trumpets that blasted forth from the citadel heights.

Both adversaries froze. Diomedes waited as if counting the notes.

Zack stammered, breathing, "What did you say about Lauren?"

"Five, Zack," he said, with eyes ablaze with a different kind of anger. "They call us to war. Go to your chamber. Gather your armor and campaign kit. Now, race me to the gate. Hermes, stand aside."

Both raced through the vines overflowing with fat grapes, and past rows of olive trees. Blacksmiths, cart makers, and herdsman halted their labor, watching the two racing for the long stone ramp. Zack's long legs gave him an advantage, but Diomedes sprinted up the ramp, passing first through the Lion Gate to the clapping of spectators.

They halted briefly, regaining their wind. Diomedes got into a sprinter's stance and Zack did the same. They bolted through the winding streets, past hoplites gathering weapons, campaign packs, and forming squads on the lower courtyards. When the two reached the megaron, high into the citadel complex, they fell and rolled, chests heaving.

"You are a worthy adversary," Diomedes, grasping for air. "Delay not, the trumpets will sound again... and we will line up."

"I won't be long."

"I will meet you at the parade ground. Do you understand my meaning, man? The Spartans are marching, the whole Spartan army. We will march behind them, drive the barbarians from Athens, and slay them on the road north as they flee. I have waited all my life to see such a line of red cloaks."

"You aren't the only one," Zack said, dashing after his friend, knowing full well what the coming days would bring.

Zack reached his chamber, kicked in the door, and threw open the double doors of his locker. A polished bronze breastplate and a dark, stiff rim of horsehair atop a Corinthian helmet with long cheek guards hung on hooks. Holding it in his hand, he wiped his elbow over a smudge marring its gleam. He had paid a sizable sum for it with Nestor's money.

A warrior shows pride in his armor.

Zack flinched and turned to see Io at his door. She shut the door behind her with a sweep of her hand. She folded her bare arms across a dark green robe, silence broken by the clinking of her gold bracelets. Zack bowed.

"I am honored, Queen Io."

"Bow not," she said, breathless herself. "Dispense with the formalities, there is no time for it. You know what the trumpets mean."

Zack turned his gaze away. He could only see her as she was in the temple that night. His throat went dry. Io reached for a linen towel and handed it to Zack.

"I watched you both run from the fields. You are a man at full strength now."

She did not take her eyes from him as Zack blotted off sweat from his brow. Her gaze left his muscled torso and settled on his eyes.

She's reading me.

Zack brought the towel to his face and wiped it again, though there was no perspiration left, more to shield him from her stare.

"I am the queen, Zack, but you must see past this."

"This is a confusing time for me, truly . . ."

"I am Diomedes's mother, but you must see past this also. He is not a boy anymore, and neither are you, Zack."

"That's not the problem," Zack countered.

The blast of trumpets ricocheted off the walls and mountainside yet again. Io parted her lips and breathed deeply.

"Neither of you may survive the battle." Io's face took on a look of desperation. Her chest heaved.

"No one knows the future . . ." Zack said.

She placed her fingertips on his lips.

"No one knows the future, except the gods. My husband is dead. Your wife is far removed and a merciless war awaits us. You may never see her again, despite your devotion to her. None of us may survive this. Those that care for each other, support each other's needs. While I am a maiden no longer, I am ripe and a woman of unquenchable desire."

Io brushed her fingertips across Zack's cheek. Zack shivered as he met her eyes.

"Perhaps in your land you have the luxury of safety and endless nights to be with those dear to you." Io wrapped her arms around Zack's waist. She pressed herself close. He drew in scented hair and oiled skin.

"Here, we do not waste the days the gods give to us, for they snatch them back from those who arrogantly take each sun and moon for granted."

She raised herself on the tips of her toes and kissed the base of his neck, just below his trimmed beard. Outside and down in the upper courtyard, the clamor of horses, wagons, and armored men rose. Io delicately brushed her fingers over him, as if checking to see if she was having the effect she hoped for. She smiled up at him.

"Would you deny that which is sacred and given to us by the gods? Aphrodite beckons."

Running in the hallway outside his door broke his attention, but Io didn't let him go.

"Tell me then, Atlantean, will you give me what I desire?"

Zack closed his eyes. Visions of Lauren battled for dominance over the carnal assault at hand.

I have to say no.

"Queen Io, I mean Io . . . I beg you. My thoughts are scrambled. I cannot devote myself to you in the manner you would require, not yet."

"A very diplomatic answer, but not bravely said. Speak with your heart."

She nuzzled his ear and ground her hip into his groin. "Look into my eyes and see that I am not a woman who plays at tops and throw bones. You are a man I could give myself to." Io scanned Zack's eyes for a kernel of surrender.

"Do not presume that I don't think about you, for I do," Zack said, breathing hard. "And I see your point, but I'm married, and I want to go back to Lauren. When the fighting is over, I will come back, but only if I am to stay here, forever, in time . . ."

What am I going to do?

A series of girlish cries and giggling erupted outside in the hallway. Zack's door took a pounding.

He heard a warrior's voice call to him. "Atlantean, do you have your kit? This is no time for a nap or a fast dive into the mirthy moss of some maiden."

Io put her hand over her mouth to hold back laughter.

Zack turned to Io.

He heard Diomedes's voice this time. "Be fast. The company is lining up."

Zack answered, "Rein in your stallions, Diomedes. I need a little more time."

"This could be embarrassing," Zack said, rotating his gaze from the door back to Io.

"Atlantean, you are truly a marvel. My son will not flinch."

Io disregarded the impetuous knocking, unhooked the top of her gown, and let it fall. She guided Zack's hand to her breast and did not let him withdraw it.

"Squeeze me, Atlantean, but it will be the last touch today that will be a gentle one." She leaned back against the door of his weapon locker, pulling Zack toward her. She pulled up the hem of her gown.

"Now Atlantean, I am here. I desire you. We may all be shades by the next moon."

"But Io . . ."

She put her finger over his lips. "I am yours. Tell me the gods would not allow it?"

She wasn't interested in talking any more. Zack lost himself in the lavender scent, her racing breaths, and the relentless pressing of her hips. He couldn't take his eyes from hers. Zack wanted to break her embrace, push her away, but he could not.

She yanked him over to the bed, hurled him atop it, threw away her gown and pushed on his chest. He saw the consummate joy on her face. Zack tried to shove her off.

"Io, please—"

She bared her teeth and said, "No longer will you tell me no."

Zack pressed his lips together. She slid onto him, deeper and faster, and with an urgency that told him he wasn't going anywhere.

Maybe he wasn't going back. Maybe he would never see Lauren again. Maybe Apollo would sentence him to the past. Maybe he would perish in the battles to come.

He let go of his past life. It could be that he would live among the ancients, permanently.

Io's lips quivered. She spoke brokenly, "I want you...you will be mine..." She moaned from a place deep inside.

Zack stared into her eyes and said, "I will let the gods decide."

Her face contorted and it looked like she would burst into tears.

She ground him into dust. Zack saw tears in the creases of her eyes. Io threw her head back and let go a primordial cry.

Zack lost control.

Trumpets blared. He heard leather snap and bronze clank. Hoplites ran in the hallway.

Io collapsed onto him. Their chests heaved in unison.

After a minute of murmurs and captured breaths, she raised and said, "I want you, Atlantean." Io kissed him lightly and with resignation, said, "Remember how I am. Remember how I will be for you."

"If the gods will that I stay, then I will be your man."

Io smiled. She put her gown on. "Come to me with more of that when you have defeated the barbarians."

She left Zack with the taste of honey on his lips and opened the door. Diomedes bounded in, tripping a little, as if he had been about to break into the room.

"The muster is nearly complete, Mother, excepting one misplaced outlander." He raised an eyebrow. "I see that diplomacy never rests."

"Go to war with our hopes and dreams to brace you, Diomedes, "Queen Io said with her face flushed. "Come back to me as you did after Thermopylae, and bring this Atlantean with you." She cupped Diomedes's cheek with her hand, kissed him, smiled at them both, threw back the long hem of her gown and retreated, clearly holding back a torrent of emotion.

Zack searched Diomedes's face for anger. Diomedes smacked Zack on the shoulder. "Do not fret. There are few secrets between my mother and me. Come, we have a long march and barbarians to slay."

Zack gathered his armor, sword, and his backpack full of kits to repair weapons and flesh. He followed Diomedes down the hallway, wondering which he feared more: battalions of Xerxes's Immortals bearing down on him or Io's amorous demands.

20

Delphi, Greece

PRESENT DAY

The bathwater turned brown. Lauren remembered another time she had turned water this dark and it was back in Mycenae. She thought about Queen Io and Prince Diomedes. She had been rescued back in those ancient times and was alive now because of Diomedes. She took the washcloth off her face.

How can you think about what someone is doing in the present term if they've been dead for over two millennia? I must be a total idiot.

The hot water soothed her muscles, but it stung scrapes and bruises, visible merit badges of her efforts from the night before. It had taken till dawn to finish her work in the cave. She woke Cassandra up when she came in the room in the morning, telling her to go back to sleep. Lauren would have to rest during the day and cancel her classes, just this once.

She shut her eyes, reviewing her strategy, as if anticipating a chess match. Her father had said that no battle goes as planned. An intelligent leader must be able to change tactics if necessary, she remembered. He always talked about the teachings of Sun Tzu, the ancient Chinese military tactician. She should have read his book.

Lauren realized she knew nothing about her opponents.

Lingering no longer in the bath, she hopped out and dressed to make a phone call.

"Why can't you push them to act more quickly?" Lauren asked Samaras. "I'm getting pressure from the police. I mean, I may be in jail by the time something is worked out."

"I've never been able to get used to Americans," he answered, his tone conveying irritation. "You want everything now, like spoiled children. Poor behavior on your part does not create urgency on my part."

"But what am I supposed to do if they jail me?"

There was no answer, just a long grumble laced with disgust. Finally, he replied, "See here, you must be patient. Use your intellect to control your emotions."

She blurted, "Trokalitis said I had one week."

"Calm yourself."

Lauren raised the phone as if to crash it onto the cradle. She bit her lip.

"I'm depending on you," she said, lowering the phone.

"Let the pot cook."

"My feet are in the pot and the water's getting hot."

A gentle laugh ensued. "Get some breakfast," he advised. "Maybe try meditation. Call me tomorrow."

"Meditation," she muttered while walking up the stairs to her room for a nap. She sent Cassandra off to classes on the ground floor and lay down on the bed. She reviewed the strategy in her mind.

At last she slept.

Startled from her nap, Lauren heard chairs scraping downstairs, followed by smashing sounds and shouting.

Demo shouted out her name—a desperate call. She sat up in bed.

Then in quick succession she heard again, "Lauren! Lauren!"

Lauren, not seeing Cassandra in the room, bolted to the door. She ran to the stairwell, saw her bare legs and realized she only had on panties and a T-shirt. She halted, but heard more voices laden with anger.

Lauren heard, "Leave her alone." She knew what it could be.

She leaped three stairs at a time and reached the first floor hallway.

Two policemen and a uniformed woman fought with Demo. She saw a jumble of legs and arms. The authorities tried to pull Demo away from someone on the floor.

Demo screamed, "Leave her alone!" He shook off the grip of one of the cops by falling to the floor. He threw himself on top of a child at the bottom of the heap.

Mr. Avtges rushed to the struggle but could not separate the jumble of bodies.

Demo screamed again, "Lauren!" He grasped Cassandra's hand, his face red with the strain.

The policemen lost their patience. One drew a billy club. The female cop shook her head at him, warning the officer not to use it. Another uniform ripped Demo away from the child on the floor. Demo struggled, twisted, freed himself and put his fists out, guarding Cassandra, who lay curled up in a ball on the linoleum.

Lauren growled and ran to her.

The policeman with the club intercepted her.

Lips curled, with her arm, she clotheslined the cop holding the club.

She could kill. The policeman covered his nose and fell away.

Mr. Avtges warned, "No Lauren, don't."

One officer picked up Cassandra, pure terror locked on the young girl's face. The female cop threw herself between Lauren and the girl. She shouted in Greek to the other officers, "Get her out of here."

The thickset cop pulled hard on Cassandra's arm. She kicked him. He pinned Cassandra's arms, and hauled her away.

"Cassandra," Lauren yelled in ancient Greek. "Don't talk, fight." Lauren pushed the policeman off her. The female officer pulled Lauren's hair.

"They'll arrest you, Lauren. Please stop this instant," Avtges warned. Lauren blared, "No, no, no." She saw the policeman dragging Cassandra out the door. "Cassandra, I'll come for you."

The last Lauren saw of Cassandra was her white sneakers. The heels made squeaking sounds as they hauled her away.

Inspector Trokalitis sauntered out of the office, a curt smile on his face.

"You unbelievable son of a bitch," Lauren roared. She glared at him with eyes that promised violence.

"Go upstairs before I throw you in jail," Trokalitis warned, withdrawing a gold cigarette case from his coat pocket and heading for the parking lot.

"And take the boy upstairs with you, professor. Defy my authority again and you will be sorry in ways you won't believe."

21

Delphi, Greece

PRESENT DAY

Later that day, Avtges pinched the bridge of his nose. A massive migraine assaulted him. The doctors called it a cluster headache. It fit the situation.

Lauren strummed her fingers on the desktop. She said nothing and looked out the window, chewing on the inside of her cheeks. Then Avtges heard her puff and snarl, like a bear defending her den.

She said low and deliberately, "I need your phone, and some privacy, please." Lauren didn't look at Mr. Avtges.

"Of course, but can I help in some way?"

She shook her head no and proceeded to gnaw the end of her index fingernail. Mr. Avtges shut the door to the office.

"Samaras, I need you to do something, now." Lauren told him in hushed tones what had happened.

"I don't know why he took the girl," the Facilitator replied. "He is a hard man and desperate. He doesn't believe you."

"I don't give a damn about him. I want her back. She must be terrified." Lauren held back the anger boiling inside her. "She's a young girl. She's doesn't know who to trust."

"You ask the impossible. I need time to sort it out."

"Did the twenty thousand dollars arrive?"

"It did."

"Then earn it," she said with venom.

"You're hysterical."

"I'm responsible for her. Do you get that?"

"Get some rest and gather your wits. We will need to go to war, and I can't have you going wobbly on me."

"Wobbly is never a word you can use to describe me," she shouted. "Call me later. Find out where they took her."

"If I know something, I'll call you," replied the gravelly voice.

Lauren hung up the phone and beat the desk with her fist. She had betrayed Cassandra's trust. The whole charade could fall apart if the girl even spoke a word.

Lauren leaped two stairs at a time to get to her room on the second floor.

Demo waited at her door. "What will happen to her?"

"Thanks for fighting for her." Lauren hugged him. "I wonder if they know something. I wonder if they've found the video as part of the investigation. They must be scouring Professor P's house and office."

"I told you where he left it."

Lauren massaged her temples with her palms. "I may have to sneak down to Athens and get into his office at the museum. It might get me in trouble with the police for leaving here, but I have to try."

"Everything is a mess, lady."

"I know, and I don't think it's going to get better. I've got to get some sleep first. And then I'm making plans to sneak down there in a few days."

Demo stood in front of her pensively, blocking the door. "It's not even six o'clock. Are you going to sleep now?"

"Can I go in my room, Demo?"

He moved aside. This time he didn't smile.

Two days later, Lauren awoke to a dirge of crying children.

"Oh my God, what now?" she said, hopping out of bed. She put on her bathrobe, white tennis socks and ran downstairs.

Some of the children were in Avtges's office.

"What's wrong? Lauren asked, pulling her hair back.

Avtges held the phone in his hand. "I'm on hold with the police station. No one has seen Demo. I'm trying to reach Inspector Trokalitis to make sure Demo hasn't been confiscated because of . . . the other day."

"They can't do that."

"I beg to differ, Lauren." Avtges held his hand up while he listened on the phone. "Oh yes, inspector. We have lost a boy, Demetrious. Do you know of his whereabouts?"

Mr. Avtges listened on the phone for a moment and then said, "I realize you don't know the children's names but he's the one who fought your policemen the other day, and I thought . . ."

Mr. Avtges went silent for almost a minute. His face changed from an expression of curiosity to shock, and then submission. He slammed the phone down.

"Inspector Trokalitis reports that there is no information on Demo so far." He took a short breath and stared at Lauren. "But . . . he says that you are to be ready. He will be here in a half hour to take you to headquarters for questioning."

The corner of Lauren's lip twitched. She covered it with her hand and dashed upstairs to get ready.

Lauren sat in the backseat.

"Is this your official vehicle?" Lauren asked while inspecting the confines of Trokalitis's aging Citroen.

"Not up to your standards? Is that what you are thinking?"

"I'm just used to seeing black-and-white cars with flashing lights."

"Not black and white? Life is not so cut and dried either, professor."

"How long will it take to get to the station?"

"In a little less than an hour."

Lauren bit her nail. "What can I answer that you haven't already asked?"

Trokalitis shifted to a lower gear driving downhill. "We are not stupid."

Lauren's heart began to pound.

"Have you even been in a Greek jail?" he asked.

"I've had no reason to."

Trokalitis lit a cigarette. "I will keep the window open if you prefer."

Incredulous, Lauren said, "It *is* December."

"Just a crack then," he said before puffing and blowing smoke out the window. "Greek inmates are not pampered like in America. The food is atrocious. You sleep in a hall with other women, hard women, many from other countries."

Trokalitis coughed and cleared his throat. "The courts are overtasked, funds meager, delays in hearings are . . . frustrating." He took another long drag and exhaled it into the car this time.

"Of course, there are many assaults in prison by other women, who prefer women of the feminine sort, and by the guards themselves."

Lauren shivered. She wrapped her arms over her shoulders.

"We do the best we can to police the inmates, but with the shortage of funds, we cannot prevent everything." Trokalitis put the cigarette in the ashtray holder. "Of course you can petition your embassy. I'm sure they'll be able to send the cavalry to rescue you in time, if that is your fate."

He downshifted and negotiated a curve in the mountain road. Clouds obscured the heights of Parnassus and filled the valleys coming down from the peaks.

"You're trying to scare me," Lauren said.

"Scare you," he laughed. "I'm explaining reality to you." The car turned off the main road to Lavadia, past modern apartment buildings, and then uphill. "When will you tell me the truth?"

"I have."

"You lie and I hold your future in my hands."

Lauren's hands began to shake.

"You have quite the dilemma. You want the girl and you need to stay out of jail." He drove the car toward a small house overlooking a sharp gorge. "What will you do to stay out of jail?"

"What do you mean?"

Trokalitis held up a folded piece of paper, bearing a stamped seal. "This is a warrant for your arrest."

Lauren gasped. The car stopped in front of a two-story house. She said, "I thought...we were going to headquarters." The house was on an isolated road, obscured by trees, but with a clear view of a valley.

"We will, all in good time." He took another drag of his cigarette.

"What do you want with me?"

"You withhold the truth from me." He raised his voice. "This has caused me a lot of trouble. I'm expected to solve the murder of the professor." Trokalitis turned toward Lauren. "I think you can provide me some relaxation from the misery you have brought upon me."

"This isn't my fault."

"Ah, but it is. I spent three months searching for you and your lost husband. You show up just as the professor from Athens is murdered. So does this kidnapper. You are involved." He waved the warrant in her face. "It's time to discuss your options."

Lauren recoiled in the backseat. "Do you want sex, like I'm some kind of whore?"

He smiled. "I have the utmost respect for you, but you must discard your emotions and think logically, professor." Then Trokalitis sneered. "This is not America. You are at my mercy. You can make this easy, or make it desperately hard."

Lauren blinked repeatedly. She zipped her parka all the way up.

"How important is this girl to you?" he asked, not looking at her.

Trokalitis squeezed out of his driver's side door. He opened Lauren's door. "Come of your own free will. Should your entertainment prove acceptable, even spirited, then I will withhold the arrest."

Lauren's eyes welled. "What you're suggesting is reprehensible."

"It's your choice. You must decide what is important."

"What guarantees do I have?" Lauren breathed fast in and out.

"There are no guarantees in life, but there is, and excuse my Latin, quid pro quo."

He beckoned with his hand. "I'm out of time, freedom or jail?"

Trokalitis held the car keys up and dropped his cigarette on the gravel driveway. He ground the butt with his loafer.

Lauren closed her eyes. Where was Zack to help her? Where was Apollo to get her out of this? She recalled the dream. Apollo told them they must fight and that Cassandra must be secured. That meant maybe she had a more important role in the future. She didn't know what to do.

She didn't know what she could do. She had to buy time.

Lauren shook her head and got out of the car.

From the corner of her eye, she saw Trokalitis pop a breath mint.

What the hell am I doing?

Trokalitis opened the apartment door for her. Stairs led to a second floor. Lauren glanced at Trokalitis and walked past him. She ascended the stairs and knew he studied her. The second floor smelled like stale cigarettes. The living room looked furnished with poorly maintained leftovers. Lauren walked to a window offering a clear view of olive groves filling the hillside. A heater already warmed the room.

That meant that he had planned this.

She didn't know whether to stand, sit, or *run*. If she ran, the warrant for her arrest would come quickly. Then she would be a real suspect. She could swing at him, but that would result in jail, too. She had been snared. He had created the perfect power play.

"May I pour you ouzo?" he asked, moving to a table that served as a bar. A few of the glasses beside the bottles of liquor were turned over and looked unwashed. He picked two off to the side and held them up to the sunlight. "An ice cube or two makes it just right."

Lauren folded her arms. "You have me at a severe disadvantage. What do you expect me to do?"

Trokalitis took a sip of the drink. "A confrontational attitude will not suffice. Be grateful I am offering you the opportunity to straighten out your...situation. At the very least you will have more time to tell me the truth and clear your name. The girl may be a different matter."

He sat on the couch.

Lauren moved one leg in front of the other, then back again. "She's scared. We are not objects for your amusement. Do you have a family?"

He smacked the glass down on the lamp table next to the couch. Then he took a deep breath and let it out slowly, in an obvious attempt to calm his temper. "You are a professor of ancient languages, not psychology. It will be of no use to change the subject."

Lauren recalculated. She wondered if she should be bold or meek. She wasn't sure what would work. She might have to make a dash for it.

"Come closer," he crooned and took another sip of the ouzo.

She froze.

This can't be happening. When I was in the tent with that monster, all I had to do was fight, just for me. Now I have to worry about Cassandra. What the hell am I going to do? Is this a test? Is this Apollo's test?

"Make this easy on yourself. You Americans are all so pure. Puritans," he laughed. "This is the dance between man and woman. I have something you want . . . and you have something I want."

"I'm a married woman. I can't do this."

"Married? Ha. I doubt it. That won't work." He tinkled the ice in his glass. The ouzo turned cloudy. "Come closer now, or the deal is off. Make your choice."

Lauren rolled her eyes. The situation was beyond belief.

She took a step forward.

"There now, was that so hard?"

"I don't know what you want. How do you expect me to—?"

He blared, "Enough of the innocent act. You know how to please a man. Get on with it."

Lauren closed her eyes and gritted her teeth.

"If you don't know what to do, then I will command you."

Her lips trembled. She felt shivers.

"Remove your clothing, down to your panties."

"What?"

"You heard me. Come closer. Don't make me angry."

Lauren let out a breath of resignation. She had to think.

She took her parka off and dropped it on the floor. Slowly, the sweatshirt came next. Lauren brushed strands of hair away from her face. She stood before him in jeans and a red blouse.

"The blouse you are wearing, professor." He eased back on the couch and opened his legs. "I see you are wearing a bra, how wonderfully chaste." He motioned with his free hand for her to get going.

She unbuttoned her blouse and hesitated. Finally, Lauren slipped it off her shoulders and let it hang from one hand. Then she dropped the blouse on the floor.

The room became suddenly cold. She shifted her feet and ballooned out a breath.

Trokalitis sat up straight. "Closer now, it is not enough just to be beautiful. There is more to being a real woman."

Lauren grimaced.

"Do not feel so sorry for yourself." He sipped on the ouzo. "A woman knows her role in this world. There will be a time when you have the advantage." He spun the ice cubes in the glass. "But that time is not now. Jail is your fate and the girl disappears into the system, maybe the favorite of some guard hired from the Balkans."

Lauren shut her eyes, her face, neck, and arms suddenly burning.

"Now," he demanded. "Decide. I'm losing my patience."

Lauren turned slightly to see if the path was clear for her to run. She turned back and saw Trokalitis holding the glass with one hand, and the warrant in the other. His smirk spoke of the unquestioned exercise of power.

She reached behind and unhooked her bra.

She held the cups with both of her hands. She couldn't look at him.

"Drop it," he demanded, like she was a dog with a sock.

He froze for a moment. Then he uttered in a slow cadence, "Magni-fi-cent."

Lauren stood with her arms by her sides. She asked, "Is this enough? Is this enough to make you happy?"

Trokalitis snickered. "Come now, professor, every woman of maturity goes bare-breasted on the beaches in Greece. Surely you have gone naked on our islands. All tourists do."

This is going to be horrible. The image of Cassandra sitting in some cell staring at a male guard . . .

"The jeans are next and I want you to turn back around as they come off."

She slid the jeans past her hips and down her legs. Her panties caught on the button and were pulled down her leg. From behind, she heard him gasp.

"Turn now, and kick those off."

Help me, Zack, help me get through this. Help me save our future. Help me save Cassandra. Is this my sacrifice?

She ran her fingers under the elastic rim of her white panties. She slid them down just a fraction and stopped.

Trokalitis unbuckled his pants and frantically slid them down to his ankles.

Lauren cringed. She folded and unfolded her hands. *How can I rescue her from a jail cell?*

"Women in the American movies are not so shy."

"I'm not one of those women."

"How long do you want to stay here?" Trokalitis curled his lips. "Enough of your drama."

Lauren could see he'd risen. *God, no, he's not going to ask me to . . .*

"I'm waiting. It's not so difficult after all."

"I can't do . . . that."

He held out his hand. "Come here and get on your knees. Do not delay."

She turned away from the sight of him. *How many guards will I have to fight off in jail? They'll overwhelm me . . . and Cassandra. We'll be raped.*

"Satisfy me now, or we walk out the door."

He looked at himself and then at her. "You have never been with a Greek man."

Lauren sobbed, "Is there something else you want, please."

"To gaze at you a bit longer and then I want you to come here."

Lauren didn't move.

Trokalitis breathed hard, like a locomotive gathering steam. His legs twitched. "Yes, you are long and lean."

She pulled up her panties, walked over to him, and kneeled.

He bared his teeth. "I feel sorry for your dead husband."

She blared, "You bastard."

"No need to be angry. You are a sight, is all I am saying. Now, no more delays."

"I mean, you've seen me without my clothes. You can easily get a girl to satisfy you."

"No, enough talk. I'm ready. Enthusiastically, or the deal is over."

The floorboards were unforgiving on the uneven bones of her knees.

"Screw the deal, you bastard." Lauren rose. She pointed a finger in his face. "You're drunk with power. To hell with you." She picked up her jeans and threw them in his face. "I'm not your whore."

He brushed the jeans away from him. He tried to rise but his underwear and pants hindered him. Sneering, he spit out, "Then you will suffer the consequences."

This is dangerous.

"Look, I have something better than . . . than sex." She stepped toward him. "I can lead you to so much money you'll be able to afford the highest-priced call girls. They'll do anything you want. Leave me my dignity, please."

"What do you mean?"

"Seriously, wouldn't you be happier with money? Real wealth, more than you could ever imagine."

Lauren wondered what she looked like standing across from this bastard. Nearly naked and desperate, she constituted a perfect pawn for this guy. He had to take the bait or she'd have to kick his lights out.

"Be more specific, professor. Did you discover something?" He started pulling up his underwear.

"You won't believe it, I promise you."

The inspector looked down at his crotch. A smile spread over his face. "Finish me first." He picked up the warrant and waved it at her.

"Put it away, inspector, along with your warrant. Let's make a business deal instead."

He bared his canines.

She grabbed her jeans and walked to where her blouse lay on the floor.

"Come back here or you'll regret it." His tone bugled anger.

Lauren halted. She turned and said, seething, "You'll get nothing else from me, no matter what you threaten me with." She pushed one leg through her jeans.

Trokalitis scrunched his lips together and appeared ready to burst.

Then his cell phone rang. He scrambled for it.

"Yes," Trokalitis said. After listening for half a minute, a smile broke across his face.

He said into the phone, "Good work. Yes, I'll be in the office right away. Hold him there."

Lauren sensed something had changed, something was wrong. "Let me make a call back to the orphanage. I'll do my best . . . to help you. Empty my accounts."

"It's bold and so very foolish to suggest bribing an official."

She waved her hand at his apartment. "It's a time to be bold. I can change all this for you, for the better. I can arrange it, and no one will know."

Trokalitis pursed his lips, ruminating. "Dress and be quick."

He watched Lauren button her jeans. "It's not over for you. You'll have another opportunity to please me, and next time, your performance will need to be far more exotic if you are to stay out of jail. And no one will know about this or you will be buried in our system or worse. Got it?"

Lauren put on her clothes like she was late for work.

"I'll return you to the orphanage. You've been saved by a phone call. We have to go."

"What happened?" she asked.

"Something that's really quite astounding, actually."

Arriving at the car, Lauren slid into the backseat and snapped her seat belt on, folded her arms, and prepared for an icy return trip. "I'm sorry," she said before he started the engine.

He didn't respond.

"Greek men are generous and compassionate. Decency, inspector, that's what being a real Greek man is."

His eyebrows narrowed in the rearview mirror.

Lauren thought that something was wrong. She knew it. This just wasn't working.

"Shut up, professor. I'm not finished with you. You suppose everything, and soon you'll find out just how little you really know."

PART III

22

Plataea, Greece

SEPTEMBER 479 BC

Raids by Persian cavalry on Greek supply lines and water sources left the allies hungry, thirsty, and hot-tempered. Zack scratched at the skin under his arms and near his groin, chafed and irritated by long days wearing bronze armor in the soaring temperatures. The Asopus River, lying in the valley bisecting the rolling hills and plains outside the town of Plataea, might as well have been in Siberia.

None of the allies could drink from it.

The Persian cavalry's hit-and-run tactics posed a serious threat to the allied army consisting mostly of heavily armed hoplites and small units of archers. They had no cavalry and therefore nothing to counter the volleys of arrows that brought casualties to their ranks, and frustration as the horsemen raced away when threatened. The Persian tactics had caused the Greeks, under the command of the young Spartan general Pausanias, to move their position into the hills and areas more protected from the missile attacks and outright charges by thousands of horsemen.

Zack leaned on his spear with two hands, wondering when the next attack would be. His bronze helmet absorbed the sun's intensity and his head felt like it sat inside an oven. He lifted the helmet off to cool his face.

"I have never seen so many hoplites," Diomedes said, wiping his forehead with a rag. Zack didn't comment but recognized, as a professor of history, that this truly was uncharted territory for the Greek city-states, whose wars against each other might only total a few thousand men each. No Greek commander had ever encountered the logistical needs for food, water, supplies, armaments, and tactics necessary for an army of forty thousand warriors. The Persian army opposing them totaled around about seventy thousand warriors, with ten thousand or more cavalry. A huge wooden stockade had been built near the city of Thebes to give protection to the Persian army. Mardonius commanded a well-supplied and rested army of elite forces left by Xerxes to complete the conquest of the Greeks.

"How is it possible to move all these men and keep them in proper lines?" Diomedes asked with an irritated tone. "Horns and flags will not keep order when dust fills the air. We cannot come down from these hills onto the plain before us. We'll be cut to pieces. Look there now." He pointed to a unit of hoplites that had stopped in the middle of a field, isolated and looking lost. "Are battles fought in your land with such hosts of men?"

"They are," Zack answered. "That is why each commander is trained to think for himself, because few battles follow the plans that are drawn up in advance. Changes will be necessary and you cannot count on getting an order from your general."

"You have told me that you did not fight in any wars, yet you understand the tactics of warriors?"

Hey, I watched a few movies in my time.

Horns and drums drowned out the hum of insects tormenting the warriors. Each man straightened himself and pulled down the helmet over his face. In the distance the battle cries of the Persians were heard, despite the muffling effect of the bowl helmets.

"Form up and be quick," Diomedes shouted with his helmet still set high on his forehead. "By the gods, there are more horsemen each time. Who are those lads caught out in the open?"

"They look to be Megarians," a man cried out. "Here come the barbarians. Signal those hoplites. They can't see them."

A mass of horsemen rode over the wooded hills, through the shallow river, and attacked the stranded unit with missiles. From a distance, shiny metal reflected from a lone rider at the head of the cavalry. Hoplites fell under the onslaught of arrows, causing gaps in their lines. When the hoplites could condense their lines and move forward, the Persians retreated, loosening more missiles at them.

Diomedes swore. "I cannot watch the slaughter of these men. March toward their standard, right now."

Two thousand men in two lines moved down the hillside, marching double time.

Another charge of the Persians brought more losses to the Megarian hoplites.

"Look at their leader, Zack," Diomedes shouted over the war cries of his men, pointing at the Persians. "He looks like a gold ingot on horseback. Wait, his horse is armored, too."

Crap, I know what's going to happen here.

Athenian archers sent by Pausanias ran forward to counter the missiles of the Persian cavalry. The Persians retreated to build another assault when the Athenians arrived and deployed their ranks behind the Megarian hoplites. Zack, in the front line of Diomedes's Mycenaeans, ran with his unit to help the Megarian hoplites. Blood pounded in his ears. Shouts erupted from the allies. His arms and legs did not tire. All the months of training with sixty pounds of equipment on him finally bore fruit.

"Here they come, run faster," Diomedes ordered.

Battle cries and rams' horns signaled the next assault. The Persian golden knight drove his horsemen forward to cast javelins and darts at the Greeks. The Athenian archers drew back their bows and fired. Their arrows dropped Persian horsemen, but those shot at the golden warrior bounced harmlessly off the rider, covered head to toe in gold scales. He rode a big charger, armored and elaborately decorated in gold as well.

"What gods protect this warrior? We can't pierce him," the Athenian captain complained. The Persian horsemen let loose a final volley, but an

Athenian archer behind the lines shot an arrow that hit the horse in a spot where the gold scales flew up when it turned.

The horse threw its owner. The Persian horsemen didn't see their leader fall and raced away to gather another charge.

Zack's unit finally reached the Megarians and locked shields with them. Cheers erupted among the ranks. The Greek allies moved together at double pace to reach the golden knight. The Greeks swarmed over him while he lay stunned by the throw and unable to rise under the weight of his armor. Lances bounced off the fallen knight. The Greek warriors screamed their frustration. The Persian squirmed and attempted to get to his knees. The Greeks knocked him back down, but no one could penetrate the body armor. In the distance, the Persians had just noticed their commander had fallen. They milled about, leaderless, stunned by the loss of their hero.

An Athenian archer withdrew an arrow and cradled the golden knight's helmet in an arm. He drove the thin iron point through the eye slit. The Persian screamed. The Athenian stabbed him repeatedly, until he could finally drive the point of the arrow far into the eye socket. The archer twisted the arrow. Blood poured from the eye slits. Spasms followed and the screams ended. The Persians watched from a distance. A great wail rose up in their ranks, but it fast turned to fury.

Zack dug a hole with his heel, as did others. The attack did not take long to coalesce. Squadrons streamed across the undulating terrain.

Diomedes bellowed to his men, "Hold now and brace your feet."

Thunder shook the ground. The horsemen crashed into the wall of shields. Zack was thrown backward against the ranks behind him, amid the chaos of horses and men, iron and bronze. He lay on his back. He couldn't turn or sit up. Spears bounced off his shield. He kicked at horse hooves. He decided to roll, keeping his shield over his body. Slowly, the hoplites regained their feet, locking shields.

The Spartans saw the Persian attack and closed in. The Persians, frustrated, unable to retrieve the body, retreated. They rode away before the Spartans arrived, shaking their fists.

The allies hoisted the gold warrior corpse atop a cart. Greek warriors disassembled the suit of gold. Each piece, removed with difficulty, was held aloft, eliciting more cheers. Finally the corpse was stripped. Hoplites craned their necks to see the tall handsomely built Persian who had caused so much havoc. The corpse was hauled through the lines of hoplites so they wouldn't have to break rank to see the trophy. When it passed by Zack, he could only imagine the horrible death this man met. This was the famous Masistius, a commander in the Persian army, ,and a most highly regarded warrior. The historian, Herodotus, had reported this event. His corpse was whole and unmarked by sword or spear thrusts. The stream of blood that ran from his eye was the only evidence that he was slain.

At Thermopylae, Zack felt disgusted by the brutality of war.

No more. Survival was at stake. He would have to kill to survive.

The Greek line consisted of Athenians on the left, Spartans on the right, and the middle formed of smaller city-states, though separated by terrain. Zack saw Diomedes nursing a sword slice on his wrist. Each warrior carried a kit bag that contained enough cloth bandages to bind the inevitable nonlethal wounds. Diomedes wrapped the cloth tightly around the wound. He pinched into it a square bronze ligature that had curved teeth on the underside. Then he heated glue normally used to keep the leather grip from unraveling on his spear shaft.

"How do you fare?" Diomedes asked, swabbing the glue over the wrap.

"Nary a cut, a few bruises." It was true. The three-foot shield Zack carried had taken the blows.

"I think they are done for now. They don't want to tangle with the Spartans," Diomedes said, checking his line of men. "On your backsides," he shouted to his line of hoplites. "Rest while we wait to see if the barbarians dare return."

For another week the cat and mouse games continued. The Greeks were not willing to attack, nor the Persians to commit their infantry in all-out assault. Zack knew the day of battle neared. The accounts of the Battle of Plataea told of a long wait before the climatic clash that decided the future of Greece, but more ultimately the future of Western civilization. Would culture be Persian or Greek? The Greeks fought for their survival and their way of life. They had no idea, in a larger sense, what was at stake.

There were more reports of treason among the allies, offers of bribes from the Persians to split city-states. Zack guarded every word he spoke with Diomedes and others. His presence here was an aberration of history and he would not interfere with its eventual course. Yet each day he felt more like a man of these times. He sat by a fire and observed. A man nearby groaned, then ran to the slit trenches that served as latrines. Illnesses were beginning to take a toll on the hoplites. The evenings were cooler and the days still charged with overbearing heat. Dysentery plagued armies from the ancient to the modern world. A warrior could only hope that his life was not taken by disease before he could gain honor in battle. Many stared into the licking flames. Did they sense that the morning might bring the final battle? No one spoke, and only the sharpening of weapons on the stones could be heard.

"Up now, we move," Diomedes ordered. Grumbling from the ranks erupted. The hoplites complained of marching in the dark.

"Where do we go now?" Zack asked.

"A runner just arrived from Pausanias. We must join the lines. Where they are in this cursed darkness, only the gods know. Stay close to the man in front, all of you, and point your lances at the stars. We needn't make the Persian work too easy."

Metal clanked and warriors swore when they fell on the hillsides or crashed into their neighbors. They wandered for an hour.

"Hold here," Diomedes said. "Relay the word down the line to strap tongues and wrap their shields with their cloaks. The Persians will hear us back in their cursed camp, and their horseman will attack us at first light. Quiet now."

Zack tripped over the man in front of him and his bronze rang. He heard a groan from Diomedes.

"Do they teach you to walk in Atlantea? You're a clod."

Zack laughed, quietly.

"Do you think I'm some cat with yellow eyes that can pierce the darkness?" Zack answered.

"You could not be a cat because you move more like an ox! Now glue your lips together or I will stick you."

"After we slay the Persians, I am personally going to kick your ass all the way to Corinth," Zack whispered. He saw the flash of Diomedes's white teeth, even in the darkness."

"You have my pledge that you will have such a chance. We will call out the city, and offer a display of arms to our citizens. Like Hector and Achilles before Troy."

"Then you are sure of victory in the battle ahead, Diomedes?" Zack asked. He had seen these men of ancient times in three critical battles now: Thermopylae, Salamis, and now, Plataea.

"Atlantean, have you no confidence in your gods? Remember how we killed so many at the Hot Gates?"

Zack said into his ear, "Could it not be that the deeds of men are of their own doing and are the result of their free will?"

Diomedes halted the march. Zack heard collisions in the dark behind them. He asked Diomedes, "Are the gods responsible for everything?"

"You must be a philosopher or a fool, questioning the veracity of the gods, even before battle when all men talk to them in earnest. You must come from a strange people. I'll have to discuss the gods with you later. We shall move again and seek the Athenians. They must be to the west."

It was clear to Zack they were lost. They heard voices and followed the sounds to no avail. The word was passed to halt when they reached a temple.

"You see, brother Zack, the gods have guided us to this place," Diomedes assured him. "To which god this temple is dedicated I do not know, but I will take this as a sign to stop here. I will not exhaust the men any longer, or I will have them falling in the ranks tomorrow. Helios will guide us then."

The warriors gathered before the small stone structure, taking an hour or so to find the lost. They slumped to the ground on bedrolls, consisting of no more than a cloak spread underneath and their pack stuffed under their heads for a pillow. With arms laid nearby, they slept in their armor.

When Diomedes had finished with the arrangement of units, he returned and settled himself next to Zack.

"I have Mycenaeans mixed with Corinthians, and Achaians with Arcadians. It will take time to organize them at dawn. Stragglers still arrive, telling us of others lost out there. Pausanias has made a mess of us, but I see the sense of what he orders. We cannot move during the day; the Persian cavalry will surround us in the open and cut us down. Already their shafts cause so much misery. Many warriors have left their lives on the banks of the Asopus and in the fields, and we have yet to strike a blow."

"How many warriors do we have?" Zack asked, already knowing the answer.

"Almost eleven thousand under my command, another seven thousand Megarians, and others that make up the left center. We are to combine and fill the gap between the Athenians and the Spartans, if we are not too far apart when the fighting begins. The Persians search for an opportunity to catch us separated in the valleys between ridges."

"I don't think we should be so hard on Pausanias," Zack pointed out. "What Greek general has ever commanded so many Greeks?"

"Your words are true. Never have the warriors of Hellas ever been united as now. The barbarians command great armies and are prepared for such numbers. We are not."

Diomedes lay down and clasped his hands behind his head.

"This is easy to see by the look on the faces of the hoplites. Food is gone and water taken away from us by their horsemen. Maybe I should not be so certain of our fortune." He made a long sigh. "The army cannot exist as it is for much longer. If we splinter, defeat will follow. Should we attack and venture from defensible land, their cavalry and numbers would flow around like an island sitting in a great river."

Timing is everything, Zack thought. *My stockbroker never thought so. The worries of my era are so far away.* "But the gods are on your side, Diomedes."

"You wish to continue our discussion?"

"Belief in the gods is a matter of faith; for any gods, among any nation of men. Where there is faith, there is confidence for the well-intentioned."

"Wise words you have spoken, brother Zack. Ask me if I have faith that you will return with me to our fair city on the mount? I pray to all the gods that you will."

"I have thought on this." Zack hesitated, weighing his decision for conviction. "I believe I will return with you. You have made a warrior of me. I owe you much gratitude."

Diomedes rested a reassuring hand on Zack's shoulder. "Don't dwell on that. Fill my mother with joy. Truly, become one of us. Join our bloodlines. She would bear you an heir, someone who will take over for me when the three sisters cut my twine. You have a home, if you desire it and the gods are willing."

"I still have a wife. I will not let her go."

"Nor will I," Diomedes mumbled.

"What did you say?"

"I said, if it is the will of the gods," Diomedes replied, laying his head back down to look at the stars, "we will see Lady Lauren again."

"I can only pray."

It was too dark for Diomedes to see Zack's face. "Tomorrow, the field of battle will be strewn with the slain. If you fall, how will I let Lauren know that fate has claimed you?"

"That will not be easy to do," Zack replied with a touch of sadness in his tone. "You would not be able to find her in Atlantea, even if you survived the journey at sea."

"How could this be? How many days must I sail to the west to find her?"

"Diomedes, you don't understand."

"Tell me now," Diomedes insisted. "The gods may not lend us a chance tomorrow. Tyche and the three sisters of fate may tug at my arm, or maybe at yours." Zack exhaled.

"You would need a broad, keeled ship to weather the seas. It would take more than thirty suns. The winds would have to be in your favor and that is only when the leaves fall. It is a voyage only an experienced mariner could survive."

Diomedes fired back. "You don't want to tell me how to reach her, do you?"

"It's not that."

Diomedes raised his voice, "I want to know. If you fall, I must reach her."

Zack shook his head. "To the west, beyond the pillars of Heracles, a long month at sea, and even then, you might land on islands with barbarians instead of Atlantea."

Diomedes lowered his voice, "I will tell her you died a warrior."

"Don't send me off to Hades yet."

"And if it is the will of the gods?"

"The will of the gods will be seen more clearly when this battle is over. It will be Europe or Asia, slavery for all, or independence and the advance of freedom-thinking men. So much is at stake."

"I had not considered what you have said. I only strive to continue the lives of my people, and in doing so, save Mycenae from ruin. You talk as if you sit up in the clouds with the Olympians and look down upon the earth to render such thoughts to me."

I wish I could tell you.

Zack said, "We should rest while we can. The morning comes quickly, like Hermes with his feet on fire."

Diomedes smacked Zack's arm. Zack rolled, stifling his laughter with his hands.

Then he said seriously, "If you fall Atlantean, I will find Lauren."

Zack replied, "I believe you will."

"And if the battle is tomorrow, do not wander from me, Atlantean. I will keep one eye on the barbarians and my other on you."

"It shall be so, brother, and I on you, too."

23

Plataea, Greece

SEPTEMBER 479 BC

First light brought disaster. From the temple where they bivouacked, Zack and Diomedes could see that the valley before them was not filled with a solid line of the Spartan and Athenian armies. Instead, the Spartans were withdrawing from a ridge on the left and the Athenians sat in an island between two rivers to their right, the distance between them dangerously wide.

"Blue thunder, Zack, we haven't closed the ranks. The Athenians are caught in the open. We must get to them before the Persians see the blunder."

Diomedes roused the contingents. "Arise," he shouted. "All of you hear me. We march at double step to the Spartan lines coming off that ridge. We must fill the center before the Persians split us in two. Hurry now. Keep the ranks."

Zack slid into the dense pack of hoplites quickly forming a line eight men deep. They set off down the hill.

"I thank Hermes I had them sleep in their cuirasses," Diomedes said, raising his spear and pointing it at the Spartans, who looked like a sea of red from the distance of a mile or more. The Athenians were forming their lines but more slowly. Suddenly, the air was split with war cries and the pounding of horse hooves. From across the shallows of the

Asopus River, the Persian cavalry discovered the Spartans on the march and surged to cut them off.

"Oh Tyche, you are a cruel goddess. They have found us out," Diomedes cried out to his men. "Faster!"

Zack felt a surge of adrenalin.

This is what it must have felt like for the Athenians when they ran at the Persians at Marathon. The training, the physical stamina: this is where it pays off.

They moved as a solid wall down the slope from the temple. Divisions of Persian horsemen shot swarms of missiles at the Spartans, who had stopped their withdrawal and crouched behind their great shields which were marked with familiar lambda and designs of snakes and other beasts. Diomedes's face bore a mask of worry.

"We'll have to divide and assist the Spartans and Athenians," Diomedes strained to say. Zack breathed hard and couldn't respond.

Diomedes yelled to an aide, "Runner, go to the Megarians. Tell them to split off from us and help the Athenians. Go!" The messenger, unarmored, flew down the hillside to their right.

"If we're late, Zack . . ." Diomedes said, puffing. Zack could see down the length of the hoplite lines, being taller than they. "You are the glue when we get there, Zack. Don't let the barbarians divide you from the Spartans."

Dust swirled as the Persian horsemen rode back and forth before the Spartans, pelting them with missiles, causing more casualties. Zack saw the Megarians and the other allies section off from his formation to assist the Athenians on the right. When the Megarians were halfway to their destination, they were struck by a sea of horsemen, catching them in the open. The Spartan army dug in. The Persian infantry now followed their horsemen. Tens of thousands crossed the river. They carried wicker shields, short spears, and swords, not in organized lines, but more a swarm of Asian warriors, eager to destroy the Greeks once and for all.

"We must reach them," Diomedes shouted in a more desperate tone. The forces joined, drowning out voices. Zack, with Diomedes just to his left, led his division to the Spartan lines on his right, like a trireme aiming for a dry dock. The Persians saw their attempt to merge the formations and cast javelins and arrows at them.

It finally occurred to Zack: *Oh shit, I really am the glue.*

Plataea, Greece

SEPTEMBER 479 BC

The jeweled princes looked toward the eastern sky, awaiting first light. A dark-robed magi priest scanned the horizon. When the first glimmer appeared, he lit the sacred fire. The magi reached for a golden chalice to make a wine offering to their supreme god, Ahura Mazda, and then began his incantations. Mardonius hauled on the reins of his white Nisean charger. Battle fever encompassed them all. The magi moved too slowly for Mardonius. The wait had been too long. All were eager.

Masistius would have led this attack. The faces of the army are lodged in despair since he perished. I will bring this victory to the king.

Dawn reached the opposing hillsides.

An aide pointed at the ridge directly before them, guarded by the Spartan army the evening before, but now held by only a small remaining unit. "Look, my lord, they flee. The Spartans have abandoned the heights."

"The mighty Spartans. Hah! The entire host of Greeks has taken to their heels," Mardonius yelled, wheeling his charger to view the enemy, and sending the chief magi diving out of his way into the arms of his fellow priests.

"Mazda will have to wait; the opportunity will not," Mardonius said, whacking his horse. "Gather my horsemen and follow me. Encircle them and fire into their ranks. Raise the banners." Mardonius saw faces keen for battle.

En masse they advanced. The cavalry splashed across the river in pursuit of the retreating Greeks, hoping to cut them down. Infantry followed, slowed by the knee-deep water. Mardonius held his golden bridle tight. His charger snorted, lifting its hoofs high. Mardonius raised his spear and directed it toward the enemy. Armored warriors, his bodyguard, and elite Immortals formed a circle around him.

Victory will finally be ours. I can return to the king, proud and victorious. I will atone for the defeat at sea, the sunken ships, and the screams of dying sailors.

The foot soldiers crossed the river, Persians on the left facing the Spartans; Thebans and Greeks allied to Xerxes on the right, opposing the Athenians.

Where is my center? If Artabazus holds his infantry back, we may miss our chance.

Mardonius said, "Rider, go to the Persian commander, Artabazus. Tell him to bring up the center now, or I will wet the ground with his entrails."

The courier slapped his pony and rode back to camp. The Persian cavalry rambled up the ridge, filtered through boulders and trees, then swarmed over the top, only to come upon a solid mass of Spartans.

Mardonius let go a stream of curses.

Behind him he heard the Persian infantry, trumpets blaring and banners furling, announcing their imminent arrival at the battle line.

The attack cannot be halted. His stomach gurgled. Visions of Spartan ruses at the pass where so many of his best warriors were slain distracted him. Mardonius directed, "Send missiles into them, wait for the infantry."

The battalions of cavalry rode up toward the Spartans, drew bows, and shot arrows into a dense packing of hoplites crouched behind shields. The air sang with the continuous rip and ricochet of the shafts. Mardonius sneered, satisfied that the missiles would hold the Greeks in place until his infantry could close in. Thousands more horsemen joined the barrage, raining death upon the Spartan ranks. So many hooves beat the dirt that swirls of dust screened sections of the battlefield. He had seen the Theban infantry attack on the Athenians to his left.

My battle plan goes well. Now we will soften that shield wall, and when the time is right, we will smash them with infantry and strike them from the sides with my Bactrian horsemen. Where is Artabazus?

An aide shouted, "My lord, the Greek center has joined the battle. The fools divide their strength, one section to aid the Athenians, the other sliding toward the Spartans before us. We can cut them down in the open."

Mardonius replied, "Mazda be praised, send half my horsemen to attack that small band heading to the Athenians. Keep the others here to shower the Spartans."

Horsemen fell upon the Greeks, smashing into them and thwarting their attempt to merge with the Athenian lines. The other half of the Greek formation escaped in the hope to bridge the gap with the Spartans.

"My lord, they're closing the line." the same aide said, his horse foaming, turning in circles around Mardonius.

"Attack them," Mardonius answered. "Hold them apart till Artabazus can bring the center up and finish them. Where can he be?"

"I know not, lord, but the time is now. We have them."

Squadrons of Persian horses charged toward the oncoming Greeks. They sent a shower of arrows at the Greeks, who raised their shields while running toward the Spartan lines.

The Persian infantry streamed past Mardonius, taking positions a short distance from the Spartans. The Immortals set up a dense shield wall of wicker in front of his cavalry.

Why do the Spartans wait? Are they fearful?

The battle cries of his army filled the air. Finally they would fight together, the whole army, in one battle. Mardonius lived for this moment. He heard cheers to his left. The Athenian swine must be feeling the sting of his infantry.

I will be satrap of Greece when I conquer them. My lord king will reward me with Europe. I will march the combined armies to the west. The Carthaginians speak of lands of wonder, fields of grain in Sicilia, seaside cities in Italia, and forests to the north and west, the riches of Africa. I will be the most favored of the king.

General Hydarnes, leader of the Immortals, asked him, "My lord, the horsemen cannot stop the Greeks from joining. Shall I send in the infantry?"

Mardonius flexed his jaw muscles. He would not start the battle at the shield wall until all his warriors were in position. He turned his head and did not see the approach of Artabazus. The Greeks closed the gap. His horsemen receded, shooting darts at the point where the enemy welded their shields together. A giant stood among the Greeks, bridging the Spartans on the right to the force that had just arrived.

"See that giant," Mardonius pointed at the seam. "When we attack, gather your bravest warriors and strike there. Slay that giant and drive a wedge between them. I will ride my horsemen through the breech and we will conquer. Until then, pass the word: close the ranks, ready your spears, and send them all to their Greek hell."

A vision of the Bactrian commander, his own giant, flashed into his thoughts. He shook his head, wondering what had happened to the smelly savage. He disappeared on the road to the temple mountain. He would be useful now. His axe would break that line.

He refocused on the struggle before him. Clumps of Greek hoplites lay before their lines, pinpricked with arrow shafts. The Spartans cowered.

"Gather here," he cried out to his elite warriors. "Not one of the Greeks is to be spared. Do you hear me? This is the only race of men that can stand in our way."

Mardonius shouted louder, "All will kiss the feet of the king. Trample them under our hooves. Destroy the Spartans here and now. Remove their memory from the records of civilized men."

The face of the dead Spartan king disrupted his thoughts.

"My lord?" his aide inquired. "Shall we attack now?"

From the dense packing of red horsehair-crested, helmeted Spartans, a call of bugles and flutes sounded. The shields were brought higher and as one, and they rose. Spears of the front rank were leveled. Missiles hit and fell away, a continuous song of metal upon metal.

Mardonius could not remove the Spartan king's severed head from his thoughts. The lifeless eyes haunted him, the darkness of them.

Mardonius shook his lance at the giant next to the Spartans, his height breaking the evenness of the line, standing like a beacon on a mountain.

You will surely die, giant. I will kill you myself. More glory will be mine.
Then the voices of the enemy army drowned out his own.

"Where is Artabazus?" he screamed at his officers beside him. "We cannot wait. Form my horsemen into a wedge and aim for the giant."

Then, a roar unlike any other drowned out all other sounds.

Momentarily, he saw himself as a boy, sent out to kill a lion, a rite of passage to manhood. He crept up upon a den. If he could slay more than one, great honor would be his, above all the other princes.

The Spartans cried out—the same "Ha!" he had heard at Thermopylae. Mardonius saw rows of spears.

They're coming. Not a few as then, but so many this time. I see too many red cloaks.

He remembered suddenly: he slew one lion back then, and wounded another, before he ran.

The moment is now.

Mardonius shouted, "Attack."

The Persian infantry parted. Dust billowed. Hooves pounded the short distance between the lines. A stampede of infantry followed. The Persian horsemen, shaking spears and axes, set a direct course for the overgrown hoplite.

25

Delphi, Greece

PRESENT DAY

No more words had been spoken in the car. Trokalitis dropped Lauren off at the orphanage with warnings on her silence. Muted sounds of sobbing reached her ears when she walked up the steps to the second floor. The children raced from their beds toward Lauren. Mr. Avtges sat in a chair in the middle of the long rows of beds, his eyes narrowed.

"What happened?" Lauren cradled the heads of the younger ones with her palms.

"Demo has been arrested."

"What? Not him!" Lauren's knees buckled. The children braced her from falling.

"He was found in the National Museum after hours, hiding in the dead professor's office. A guard heard noises coming from the room. He found Demo making a mess of the late professor's bookshelf," Mr. Avtges said, his forehead glistening under the lightbulb.

"Why would he . . ." Lauren swallowed three times.

"Do you have anything to do with this?" Avtges asked. His lips were tightly drawn, his gaze unwavering.

"I told him some time ago that I knew Professor Papandreou and that Zack and I had left something in his office, but I never asked Demo to get it."

Avtges waved his hands. "You have to be careful with my children and what you say to them." The little ones started to cry again. Avtges led them back to their beds, assuring them all would be fine. When all were tucked in, Avtges motioned for her to come downstairs.

"I'm so sorry," Lauren blurted out. "I'm not sure what I'm doing. Everything is so out of control. I can't trust anyone but you." She latched onto him, her breathing life preserver. "My family can't help me, even the embassy seems powerless. I've lost Cassandra and now Demo, too." Her voice cracked.

"I don't know how to help you," he said, holding her at arm's length. "There is such corruption everywhere. I know you are honest, but you have embroiled yourself in something only lawyers can straighten out."

"I can't bear they've been taken from us."

"It breaks my heart. Demo is special. I've watched him mature."

"I know, I know." Lauren wagged her head up and down. "He looks up at you with those big eyes that you can barely see with his hair so long and frazzled."

Avtges hugged her, saying, "How do I get him out of jail?"

"How can you get us both out of jail?" Lauren asked, sniffing a few times.

"The police arrived while you were gone. They had a warrant to search your room. I had to let them in. I don't know . . . if they found anything."

"There's nothing up there to find." *Thank my lucky stars I kept Zack's letters and any of Nestor's treasure back in the cave.*

It was Wednesday night. She wished she had a knife that could just cut this day out of the calendar. She looked in the mirror. Dark circles had taken residence under her eyes. Trokalitis terrified her. He had the power of the law behind him. She had parried his advances this time. Could she fight him off again? Veins pulsed on the side of her forehead.

Reeking of cigarette smoke and reeling with the disgusting memory of Trokalitis's touch, Lauren headed to the shower.

Maybe she should have gone ahead with Trokalitis. Maybe it would be a bargaining chip for the next disaster. Now both children were held.

What would she have to do to get them both back? She pictured their terrified faces. She wondered if she could sleep at all. She had to get rest, with important calls to make in the morning, and whatever else they could throw at her.

Lauren was out of her league, way out.

In the morning, the conversation wasn't going too well.

She called Samaras as promised, talking quietly so Mr. Avtges couldn't overhear her. She laid out what she wanted: a signed release from the investigation of Zack's disappearance by Inspector Trokalitis, the police, or whoever had jurisdiction. Then, she wanted legal custody of the children in Greece while she waited to go through the adoption process, and any record of Demetrious's arrest removed. In return, she offered portions of Nestor's treasure. She didn't tell him about everything she had. She mentioned coins, gold sticks, and gems, but not how many. Samaras didn't seem too excited by the offer.

Samaras laughed a long time. Then, he coughed for half a minute.

"I have to stop smoking," he said when he could breathe again. "Do you know what the penalty is for black market antiquities?" he asked coldly.

"This is a proposal, sir. That is all, at the moment. I want to know if you can grease the wheels, so to speak. I know the penalty is probably very stiff."

"Stiff! Stiff is what you'll get nightly from the prison guards, over many years while your beauty holds, and maybe even afterwards."

"I've gone out on a limb here, sir, and there's no need to be crude. If you think it won't work, then we'll forget it. I gave you twenty thousand. I'm offering you a hell of a lot more to make this happen fast, with legal results."

"Do you think I am some god who can hurl a thunderbolt and force everyone to do my bidding? Negotiations are done carefully, over time."

Lauren raised her voice. "There is no more time." She looked at the door, expecting to see Mr. Avtges barging in, asking what's wrong. She returned to the phone. "Let me tell you again, you won't believe your eyes. You know how to move these coins. I may be American and ignorant, but I know money talks in any language, given enough of it. If we make the deal, I know you'll be happy. If not, and I go . . ."

"Professor, I will make inquiries. I will let you know. Let us say the offer is tempting. There are risks for everyone. I will call you back in two hours. Do you have a sample, so I can see that you are able to keep your word?"

"I've buried a small sack of them. I'll give you the location when you agree to go ahead."

"Professor, why do you trust me so?"

"You said I had to."

"The world is not a trustworthy place."

"The ancient Greeks searched for truth. Didn't Socrates strive to get to the core of what it meant to live a just life? He said for men to be happy they must be good to each other."

"You attempt to teach a Greek about his past."

"I'm desperate." Lauren didn't know what tack to take. You can't bullshit a bull-shitter. She knew that.

"Await my call." He hung up.

Lauren twisted her neck, trying to snap it like a chiropractor would. She looked at her shaking hands. Even with the tremors, she could see the skin was cracked. They were a mess, and a lot else at the moment was, too.

By late morning, she was on the phone again. Mr. Avtges complained that he couldn't get any work done with all the calls coming in. Lauren apologized. He left with shoulders sagging, shaking his head.

Samaras talked fast. He said he'd worked out a deal for her. Satisfied, Lauren gave him the location of the sack of coins.

There was more to negotiate.

Lauren asked, "And if you're happy with the coins, what's the next step?"

"Then you tell us where a larger sum of them is."

"What assurance will I have?"

"All involved see the value in this transaction succeeding," he said less brusquely.

"When do I get to see the children?" Her heart jumped. A moment's silence ruined her confidence.

"The paperwork is being prepared. When a larger measure is in our hands, we will see what we can do."

"And Trokalitis is on board with this?"

"It's best not to ask too many questions."

She raked her fingernails on the desktop. "I get to see the children and they come back to the orphanage to stay, right?"

"If you frighten easily or are impatient, this will be long process for you. Wait for my call."

Lauren walked beyond the trees behind the orphanage. She had buried the sack up behind the temples. She figured it would take them an hour to find it, if someone under their pay was nearby.

Lauren wondered if she was too predictable. For a moment, she imagined her head on a platter. She walked in circles, reviewing the locations of the terra-cotta pots holding the coins. Had she hidden them well enough? She suddenly worried that she'd been followed all along, and that she'd end up in jail.

She imagined her head on the platter again.

Lauren smacked the flat of her hand against the trunk of a pine tree, whirled, and kicked it with her heel.

She hadn't sparred in so long. She'd love to hit somebody right now—crack limbs, maybe even heads. This was no time for civility.

Plataea, Greece

SEPTEMBER 479 BC

Zack stopped counting the numbers of times arrows bounced off his shield or zipped through his horsehair crest. He kneeled and caught his breath, as did the other hoplites that ran with him to close the lines. He turned to look at Diomedes but only saw his eyes, his face covered by his Corinthian helmet. Zack nudged him with his elbow.

"Now you know why we ran so many times in full armor from the groves up to the citadel," Diomedes shouted. More arrows chattered on their shields.

"Do you know why I always tried to beat you?" Zack asked.

"Why is that?"

"So I wouldn't be struck by the olive pits shooting out of your back-side while you ran."

Diomedes cackled, then coughed and gripped his side.

"Enough, I beg you. No more amusements, I need to catch my breath." Diomedes wiped his eyes. Arrows ripped the air.

"Take a look and see where the Persians are, Zack."

Zack lowered the rim of his shield just a second. He saw a sea of horsemen organizing directly in front of him and a wall of wicker shields beside them. A shaft flashed past his vision, impaling someone behind him. The man fell, opening a hole that was quickly filled by a man from the rank behind.

"Shit." Zack raised his shield.

"What is Pausanias waiting for?" Diomedes asked, turning his head to Zack, shouting each word.

"Omens."

"They had better find the right pigeon guts or we'll all be wearing darts. Almost time to stand, Zack."

"I'm surprised. Do not the gods decide when to attack?"

"Do not start with me now, Atlantean."

Zack searched the faces of the others in the unit to his left. He saw the future of Western culture in their crouching determination. Some eyes bore fear, others looked undaunted. They held the grip cords of their shields close. On his right side, Zack locked shields with the warrior next to him.

The Spartan hoplite did not break his gaze from the Persians.

"Not too fleet of foot, are you, Mycenaean?" the Spartan said wryly. Zack grinned, noting the long hair lying over the Spartan's red cape, the molded breastplate over his torso, and a face that reminded him of the others he had met back at Thermopylae.

Zack never dreamed he would be standing with the Spartans in battle. Yet here he was, ready to share the danger.

"Speak up. I know you are Mycenaean by the double axe painted on your shield. Since when does Mycenae grow giants?"

"I'm not Mycenaean," Zack answered. "I would be proud to say I was, but I am Atlantean." The Corinthian helmets muffled the Spartan's words, causing him to yell over the bedlam of the armies and smack of the arrows.

"Atlantean?" the Spartan replied, in a voice that registered surprise.

"What?" Zack turned his face to the Spartan hoplite.

"I know an Atlantean, a woman; one that would cause Aphrodite herself to cower. Lean closer so I can hear you. They look like they will charge. Do you know the woman?"

The enormity of what Zack had lost dealt him a blow far worse than any the Persians could deliver. Horns blared behind the dense packing of the Spartan army. "She's my wife."

The Spartan spoke quickly to the man beside him, and both looked upon Zack with amazement in their helmet-shrouded eyes.

"You are brave to be here, but a fool for letting her from your sight."

"I know too well."

"Don't leave my side today, Atlantean. There can be no breach in our line. We delivered your woman to Delphi, me and this nasty-smelling Spartan next to me. We brought her safely, by order of Queen Gorgo."

"Then I am in your debt. What's your name?"

Drums behind increased their beat, joining the trumpets. As one, the Spartans all stood. The allied hoplites holding the line to their left did the same.

"Posidonius is my name. My barracks mate here is Arimnestus. Can you be counted upon to hold the line?" the Spartan asked, searching Zack's face for confirmation.

It was a question asked of generations of warriors that held the Western kingdoms against invasion throughout history: Charles Martel and the Franks facing the Moors at Tours; Romans and Visigoths against the Huns; Genghis Khan stopped at the gates of Vienna; Allies landing at Normandy beaches.

"I can. I made a promise to Leonidas, a year ago."

The Spartan scrunched his face and then nodded. The scene hit Zack as beyond surreal. Shields deflected the hail of arrows continuing to pelt their ranks from Persian archers. Yet this Spartan wanted to talk as if they lay on couches in symposium with cups of wine.

"I understand you were at the Hot Gates. Then you know what we are about," Arimnestus said.

Zack set his eyes on the enemy. The shrill voice of flutes sounded from behind the Spartan lines.

"The omens are good. Prepare to attack," Posidonius said to Zack.

Zack's throat went dry. A cross-crested Spartan officer stepped from the ranks and pointed his dory at the enemy, shouting, "*Epi dori*, level spears."

Zack's heart pounded.

This is what it feels like. I'm scared shitless.

Then the Spartans did attack, a solid mass of bronze and iron, muscle, bone, and determination. Spears of the first rank leveled straight ahead, the second and third lines held theirs at shoulder height, ready to strike. It was as if a savage beast were unleashed, the deep growl of which would not just be heard, but felt in both Greek and Persian lines.

Zack lowered the rim of his shield, crouched to lower his profile and stepped forward. The Persian missiles leaped from bows, thirty yards or so between the battle lines.

Diomedes hollered into the ear hole of Zack's Corinthian helmet.

"Lock shields with me and the Spartan. No mercy today, Zack."

Zack lost his voice. He gulped. The drums beat from both sides. The far right end of the Spartan line, the position of honor, surged ahead, emitting a roar that caused Zack's heart to race.

The Persians, seeing the Spartans come forward finally, attacked with a fury. The Persian cavalry opposite Zack formed a triangle, kicked up dirt, and launched themselves.

Directly towards him.

"Steady, Zack," Diomedes warned. Zack knew enough to set his right foot back and sideways to absorb the impact. The shield of the man behind him pressed into his back, as did the succeeding lines behind him. They condensed into a solid wall of bronze.

The horsemen gathered speed. Just before hitting the Greek lines, they threw heavy axes that hissed, slamming onto the shields of the front line.

Shields fell, as did men. The cohesion of the line faltered and then the horsemen hit.

Zack gritted his teeth.

Three massive warhorses and riders, the tip of the charge, crashed into Zack as if one, hurling him off his feet.

Crushed between the onslaught of horsemen and the weight of hoplites behind him, the air left his chest. He dropped his spear.

The cries of men and the scream of horses filled the air.

Zack couldn't move.

It seemed an eternity before he could set the tips of his sandals on solid ground. Spears struck at him, seeking a soft spot beside his bronze cuirass. He crouched when his feet landed, and let the long spears from the lines behind him unhorse the riders.

His helmet strap snapped, allowing the helmet to rise up on his face. With his arms pinned, he shook his head to reseat it. Another double-ended axe hissed past his head. Diomedes hoisted Zack's shield higher to thwart a slash that would have killed him. Zach reached for the Spartan to his right and locked shields with him. From behind, he heard the call to push forward.

"Omphimos, Omphimos, Omphimos."

Spearheads jabbed back and forth from over Zack's shoulder. Persian warriors and their horses shrieked. The momentary relief of pressure allowed Zack and others to regain their stances. Zack set his shield squarely in front and pushed with all his might. A bearded Persian swung a heavy sword at him but it glanced off of Zack's shield and caught the side of his helmet instead. Zack reeled. The hooves of horses clubbed his shield. Diomedes stabbed a rider with his spear. The warrior toppled from his mount and fell onto the shield wall. Wounded Persian warriors lay in clumps at their feet. Rocks and brush hindered their footing, threatening to break the integrity of the phalanx.

The ground slickened with the blood of warriors.

Diomedes shouted at Zack to close the ranks. A Persian lance lay at Zack's feet amid broken swords and spent shafts. Picking it up, he knew immediately the disadvantage the enemy faced. Their spears were easily three feet shorter than a Greek dory and not counterweighted by the butt spike. It was tip-heavy and ungainly. He pointed it at the enemy but heard the cackle of one of the Spartans next to him.

"A little short, like your phallus, eh Atlantean!"

Zack would have laughed but a new surge of cavalry pounded the fragile integrity of the line. Horsemen flung lassos out over the hedgehog of allied spears trying to catch and pull the lances from the hands of the Spartans. Javelins hurled from helots behind the front lines dispatched them quickly.

Behind them, more Persian cavalry, black-suited and holding studded, round shields, threw javelins all at once, wounding hoplites all along the front lines.

An enemy warrior on the ground wrapped his arms around Zack's legs. Before Zack could stop him, the warrior drew a dagger and plunged it into his thigh. Zack shrieked and kicked at the Persian with his other foot. Diomedes thumped the Persian with his heel. The Persian screamed when a butt spike from behind Zack's line impaled the man on the ground.

Blood ran in rivers down his leg. Zack didn't have a free hand to stop the flow. He pushed onward with his back leg and joined the collision of two cultures intent on victory. The battle became a contest of bull determination. Zack could only concentrate on the task he vowed to carry out.

Hold the line.

Bridge the allied units.

The Spartan flutes played high-pitched notes. Zack limped forward. He locked his shield once again with Posidonius on his right. Their eyes met. A quick wink from the Spartan acknowledged his efforts. He felt a kind of vindication of his transformation to a warrior.

I'm no longer just a scholar. Can you see me, Leonidas?

No longer observer and critic of those who sacrificed all for their people, Zack drew the depth of his voice and discharged a war cry that was heard on both sides. His companions joined him. They crashed their bowl-shaped shields into the enemy.

Zack had always wondered how it was that ancient battles were carried out tactically with limited means of communication. The average hoplite's vision was restricted by the enclosure of his helmet with narrow eye slits. He could listen for drums and trumpets that might tell him to change directions or charge to a landmark. He could follow the battle flag. In the end, the warrior who endured strenuous training, and could think when cut off from his commanders, would likely win the day.

The Greeks bred such warriors.

Zack stared at his hand gripping the *hoplon* cord inside the wooden bowl of his shield. He smelled smoke, ripped intestines, and the sick sweetness of bloodletting.

Diomedes stood with him, as did Posidonius, like his bookends.

They were still alive. He heard drums. Smoke from fire-tipped arrows zipped past him. Zack raised his lance.

Resistance in front of him eased momentarily. Zack fell forward from the release of pressure. Peering over the edge of his shield, a new threat emerged. He could barely swallow. The sun had risen higher and he suddenly felt consumed with thirst.

Horsemen charged through Persian lines yet again. These were not the professionals of the Persian army, but wild men with tattered rags and earsplitting battle cries. They hurled axes and javelins before crashing into the Greeks in an all-out assault.

Bactrians.

The impact knocked Zack to his knees and broke his shield in two. An axe smacked into what was left of the crest of his helmet, stunning him enough to make him drop his short spear. The enemy cursed in their foreign tongues. Zack let go his fractured shield and gripped the shoulder of the Spartan to keep from falling backward. Diomedes pressed into Zack from the left, covering him with his shield.

The berserkers from Bactria flung their axes at the Spartan helmets, cutting heads from shoulders. The line began to buckle. Hoplites from the second line tried to fill the gap. Bactrians leaped from their horses onto the spears of the Spartans, hoping to break the integrity of the shield wall. Warriors fell on both sides. The Spartan line bowed inwards. Zack lost his grip on Posidonius.

A spearhead bounced off Zack's cuirass. He rose on one knee. Posidonius yelled something at him. His wounded thigh refused to give him a second leg up. A Bactrian jumped at Zack with a sword, emitting some unintelligible battle cry. He hit Zack like a linebacker and knocked him backward. The Bactrian's blade swiped across Zack's helmet, glanced off, and hit Diomedes's shield. Zack drew back and slugged the warrior in the face. Blood burst from the Bactrian's nose. Diomedes swung the edge of his shield at the

Bactrian. The warrior's head fell to one side, neck broken.

Zack reached for Posidonius, stretching his hand to clasp onto his leg or arm, anything to hold onto and bridge the seam. More Bactrian horsemen smashed into the Spartan line. Hoplite spears unhorsed the riders, but that meant more of the Bactrians would fight on foot. They reached for the Spartan spears and tried to wrench them from their hands. Zack held on to Posidonius's leg. Arrows flew past him with such speed he only heard them whiz past his ear.

Then he heard loud trumpet calls. Three long blasts.

Zack could only throw a glance in the direction of the trumpet calls. Diomedes slid over to him and again covered him with his shield. Did the trumpet call mean another cavalry attack? He couldn't get enough air. Another of the Bactrian savages fell in front of him. Zack kicked out with his foot, momentarily keeping the warrior from stabbing him.

"Draw your sword, Zack!" Diomedes screamed at him.

On both sides of Zack, the Bactrian horsemen perished at the points of the hedgehog of Spartan spearheads. Zack couldn't stand. The bleeding gash in his thigh ached. His leg failed. A Bactrian dove at Zack, weaponless, teeth bared and looking to rip out Zack's throat. With one arm wrapped around the Spartan's leg, Zack only had one hand free, but he couldn't raise it fast enough since he was reaching to draw his own sword. Zack could only see the Bactrian's wild eyes coming for him. He smacked the Bactrian in the face with his helmet, a head butt. The Bactrian crumbled.

Zack heard the trumpets again. The Bactrian horsemen continued their assault, but now Persian cavalry appeared. He heard someone shout out, "That's Mardonius."

Zack swallowed blood and spit. His vision blurred. He braced himself against the Spartan and tried to stand on his good leg. He saw a whirr of motion and the scream of horses.

Can we survive another charge?

With Mardonius in their midst, the Persians would fight with renewed vigor.

This is bad.

Zack made it to his feet, bolstered by his hold on Posidonius. He saw Mardonius on a white horse, black-clothed, extending a spear and pointing it directly at him. Hoplites took wounds. The Bactrian charge succeeded in stopping the hoplite advance, and worse still, holes were opening up in the Greek lines.

Now the elite Persian bodyguards surrounding Mardonius charged. The force of the horsemen had them reeling. More javelins flashed past him, reaching their targets in the lines behind. The shield that had been jammed in his back, supporting him, dropped suddenly.

Diomedes screamed at Zack, "Hold onto me."

Zack reached for Diomedes but didn't see the spear till it tore into the flesh above his collarbone. Zack screamed, looked up, and saw savages and black-dressed Persians everywhere in front of him. He couldn't pull the spear out of his shoulder. The pain consumed him and he fell to his knees again. Diomedes let his spear go.

He covered Zack with his shield.

"You're coming home with me, Atlantean," Diomedes declared. A split second later, with Zack protected, a spread of javelins raked Diomedes. He spun. Some bounced off his armor, but one pierced deep under his armpit.

Diomedes fell.

Mayhem ruled. Hoplites moved to close the line.

The Spartan hoisted Zack up, in time for him to see Arimnestus, to his right, throw a rock at Mardonius. It hit the Persian marshal in the face. Mardonius dropped the reins, lost consciousness, and fell from sight. A raucous cheer erupted in the Greek lines.

Zack heard all around him: "Praise the gods. Mardonius is down."

Diomedes squirmed at Zack's feet. Zack teetered, the spear still stuck above his collarbone. He let go his grip on the Spartan's arm and fell beside Diomedes. Feet trampled over them.

The phalanx advanced.

Zack saw sandaled feet, covered with blood and gore, and agony forever cemented on the faces of the dead. Broken swords, shattered spears, staved-in shields, and the eyes of Diomedes filled his view, eyes blinking as he struggled to speak. There were bubbles in the blood that leaked from his lips. Diomedes extended his hand.

"It is a good day . . . to die," Zack said, reaching for Diomedes with his sticky hand.

Diomedes tried to speak, but couldn't.

"Be comforted . . . the day is ours," Zack said, but cringed himself, absorbing waves of pain. He felt faint, and Lauren's face came to him suddenly.

Am I to die here? I'm going to miss you, Lauren.

Diomedes coughed up a gush of bright red blood. Finally able to talk, he said, "Atlantean . . . come home to us."

They fumbled to join their slippery fingers, trying to lock them together, like shields in the line.

"My mother, save . . . her."

"If I can . . ."

"Lauren . . . I love her . . . too," Diomedes managed to say, locking his eyes with Zack before he vomited more blood.

When he cleared his throat, Diomedes gasped out, "It has been her . . . all along. I thought . . . if you favored another . . . she might be with me." He drew strained breaths. "At times . . . I wanted you dead. But you became my brother. Where is she?" The yearning in his friend's eyes caused Zack to tell Diomedes . . . the untellable.

"She's gone. I may never see her again, either. Apollo has her." Lancing pain caused him to draw up his legs, fetal style. More lines of hoplites marched double time over them. The din of battle continued fifty yards in front of where they lay.

Surprise registered briefly in Diomedes's eyes but it was quickly replaced by a look of exhaustion and agony. "Never," he coughed out, "trust a god . . . with a beautiful . . . woman."

Zack cackled but cut it short. He couldn't raise himself up and didn't have the strength to pull the spear out. He blurted out through the pain, "The battle that you have won here . . . today . . . will save the future for free people."

Diomedes's eyes blinked fast. He breathed rapidly, straining to speak. "If Lauren is gone . . . marry my mother . . . give us an heir . . . don't trust Argos."

Then, it finally hit Zack. The *something* he had been trying to remember, the unknown fact he could not recall about Mycenae. Ten years after the Persian Wars ended, Argos conquered Mycenae. That meant Queen Io would have been killed or enslaved. Zack groaned aloud. Now he knew that Io, this beautiful woman, priestess of the earth goddess, had an appointment with disaster. She was someone he could be with, if he couldn't return to his own time . . . if Apollo wouldn't allow him to return to Lauren.

He felt his own strength leaving him. Diomedes's grip on his hand weakened.

"Tell Lauren," Diomedes strained to say, "tell her I loved her." Bloody bubbles burst from his lips.

A lot made sense to Zack now, but he couldn't hold the realization of his friend's frank revelations, because his vision clouded and both sets of their eyes lost sight at the same time.

Delphi, Greece

PRESENT DAY

Professor, you have another phone call." Mr. Avtges tapped on the door with his knuckle.

"The man says it's very important."

"Another seven a.m. wake-up?" *I'm getting tired of this.*

Lauren grabbed a bathrobe, cleared hair away from her face, and rushed downstairs. Mr. Avtges sat in his chair, rotating it slowly on its swivel. "When you finish this call, I want to speak to you." He handed her the phone and walked away.

"This is Lauren."

"Professor, gather your belongings and take a cab to the airport in Athens. A private jet will await you there with your passport."

Frantically she shouted, "Where are the children? I want to know where the children are, now."

"You are extended this one opportunity to leave the country and be free from incarceration. The adoptions will take much more time. The problem is that the other party believes you are lying about a number of issues, including antiquities you may have discovered. You are, of course, aware of the double jeopardy you are in. You can be easily arrested for dealing in the black market. This would be a sizeable sentence for a foreigner."

Lauren's mouth went dry.

They're screwing me.

"But . . ." she began to say.

"No buts. Leave now. Fly back to your own country. Perhaps the adoptions can be approved later."

"I gave him enough to buy a goddamned island and set him up for the rest of his life. I'm positive everyone is profiting from this."

"Take the deal, or go to jail. It will take you three to four hours to arrive at Athens Venizelos International. Go to the corporate terminal."

"You bastards, you've gone back on your word."

"I'm offering you freedom. Is there anything so dear, professor, whatever the cost?"

Lauren slumped in her chair, but only momentarily. She erupted out of it and slammed her fist on the desktop.

"But the children, I can't leave them. You know I can't."

"You have to, or you will have no chance to adopt them later, being that you will have been convicted of a felony in this country."

Lauren screamed, "No, you have no proof." She heard a rapping on the door.

"Lauren, are you all right?" Avtges asked.

She placed the phone over her heart. "Don't worry, Mr. Avtges. I'll talk to you in a minute." Lauren walked circles in the office, holding a hand over her mouth.

There's no more time. I'm trapped.

Lauren said, "You leave me no choice. I'll be at the airport on time. Is there nothing else I can do to change this?" Her tone conveyed resignation.

"You have stated that you have nothing else to offer us. If that is true, then you will be given your signed release from the police and transported on my private jet once we have procured the second deposit. Look for a white limo with a Greek flag on the antenna. The driver will be wearing a blue cap. Do not delay your departure; traffic is always heavy. The driver will hand you a phone and the documents. Call and give us the directions to the deposit. Do you fully understand?"

"Yes, I understand I've been hornswoggled."

"How colonial, too bad this is not a Hollywood western, professor. This is your future. Be wise."

"I'll be there." Lauren hung up. She massaged her temples. She opened the door. Mr. Avtges came around the corner from the cafeteria.

"What on earth is happening?" He looked at her over the rims of his glasses.

Lauren ran to him and enveloped him with her arms.

"I'm so sorry. I cannot explain fully to you what is happening, but if I don't leave now, I'll be in serious trouble. I want you to know that you are a most wonderful man. You will hear from me when matters have . . . calmed down." Her voice cracked. "I love the children. I'm going to fight for them. Tell them, please, I'll be back for them."

"This is such lunacy. Who is the source of this trouble?" Avtges asked.

"I think you know. My husband is missing and no murderer has been found. They consider me a suspect, but I guess I am being deported."

Mr. Avtges sucked in his breath.

"I must leave. Thank you for everything, I'll never forget you." Lauren kissed his cheek, once on each side. "Please call me a cab. Good-bye for now." She wiped her eyes with the back of her hands, ran for the stairs, weighing her time constraints to shower quickly and pack.

Lauren squeezed the letters she had retrieved from the cave into her parka. She stuffed her clothes into two large green suitcases she had acquired over the past couple of months. She left Cassandra's clothes in the drawers. She had no time to retrieve Persephone's snake bracelet and jewelry box hidden in one of the pots of treasure back at the cave.

I'm really leaving her. Shoot me now. I don't know if I can live with this.

She reviewed the secret locations of her bribes, all separate from each other, but in close proximity to Delphi.

Helping her into the cab, Avtges said, "Do not forget about us." His voice cracked. "Who else would lead us in a campfire and barbeque? Be well, Lauren."

Lauren blew him a kiss while squeezing into a dirt-shrouded cab that promptly took off with a burst of blue-gray diesel exhaust.

Avtges settled into his office. He hadn't cried since the death of his wife, twelve years past. He stared into the polished brass of his desk lamp. He saw deep creases in his face. Eyes devoid of joy stared back at him. The sudden departure of the professor would bring more anxiety and disappointment to the children. Intruders, kidnappings, murder—what had become of their quiet little corner of the country? His phone rang.

"Avtges, here."

"This is Mr. Parsons from the US Embassy. Could I speak with Professor Fletcher?"

"I'm sorry. She just left in a hurry, claiming she might be deported. She had her suitcases."

"Is she going to the airport?"

"Yes. Sadly, she is."

"I agree. Thank you."

Mr. Avtges shook his head at the idiocy that was transpiring before his eyes. He touched his cheeks where Lauren had kissed him.

He wondered what to tell the children. More tears, more pain. Would it ever end?

Lauren tapped her feet on the floor of the cab, a native drumbeat to absorb the angst of what the future would hold for her. She wanted to kick her foot through the back of the driver's seat.

"Lady, are you some drummer in a rock and roll band?"

A comedian in every culture, she thought. She answered, "No, I'm just ripping mad." Lauren stared into the dark eyes of the driver, all she could see of him in the rearview mirror. Traffic was light and they made good time until just outside the city limits of Athens.

"We're almost there," the driver noted.

"I wish it were still miles away."

"What, lady?"

"No matter, keep going." Lauren checked her watch: the trip had taken three hours and ten minutes, with only one bathroom break. She felt tortured with the image of Cassandra's face; the disappointment, betrayal, and loneliness she must be feeling.

Abandonment. She had abandoned her.

I'm a horrible mother. I don't deserve children.

A half hour later, their vehicle pulled up to the airport access. As promised, a white limo sat at the far end of the driveway. Outside, a man stood, wearing a blue cap. When her cabbie unloaded her bags, she paid him well and was ushered toward the stretch Lincoln bearing a tiny Greek flag, which fluttered with the rush of vehicles streaming past.

The black-suited driver held the door for her to get in. "Good morning. Make yourself comfortable."

Sunglasses hid his eyes. Lauren entered pensively, sniffing the half-smoked cigarette hanging from his lip. She sank into the lush comfort of deep leather seats, next to the well-stocked bar accompanied by ice tongs and crystal glassware. The driver offered to make her a drink. When she refused, he shut her door and assumed the driver's seat. Lauren noticed both doors closed with the precise concussion of a luxury vehicle, comforting her, at least temporarily.

The driver's glass panel opened.

"This is yours, professor."

He handed her a yellow manila folder. One of her hand's accepted the folder, the other trembled along her thigh. The interior lights heightened. Lauren opened the flap. She took a bottomless breath and then let it go. The document, written in Greek, announced her release; all signed by Inspector Trokalitis and another official that appeared to be the local attorney general, followed by the signature of her lawyer. Zack was declared missing; the murderer of Professor Popandreou unknown, and she was absolved of any blame.

Lauren breathed deeply. She had her freedom, but it was a Pyrrhic victory, at best.

"Are the documents quite in order?" the driver asked, displaying white teeth against dark glasses and hair.

"They appear to be." Lauren managed a weak smile. "Damn good thing I can read this," she muttered.

"I have a cell phone to contact the Facilitator. Do you care to speak with him?"

"I imagine so." *More poker to be played; I can't wait to get back to the States.*

She put a cold phone to her ear.

"Are the papers satisfactory?" Samaras asked.

"They are as far as I can tell. And how are the adoptions going?"

"Be happy you have gotten this far, Professor Fletcher. Goodwill can be fleeting."

Another veiled threat, she thought.

"Now my dear, give me the location of the second cache, if you please."

With no place left to dance, she told him. "Go to the same location as before, up the next bend in the path and look for a picture of a bird with outstretched wings drawn on a rock. Dig beneath and you will find another pot of pristine coins." She felt breathless. Each word brought tortuous visions of her children held in some police station cell. "Are there any last-minute deceptions coming my way?"

"Dispense with the quibbles. I trust you will be comfortable until we confirm receipt of the package. The driver will provide you refreshment or order you a meal if you wish."

"I don't have much of an appetite." The vision of Cassandra receiving the yellow lighter from Zack back at the farmhouse in ancient Greece occupied her thoughts. She reached for a tissue.

"Now is not the time to crumble. Was there not a famous man in America's past who said that there are times that try men's souls?"

Lauren squared her chin and took courage from the challenge he voiced in describing a statement when all seemed lost at Valley Forge. Her voice quivered, but she spit out, "That was Patrick Henry and do not suppose that I am some helpless woman."

"On the contrary, professor, you are respected, though desperate at the moment."

"When you receive the second lot, then I will be given my passport and be allowed to leave?" Lauren snipped off the edge of her fingernail.

You're a traitor. You don't deserve to be a mother.

"This will take a few hours, but when we are satisfied, your passport will be delivered. Will this be satisfactory?"

"What else can I do?"

"This is my business. Perhaps you should watch television to pass the time, although I do not recommend the news; far too much negativity."

"Where are my children?"

"Perhaps you should not speak in the possessive tense. They are not yours, and it took significant terms to convince Trokalitis to overlook your deceit. Should such a person be allowed to adopt children, professor?"

"Bastards, you know I love those children."

"Calm yourself. The adoptions you desire will take a long time. Something you can pursue from your home. You cannot always bend the world to your desires. Life is a journey of joy and agony. Perhaps your life in the United States is orderly and without strife. Here, and in many other countries, people endure disappointment, unspeakable tragedy, and yet they go on. You should do the same."

No goddamned way.

"It is unfortunate that you will leave without them but what more can be done? Stay in our good graces; one never knows the future. I will call you back."

"But wait—" *Zack knows the future where he is.*

The line went dead.

"Can you call him back?" she pleaded.

"My employer will not wish to be disturbed if he has ended the call. Can I get you anything until he gets back to you?"

"No," she replied, already distracted with her dwellings on the children and Zack. Her heart felt pierced. She curled up and willed a fretful sleep to overcome her, but it never arrived.

The muffled ringtone phone startled her. The driver bared his white fangs once more and handed the cell to her. Lauren checked her watch.

It had taken three hours to locate her planted treasure, collect it, and assay its value and authenticity.

"Professor, all is in order," the leathery voice of Samaras proclaimed. "It is quite impressive actually. You have given us Corinthian coins, and others from Aegina and Ionia as well; a tidy sum on the market."

"Then carry through on the original deal."

"Do you see a gray sedan approaching; little flags with the red, white, and blue?" Lauren lowered the cell.

The sedan pulled up next to theirs. Men in long overcoats got out and walked to her door. They stood there smiling while the window lowered electronically.

"Professor Fletcher. I'm Jack Salusti, aide to Mr. Parsons. He asked me to deliver your passport." He handed her an envelope. When she opened it, the photo Mr. Parsons took of her at their first meeting stared back.

"Can I thank him?" She looked horrible in the photo: eyes like a raccoon's and hollow cheeks.

"Maybe later you can. He's been delayed at the embassy but he's going to bust gears to see you off." He grinned and she felt comforted.

"You don't know how good it feels to have an American here . . ."

"It's our pleasure, Professor Fletcher."

"I need to finish this call. Could you wait a moment?"

Salusti checked his watch. He nodded.

Lauren raised the cell. She would leave Greece, and her heart would tear in two, maybe irreparably. Zack remained in Greece, albeit in another time. Lauren opened and closed the passport, unable to look at herself.

Where are you, Zack? Should I l fly home and slug it out for Cassandra's freedom from the US, or maybe screw it all up by refusing to leave Greece?

Samaras said on the cell phone, "The driver will take you to my private jet. Go quickly, before someone changes their mind."

Lauren's voice broke. "I can't leave them. I can't!"

"Your emotions betray you. If you destroy the arrangements as they have been worked out, your chances to adopt later will be made impossible. It is not desirable for you to stay here. The children are collateral against your silence. Go now."

Lauren pounded her fist on the leather beneath the glass partition. "Don't make me leave them!" The embassy officials both raised the sunglasses from their eyes. One rapped his knuckle on the window.

"Is there a problem?" he asked.

"No, Mr. Salusti. Thank you."

"Then we'll take our leave if you're sure."

I'm not sure of anything. Cassandra fought for me. She stabbed Bessus. She's only thirteen and tougher than I am. She didn't hesitate.

"Just please ask Mr. Parsons to meet me at the airport. I want to thank him."

"We will, professor." They left, turning once to look back at her.

The limousine motor roared. The locks clicked suddenly. The driver screeched his tires and sped toward the private plane terminal.

She was trapped.

"Sir, please wait," she said into the phone. Hopelessness swamped her, like when she left Zack holding the door against Bessus.

Do I always leave the ones I love? Is this me?

Samaras said, "Your resources are spent. No more can be done. Go."

"With everything I gave you, isn't it enough for the retirements of all of you? You're still only getting me half the way. Let me stay as their foster parent until—" She was interrupted and not too kindly.

"You have exhausted my patience. I should not have underestimated a woman's inability to control her emotions."

"Still, I can still do more for you, sir."

Dead silence.

"Whatever are you talking about?"

"If you are such a man of influence . . ." Her voice fractured while she scrambled for tactics. "Then you can push through almost any deal."

"Come to the point. I have a prior engagement to attend to."

"How much of an expert are you on the coins you have procured so far?"

"I consider myself well-versed. The gold ingots, the coins from different cities, as well as the silver tetradrachmas constitute a small fortune. How do you think you were released?" Samaras answered.

"Produce paperwork that guarantees me title as foster parent for both children while I petition for the adoptions, and I will make it worth your while."

"Why professor, you surprise me. A man of my advanced years and you offer yourself to me? A younger man might be interested. Not me."

"Oh God, I'm not suggesting that. I have something far better than my skinny bones to bargain with. I have special coins, imprinted with fennel pods, shaped to resemble the four chambers of the heart."

She heard a gasp.

"You have Cyrenian Valentines?"

"I have a very large sack of them."

"Say that again and do not play games with me."

"A sizable load; North African, little hearts, very rare, I think."

"Are they as pristine and unpolished as the others?"

"Precisely. Are you interested?" Lauren had to consciously slow down her breathing.

"Can we access them immediately?"

"Yes, with the simultaneous security of my children. Take me to them, produce the foster parent paperwork, and they'll be yours."

"Not so fast. You would have to be flown to them and the arrangements you desire are nearly impossible to finish today."

"Make . . . it . . . happen," Lauren demanded, with accent on every word.

"Stand by and I will see if this is enough incentive."

Lauren's heart wanted to burst past her ribs. She handed back the phone. A sly grin broke the sides of her lips.

I found a lever. Take that.

She slid back in the leather and stretched out her legs. Not exactly the skinny bones she had described. They had regained their musculature hiking up and down the mountainside these past months. She even had biceps, lifting the heavy clay pots in the middle of the night, and loading the valuables into sacks and hiding them in pots. With so much at stake, she wondered what would happen next. Any deal with these people could easily turn against her.

Lauren had the phone back in her hand.

The words came fast and brusque. "Professor, in case you are playing poker with us, we will not look kindly upon such tactics to gain your end."

"I assure you I can produce what I suggested. Would the tinkle of silver barley Nomos from Metapontum sweeten the pot?"

"My driver will escort you to the terminal waiting area. Bring your bags. There may be a long wait while we present the offer."

"I want to be with the children. You get nothing else if I am not given legal guardianship while I stay here and fight the system."

"You are a complex woman; one moment, a sea of churning emotion, the next, calculating and confident."

"I don't care what your assessment is. I am bargaining for their lives."

Samaras said, "The girl who does not speak only produces tears, and is consoled by the boy. So strange; the tears come, but no voice."

Lauren exploded, "Do you enjoy torture?"

"Believe it or not, I am on your side. These dealings are fraught with complications."

Lauren found her nails making prick points in the flesh of her palms.

"You will get the Valentines when I see the children and the Nomos when I am made their guardian."

"Do not overplay your hand. Every effort is being made. Wait in the lounge for my call, but do not get your hopes up. The parties involved want you out of the country."

There was only herself, staring eye to eye with her opponents, just like in karate matches in high school. Some she had defeated—bigger opponents that walloped her with roundhouse kicks. She would take the punishment to get inside and punch, then grapple with them, get her adversary off balance, and take them to the mat. This was a different arena, but in the end, perseverance and a plan won the day.

Lauren knew the Valentines held allure for a coin collector. They came from the city of Cyrene on the coast of North Africa, known for the extinct plant silphium, which they grew and exported to great demand in the ancient world. This special plant was used for simple illnesses and as a remedy for the flu. Yet, its most valuable use was as an ancient form of birth control. Cyrene became wealthy and the coins it used for currency were imprinted with the image of the silphium seed pod, which had four chambers, resembling a human heart, hence the Valentine connection. The enormous cache of these coins and others of great value set her to wondering about the career of Cassandra's Uncle Nestor. Had he gone to Cyrene as a consultant for some architectural project? If he did, the work must have been substantial and there most likely was a very interesting story attached to it.

But he had died long ago and she thought about the loneliness Zack must feel. If there were no way for him to return, he would have to start his life over. That meant a new woman in his life. She wrapped her arms tightly around her chest, suddenly chilled. She saw no immediate end to her chaotic life. She extracted a single Valentine from her pocket, spun it with her fingers, feeling the uneven edge of it. Like most coins of the ancient world, it was not a perfect circle, nor was the image of the seed perfectly stamped on the surface. She kept a bag of different coins and uncut stones in her gym bag.

The phone sang out again and she dropped the coin on the floor of the limo.

"Come this way," the driver said, extending his hand.

He opened the door and offered to carry her suitcases. Lauren snatched the coin, clutched the gym bag, and pulled her parka close as she followed him to the terminal. She would never let the gym bag out of her possession now. She had transferred Zack's correspondence on papyrus and lambskin manuscripts of his subsequent travels in there, too. They held an enormous treasure of knowledge about the civilizations lost to history. He suggested that there were others buried elsewhere. Then his accounts abruptly ceased. Maybe he was wounded again, or worse. This was more uncertainty for her to contend with. She choked on a sob rising in her throat.

They reached a glass enclosure in the terminal. She handed her passport to the uniformed agent sitting behind it. Seemingly bored with his shift, the agent opened it, studied her face briefly, and pounded a small stamp onto the first blank page. He slid the passport back to her.

The driver directed her to the passenger lounge. She sat on a leather couch, not the plastic molded chairs like in the commuter terminals.

I hate couches. Trokalitis sat on a couch when he wanted me to . . .

The driver dropped her suitcase beside her and suggested she stay put. He glanced around and then lit a cigarette, shifting his weight from one foot to the other. Lauren attempted to slow her breathing. Her guts were telling her that something was wrong. She heard the whine of jet engines being warmed up. A voice announced flight schedules to the thinly populated waiting room.

What could happen now? How would they screw her this time? She would give them the Valentines just to see the kids. Then, she'd direct them to the separate caches she planted in different areas of Delphi, bargaining with them until she could be near the children and go to war for their futures.

She had to see them. Cassandra would have to keep her charade going on faith since they had been separated a few days now. Maybe the police had broken her silence already, but got only foreign words and simple broken English and Greek. They would know this was all a ruse and she would be busted.

Yet, Lauren had the passport and her release. Maybe they could still hold her and not allow her to leave with some new charge.

She looked at the signed release again and wondered if it was real.

The driver strutted off to a corner of the waiting area and punched numbers into the phone. He waved his free hand while he conversed in muffled tones. If they didn't take the deal, she would have to fly away and fight a legal battle from San Diego. The driver walked toward her, his coattails flapping as he quickened his pace.

"My boss is on the line." He handed the annoying phone to her and looked away.

"Professor, you have delivered so far on your side of the deal. I have arranged for you to see the children."

Lauren yelped, jumped, and pumped her fist.

"You did not allow me to finish."

"What?" she said, plummeting back down to earth.

"We want the Valentines now. When we have them in our hands, you will be transported to visit the boy and girl in their holding cells."

"Holding cells, in a prison?"

"I will ignore that. You will board my jet and be brought to them."

"What about the guardianship?"

"It cannot be guaranteed."

"How can I see them and then leave?" Her tone escalated. "Can you imagine what this will do to them?"

"Life is hard choices. Such dilemmas confront parents all over the Third World on a daily basis. You Americans; you expect a happy ending, like this is some Hollywood picture story. Risk is being taken all around. Do you want the deal or not?"

"Fly me to them, now."

"Lead me to the Valentines."

They outplayed me again.

Lauren withdrew the map sketch from her parka's side pocket. With resignation, she read the directions. This next cache she buried under a stone arch near the gymnasium, close to the temple of Athena Pronaia. She placed one more condition on the transfer of the coins.

"When we have them, you will board the plane and be flown to the children's location. Pardon me while I pass these directions on."

"Will you drain every last drop of my blood before I can have them back?"

I'm so out of my league.

"You do not seem to realize that what you give back to us is rightfully Greek property."

"Somehow, I don't believe these coins will get to the Greek people."

265

"They're better in our hands than that of a foreigner. This whole affair can still be turned against you in ways you cannot imagine. You will of course never speak of these proceedings, ever, professor. For if you do, there will be dire consequences for you and yours, no matter where you reside. Is that clear?"

"You take my money and threaten me?"

"I am the mediator who has arranged your escape from jail. Tell me if you would prefer to reverse this course and go back to where you were days ago?"

"I see your point."

"Then shut your mouth, girl. There are those who do not desire to see this foreigner, who deceives and bargains, achieve her goals."

"I see that the exchange is complicated, especially since I am a woman."

"This is not America. Our men are not feminized as yours are."

"What?"

"Leave to men that which is their domain. Tell me, educated lady, how do children prosper when there is no mother at home to care for them and their rearing is given to others who do not care as much?"

"Women are far more capable than you know."

"For some that is true, not necessarily so for others. Many women are happily centered in primarily raising a family and taking care of their husbands. Males and females each have their roles, developed over thousands of years. Do you attempt to manipulate nature, professor?"

"Yes I do, and how convenient it is of you to choose to dominate a woman at this very critical moment in her life."

Have I been set up?

"I beg you, no more boorish comments. I will contact you again when the package is secured." Samaras hung up.

She wondered if once she met the children, could she refuse to leave, call her lawyers, and waive the release that guaranteed her freedom. Then go to the press and get them on her side? Would this course of action make matters worse or better? Each action had consequences. There was no way to know. What would her father do?

The driver paced in front of the door that led to the tarmac. Two dark-haired men in black leather jackets joined him. The driver turned his back on Lauren. While he spoke, the other men lifted their eyes and glanced at her. Lauren shifted in her waiting room seat, suddenly uncomfortable. She coughed and wondered if she should run. If they came over to where she sat, or in any way threatened her, she would clobber them and scream at the top of her lungs.

The driver raised the phone to his ear. He abruptly turned and pulled his friend toward Lauren. She leaped off her chair and set her legs for balance. She dropped her satchel to free her hands. "Talk with your hands raised," her sensei would say during karate training. "If you think you're threatened, get your hands up and try to confuse your adversary with words. Meanwhile, you're ready to defend yourself."

"Professor, come this way." He touched her elbow as if to guide her.

"Get your hands off me." She recoiled and clenched her fists.

"Relax. We're taking you to the plane."

Lauren didn't move. She narrowed her eyes and took a deep breath, unconvinced by their smiles.

In the movies, the crooks treat their prisoner really well before they lower the boom.

The driver's friend chewed on a toothpick while holding the door to the runway open.

"Professor, come now," he said again, motioning for her to come through.

Lauren peered through the doorway toward a small jet where a technician was removing triangular blocks from under the wheels. The loudspeaker announced a series of flights: to Chania in Crete, Larissa in the north, and other locations outside the country. Lauren calculated that the flight plans meant they took the kids to either a holding cell in Crete or to Larissa, probably Larissa and less than an hour's flight away. A jet engine whined as it revved up to taxi.

"We cannot stand here all day, lady." The driver's phone went off again.

"She's frightened," he said into the phone.

"Don't tell me I'm scared, asshole." Lauren slung her gym bag, grabbed the suitcases and headed for the plane, one step, carefully measured, after another. She searched for more of the Facilitator's henchmen.

Will they fleece me for more concessions?

The henchman placed a phone in her hand and said gruffly, "My boss."

"Where are they taking me, to Larissa?"

Samaras answered, "My dear, you have such little confidence in me."

"Cut the crap. Did you get the Valentines?"

"They are exquisite. Would you care to tell me where you found them?"

"I think not."

"Maybe someday you'll reconsider."

"I'm not that fond of you."

"You wound me," his voice feigning offense to her unveiled insult.

"All right, I'll get on board. God help you if this is another trick."

"Good-bye for now, Professor Fletcher. It has been wonderful doing business with you," he snickered, but then it blossomed into a deep belly laugh that made her shiver.

"Wait, how will I get guardianship?"

"One step at a time, my dear. Now stop wasting my time, jet fuel is expensive."

"Do I call you when I see them?" She reached the stairs that had been set up against the body of the jet. She heard the whine of the engine turbines. A man in a blue blazer waited for her at the top. Lauren felt her heart thumping in her temples. Her mouth was suddenly a desert.

"I assume you still hold the Nomos?" the Facilitator said, testing. "I may be able to arrange for you to stay with them a few days. Do we have a deal?"

"You get tens of thousands of euros more for a few days?"

"Can you put a price on children? I believe you would pay far more. How can you blame the parties involved for recognizing an opportunity, especially when most feel that you belong in jail? I cannot control every aspect of this deal, professor. Other authorities may hear of this and arrest you for black-market activities. Even my own associates want their piece of you. When you meet the children, I expect another payment."

The driver followed. Her legs felt weak. After she entered the plane, there would be no escape. She heard a siren in the distance and it came closer with each step up the stairs. She was at their mercy.

"I will fight for them, tooth and nail. You will have the Nomos."

"Tell me now, and we will fly you to see the children first."

I'll do whatever it takes.

"You hear that car with the siren?"

"Yes," her voice trembled.

"They may be coming to arrest you. I will not be able to stop them."

"Oh my God!"

"Now, professor, before there is no time to shut the doors and taxi the plane."

Lauren gulped. "There's a bag buried underneath the trash cans in the back of the orphanage." She saw a car racing toward them. "You'll have to trust me."

"If you're lying, I cannot guarantee that you'll go straight to the States. No children. No adoptions . . . ever."

Panicked, she screamed into the phone, "The coins are there, dammit. Don't you have enough? Oh no, I can see the car."

"Get in the plane quickly," Samaras said.

She reached the top and ducked her head to enter the doorway.

The steward stepped back. She turned the corner, looking for another set of Greek knuckle-breakers, but instead, stars exploded before her eyes. She reeled, dazed, and then fell to her knees. She drew in a gasp and the breath left her.

Cassandra and Demetrious sat on the left side of the cabin, side by side. They dropped their half-licked ice cream cones and tripped over each other to get to her. Lauren extended her arms. A cry came out from her core. They all embraced. When she could, she lifted Cassandra's head and caressed her tear-streaked face.

"Did you know I would not leave you?" Lauren swhispered into her ear in Ionian.

Cassandra held back her voice. Tears cascaded. She wiped her nose.

So help me God, if they try to . . .

Demo stood over them, his hands on each of their shoulders. Lauren, with Cassandra clinging to her, wrapped her arms around him.

"I'm so happy you're safe. I was so worried," she said, staring into dark eyes shielded by his curly locks.

He said quietly in her ear, "I told them nothing, even when they threatened to take away the video games."

Lauren burst out laughing.

"Will they separate us again?" Demo asked, nodding toward Cassandra. "She's had a tough time. She still doesn't talk, although I know better."

Cassandra lifted her head, unable to understand the conversation. Her face bore the evidence of days of terror. She searched both faces for assurance and saw concern. The oncoming car siren stopped. There was commotion outside the plane.

"I don't know what they'll do. I'm hoping to stay in Greece and fight for the both of you." Lauren hugged them closer.

Please don't take them away.

She heard footsteps coming up the stairs.

Lauren turned and screamed at the men around her. "You sons of bitches, I'm gonna stay in this country and these children will be mine!" She shielded the kids with her body and turned her back on the airplane doorway.

"There's going to be a slight change of plans," a voice entering the plane declared, but one she recognized.

There stood Mr. Parsons, bearing a wide smile and holding a blue folder.

"What?" she said, a slew of questions erupting in her mind. "Oh my God, it's good to see you. What's happening?"

"I have in my hands two more passports and legal documents announcing the adoption of these two fine children. They're yours, Lauren."

Lauren let loose a primal scream, one that shook the interior of the plane. Cassandra and Demo gripped her tighter.

"Yes, yes. Thank you, and thank you, Mr. Parsons. How can I . . . ?"

"We'll have a little lag time in the US to make this official. I'm calling in a few favors."

"But how could this all be accomplished so quickly? Just a few minutes ago I didn't know if I could even stay?"

"I was told to prepare this paperwork a week ago, but sworn to silence in case . . . problems arose."

"You mean? I can't believe it." She bent down and looked into the worried face of her new daughter. She stroked her hair and said in Ionian, "Sweetheart, they're going to allow you to stay with me. And now you may speak or cry or scream to Athena all you want."

Cassandra lost all control, weeping and laughing at the same time. Demo, unable to understand the ancient Ionian, nor the English, looked confused. "So that's what she sounds like. Is she going to scream like that all the time?"

Lauren belly-laughed. "Demo, how would you like to be my son? We could become a family if you will have us?" She smiled and laid her hands on his shoulders.

"Do you mean I will live with you always?"

"Yes, I do. We're going to America. We'll start a new life together." Lauren embraced Demo and felt him shudder.

"I want to be your son." He lost his steady voice. In a series of broken words, he said that this was the best day of his life.

Lauren finally detached herself from her children and hugged Mr. Parsons. She sensed his embarrassment, but squeezed him tighter.

"How can I possibly thank you for all you've done?"

"It is my pleasure, Professor Fletcher. You never know, someday there may be a favor you can do for me."

"Just name it and I will move heaven and earth to make it so."

"Thank you," he replied. A cell phone jingled. The driver placed it in her hand, giving her a look that said, "I knew it all the time."

"Professor, are you pleased with my arrangements?" It was Samaras. She could imagine the smile on his face.

"I can't believe this. I'm so happy. Thank you from the bottom of my heart."

"Do not think badly of me when you dissect the progression of this transaction. This is business, purely business. We Greeks are a people that hold the family dear as well. I know that you will make a good mother."

Lauren asked if she would ever meet him.

"Not likely, my dear. Yet I do have one more question from Inspector Trokalitis. Do you have any more information that would lead us to the killer of Professor Papandreou? It would be much appreciated."

"I'm sorry. Please ask him to continue the search for my husband. The kidnapper only spoke a few times, the only word he repeated sounded like "Bessus". It might be his name."

"Not much to go on, but I will tell him."

"Can I expect a Christmas card from the both of you?"

Samaras cackled. "There's that one last task you asked for. Parsons will hand you a pen, paper and envelope."

Parsons whispered in her ear and Lauren grinned. She scribbled quickly on the paper and folded it. She licked the glue and sealed the envelope.

Samaras said, "Good-bye for now, and remember, not a word to anyone." The line disconnected.

"I cannot believe how this all worked out," Lauren said to Parsons.

"Whatever deal you made, it worked. Would you care to tell me how it was accomplished?"

"I'm sworn to secrecy, I'm sorry to say."

"It's best I don't know anyway. It's time for me to depart."

"You have in your packet my contacts in Immigration. They've been informed that all of you will be arriving in New York via London. You'll be whisked through Immigration without having to stop for inspection." Parsons checked his watch.

Lauren made a quick exhale. Now she wouldn't have to toss the valuables in her bag.

"Good luck to you, Professor Fletcher. You are a very courageous woman."

"How can I thank you? You calmed me when I was frantic . . ."

"Who knows? I will let you know, but until then, travel safely." He smiled, turned on his heel, and left along with the Facilitator's employees. Flight attendants sealed the hatch door and asked passengers to fasten their seat belts.

Lauren danced back to the children.

"Cassandra, we are embarking on a great journey. You may not believe what is going to happen next, but do not be frightened. Like the kite we made back in Delphi, we are about to fly into the realm of the gods."

Cassandra eyes widened and she spilled out a sea of questions.

Demo's mouth dropped open. "What is she saying? I've heard tourists from all over and I can't understand any of that."

"Demo, it's a long story and we'll have plenty of time to talk about it."

Cassandra blared, "Lady Lauren, what is the chariot we sit within? It whines and shakes beneath me."

"Sweetheart, you know of the winged horse, Pegasus? This invention will lift and fly us through the sky all the way to our new home."

"Athena! I must pray to her and Hermes. We cannot enter the realm of the gods without their approval." She parted her hands and raised them, palms out.

"What's she doing now?" Demetrious said, squinting at her.

"She doesn't understand. There is a lot she needs to learn. Will you help her?"

"She's my sister now, right? Then I will be her protector and yours. Hey, I've never been on a plane, either. This is going to be fun."

"Hold on to your seat, Cassandra. We're ready to fly."

The plane accelerated and they were thrust back in their seats. The look on Cassandra's face was of pure wonder. She scrunched her face, closed her eyes, and burst out laughing.

28

Delphi, Greece

PRESENT DAY

Samaras crossed his legs and sipped on an iced Sambuca. He emitted a long sigh. A vested waiter set a generous plate of lamb shanks and green beans in tomato sauce in front of him. He dragged a knife through succulent meat that fell off the bone. Chewing vigorously, he silently marveled at the precision with which the deal had just been completed.

The professor proved an easy mark; so desperate that she would pay any price for the children. A mute girl and a boy saddled with chronic hepatitis would be expensive wards of the country for many years to come. Children with compromised medical issues were exceptions by which the Greek authorities would allow adoptions by foreigners. A simple phone call to his former associates set the wheels in motion. After all, the medication the boy required each month was a drain on a system that was already short of funds. Strategically placed bribes worked wonderfully. His cell phone rang.

The voice on the phone asked, "How is the last cache?"

"Wonderful. We have a few thousand Ionian bumblebees and silver barley Nomos from Metapontum. Amazingly, she had Cyrenian

Valentines, too. I am still calculating the values of cut and uncut rubies. Then, there's a full pot of gold sticks. Your portion of each of the loads will bring you a tidy retirement."

"I received the first wire into my Swiss account. You played her exceptionally well, ratcheting up the pressure and forcing her to deliver for each small concession."

"It's a simple matter of business. My former colleagues were only happy to assist once they received their payments. The law firm she hired was easily convinced to drag their heels."

"You have to admit, she certainly was full of surprises. At first it looked like just a matter of some tens of thousands of euros in cash. I would still love to know where she found all of the coins. The final cache had to be in the millions on the black market."

"A very profitable enterprise, but I wonder where her husband really is. The murder of the professor is still an open case. Considering all the secrets she holds, do you think she is involved?" Samara drank the last of the Sambuca and turned the glass over.

"So much of this does not add up. Either way, we have secured our retirements."

"What will you do with yours?"

"I'll purchase a quiet beach house on Patmos. I much prefer islands to the mainland. It will be easy to rent out until I retire."

"That's a fine choice. The next payment should enter your account in a couple of days. Perhaps we will do business again?"

"Possible, but I will be leaving soon."

"It's been a pleasure doing business with you, Mr. Parsons. Such a pity you're leaving. Are you going back to the States?"

"Yes and no. I have applied for a rather sensitive position in the State Department and it looks like I will be transferred very soon."

"Anything you can tell me about?"

"Actually, I can't."

"Delving in secret activities? You Americans are rather predictable."

"It's a difficult world out there."

"In the end, I agree with you."

"Oh, a last question. What did you think of her written request found inside the last jar? I had her sign a note before the plane left."

"I'm happy to take care of it." Samaras paused. "Did you desire her, Bartholomew?"

"Didn't we all?"

"What stopped you?"

Silence lasted for half a minute. "There is a time for women and a time for business. I think she is a woman of virtue. I respect her."

"The next one may not be so lucky," the Facilitator jeered, and cut the line.

Trokalitis neatly folded his official retirement request. He pushed the letter into an envelope, licked the label, and set it aside on his desk. Quick approval had already been arranged as part of the deal. There might be questions from the newspapers and the media, but the murder investigation was a disaster and it would be assumed that he had given up or was forced to retire.

He didn't care anymore.

There was the issue of honor, but the embarrassment would have to be tolerated so he could take his leave and escape. It would be far safer to leave the country, and soon. It would take two or three days to travel by train to Austria, where he would draw on the account. The pension he would receive from his twenty-five years of service to Greek society would provide a minimal, but reasonable screen for his activities. He could return later when the publicity and furor over the professor's murder had died down. He wondered where the mysterious murder suspect had taken refuge this time. If the trail led to Turkey again then it was likely he was beyond the grasp of Greek law anyway.

Conveniently, the staff members of his department had left for the weekend, leaving darkened rooms.

He organized and cleaned the contents of his desk drawers. Not that the case didn't still interest him. Perhaps he would continue the investigation on his own. He was positive the woman professor had concealed the truth. She was guilty of something, and it took the substantial payments of the Facilitator to budge him from searching for the whole truth. He slid his top desk drawer out further and removed the bronze armband from underneath the wooden frame. This would remain his. He double-wrapped the armband in tissue, tied it with a rubber band, and slipped it into his jacket pocket.

His family would suffer embarrassment also. He had been trapped in a no-win situation. Lucky for him and others, there was enough money from the professor's cache to pay off the involved parties. He still had sore legs from going up and down the mountain paths finding and carrying jewels, gold, and coins each time the Facilitator called.

He chuckled, recalling the reaction of the woman when he had the children taken from her. She might have struck him and ended up in jail. He wisely brought a female officer and a social worker to help defuse her objections.

But she was a desirable woman nonetheless, and one without a man. She needed a real man to delight her. He had dreamed of ripping her clothes off and plundering those long legs that seemed to reach from her heels to her shoulders. The vision of her wanton face under his passionate attention haunted him. He had come so close in his apartment with the fake arrest warrant.

Still, he shook his head at the only opportunity he had to realize his dream. She was an exquisite woman, and he had seen her in all her naked beauty. Now, she had been released and a big deal struck. There are times when you can't have everything your way. Such is fate.

How cruel are the gods.

Alas, he had decided to maintain his professional dignity with so much money at stake. Yet, soon that would not be an issue. Perhaps he would make a play for her at some other time. Surely, she understood his devotion to his duty and would only admire him the more for it.

Or she was right. Maybe, he did have a conscience.

He coughed and reached for a nearly empty pack of cigarettes.

This is what women do to you.

Trokalitis shut off his desk lamp. He grunted, lifting the box with his personal items inside. Hauling it to his car, he turned one last time to view the building he had worked in for so many years. Had they appreciated all the work he had done for them? He doubted it.

People only thought of themselves, and it was time for him to do so as well.

29

San Diego, California

PRESENT DAY

Cassandra and Demo pressed their noses to the jet window. The stopovers in London and New York had resulted in more than a whole day of flying. The exhaustion disappeared when the flight attendant announced that they would be landing in San Diego within minutes.

Mountains and desert landscape merged with a sea of houses as the American Airlines jet descended toward the shoreline.

"I see the ocean, and a long bridge," Demo said. "And are those ships of the navy? They're *huge;* two are flat, over there. They have jet fighters. I love fighters."

Lauren saw the awe in their faces. They both abounded with questions over the many hours they flew. She answered each in turn in the language they best understood. Cassandra sometimes had no words and only showed her wide eyes and silent murmurings of prayer. She pulled on her mother's sleeve.

"Helios shines in this place. It is a good omen."

"Yes it is." Lauren patted her hand as the wheels underneath the plane rumbled and grinded, lowering the landing gear.

"Where will I go pray to the goddess? Surely we will give her thanks for bringing us to this place unharmed." Cassandra reached for a candy bar stuck in the seat pocket in front of her. "Will this be a sufficient offering?"

Lauren stared at the untouched chocolate bar, wondering how she would finally explain to her daughter that the gods of her time no longer were worshipped. Perhaps she didn't have to. After all, this was California. There had to be a cult to Athena somewhere.

"We will find a sufficient location to make an offering to Athena. First, we will land and make a long walk to where we will collect our belongings. They sit now in the belly of this winged chariot. Then we will be joined with the members of our family who wait anxiously to meet you and Demo."

From the row behind them, Demo poured out a stream of observations, each one voiced with more excitement than the one before.

"Lady Lauren," Cassandra continued. "What if your family does not approve of me? Can they not see that I am not of your blood and therefore an outsider?" Her lip quivered.

"Here, snuggle up to me, sweetheart." Lauren drew her in and wrapped an arm around her. "They will love you as your mother and your uncle did. You will see. They know that I love you and that a battle was fought for you and Demo. Be confident, my love. There are only bright days ahead."

Cassandra sighed, but then felt the jar and squeal of their plane landing on the runway.

They stood at the top of the escalator, seeing cardboard signs of welcome held high and the family down below screaming and waving to them. Cassandra froze.

"The moving steps, they will devour us. Must we?" she said with trepidation.

"Hop on my back, like you did when we walked up the steps from the cave. Hold your feet high." Lauren broke a smile from ear to ear when she saw her parents.

She stepped onto the moving steps. Cassandra gripped her until they reached the bottom. Her mother broke ranks, ran to her, and then deluged Lauren with hugs and kisses. Lauren's father raised himself from a wheelchair and enveloped her in his embrace.

He said, "I knew you would work it out. Welcome home, honey. You're here, safe and sound."

"I am, Dad, I am. I love you." Lauren did not leave his embrace until her Grandma Cassandra Asimos parted the crowd with her hands and a voice that demanded attention.

"Where is my *Cardia*? Where are you?" Lauren savored the nickname her Greek grandmother had given to her as a little girl. She always treasured being called a sweetheart by her.

"Oh, Grammy," Lauren swooned and hugged her. "I have a surprise for you."

Cassandra hid behind her. Demo swept his eyes from face to face. Lauren's brothers were next, then colleagues and neighbors swarmed her and there were more people behind them.

"Mom, Dad, Grammy . . . everyone, I want to introduce you to my children." She placed them in front of her.

"This strong, young man likes to be called Demo. And this beautiful girl is Cassandra."

Lauren's grandmother gasped. The crowd broke into applause and laughter.

The two children raised their eyes into a crowd of smiling faces. Lauren's mother approached first and knelt in front of Cassandra. She brushed the girl's cheek with her fingertips.

"Cassandra, welcome to our family. I've waited so long to meet you."

Cassandra smiled back, unable to understand her words but easily able to discern the message of love that effused from all present.

"Sweetheart," Lauren said to Cassandra in Ionian, "this is your great-grandmother and the gods must truly favor you because her name is Cassandra also." Lauren's grandmother handed Cassandra a brown teddy bear.

Cassandra discarded her reserve and laid her head onto the old woman's shoulder. Demo was next and Lauren could see the difficulty he had with the obvious displays of affection that were being rendered to him.

Lauren held his hand and told them all the story of his life in the orphanage and how important he was to their successful arrival in San Diego.

"What language are you speaking to her, *Cardia*?" Lauren's grandmother asked.

"It's a very long story, Grammy."

"If I know you, it must be a good one."

"It truly is, one that would rival Homer, Grammy."

"Then I must hear it, but let's get these children to their new home first."

Lauren held one hand of each child in hers and asked each in turn if they were ready for their new life. Each nodded and smiled up at her.

"Then let's go." She led them away. Zack might not ever see the happiness that they would all share. Questions about Zack would come, she knew. She said a silent prayer and choked back the emotion gathering within her.

We're a family now, Zack. You made it possible. Wherever you are, you're not forgotten.

30

San Diego, California

PRESENT DAY

Goodnight, sweetheart," Lauren said. She flicked off the light, left the door open a crack, and leaned against the wall. She almost couldn't believe her fortune. Cassandra slept in her bed, and would probably do so for some time, until she adapted. Demo had no such problem.

Lauren found him watching football on the television in the family room. He shoveled potato chips in his mouth and changed stations with the remote.

Just like Zack.

"Demo, you think it's time you got to bed?"

"I'm too excited to sleep." He crumpled the empty bag of chips and tossed it at the wastebasket. It hit the rim and bounced in.

"Maybe it would be best to try. Tomorrow I'm going to take you both to the beach. We're going to have lunch at a beautiful hotel called the Hotel del Coronado. They have the biggest Christmas tree you'll ever see, decorated with presents and lights."

Demo shut off the television. "What school am I going to?"

"It's nearby. You're going to love it."

"Is Cassandra going too?"

"Yes, but she may need a special school at first also. She has a lot to learn. I want to ask you one favor though." Demo smiled.

"I need you to support her. I think in time you'll see that she's a very special girl. I know she is."

"She's my sister. I've never had a sister. I'll take care of her."

Lauren ruffled his hair. "Look, we have a big day tomorrow. We're going to run on the beach. Maybe we'll play volleyball, too."

"Can we go fishing in that lake down there?"

"We'll do whatever you want."

"Maybe I am a little tired. I guess I'll go to bed."

"And you get your own room."

His face beamed. "I saw it. There's a TV in there."

"Yep, it's all yours."

Demo hugged her. "Thanks for wanting me. I never thought anyone would want me."

"Well I do, and so does Cassandra. One last question though?" Lauren sat on the couch with him. "With so many people on the plane, I didn't want to ask questions. What happened at the museum? Did you ever find the movie camera or the memory stick?"

"It wasn't there. I looked all over his office. Guess that's why they heard me."

Lauren cupped his chin. "I wish you had asked me first. It made a lot of trouble for me at a bad time."

Demo said, "I'm sorry. I thought I could just get rid of it. I was the only one who saw where Professor Popandreou hid it."

She put her arm around him. "In the future, we make decisions together, okay?"

He nodded his head.

"We'll discuss the options and pick out the best course of action. All three of us decide as one. We're stronger together than alone."

Demo looked up at her. "Where is your husband?"

Lauren squeezed him tighter. "My best guess is he's a long way away and I don't know if he's coming back."

"Then I'm the man of the house."

"You are, but even big men need their sleep. Good night, Demo."

Lauren watched his curly-mopped head as he walked to his room. He stopped in front of the open door, counted to three, ran and jumped onto his bed.

She went to the kitchen and decided to open one of the "welcome home" bottles of wine.

It just happened to be the resin-tasting retsina.

Maybe I'll have to get used to this. It'll be my lent, until Zack comes back.

She took her glass to the backyard and headed to the swing love seat they had set up to look out at Lake Murray. House lights ringed the lake and she'd forgotten how much she loved the view from their perch. She stood and slapped the big boulder sitting at the end of the property. Her mother had a spare set of keys so she didn't have to dig up the Altoids box and get the spares Zack always buried there.

Lauren covered her face with her hands.

She would have to start a new life without Zack. He wasn't the same man as before. He was a far better one now. She put her hands on the boulder. She wanted something solid, something dependable to hold onto.

Lauren said aloud, "Thank you, Nestor, thank you, Zack, for the treasure." Crickets and a lone coyote answered her. The call of the coyote sounded strange, more like the ones she'd heard on old western movies rather than the normal high-pitched yipping. More coyotes started yelping out along the hills and their cries overcame Lauren's desperate pleas to Apollo to let Zack return. She said loudly, "I did what I thought would work." She thought back on the terror she felt in Bessus's tent and the power play of Trokalitis. Did men only want her for one thing?

"Hasn't Zack done enough for you?" she cried out to an absent Apollo. "Hasn't he served you well?"

Lauren didn't expect an answer. She had met Apollo twice before, once as the waiter, Calchas, in the Plaka restaurant, and then in the dream. In that hazy memory, Zack said he had saved Athens in the future and that disasters were on the way.

"How much pain must he endure?" she shouted.

She expected Apollo wouldn't hear her. Why should she bother calling to him? She'd have to do the best she could. Everything was upended. Bessus's body was gone at the cave, too. That meant he had to be somewhere. She shivered. The image of his dirty fingernails and the crush of his grip around her throat, caused her to shake her head to destroy the memory. She had to refocus.

She closed her eyes, fell to her knees, and prayed, "I'm begging you, Apollo. I need Zack, too. He's in trouble. I know it. Please help him and let him come home to us."

A flash penetrated her eyelids and she opened her eyes, but the burst of light was gone and left her staring at the infinite overhead display of the nighttime sky.

In this play of nations, generations, and conviction, there wasn't much she could do at the moment. She would have to wait for her chance. She had the children and must concentrate on what went well; her cup was more than half full.

31

Plataea, Greece

479 BC

Zack floated in a calm, tepid pool of water. He tried to propel himself within it, but drifted aimlessly instead, beneath a blinding sun. He closed one eye, turned his head, and saw a flight of birds settling down among the slain.

They worked their way toward him..

Curved beaks and with extended claws, these birds were larger than they seemed from afar. Muffled cries invaded the calm, but those sounds were muted, distorted, and distant.

One bird hopped onto his chest and stared him down with black eyes. Satisfied with his prey's immobility, the bird picked at Zack's splayed flesh above the rim of his breastplate. He heard voices, the moans of dying men and others, urging their comrades to fight on. The bird ripped more flesh from him. Zack watched, faintly sensing the stab of the rapier beak digging into him. Awakening finally, he tried to swipe at his assailant but couldn't raise his arms. In the distance, he heard the crescendo of battle continuing on: drums, the incessant ring of metal, the pounding of the earth. He smelled the sick odor of blood and the disemboweled, mixed with a dense smoke on the wind.

He ventured to raise his head but his body refused. Breaking a seal of dried blood, he separated his fingers. His tongue seemed permanently fixed to his palate, like a slab of stuck leather. He lay in a sea of corpses and those that soon might be.

The bird wrestled with a flap of Zack's skin. It stared him down and finally ripped his flesh away. It gobbled up the piece. Zack wasn't sure if he could even blink, or shake his head to shoo the bird off.

A predator knows when you're toast.

Maybe the Native American chief, Crazy Horse, was right; this was a good day to die.

The bird pecked on his cheek now. Zack felt the sting but then it dulled. He didn't care anymore. His eyeballs would be next.

He had given his all.

He began to spin, slowly at first, and then faster. Then he started to sink within the revolutions. He'd lost control. He couldn't move. In a few more sweeping rotations, he would be fully immersed, swallowed up, and gone forever.

Forgive me, Lauren. For all I've done.

32

San Diego, California

PRESENT DAY

Only Apollo did hear Lauren. He heard her pleas over those of the coyotes that he tried to mimic.

Golden Hair has a point. When do I decide Traveler has served enough? It is just that the time for mercy is not yet here. It does remind me, though, that I should check on his progress. My, it is a struggle to keep an eye on that young man.

From his hidden gully below Golden Hair's home, he enveloped himself in blue charge. He must travel back to Delphi and enter the portal. A moment later, a blue flash sent him skyward.

Arriving, Apollo approached the battlefield at Plataea from the south. The struggle between the free Greeks and the Persian army had moved toward the timber stockade Mardonius had ordered built months earlier. The Greeks stormed the wooden palisade and the air was thick with cries, cheers, the chopping of wood, and the ring of sword and spear.

A battlefield strewn with the dead and wounded offered no clear path to travel. Nevertheless, Apollo scanned the corpses for signs of life and for the Traveler. Then he saw Traveler's body signature in the distance, lying among the red capes of the Spartan dead, a yellowish hue that pulsed with his vitals. He also lay among Persian horses, their riders, and the torn Persian infantry. Zack's yellowish glow beat faintly and now Apollo worried. He found a cart large enough to carry a body and pulled it toward his fallen apprentice.

He had left Traveler alone for too long, as he had been immersed in viewing the events transpiring for Golden Hair.

They have to survive on their own, by their own guile. I cannot always continue to rescue them from their fates. The cart bounced over a wounded hoplite, causing the man to groan. Apollo stopped and checked the status of the warrior. The man would live, but only if someone could stop the flow of blood. He shouted for help, and his voice carried to Spartan helots who answered his call.

Apollo hurried toward Traveler's position. He thought back to the last meeting he had with his fellow gods. All he had now was his memories of them, and he wondered if the other gods would be pleased with his handling of the sacred mission to which they all had committed. Each of them knew there might be limited opportunities to avoid the disasters and effect the changes they strived for.

He would never know the answer to that question, because the other gods never returned.

Only Tyche, the goddess of outrageous fortune—his nemesis—remained to disrupt his plans, though she was a spirit more than an embodiment.

His thoughts wandered back to one of the last times the Olympians debated their plans; it was a course of action that would alter the course of history, and also ensure their communal destruction.

Apollo craved the counsel of his fellow gods. But now he must make all the decisions and, self-assured as he was, lingering doubts still plagued him.

Philosophy had its merits.

But survival is a practical business.

And altering what has already been recorded as history would be a tortured and tenuous task. One he must relish for it to succeed.

A great cheer interrupted his revorie as the Greeks were able to breach the wooden palisades and open the gate. There would be a terrible slaughter of the Persian warriors who had retreated to their stockade.

This would be no day for mercy.

Apollo dodged more corpses with his cart on his hurried way to Traveler, and fell back into his thoughts and memories.

He remembered that on that fateful day, the gods sat around an unadorned stone table. Taller than the others, Apollo stretched his legs and nervously twirled the long forelock on the right side of his head. Two chairs remained empty, their occupants delayed for reasons unknown. He stared into the eyes of his fellow gods and registered their trepidations. The entrance to their enclosed chamber remained sealed shut. A subdued reddish glow lit the room just enough so that Zeus, Hera, Poseidon, Hephaestus, and Apollo could see each other. Symposiums must be held in total secrecy.

But now Apollo sensed disaster, too. The other gods said nothing. Patience, one had advised earlier, would serve them better than jumping to conclusions. There was no reason to suspect the other gods had been discovered. The enclave they occupied was secure, free from the intrusive discovery of all they thought, all they felt . . . especially all they plotted.

"We need a distraction to pass the waiting," Zeus advised, standing to stretch. He scratched his straight gray hair and the weeklong whiskers darkening his face. He wore a knee-length robe and held one drape over his forearm, as all the others were required to do for their meetings. At the inception of their confederation, they decided gods must dress like gods. "Let us review what we have agreed upon."

Poseidon drew in a sharp breath and let it out. "We must meet the need, and I believe it should be done unconditionally, otherwise it is not *agape*. Love and benevolence shall be extended to them, regardless of their mistakes. We will ignore their wrongs and effect the change with no strings attached." Black-skinned and muscled, he stood and tightened the belt around his waist. "I can guarantee success."

Apollo, wearing a white himation, strummed his clean-shaven chin with his fingertips, thinking. Then he brushed back his long, wavy hair and tied it in the back with a string, leaving only the forelock to dangle.

He ran his hand over the top of the table and cleared away drawings on its surface. "Unconditional love? Where is it in our time? No such ideal exists. Where we are now, in fact, *is* a function of mankind's wrongs, their excesses. They appear to only be in love with themselves."

Zeus paced the room. His leather sandals clapped the hardened floor surface. "I agree. Love, regardless of its lack of conditions, will not suffice. We will help them, but love and giving unconditionally will not likely change their ways. They must be warned. They must be taught. They must change in order to endure...to survive."

Poseidon extended his hands, palms out. "You expect too much from them. They are not enlightened, not capable. They will self-destruct. We cannot trust them with the future, our future . . . our inevitable existence." He raised his voice. "We, the gods, should effect this change. We will not fail. Together, we should go back and change history ourselves. We must not depend on them."

"Shush," Apollo said. "Lower your voice." He traced a design on the tabletop with his fingertip.

"Fear not, Silver Bow. I ensure that we are not heard or known. The chamber is intact. I promise you," Hephaestus said, wearing a blacksmith's apron tied about his waist but speaking in hushed tones nevertheless.

Poseidon continued, "We should give them what they need: unconditional benevolence, brotherly love, security. Only that is true *agape*. That is how the *Histories* have told us to act."

"I disagree," Apollo replied, hands on his hips. "If we do everything for them, they will never learn to care for themselves. We will have to return time and time again to correct their course. We must be prudent schoolmasters, hard at times, benevolent at others. The *Histories* are wrong in this."

"Wrong?" Poseidon blurted out. "Can the *Histories* be wrong?"

"They are a reporting of events. They do not suggest right or wrong. If we learn anything from the *Histories*, it should be that these mortals of the modern day and their attempts to balance society... failed."

"I concur," Zeus said. "We will travel back together, though I think one of us should go back and prepare the way. One must take the risk in case there is a problem with the transit."

Apollo raised his hand. "I volunteer. I will research the mortals whose names are listed in the *Histories* and see if they can be of assistance. I will ensure that our beloved Parthenon does not suffer ruin again, also."

Hera, dressed in a red robe that accented her jet-black hair, pursed her lips. She sniffed the stale air in the enclave. "And if you discover that your method is not successful, will you reverse course and allow them to be saved unconditionally?"

Apollo nodded. "If we cannot convince them of the merits of moderation and the need to fight for their way of life, then I'll reconsider your plan."

Zeus looked at the plug of bronze in Apollo's hand. "Your medallion has an archer on the face."

"Is it not appropriate? I am Apollo."

"Then I shall have a thunderbolt. Poseidon will sport a triton; Ares a sword; Athena an owl; Hephaestus an anvil; and my darling Hera, a pomegranate."

Hera smiled.

"How conventional," Poseidon said brusquely.

Apollo pulled a second medallion from his pocket and threaded a thin leather cord through the hole in each one. "Hephaestus has made two for each of us. You are a fine tinkerer."

Hephaestus smiled and returned attention to his calculations.

Zeus checked the security of the room. They were safe, for now. "Where are Ares and Athena?"

No one could answer. Apollo knew in his heart that they couldn't wait much longer for the missing gods to return. Within the security of Olympus, they could be confident that all they spoke of and thought about, would be just between them. That's why they rarely left. But what if the two gods were compromised? He, any of them, could be discovered in their treachery. They would be violated, physically and psychologically, and all would be revealed. All their planning, all their successes, their discovery that free societies existed in the past, would be snuffed out.

Silence ensued. Apollo tied the string around his neck. "Speak to me of immortality, Zeus."

Zeus, the thinnest of all the gods, with narrow eyes and a yellowish tint to his skin, gray-haired and balding, halted his pacing. He thought for a moment before saying, "I will *not* speak to you of the immortality of the body, only of the spirit. Immortality can be the result of heroism, or of despicable acts, too, because they are remembered by all. What we propose is to promote acts for the betterment of people, societies, countries, of the community of men and women on earth. If we achieve this, then we will be immortal, because our philosophy and our deeds will be remembered with reverence."

Poseidon asked, "And if all we have accomplished thus far, our discoveries, our ideas, the freedom to think and do, is eliminated and never known?"

Zeus replied, "That would be failure. We have to believe that what is good will in the end prevail over that which is evil. We have seen how fast slavery can return. Humanity deserves the liberty to think freely and to act independently."

"But only if they are willing to fight and die for it. Therefore, we act not just for lives, but for ideals, too," Apollo countered. "They must voluntarily choose moderation over excess. Manipulating their fate will not give us a true sense of their ability to survive and prosper. Tyranny will trump intellect and the good acts of men will not survive. Everything of value will be buried in the interest of preserving power, as we have already seen."

Poseidon peered at the entrance. "Perhaps we will know soon enough if gods themselves are mortal or immortal."

Apollo declared, "We must act, and not be reactive, for our invisible adversary, Tyche, too is unforgiving and I fear she will gleefully ruin our plans. Furthermore, there will be a breach in our security at some point. We don't know when, but they cannot be fooled for long."

"We will try your way first, Apollo, but if it fails, my plan will be enacted," Poseidon said. "We will engineer the change in history ourselves."

Zeus nodded his approval.

It turned out Apollo was right, at the time, even prophetic.

Athena and Ares did return, but it didn't matter in the end. They had all died, sacrificed themselves, so he could go on. Apollo was left alone to execute their plan to change history.

Traveler's yellow glow weakened further. Apollo hurried to where he lay. He would have to arrive before the pulse disappeared, or Traveler would expire. He had come to like his trainee. The man had changed. He was a warrior now.

Apollo broke into a run. The Travelers vitals faded fast.

Dear, dear, Traveler. Perhaps I have pressed you too hard. I hope that you do survive. The struggle is imminent and I do not want to send Golden Hair into the fight if I do not have to. Soon, I will have to check on the Beast also, for he will have a role, too, in the destiny of nations.

The yellow signature barely registered. Apollo raced to Traveler's side, shooing away the rapier-beaked carrion with a flap of Traveler's skin in its claws. Slain warriors lay in clumps and in rows. Horses screamed their agony. Apollo pulled Traveler into his arms. Blood shrouded Traveler's face, made more horrible by the visibility of a bared cheekbone.

"Oh Traveler, you are a sight." Apollo yanked the spear out of Traveler's upper chest. The man didn't move. Blood oozed from the wound. The yellow glow halted.

Apollo gasped.

He raised Traveler's chin and opened his airway.

The yellow glow beat faintly.

Apollo pulled the silver flask from his hip pocket.

The yellow glow halted again.

"No, Traveler. It's too soon. Your work is not done."

He dribbled the nectar into Zack's mouth.

"You are needed, and so is Golden Hair."

The yellow glow resumed. Apollo compressed the wound with the palm of his hand. "We will go someplace quiet and reflect. If you live, maybe I will let you think you are dead. Yes, if you think you are dead then perhaps you will risk everything for what is to come."

Delphi, Greece

PRESENT DAY

Mr. Avtges arranged the smorgasbord of desserts on the table. He and a few ladies from the town had spent the last two days baking honey-drenched, custard-filled phyllo *galaktoboureko*, *kourabiethes* white powder sugar cookies, and pistachio-coated *baklava*. They hoped to raise a hundred euros to pay the bills. The orphanage was in danger of closing and the children would be dispersed. Avtges wasn't sure how much more disappointment he could endure.

He said to one of the townswomen, "If we only had Demo, he would go into the town and get lots of people to come by the stand. Maybe a hundred euros is too much to expect from the sale. I wonder which of the children could take over for him?"

"You miss him, don't you?" said a woman in a black kerchief.

Avtges had not smiled in the week since the professor and the children had departed suddenly. News had filtered back to him that by some miracle the lady professor had taken the children with her to America. The other children missed Demo, too, and the strange girl who never talked. And they had fallen in love with the lady professor. He couldn't continue the language lessons she had begun. Even the knowledge that Demo and the girl would be better off in their new home could not lift the pale of depression that overlaid the orphanage.

"We all miss them," he said, hoping he did not reveal just how devastated he really felt. He considered seeing his doctor and asking for an antidepressant. "I'll be back in a minute. I have to go back to the orphanage for some smaller bills to make change."

He unlocked the door but was interrupted by the screech of brakes. He turned and saw a white limousine pull up next to him.

The window powered down and the driver looked at him and then at a photograph he held in his hand. "Are you Mr. Avtges, the caretaker of this orphanage?"

"I am. How can I help you?"

The driver got out of the car. He held a manila envelope. "I've been instructed to give this to you."

Avtges accepted the envelope with a blank look. "What is this?"

The driver smiled and replied, "Compliments of my boss." He got back in the car.

"Who's your boss?" Avtges asked, but the window closed and the car tires spit stones and headed back down the mountain.

Avtges slid his finger through the seal and pulled out a single sheet of paper with a letter-sized envelope paper-clipped to it. He realized he didn't have his glasses so he walked to his office.

Please accept this donation to the orphanage. I know this will be put to good use. Perhaps it will be enough to make some great headdresses for the buffalo hunt.

I beg you not to ask too many questions for it would be impossible to explain. Just help the children and know the gift comes from my heart. Please accept this as an anonymous donation.

Avtges swallowed hard. He opened the envelope.

"Am I seeing this correctly?"

His hands shook putting his glasses on. There was no mistake. He held a banker's draft for one hundred and fifty thousand euros, made out to him.

He collapsed on his desk chair, set his face in his hands, and let go tears of relief and thanks. He said aloud, "You will be remembered here,

Lauren. Bless you and I can only hope you will find your husband. One person can make a difference. You made a difference for those children . . . you made a difference for us."

34

Delphi, Greece

PRESENT DAY, BUT A YEAR EARLIER

Bessus awoke and shivered. He watched the spinning mud harden into solid rock. The first time he had been sucked into the mudslide, it nearly ripped him apart.

Not this time.

He'd been laid down carefully on the stone floor, like a swaddled newborn.

He could only guess that the Sorceress still controlled him. He would give anything he owned—cattle, gold, even all his fields full of wheat, if he could just slay her and be free. Earlier, when he jumped after the Sorceress and the girl, the Mumbler had lain behind him on the stone floor, beaten and weakened. But now, he was gone, too.

Nothing made sense.

Bessus felt a throbbing in the unreachable part of his back. Then he remembered that the Sorceress had been in his clutches in a cave with fire and smoke. She had squeaked under his grip and he had heard her death rattle. But he had wanted her alive just for a short time longer, until he could fill her with his seed and reverse the curse.

That was his mistake. The girl had plunged the knife into his back thrice. The two escaped and left him to burn. How had he survived wounds and fire that should have ended his days?

Spinning stars filled his head when he stood. Bessus breathed in deep and again felt the sting of the dagger in his back. How could he have been stabbed with his own blade by a girl with sticks for arms and legs? He ran his fingers over his chest and realized he had his bull-hide armor back on. This confounded him, too. He had taken it off at the stream and didn't remember putting it back on. That's why the girl was able to stab him in the back.

A rush of air beckoned him up the stairway he had climbed earlier when he killed the old man. Reaching the top of the stairs he saw stars overhead. When he climbed out of the hole, his head filled with sparkles of fire. He pounded his fist on the ground and words would not come forth. The Greek temples were old and broken. That meant he still lived in the Sorceress's world.

He didn't know what to do now. No axe, no helmet, not even his dagger, or a torch to light his path.

Nothing made sense.

Were his horsemen still down the road from here?

He ran his hand over his head and found no hair. Again, he remembered fire falling on him from the cave ceiling. His face bore scars. His fingernails told him so. The first scar was given to him by "Blue Eyes" at the battle on the beach with the Greeks; the second by the Sorceress in his tent, with his own dagger.

He put his forehead on the ground and moaned. Only the wind coursing along the mountains heard his cries.

Would he ever be delivered?

After a time he stood. Darkness kept clear sight from his eyes, but he sensed dawn coming. Bessus made his way down the snaking path between the ruined buildings. To his left, the road lay covered with a flat blackness. On top rested a metal chariot, unlike any other he had ever seen, even on the richest streets of Babylon. Silver decorated its head and flanks, while black orbs held it up off the field. He searched the brush for a club. He would need a weapon to defeat the inventions of the witch's world. He breathed slower and his calm returned.

Bessus could not let the sorceress win. He felt around his chest, remembering the archer medallion he took from the Mumbler. Maybe it would be magic against the sorceress, but it was gone, too.

From around the building, a metal beast with two blinding eyes emerged from the roadway, coughing and rumbling toward him like the one the night before, except this one was bigger and more fearsome looking. He needed his axe. A club would be useless. The beast stopped in the black field, its yellow eyes seeking only him. Fleeing deeper into the trees, Bessus turned to see the metal beast open up one of its sides. He threw the club away. The beast roared like a lion, spewing gases from its rear end. Arms came from the side of it, extending to grasp the large silver jars left by the side of the black field. It lifted the silver jars and dumped the contents into its empty back.

This is what it would do to him, if it could catch him. He ran with all the breath left in his lungs, across a field and down a hill, until he heard running water. Bessus groped in the darkness. His boot sloshed into a brook coming down the mountain. He felt safe now. He had been here before. The mountain air revived him and reminded him of his home-land. An early morning wind whipped leaves overhead. He had to sit and make sense of all this. His guts burned inside, like the embers of a dying campfire. Bessus shut his eyes. *Mainyu, I don't understand Greeks. How had we not encountered such weapons in the north? Why did they hold them back when we defeated the red soldiers? Xerxes must know of these char-iots that shoot vapors like dragons and need no horses to pull them.*

Dreaming could be the cause of his misery. Bessus opened one eye slowly to see if it all was as before. Cursing, he knelt at the stream and scooped water into his mouth. He remembered he had lost an armband in this place earlier. He searched the streambed for it unsuccessfully. The water settled his stomach, but it didn't quench the burning inside him as the milk had.

Bessus bit his lip and sucked air through the spaces in his teeth. The metal beast coughed in the distance. Was it after him again? He could stay no longer. The beast would have trouble seeing him if he moved within the trees. Bessus headed to the temples, to retreat through the mud hole and to the world he left behind. He crept silently between the trees until he found the road. Then he ran, turning to see if the beast saw or smelled him.

Hiking back uphill along the snake path and then beyond it, Bessus found where the mud hole had been. He listened for groans coming up from the earth, but it was quiet. The mud hole was closed up, dead. He was stuck here.

The only answer was to find the Sorceress and slay her.

Bessus rambled back downhill again. He reached the gate and listened. The two-armed chariot had left, leaving only a silver chariot on the black road. He approached it slowly, with his hand out, in case it awakened. He couldn't tell if it was alive or dead. Cautiously, he touched the chariot with his fingertip, then drew it away. Cold. He pressed both hands on the top of the chariot and pushed gently, at first. Then he pounded on the metal surface. Before he could raise his hands again, the chariot gave off an earsplitting shriek. He blocked his ears and ran back to the trees. The chariot wailed and didn't stop. The dwelling he had been in earlier, where the young wildling had bit his hand, came alive inside with torches. He bolted, sticking to the side of the black road when his leather boots made too much noise. Bessus returned to where he thought he had left his horsemen, but they were gone, too. *Curse that scout, taking my men away, and leaving me all alone to fight the Greeks myself.*

Bessus found a mound of rocks and a perch to sleep on. He scattered branches around his camp, so he could be awakened if anyone came after him. After settling into a comfortable spot, he clasped a rock in his hand. In the morning, he would make a wooden spear. Turning fitfully, sleep finally claimed him.

The sun was halfway up when Bessus awoke. He heard another chariot, but this one was different than the others. It was long, and the color of the sun. It groaned and squeaked as it moved uphill. Even worse, there was a long line of them, with Greeks inside, sitting in rows, peering out at the mountain. Bessus ducked.

How could he defeat them all himself?

He had to rejoin the king's army. After hiking down the mountain, he found a town with hundreds of Greeks shopping and more horseless chariots. Staying out of sight, it took till midday to sneak around the town and continue his descent, concealing himself within the bushes of the switchbacks. Thirst and hunger ate at him. He wouldn't be able to endure the hot sun of the Greek lands without finding a stream. That would drive him to encounter the Greeks and slay a few to steal their food. Reaching a city, he halted and stared at the buildings the Greeks had erected. The dwellings were ablaze inside with torches and orbs of light. Not a horse could be seen, only endless streams of chariots with their Greeks inside, crowding each other, racing and dodging each other as they sped along the black roads.

And not one sign of the king's army. *Could it be that the king had met with some disaster?* At dusk, he dared to venture from the trees when a huge silver bird thundered over him. Bessus dived to the ground and curled up, seeking to escape the roar and the imminent attack. Then, to his relief, it flew away, leaving him unharmed. He stood and shook his fist at the bird that left a trail of smoke behind it. "You will not catch me, you stinking Greeks. Your magic may be strong, but I am far too clever. I will return to plague you and I will leave no one standing. Hear my words and keep watch, Sorceress, the Mainyu will surely deliver you into my hands and I will return you piece by piece to his flames."

He spit, securing his vow, and made his way down the blacktopped road.

Near nighttime, he found a stream, cupped his hands and drank from it. Another town came into his view. He crept along the outskirts and waited for dark.

When the Greeks retired to their hovels, Bessus looked into a shop and saw food and drink. He tapped his finger on the clear wall that he could see through, remembering how the covering of the torch in a ball had shattered when he had hit it with something hard. He lifted a rock with both hands and shattered the clear wall into pieces, leaving him a way to climb into the shop. But now, the wailing began anew, like the chariot had done. Inside, he grabbed bread and packets of meat. He found a knife to cut off pieces of fowl spinning on a cooker. Jars of cow's milk and other drinks sat within a clear closet. He couldn't take too much more time. Certainly, the Greeks would follow the sound of the shrieks, because now he understood that the noise was designed to ward off thieves.

His arms loaded with the precious loot, he climbed back out of the shop and ran into the trees just as two men arrived. Bessus stuffed the fowl into his mouth, watching them. The meat was hard from being overcooked but he devoured it. The men looked around and then one put a small square to his ear and talked into it. Bessus ripped open the cow's milk container and drank it down. He wiped his mouth, tore the slimy covering off the bread and had his cheeks half-stuffed when he heard the wail of more birds. A blue and white chariot with a whirling light sped toward the shop. Bessus gathered his cache and slid down a bank into a ravine. He would have to eat fast. The swirling light scared him. Were they guards? They would be armed, and still he had nothing but a sharpened stick and a knife to defend himself. He retreated into a long gully and devoured most of the meat and bread. He could find another shop. They were easy to steal from. Nighttime would be his ally. He would be a ghost that the Greeks would never see.

Bessus trekked north, tracing his steps back towards the Greek capital, wondereding if Xerxes was still there. Threatened with all these inventions of the Greeks, the king would have taken his army back home and saved his warriors to hold the empire. He must march north, back to the bridges. This would be his best chance.

Bessus walked all night, guided by the stars. He sat on a hill and watched the stream of yellow-eyed chariots race up and down the black-topped roadways. He listened to them drone like a swarm of bees. After a while, safe on his roadside perch, the mesmerizing trail of lights and the constant hum from the chariots brought sleep to his eyes.

In the morning, the last of the food filled his belly. He wanted to keep the flimsy container with pictures of cows on its face, but it crushed in his hands. He could hunt with his spear, or even raid another shop. *This land of the Greeks might not be so fearsome.* Bessus hugged the underbrush along the roadway. Across the roadway, he saw a smaller road, not so busy. Three nearly naked girls with tight-fitting clothes walked along it. Bessus could have all three, if he could just get over to them. There was no break in the fast-moving chariots on the road. The women would escape him, but now his loins were fired, and he must have a Greek girl before long.

Even with the tall buildings and the black roads, Bessus recognized the land. He and his horsemen had traveled through here on the way to the Greek capital they had burned. *A Bactrian warrior needs no guides.* He crept along a ditch and across fields of wheat but had to hide behind a tree, for coming up the road, a group of Greeks sat on iron chairs with two wheels. They pumped their legs and the wheels moved fast toward him. He couldn't tell if the riders were men or women as they rode past him.

Night would soon arrive. Then he saw a lone rider on the two wheels. This one was going fast, too. Maybe he could catch the rider and have one of these inventions for himself. He hid along the ditch and waited, imagining himself a great cat from the eastern realms. Bessus ran up the ditch incline, carrying his wooden spear. He set himself in front of the approaching riderchair. The Greek on two wheels swerved to avoid him. Bessus threw his spear and hit the rider, who fell, yelling in Greek.

A female's voice.

The girl scampered away from him. He dashed to grab her. She detached her battle helmet, swung it at his head, connected, and Bessus fell backwards. Curling his lip, he blared, "Now Greek whore, you are mine." The Greek wench reached underneath her loincloth and pulled out a small flask. She pointed at his eyes. A mist clouded his face and Bessus screamed. He gagged and his eyes poured tears. She picked up her two wheels and rode away. Bessus rolled onto his stomach and vomited. He could not rub the sting from his eyes. He staggered around with his hands out, trying to find the ditch he had hidden in. He tripped and fell, finally crawling to where he thought his hiding place might be. He drooled from his mouth. Sweat from his eyes made it worse. Would the agony ever go away?

Near nighttime, the sting subsided. Bessus wiped his eyes with his sleeve. He had rarely known fear since he was a boy. On this campaign, he had felt the spidery grip of it a few times now—when the red warriors stabbed him and took his helmet; when the young girl cut him with his own knife and left him to burn in the cave; and now, in this world of horrors, where magic and Greek inventions plagued him at each turn. He had to get out of these lands . . . and return home. He had to reach the bridges before they were destroyed. It might be his last chance.

Maintaining a course along the waterways, he kept to the long island to his right. Ships moved silently up the channel, and in his head, he could see the great fleet of his king, the oars pulled by slaves dipping into the sea. He wondered if the king's navy had met defeat, too. *Why did they all abandon me?*

He strode alongshore by moonlight until the mountains and the curving bay held his gaze. He had surely been to this place before. Up ahead, he saw a statue. Bessus cautiously approached it, looking to see if any Greeks were around. The Greek warrior, carved in stone or maybe iron, looked familiar. It held a large oval shield and a long lance. Bessus remembered he had felt the sting of such a lance before. He scratched at the wound he had received a month earlier which still had not completely healed.

This is truly the site of the great battle that cost the king so many of his men.

Bessus shouted and shook his fist. "Is it you, Spartan king of the red capes? You thought to defy the king's will. My people shall sing my praises always for the deed of removing your head. Could the Greeks have already built your memorial, a king disgraced? Your men were all slain. You are nothing."

The sweep of the bay was different now. Before, the narrow pass was bracketed by the mountains on one side and the bay on the other. Now, the mountain was not so steep, and the edge of the bay was much farther away. More tricks to confuse him.

Bessus walked toward the mountains beyond the battle site. He needed to retrace his path from the north and find the bridges.

After stopping to retie the worn leather strappings that reached to his knees, he hiked till sundown, relieved finally to find a horse on farmland enclosed by a rickety fence. Bessus approached the horse slowly, whistling low and singing words that his father had taught him. Following some fuss by the horse, Bessus rode the rest of the night behind the line of trees that ran parallel to the road. He made great distances now, ceasing his hunt for harlots and stopping only to find foodstuffs for himself and his horse. He felt himself again and, only incomplete by the loss of his double-ended axe and his prized horned helmet.

Bessus rode hard for many a night until hanother of the two wheels approached. He tied his horse to a tree and readied his ambush. Under his breath he said, "You will not get away from me this time." He timed his attack better. A well-thrown stone connected with the rider's head. Bessus ran to his prey with palm extended, in case the rider had the devil's spray that brought him such pain the last time. He saw the rider was alive, but knocked out, lying on her stomach. A knocked-out harlot was just as good. He tried to take off the battle helmet, but a strange clasp held it on the rider's head and no matter how hard he yanked it, it would not come off. He pulled the rider's tight-fitting pants down to the knees. He turned her over.

"Damn the stars!" Bessus shouted. A man lay before him. He clubbed the unconscious man with his fist. "I thought only harlots rode on the two wheels." He dashed to his horse and rode into the cover of trees, leaving the rider by the road. Foiled a second time, he decided to not prey on the two-wheelers, and look for walkers instead.

Another night's ride brought him east of some magnificent city in the distance. At the top of a hill to get a better view, he met a pair of hikers. Clearly women, they looked at him pensively, backing off. Bessus smiled, but it did nothing to allay their apprehension. Bessus kicked his horse's ribs and seized one of the women by the shirt. She twisted, but he held on tight. The other screamed and tried to pull her companion back. Bessus won the contest, and hoisted the woman face down over his lap. The other woman pounded his leg with her fist to no avail. Bessus swung the horse, knocking the companion down. He made a getaway with the companion chasing him and throwing rocks. Finally, she stopped.

Bessus turned his mount and saw the companion pull a small box from her pants and talk into it. Something about what she did made his stomach twist. Who could she talk to? His guts told him to ride away fast and stay out of sight. The girl over his lap thrashed. He slapped her hard on the back with the palm of his hand. The air left her lungs. "Shut up, whore. Service me quietly and I may let you go." She gasped and coughed, and restarted her kicking. He rode into the safety of a forest. Finally, he stopped and lifted her off the horse. She cried. Bessus got his first good look at her— dark-haired, and built for his pleasure. She screamed at him in Greek. Bessus backhanded her hard across the face. She fell and he was on her, ripping off her loincloth. The screeching did not cease until he tightened his grip on her throat. He filled her, then lay on top of her. His weight brought the last breath from her chest. Finally, her eyes turned up and Bessus knew he had sacrificed properly.

"That was a good one," he shouted. "I have not sacrificed enough in your name, Mainyu, Lord of Darkness. Do not be angry with me. Your power must overwhelm that of the Greeks. I beg you to lead me to the sorceress." Bessus shook his fist. "If you demand more of the Greek women as a test, I will do your bidding." He left the Greek woman where she died. He mounted his horse and traversed his way down the mountain in the other direction. Darkness had come now and he heard the wail of the blue-lighted chariots in the distance.

Bessus rode all night again. Morning delivered him another Greek harlot running by herself on a trail. His hunting skills had improved.

She was easy, too.

He recognized the rise of mountains not far off, having ridden this way south at the head of Xerxes's army. He shook his head, deciding it would do no good to dwell on the fate of the Persian king for now. Bessus's fortune had been good since he had begun sacrificing the Greek girls. Food and drink were easily stolen from shops.

After two more women the next night, surely, he had earned Mainyu's favor by now? The wail of blue-lit chariots seemed to follow him and from more than one direction. *They're hunting me.* He recalled that his horsemen were ordered to turn north after crossing the bridges, up a long peninsula, then inland as part of a covering force to protect Xerxes's main army. That meant he would have to continue heading toward the rising sun. Somewhere, he would recognize the lay of the land again, and find his way down the long peninsula to the bridges made of ships.

More riding until he slipped past a guarded post in the darkness and saw the Greek lettering had changed. The writing was curved now and singing was heard far away. He followed a wide road, thick with chariots, until he saw a great city in the distance.

Tall, thin spires sat against the dusk of the evening sky. An unusual building, one with an onion on top, beckoned him closer. Streams of chariots rode into the city, seemingly converging toward the towers that reached to touch Ahura Mazda himself. Then he heard music, loud in all directions. It was not the voice of some honey-scented concubine. It was a man's voice. He stopped to listen, tying his horse's tether to a branch. He could not leave until the man sang again. Could there be a festival? Bessus crept into the city on foot and made his way to a dark corner. He had to get to the onion building. It might be a temple.

The temples—I remember the temples hold the wealth.

Now he could see that there was more than one temple. He walked along the roadway, marveling at buildings that towered above him and watching crowds of Greeks strolling in the early evening. Nearer the onion-topped building, he craned his neck around a corner to get a clearer view of it, when he heard voices behind him. Bessus turned to see two men, dressed in tunics the color of the evening sky, braced for battle, shouting at him. One carried a small club. They motioned for him to come nearer, but Bessus froze. He could see they were angry and warriors of some kind, but he needed time to think. One shouted at him again, an act Bessus could not tolerate for long. They separated to come at him from two directions. One warrior talked into his hand, which crackled and spoke back to him.

Dare I challenge these warriors, the owners of so many inventions?

There was no more time to consider what to do when one ran at him swinging his club. Bessus seized it, snapped the fool's wrist and then swung him into the other warrior. Just as the two men collided, there was a crack, and fire leaped from one of their hands. Bessus heard a wasp fly past his ear and smack into the bricks behind him. Unsettled by the new magic, he dashed away. Lumbering between brick dwellings, he heard shouts and more cracks that caused doorways to splinter in front of his path. He turned corners, racing past Greeks who cringed in fear and made no move to confront him.

Soon, the onion tower rose in front of him. The voice called to him from another tall, thin tower. He ran toward it and saw lines of men entering, dressed in long robes and cloth caps. Bessus heard more shouts behind him and reached the entrance, just behind the last of the men entering.

Pushing his way in, he sent a man crashing onto stone floors and scattering sandals and boots. Bessus withdrew himself into a corner, catching his wind. The man he knocked down took one look at him, dusted off his robe, and hurried through a portal. Onlookers drew a circle around him, pointing and putting their fingers to their lips. Bessus stood straight, drew his knife, and waited for the warriors who had pursued him to come in, or for any of the others before him to make a move. He would cut off the fire hand of the warrior before it could harm him, and easily kill any of those who now blocked his escape.

Beyond the antechamber where he stood, Bessus could see men kneeling in a room with brightly colored and intricately arranged tiles, pictures upon the walls and polished stone columns and flooring. Incense sweetened the air. Elaborate rugs beckoned for Bessus to lie upon them and rest. He watched the crowd of men put their hands to their ears and then fold their right arm across their left over their breasts. Many of the men in front of him left now, moving quickly to where the others bowed down in a great room, putting their hands on their knees and then standing while someone chanted. *This must be a temple.* The worshipers then prostrated themselves, touching their heads to the stone floor. *Do they worship the Mazda?* He held his dagger higher when the dwindling circle of onlookers opened and a short man with a gray beard stood before him.

Imam Abdul Mohammed al Azul made his preparations for the evening prayer. He was especially proud today, this being the tenth anniversary of his ascension to the position of prayer reader and leader of this Sunni community at the prestigious Selimiye Mosque in Edirne, Turkey. An architectural masterpiece designed by the legendary builder of mosques, Mimar Sinan, in the sixteenth century, this mosque was an artistic showcase of Turkish handicrafts, artwork, and architectural elegance.

Echoes from above sounded, the last of the song of the muezzin calling the faithful to prayer from loudspeakers atop the minaret. He must hurry. The worshipers of Almighty Allah would already be kneeling in front of the qibla, facing Mecca, and prepared to pray. He smoothed slight wrinkles from his richly embroidered gown after the ritual triple cleansing of his hands, mouth, and feet. He loved the evening prayer, the last of five each day performed for the glory of Allah. Abdul planned to read one of the shorter sura, number 106 of the 114 suras—or miracles—that make up the Koran. The atmosphere would be charged tonight; all knew this was a special service. He could think of no prouder accomplishment than to serve God each day in this manner: helping create the divine presence of Allah on earth, breathing spiritual unity into the community, and assisting the needy. He strode through marbled corridors and tiled floors in his haste to reach the mescit. There, his worshipers awaited his ascension onto the minbar, where the holy Koran awaited him on a low table.

I will sing today in my best voice, "Peace on you and the mercy of Allah." I trained long and was taught well. This will be my finest service, one that will bring pride to Mohammed, may peace be upon him.

He was met with commotion near the front entrance. A crowd had gathered, shouting, unheard of within a mosque ready for services. He reached the circle, declaring in a firm and reserved tone, "Allah is most great, come to prayer."

The faithful opened a path for him, revealing an enormous stranger in a corner, unclean and wielding a knife. The footwear the worshippers had removed upon entering was scattered. Abdul took stock of the stranger. He was surprised by the size of the giant, who was crouching in the dim lighting of the entrance. Abdul could see two long, jagged scars etched on his cheeks and crisscrossing up over his nose. His clothing was tattered and filthy, and he wore a rugged black leather jacket. The stranger appeared ready to fight, slowly moving his knife in a circular pattern. It occurred to Imam Abdul that the man was no stranger to scrapes so he would have to tread carefully.

Abdul said in a pleasant tone, smiling, "The peace of Allah is upon you. Is there some assistance we might extend you?"

The stranger didn't answer. He just stared at him with pursed lips and dark cavernous eyes.

"If you are a Muslim, you must know it is blasphemous to enter the house of God uncleansed. What is your name and why are you here?"

Once more there was no response from the stranger. The Imam knew he must be extra careful. He was used to refugees, many as desperate-looking as the stranger in front of him now. Even they, however, were respectful and requested immediately to perform at least a partial ablution of the dirt and grime from their persons. This one was different. Outside, a police siren called. The stranger turned to the sound, cringed slightly, and raised his dagger higher.

"Allah be merciful, we shall offer you sanctuary and peace," the Imam said, taking two steps closer, his palms turned toward heaven. Then he brought them together over his chest, right over left. The stranger visibly eased his fighting stance. Imam smiled, happy that he had lessened the tension in a manner that had worked many times previously. The stranger lowered the dagger but shouted a stream of unintelligible words. Imam had no idea what the man had said and looked to his circle of worshippers for assistance. "Do any of you recognize his words?" he asked.

One man said, "Most holy one, the blessing of Allah is upon you. I almost cannot believe it, but he has spoken a word I have not heard since I attended the university in Ankara. He said an Iranian word I think, Persian more so, from many years past. It sounded like Khshayarsha. This is the name of an ancient king of the Achaemenid period from many thousands of years ago. The Westerners would call this king *Xerxes.*"

The giant stranger repeated the word again, and others, as if testing their understanding of his language.

The man who understood the Persian word said, "I apologize, Imam, but I cannot comprehend his meaning. He speaks far too fast."

Imam Abdul turned back to the stranger. "Do you speak Arabic or Farsi? How can we understand one another?"

The stranger's face showed frustration and he seethed words under his breath. Imam was expected within the mescit to begin the worship and could wait no longer, yet the man piqued his curiosity. Imam asked a worshipper to assist him in bringing the stranger to one of the rooms where refugees could stay until they were moved to other areas or assimilated within the community. The other worshippers left for the prayer room. Imam Abdul and his assistant motioned for the stranger to follow, making the motion of eating, which the enormous man clearly understood. They opened the door to the room and stepped aside as the giant entered with hesitation. Both caught the horrific odor emanating from him and looked toward heaven momentarily, as if in prayer.

Imam made motions with his hands for the giant to lie down. "Feed him quickly, Ali, I beg you, before the lion returns in him."

The man, appearing as if he had ascended from the bowels of the earth, nodded his understanding and approval. Imam turned to Ali, whispering, "Make haste, Ali. After the prayer, I will make a phone call. I have a friend who may assist us."

"Forgive me, Imam, must I stay with him by myself? My body shakes in his presence. He peers at us like he would kill us with his hands."

"Stay outside the door and be careful to keep your hands away from his mouth." Imam flashed a smile and strode away down the hallway.

The next day, Mullah Abu Mahmoud stood with arms folded as he viewed the giant sleeping on a mattress. The ugly visitor had placed the mattress on the floor. The bed frame was thrown to the corner of the room, twisted and bent back so it would be out of the way. The mention of this stranger speaking the words of the ancient kings of Persia interested him, too, enough that he drove six hours from Istanbul to the westernmost border of Turkey to be of assistance to his friend, Imam Abdul. Now, he watched the giant roll and turn, possibly tortured in his sleep by dreams. He wondered what would cause a man to have such an appearance. What deeds had he performed, or maybe, what crimes?

Imam Abdul joined him at the window. "Allah, be merciful," Abu said. "You say that he had no concept of Islamic law or how to enter and behave properly in a mosque?"

"My friend, he knew not how to even use the toilet or a shower. We discovered him defecating among the hedges in the rear grounds."

Abu cringed. "Then he must be an infidel. Why do you harbor him?"

"We offer sanctuary to all strangers, but also for the same reason that you are here yourself, Abu. There is something about this man that intrigues me, but I am not sure what exactly. Do you think you can speak with him in a language that mostly has been unspoken for many centuries?"

"It was my passion some years at university. Of course, you know how my studies were interrupted many years ago and I chose a different path."

"I do, my friend."

"Look, he awakens."

"I always have a tray of food available when he wakes. If he angers, I fear he will have far less difficulty snapping us in two than he did that bed frame."

Inside the room, the giant stood, scratching his head and yawning. He appeared to anger when he realized he was watched from outside the door. The giant motioned for them to enter.

"Salaam," Imam said smiling. The giant grunted. Imam Abdul and Mullah Abu looked at each other.

"Do not dismay, Abu. He is far cleaner now than when he entered."

"Imam, he is enormous. Might he be a wrestler?"

"We are hoping you can learn something from him. I don't know how long I can stand to be in his presence."

They both entered the room, Imam with his palms outstretched, a non-threatening gesture. The assistant Ali held a plate filled with grilled chicken and couscous, offering it to the giant. He accepted and ate his meal with his fingers, sitting on the floor.

"Imam, does he not wash before he eats? This is a violation in the house of God."

"Perhaps you could inform him." Imam winked at his friend, who addressed the giant in the language of the ancient Persians.

"Did you speak the name of the king, Xerxes?"

The giant raised his head from the steaming plate of chicken. "You speak the king's tongue poorly, small man."

Abu clearly did not like the insult but did not escalate the tension.

"We mean to assist you. Who are you?"

"Bessus," the giant answered flatly. He continued to devour the rest of the meal, barely stopping to breathe. Finishing, he ran a finger inside his mouth, around his teeth and cheeks, swallowed, and belched.

"He has the manners of a swine, Imam." Abu turned his attention back to the giant sitting on the floor.

"What country are you from?"

"Bactria."

Abu narrowed his eyes. He thought for a moment and then continued.

"What God do you worship?"

"Angra Mainyu."

Abu gasped. "Allah be praised, Imam, he worships a false god long dead."

Abu spoke again in ancient Persian. "How did you come to be here?"

316

"I came with the king's army. Where is he?" the giant asked, face full of jagged scars and flushing with rising anger. "How far is the bridge of boats? It is nearby, I know it."

"Forgive me. There is no bridge of boats."

The giant stood and blared, "You lie. Are you stinking Greeks? If you are, I will kill all of you now."

"No, no, no, we are not Greeks and we do not lie. We are the faithful of Allah, he is God."

"What?" the giant answered. "You do not worship Mazda or Mainyu? Your god has no power then, just like the Greek gods are weaklings."

Mullah Abu turned to his friend, shaking his head. "This man is deranged. He thinks he lives thousands of years ago."

Bessus spoke to Abu. "Is this a temple of your god? Is the man next to you a priest?"

"Well, yes, and he seeks to help you."

"If that is so, then show me the bridges and tell me where Xerxes is."

Abu scratched his temple. "Allah be merciful, this man is difficult."

Bessus spoke again. "Return me to my homeland. I will raise a new army to return and kill the Greeks. Then I will find and slay the golden-haired Sorceress."

"Are you a warrior?" the mullah asked, but his words were interrupted by the song of the muezzin calling the midday prayer.

"The song," Bessus said, "it soothes me. I trust only the song. Go and worship your god. I only believe in the gods of my mountains and the sacred fires of the Mazda and the Mainyu. Now leave me."

"We will think on your desire to return home, stranger, but this temple is a holy place. It cannot be defiled. No one here will harm you, but we ask you to cleanse yourself daily, use the latrines that are shown to you, and do not threaten the worshippers here. Can you do this?"

Bessus grunted, nodded his head, and sat back down on the mattress. He wore a long white robe now, his clothing having been sent to the washwomen, excepting the black bull-hide armor.

"Consider quickly, priests. I want to return home after I rest. Does your god have magic strong enough to counter that of the Sorceress?"

"Our God is all powerful, praise to his name. All submit to his will, even this sorceress you speak of. She is but a female and God is God."

"And Bessus is Bessus, now go."

Mullah Abu and Imam Abdul entered a spacious library, decorated with carved mahogany and an intricately designed Persian rug.

"He is a puzzle, Imam. He sticks to his story, but there is no debate he is an infidel. He has his possibilities, though, and I wonder if he might become one of the faithful if properly educated."

"God willing, Abu."

"He says he is from Afghanistan, but he uses the ancient name of the land, called Bactria. He mentions a golden-haired woman. She must be either European or American. I neglected to ask him if he was a refugee from some struggle."

"He has the eyes of a killer."

Abu looked to the side, considering what the imam had said. "He has the aura of a warrior, even if he is a dreamer. He may be a useful martyr for Allah's glory."

"If this is God's will, but I will not entertain such a possibility. If he stays here, he will be assimilated into the community. If he chooses to go with you, then I leave him in your care. He has a look in his eye, quite imposing, quite sure of himself, and he frightens me."

"Surely, it is risky to send him by plane. He has few belongings—just a dagger, a chest of leather, and the leather pouch he has tied around his waist. He has no passport. Could not some funds be sent by courier for us to ship him?"

"Ship him to where, Pakistan?"

Abu said, "Yes, I will accompany him. I expect we could board him in Istanbul. I have an agent who will assist us. We'll travel through the Dardanelles to the Suez Canal, then around Saudi to Gwadaron on the Pakistani coast. It is a simple matter from there, rail and then truck to the camps. There will be plenty of time on this voyage to see him submit to Allah's will. I will procure the medications to sedate him and produce the truth from his lips. If he does not see God's will, I will cut his throat and dump him overboard."

Imam Abdul raised his finger. "We do not need more killers, Abu. We need worshippers who live within God's law. Peace is what Islam seeks. Will there never be an end to the killings?"

"Only God knows. But God also knows that the struggle for justice and the security of our lives within Allah's embrace is never-ending."

Imam Abdul took a deep breath and let it out, an exclamation of exasperation.

Later, Imam stood beside the truck that would transport Mullah Abu and the giant to the docks at Istanbul, another six-hour drive from Edirne. The giant appeared pensive when brought out of the mosque and asked to sit within the vehicle. He dug in his feet outside the truck.

"Did you not explain that he would be driven, Abu?" Imam asked.

"I surely did, Imam, but he confuses me each time with his gibberish and falsehoods. He says he has never ridden upon the metal chariots and asked if this one could destroy the chariots with the whirling lights. He truly believes what he says— that everything he sees is magic and the work of this sorceress he speaks of. He says she brought him here, through a chasm of some kind, near a mountain temple among the Greeks. He will not accept my explanation that King Xerxes was dead long ago. Perhaps he is mad after all."

"You should have been with us on the first day when I switched on the lights in his room. He leaped backwards with a wild look in his eyes and he yelled at the top of his voice. Alas, be careful my friend, he has a sinister look about him. God-willing, may your journey be safe."

"It will. We might meet again someday."

"We are all God's children, Abu." the imam said.

"We, I can confirm. Him," Abu said with a head nod while walking towards the truck, "not likely."

Imam took one last look at the giant stranger, who clenched his fists as Abu talked to him. With another passenger already sitting in the front seat, and apparently assured he would be safe, the giant sat on the backseat of the truck. His seat belt was being fastened just as the motor started. The giant jumped up and hit his head on the inside roof of the vehicle. He blurted out a stream of curses and fought to get out of the vehicle. Abu calmed him down once more with soothing words and promises of his homeland, finally engaging his seat belt. As the truck drove away, the Imam saw the giant grip the metal frame around the open window and scream at the top of his lungs. Just then, the passenger in the front seat removed his floppy hat. A long curl fell.

The passenger turned to the giant, touched his shoulder, and said in ancient Bactrian, "You have much to learn before I send you over the seas. There, you will threaten Traveler and Golden Hair so they will leave for the land of the Greeks."

No movement or words came from the giant. He froze and fell asleep just as the truck passed the gates of the mosque.

"You will not sleep too long, nor comfortably, Bessus," the passenger said. "And neither could you begin to imagine the role you will play in my plan."

END OF BOOK TWO
The Story Continues

Greek Gods and Goddesses

Aeolos	God of the wind
Apollo	God of knowledge, prophecy, order, music, archery, and the healing arts
Athena	Goddess of wisdom and protector of cities
Aphrodite	Goddess of love and beauty
Artemis	Goddess of the hunt, animals, and childbirth
Ares	God of war
Atropos	One of three sisters of destiny and fate; Atropos cut the cord of life
Castor and Pollux	Twin heroes revered by the Spartans
Dionysus	God of wine and festivals
Demeter	Goddess of the harvest
Hades	God of the underworld and death
Helios	Titan sun god
Hera	Queen and wife of Zeus; goddess of women and marriage
Hermes	Messenger god of travelers and communication
Hephaestus	God of fire and metallurgy
Hestia	Goddess of the home and hearth
Gaia	Great Earth Mother
Muses	Nine goddesses of dance, music, knowledge, and singing
Persephone	Goddess of spring growth, daughter of Demeter, queen of the underworld
Poseidon	God of the sea and earthquakes
Titan	Primeval race of giant gods descended from Gaia and Uranus
Tyche	Goddess of fortune, chance, and fate
Zeus	Father of the gods; god of thunder, lightning, and justice

PERSIAN CHARACTERS

Masistius	Persian commander
Artabazus	Persian general
Mardonius	Marshal of the army
Xerxes	King of the Persian Empire

GREEKS CHARACTERS

Argos	City-state in the northeastern Peloponnese
Arimnestus	Spartan warrior Lauren's guide
Attalus	Foreman of the olive harvest
Cassandra	Orphan daughter of Persephone, Nestor's niece
Diomedes	Prince of Mycenae
Eurybiades	Spartan admiral
King Andokides	King of Mycenae
King Pheidon	King of Argos
Minander	Greek physician
Meanna	Physician's assistant
Nestor	Retired architect living in Delphi
Pausanias	Spartan general
Persephone	Nestor's sister in law
Plataea	Site of climactic battle between Persians and Greeks in 479 BC
Posidonius	Spartan warrior Lauren's guide
Queen Acantha	Queen of Argos
Queen Io	Queen of Mycenae
Salamis	Site of climactic sea battle between Persians and Greeks in 480 BC
Thera	Ancient name for Santorini

MODERN DAY CHARACTERS

Bartholomew Parsons	US Embassy representative
Demo	Young teenager at the Delphi orphanage
Imam Abdul	Imam of the Edirne Mosque
Mr. Avtges	Orphanage director
Mullah Abu	Ancient Language expert
Samaras	"The Facilitator"
Peter Trokalitis	Greek Police inspector